Friends with Benefits

Friends with Benefits

Lisa Swift

San Diego, California

Canelo US
An imprint of Printers Row Publishing Group
9717 Pacific Heights Blvd, San Diego, CA 92121
www.canelobooksus.com

Printers Row Publishing Group is a division of Readerlink Distribution Services, LLC. Canelo US is a registered trademark of Readerlink Distribution Services, LLC.

This edition originally published in the United Kingdom in 2021 by Hera Books.

Published in partnership with Canelo.

Correspondence regarding the content of this book should be sent to Canelo US, Editorial Department, at the above address. Author inquiries should be sent to Canelo, Unit 9, 5th Floor, Cargo Works, 1–2 Hatfields, London SE1 9PG, United Kingdom, www.canelo.co.

Publisher: Peter Norton • Associate Publisher: Ana Parker
Art Director: Charles McStravick
Editorial Director: April Graham
Editor: Traci Douglas
Production Team: Beno Chan, Julie Greene

Library of Congress Control Number: 2024934581

ISBN: 978-1-6672-0890-9

Printed in Faridabad-Haryana, India

28 27 26 25 24   1 2 3 4 5

For Mark

Chapter One

'Sophie asked if I can stay at hers on Friday. That's OK, right?'

Lexie tore her eyes from the morning paper to look at her stepson Connor, sitting across from her at the breakfast table. He was shovelling mountainous spoonfuls of Cheerios into his mouth with one hand while tapping at his phone with the other, his face half-hidden by the oversized Warhammer hoodie he'd pulled on over his school uniform.

'Sophie invited you to sleep over?'

'Yeah. I said you'd be fine with it. You are, aren't you?'

'I thought me, you and Uncle Theo had a date this Friday night. Homemade nachos and the new Spider-Man film, remember? Last one in our Marvel marathon. You said you couldn't wait.'

Connor looked up from his phone. 'Well yeah, I couldn't, but we can do that any night though. Soph got the MTG Ikoria booster packs for her birthday and I really want to play with her.'

Lexie hesitated, pretending her eye had been caught by a headline in the paper as she tried to decide on the right approach to this morning's out-of-the-blue terrifying parenting challenge.

'Which birthday did Sophie just have?' she asked casually. 'Fifteen? She's four months older than you, isn't she?'

Connor had already reattached himself to his phone and only nodded vaguely.

'Look, Con.' Lexie folded the paper and dipped her head to catch his eye. 'I know I'm not your mum…'

He smiled. 'You're always saying that.'

I

'I know. Sorry. What I mean is, I don't want to be some bossy parent person throwing down rules all the time, and I know I can trust you, but I'm not sure I'm all that keen on you staying overnight at your girlfriend's right now. Not until you're a bit older.'

Connor looked up to blink puzzled brown eyes at her. 'Why not?'

Oh God. Lexie had known the day would come when this was all going to get complicated. Fourteen was exactly the age a growing lad could use a father figure around to counsel and advise him. But Daryl was no bloody use to them where he was – in fact he'd not been much bloody use when he was at home – so Connor was going to have to make do with her.

Her stepson had always been a sensible boy. Lexie had been both surprised and pleased when he'd announced that he and his bright, pleasant friend Sophie, one of the little gang of role-play gamers he hung out with at school, were now an item. But sensible was one thing, and teenage hormones were completely another. Plus Sophie was older than Connor – not by much, perhaps, but a few months made all the difference at their age. Obviously no such thoughts had occurred to Connor, who was still rather naive about the opposite sex, but who knew where a moonlight game of Magic: The Gathering over a romantic glass of banana Yazoo could lead? When Lexie remembered the sort of thing some of the kids she'd gone to school with had been getting up to at that age... God, she shuddered to think.

'Are Sophie's parents happy for you to stay over?' she asked, deliberately dodging his question.

'Yeah, they said it was fine.'

'And you'd be sleeping in separate rooms?'

Connor nodded. 'Me and Oli are going to sleep on the bunkbeds in Sophie's brother's old room.'

'Oh. So it's not just... Oliver Foster's sleeping over too, is he?'

'Mmhmm,' Connor said, still fixated by the all-absorbing phone. 'It's sort of a late birthday thing for Soph.'

'In that case... look, let me have a word with Sophie's mum and check on the arrangements. I'm sure it's probably OK.'

'I don't have to tell Dad about it, do I?' Connor pulled a face. 'Every time I mention Soph, he starts coming out with all that lame "so my boy is becoming a man" crap. Soooo embarrassing.'

Lexie smiled. 'Well, not if you don't want to. Come on, finish your breakfast. You don't want to miss the bus for school.'

–

'I really don't see what the problem is,' Theo said as he and Lexie laid out fresh tablecloths in the Blue Parrot that sunny April afternoon. 'This is Connor. The most debauched thing he's likely to get up to with a girl is letting her paint one of his orcs.'

Lexie sighed as she smoothed out the wrinkles in the vintage floral tablecloth. 'Still, I can't help worrying. I feel completely out of my depth with him these days, Theo. This is dad territory, all this teenage stuff. And let's face it, I was struggling enough in mum territory.'

'Give over, you've done great. I could never have coped the way you did, getting thrown in at the deep end like that.'

'Thirty's too young to have to deal with this. I feel like I need at least another decade of life experience to handle it.'

The door to the restaurant opened, and what appeared to be a cloud of rainbow in human form floated in. A woman in her sixties approached them, sweeping the floor with her oversized boho dungarees.

'Hiya Tonya,' Theo said to her. 'If you're here for the meeting, you're a bit early. It's not until four.'

'Hello, darlings. No, I just dropped in with some bunting on my way to town. I'll be back later for the meeting.' She gave Lexie a kiss and helped herself to a seat. 'Sewed my fingers to the bone, so the pair of you had better be grateful.'

'Well, we are grateful,' Lexie said, smiling. 'Let's face it, we need all the help we can get.'

3

Tonya rummaged in her canvas bag and handed Lexie a folded string of handmade bunting. 'Here you go. Now don't say I don't love you, Lexie.'

Lexie frowned as she unfolded it. 'Rainbow bunting? I mean it's very you and all, Ton, but it's a bit more Pride than 1940s festival, wouldn't you say?'

'Well it can't be all red, white and blue. The village'll look like a National Front rally.' She pursed her lips as she glanced around at the Union Jack bunting and wartime propaganda posters that adorned the Blue Parrot. 'This place is bad enough.'

Theo leaned over Lexie's shoulder to examine the bunting. 'It's not very historically accurate, Tonya. I don't think you could get those dyes in 1945.'

'Oh, sod historical accuracy,' Tonya said, tossing her own multicoloured tresses. 'If I have to help out with this jingoistic celebration of Empire you two insist on organising, I need to do it my way.'

'Well, we're hoping we won't actually have to organise the thing – at least, not all of it,' Lexie said. 'I see our role more as a sponsor. You know, getting the ball rolling with this new committee so Theo and me are free to focus on the restaurant. That was the whole idea behind us putting it to the parish council, to drum up a bit more business for this place – not that we don't think it'll be a good thing for the village too, obviously.'

'You actually don't have to help, Tonya,' Theo said. 'You volunteered, remember? Resisting all efforts of both me and your soon-to-be-ex-daughter-in-law here to talk you out of it.'

'Soon-to-be-ex-daughter-in-law by marriage,' Lexie corrected him.

'Is that right?' Tonya said. 'I think you need to add "once removed" or something.'

'We really ought to find a snappier term to describe how we're related, Ton.'

'Oh, but it's such fun to watch people's eyes glaze over when we try to explain it.'

4

Theo ignored them. 'Anyway, Ton, it's not a jingoistic celebration of Empire. It's a celebration of our triumph over the forces of darkness. Of Home Front camaraderie, the Dunkirk Spirit, survival against the odds, and... I dunno, George Formby.'

Tonya snorted. 'You'd think that'd be reason enough not to bother.'

'Look, you don't have to help out. You don't even live in the village. Don't you have a cruise to go on?'

She grinned. 'No, I've made sure I'll be between cruises for the festival. Just for you, Theo.'

Lexie shook her head at Theo, smiling. 'I don't know why you let her wind you up, Teddy.'

'Because I know it's the highlight of her week,' Theo said, patting Tonya on the shoulder. 'I'd hate to disappoint her by not rising to the occasion.'

'What the festival will actually be – we hope – is an excuse for adults to play dress-up, everyone to have a lovely time and us to make a bit of dosh.' Lexie folded up the bunting and went to stash it under the bar. 'Anyway, thanks, Tonya. I hope we get a few more crafty-type people turning up for this meeting later or you might find yourself becoming a one-woman bunting sweatshop.'

'Where did you announce it?'

'I put a notice in the window of the post office, and posted in that Leyholme residents group on Facebook. Plenty of Likes, and Stevie Madeleine said she'd definitely join, but mostly it was just noncommittal "see if I can make it"-type comments. I hope we get enough for a decent committee.'

'We'll be fine,' Theo said. 'It's Leyholme. There's never any shortage of busybodies with too much time on their hands willing to join things.'

'And how's my handsome grandson?' Tonya asked, retrieving her bag from under the table as she prepared to leave. 'Breaking hearts, I hope.'

'Breaking hearts is the least of my worries,' Lexie muttered.

When Tonya had gone, Theo and Lexie went back to setting tables.

'The committee's going to have fun with her,' Theo said. 'I can just see Ryan Theakston's face if she starts up with that "jingoistic celebration of Empire" stuff.'

Lexie frowned. 'Ryan's not joining, is he?'

'I've got a strong suspicion he will do. He's in one of those war re-enactment groups. Anyway, you know he's addicted to joining committees. I think it might actually be some sort of fetish for him.'

'Christ. You're right: him and Tonya are a punch-up waiting to happen. I don't think her pacifist principles would stand a chance against Ryan in full bureaucrat mode.'

'Ah well, it'll keep things interesting.' He glanced up at her. 'You all right, Lex?'

'Why wouldn't I be?'

'You look worried, that's all. You're not still brooding about Connor, are you?'

'No.' She sighed. 'Maybe.'

Theo finished smoothing his tablecloth and straightened up. 'All right. Let's do this properly then.' He took her arm and guided her to the restaurant's bar.

She laughed. 'You what?'

'Come on. You round that side.' He unbolted the hatch to go through to the other side of the bar, then picked up a bar towel and started wiping down the surface. 'Right then.' He assumed a sympathetic expression. 'Rough day, darling?'

She smiled. 'You daft sod.'

He poured a gin from the optic, topped it up with tonic and pushed it to her. 'There you go, on me. Now, let me provide salve for your troubles by drawing on the ancient, mystic wisdom of the barman. What's up?'

She sighed as she took a sip. 'Oh God, I don't know. Some-times I wake up in the middle of the night and wonder how the hell this turned out to be my life. I mean, I always wanted kids, but I never expected to suddenly find myself playing mum to a seven-year-old at twenty-three. It was hard enough when Daryl was still around, but now he's gone, I'm having to be both mother and father to a kid who's only sixteen years younger than I am. And when I've got adolescence to cope with as well… shit, it doesn't feel like yesterday that I was going through the whole wretched business myself.'

'Lex, you worry too much,' Theo said. 'Connor's got his head screwed on.'

'Yes, but he is also fourteen. What did you used to spend all your time thinking about at fourteen?'

'Well, girls, obviously. I'd estimate that the opposite sex, their attached breasts and how I might achieve greater intimacy with all of the above occupied about 99.9% of my thoughts.'

'Exactly,' she said. 'You know where I'm coming from, don't you? The two of them spending the night together, hormones, one thing leading to another…'

He picked up her G&T and helped himself to a mouthful. 'Course I do. But honestly, Lex, you don't need to worry. If I didn't get laid at fourteen then Connor sure as hell isn't going to.'

She jabbed him in the arm. 'Don't be rotten. Connor's a good-looking boy, why shouldn't girls be interested in him? Anyway, you like *Star Wars*, you big geek. Stop pretending to be so bloody cool.'

'I'm not being rotten and I'm not pretending to be cool. And by the way, actually everyone likes *Star Wars* but you, so…'

She raised an eyebrow. 'Well then, what are you trying to say?'

'All I mean is, kids like Con who are hard into all that spaceship and wizard stuff, they're always late bloomers, aren't they? The whole idea of sex probably scares the bejesus out of the lad, which is very definitely a good thing from our point of view. As his surrogate parent, seems to me you should be falling to your knees in gratitude in front of the nearest branch of Forbidden Planet.'

'Hmm.'

'Look, do you seriously think Connor, our Connor, is at risk of getting this girlfriend pregnant or catching the clap or something?'

'He might be.' Lexie propped her chin glumly on one fist. 'Then the next thing you know he's walking the streets, selling his body to pay for his crack habit, and it's all my fault because I didn't want to sacrifice my reputation as a cool young stepmum by saying he couldn't stay over with Sophie.'

Theo shook his head. 'You've watched too much *Grange Hill*.'

'Well, maybe it's not that which is bothering me so much – not that there isn't a part of me that can't help worrying about him having sex before he's ready. It's more the feeling that he's getting further and further away from me, the older he gets.' She smiled wistfully. 'He was such a sweet, shy little thing when I met him. Six is no age to lose your mum, is it? I half expected him to resent me for trying to take her place, but he just seemed to blossom after I moved in with Daryl.'

'Yes, well, you can thank Daryl for that,' Theo said, his lips tightening. 'He was hardly the most hands-on dad.'

'No. I've loved being Connor's stepmum though. Watching him grow into a young man his dad and me could be proud of, and feeling that a big share of that was mine.'

'I know you have,' he said gently. 'It's thanks to you that Connor still is a sweet lad, despite an occasional attack of the Kevins. You've done a cracking job with him, Lex.'

'Thanks.' She sighed. 'He's just got so much going on now; this whole world I can't be any part of. His life revolves around his friends, his phone, his bloody gaming PC, and I'm lucky if I can get a grunt out of him. I miss the days when he used to tell me things, you know? When he was still all about *Minecraft* and *Doctor Who* and life was simple.'

'No offence, Lex, but if you were my stepmum and I was fourteen, you'd be the last person I'd want to tell things to,' Theo said, smiling.

'Oh, right. Thanks for the vote of confidence.'

'Come on. You think he could talk to you about girls, puberty, changing bodies and all that business without feeling embarrassed? Would you have talked to your dad about that stuff?'

'I guess not.' She looked up. 'I don't suppose you'd be able to have a word with him, would you?'

'About what?'

'Well, all that stuff you just said. Bodies, girls and so on. His dad's not around to do it, and you are his godfather.'

'Ugh. In that case can I not just scare him off sex by leaving a horse's head in his bed?'

'Come on, Theo. He respects you.'

'How would I open that conversation? "So, young Connor, I'm told you're growing into a man. Let's shoot the shit about our penises for a bit, shall we?"'

She laughed. 'All right, maybe not that. I just mean, you could have a chat with him before he stays at Sophie's on Friday. He told me he's sleeping in a separate room with Oliver, but it's natural the pair of them are going to want to experiment at some point. I think he'd feel a lot less awkward if you were the one to do the safe sex talk.'

'Jesus, that sounds excruciating,' Theo said, pulling a face.

'Come on, Theo, you've had enough bloody practice. The least you can do is help out an old friend by putting your years of lecherous dissipation to good use.'

'I thought I paid taxes so that schools could have these humiliating conversations on my behalf.'

'Look, one of us needs to do it and I think we've already established why it shouldn't be me, with my unsympathetic lady parts and undulating rivers of oestrogen. Go on, for me.'

He swallowed another mouthful of her drink. 'Why don't you ask Tonya? She's a sexually liberated modern woman.'

9

'Yeah, I bloody know she is. She'd be round ours with her pop-up *Kama Sutra* and joint-rolling kit before I hung up the phone, talking him through all the positions he ought to try out. I really don't think Tonya's particular brand of libertarian grandmothering is going to help here.' She took the G&T from him and finished it. 'No, it'll be best coming from you. Why don't you come over on Friday, before I drive him to Sophie's?'

'Can't. I've got a date that night.'

'You're right, you have got a date,' Lexie said. 'With me. The three of us were going to watch *Spider-Man: Far From Home* before Connor got a better offer, remember?'

He grimaced. 'Damn it.'

'So you'll come? Please, Teddy.'

Lexie made her eyes wide, Puss-in-Boots style, then fluttered her eyelashes a couple of times for good measure. Theo flicked her cheek with the corner of his bar towel.

'All right, all right, I'll do it,' he said with a sigh. 'I ought to know resistance is futile once you roll out the pet names. But you owe me one, Alexis Whittle. A big, big one. Like, King Kong's schlong level of huge.'

'Ooh! Band name klaxon.'

'I know, right? It just came to me.'

'You've got a real gift for them.' Lexie slapped his arm. 'Cheers for helping me parent this one out, mate. It's not every business partner who'd be willing to offer free sex education classes on the side.'

'Oh, for the days when that might've been a come-on,' he muttered as they got back to work.

Chapter Two

The inaugural meeting of the Leyholme 1940s Festival committee was to take place in the Blue Parrot at four o'clock that afternoon. As the time grew closer, Lexie found her eyes wandering between the clock and the door with increasing frequency.

'Shit, Theo. What if no one comes?' she whispered, lowering her voice so Charlene, the waitress who'd just arrived to do the late afternoon shift, wouldn't hear. 'What if we have to scrap the whole idea?'

'We won't. We've already got Tonya, and Stevie Madeleine said she was a definite. That's two already, plus us, and there's bound to be more.'

Still, Lexie's stomach churned uncomfortably as her eyes once again flickered to the door.

The Blue Parrot was a cute, quirky little place somewhere in between a cafe and a restaurant, with an eclectic menu, a cracking cook and a drinks licence. Profit-wise it wasn't exactly a goldmine, but nevertheless, business had built steadily since Lexie and Theo had opened the place a year ago. The 1940s theme seemed to be popular, and the Parrot pulled in trade from both the village and the walkers who came to explore the stunning moors and valleys around Leyholme.

For all that it hadn't exactly been a runaway success, Lexie was quietly proud of everything she and Theo had achieved together. She could wish the place earned her a bit more money – life as a single mum was a constant struggle in that respect – but she loved being her own boss, and having the flexibility to fit around Connor's schedule. Even more than that, she loved being in partnership with someone she now thought of as her best friend.

The two of them had discussed long and hard the type of place they wanted to open together. It couldn't be anything like Bistrot Alexandre, the restaurant Theo used to run with Daryl; not way out here. Leyholme was a pretty little place in the heart of rolling Yorkshire moorland, and a lah-di-dah haute cuisine establishment just wouldn't fit. A teashop had been dismissed almost as soon as it was suggested. There was far too much competition in the local area for yet another chintzy Nan's Pantry-type establishment to be a success. A bar, too, had been considered and quickly discounted. When it came to nightlife these were pub people, not wine bar people, and the Highwayman's Drop and the White Bull Inn in neighbouring Morton had already cornered that market.

It had been Lexie who hit on the idea of having a theme: something that would set them apart from other local businesses. Theo, with his love of all things retro and vintage, had been the one to suggest the 1940s. There was nothing else like that around here, it suited the character of the place, and it was just the sort of thing to pull in people from outside the area as well as villagers. Which was why Lexie now found herself wearing a stuffy button-front black dress with a white collar and frilly pinny, surrounded on all sides by Union Jack bunting and posters reminding her to make do and mend, keep calm and carry on, and that loose lips might very well sink ships.

Still, Theo had felt they were failing to promote the place as well as they could do. Villagers loved the Parrot, and walkers who stumbled in after a day's hike always left pleasantly surprised, but it wasn't pulling people in from outside the area the way it had the potential to. Too often their TripAdvisor reviewers included the loaded phrase 'hidden treasure' – a compliment, obviously, but from a business point of view, not so great.

Between them, they'd come up with the idea of a Leyholme 1940s festival to take place that summer. Not a huge event; more a sort of family fun day with the Parrot at its heart, with period costumes and vehicles, music, dancing and so on. It had seemed like a great idea at the time: free publicity for the restaurant, and a way to bring in business to the village. But now, as Lexie's gaze once again flicked from the clock to the door while butterflies Lindy-Hopped in her belly, she was starting to wonder.

She let out an audible sigh of relief when Stevie Madeleine walked in.

'Hi guys,' Stevie said. 'Am I the first one?'

'Er, yes,' Lexie said. 'Well, apart from us, obviously, and we've got one other guaranteed. We're hoping we'll get more, though.'

'Who's the one other? Your mother-in-law?'

'That's right. Well, she's not actually my mother-in-law.'

'Isn't she? I thought she was.'

'No, she's Daryl's mother-in-law.'

'Oh, right.' Stevie frowned while she tried to calculate this. 'So... she's your mum then.'

'No, she's Elise's mum – his first wife. I suppose that makes her my mother-in-law by marriage or something. We're never quite sure how to describe it.' She smiled at the expression on Stevie's face. 'Sorry. We're one of those complicated families.'

Stevie laughed. 'Oh, don't worry. You're talking to the queen of complicated families here. Where are we sitting, then?'

'Over there,' Theo said, pointing to a couple of tables that had been pushed together. 'I hope two tables wasn't too optimistic.'

Stevie went to claim a seat.

'Well, that's one,' Theo murmured to Lexie.

To Lexie's relief, the table soon started to fill. After Stevie came Ryan Theakston, chairman of Leyholme Parish Council, Leyholme Gardening Association, Leyholme Drystone Wallers, Leyholme in Bloom and just about every other village committee going. Tonya arrived next, followed by Janette Cavendish – Connor's girlfriend's mum, who lived in the neighbouring village but ran the bakery here in Leyholme – and finally Brooke Padgett, the pretty young landlady of the Highwayman's Drop.

'I knew we'd get Ryan,' Theo said. 'The man's a committee junkie. He'll try to appoint himself chair in a minute, just watch.'

When he and Lexie joined the group, they discovered an argument was already in full swing between Tonya and Ryan.

'Mrs Hodges—'

'Ms,' Tonya corrected him.

'Oh, well. Naturally,' Ryan muttered. 'Ms Hodges, I'm not sure you understand the tone of this event. We're trying to evoke nostalgia for a much-missed golden age here.'

Tonya scoffed. 'Golden age my shapely little arse. Nostalgia for what, Ryan? The millions of pointless deaths? The people who lost homes to the Blitz? The kiddies ripped from their parents' arms? Or maybe the semi-starvation diet people had to survive on?'

'Oh, I like her,' Stevie whispered to Brooke.

'Nonsense,' Ryan said stoutly. 'People ate more healthily during the war than they ever have.'

'Those who could afford it did,' Tonya snapped. 'The working classes could barely—'

Lexie held up a hand. 'Sorry, could someone fill us in?'

Ryan turned to her. 'I'm just trying to explain to your mother-in-law that the purpose of this event is nostalgia for a bygone age, and to educate younger generations about this glorious period in our history—'

'Oh, so you're that sort, are you?' Tonya said, snorting. 'Who remembers rickets, eh, fellas? Ah, those were the days. Bring back the cane! String up the criminals! Hurrah for the Blackshirts!'

'—all while showing respect for those who made the ultimate sacrifice,' Ryan went on, ignoring her. 'I don't feel performance art featuring a drag-queen Winston Churchill is the sort of thing we want.'

'Why not?' Tonya demanded. 'We ought to challenge people's preconceptions. Force them to confront what they think they know about this nation's so-called "glorious" past. Besides, Lola's an old friend and she says she'll do it for a free pint.'

'Look, love, you don't even live round here. It's not up to you how this village chooses to celebrate its history.'

'Right. "This village" meaning "Ryan Theakston", clearly.'

'We don't want any of your "woke" PC nonsense here, thank you very much,' Ryan said briskly, rather making a meal of the air-quotes. 'My military re-enactment society can provide entertainment of a far more suitable nature.'

Tonya shook her head. 'Oh, no. Absolutely not. We won't be having that fascist bullsh—'

Theo coughed loudly.

'Um, well, it seems as though we all have different ideas about the sort of event this should be,' he said, smiling weakly. 'Perhaps we ought to have a brainstorm and... see if we're on the same page, eh?'

'I'll be chair,' Ryan said, inflating his chest like a particularly self-important frog. Lexie felt Theo nudge her knee under the table.

'But it's not your event, is it, Ryan?' Stevie said. 'Theo and Lexie came up with the idea. One of them ought to chair.'

'Oh, no, that's OK,' Theo said, glancing at Lexie. 'We'll be too busy looking after the restaurant to be in charge of the whole thing. It ought to be someone unattached to any of the village businesses, really – someone impartial.'

'Why don't you do it, Stevie?' Lexie said. 'I'm sure Ryan's got enough on his hands with his other committees, and you don't have any business interests around here. Besides, I reckon you'd suit chairmanship.'

Stevie laughed. 'Because I'm bossy, you mean.'

Lexie smiled. 'Let's call it Churchillian. In keeping with the theme.'

'Well, I'm happy to do it if everyone else is.'

There were approving murmurs around the table from everyone except Ryan. He maintained a sulky silence but didn't make any objection.

'We wondered if the last Sunday in August would be a good date to hold it; the bank holiday weekend,' Theo said.

Stevie nodded. 'Yes, that sounds good: right before the new school term. Milly's doing World War II in history next year so it's perfect timing for the Year Threes.'

'What will we have on the day?' Janette asked.

'Well… I'm sorry, Tonya, but I'm not sure Churchill in drag is really all that Leyholme,' Stevie said with an apologetic grimace. 'Although please tell your friend we're grateful for the offer.'

'Huh. Suit yourselves.' Tonya cast Ryan a resentful look. 'Let him play at soldiers then, if that's what you want.'

'I think we should avoid battle re-enactments too,' Stevie said. 'We want to show we're being respectful of people's sacrifices without glorifying war, don't we? It's a fine line with that sort of thing. Besides, if it's too realistic then the little ones might find it upsetting.'

'Nonsense,' Ryan said. 'It'll be educational. Sod the snowflakes.'

'Sorry, Ryan, but I agree with Stevie,' Theo said.

Tonya nodded. 'Me too.'

'And me,' Lexie said. 'I mean, I'm sure your group are all about remembering history rather than promoting violence, Ryan, but we want to focus on the Home Front side of life. You know, the sense of community.'

Ryan didn't look too happy at having cold water poured on his suggestion, but he settled for humphing to himself.

'So what will we have?' Brooke said.

'How about a procession through the village, if it's not too big a thing to organise?' Stevie suggested. 'You know, period vehicles and things, with people in costume?'

Everyone nodded, and Stevie made a note on her tablet.

'I thought we'd have a swing band on at the pub,' Brooke said. 'And how about some fairground rides in the park for the kiddies?'

'That sounds good,' Lexie said. 'We ought to hire a brass band for the bandstand too, and maybe get the Leyholme Dance Society to perform.'

'Oh! How about a flypast?' Janette suggested.

Theo frowned. 'What, like the Red Arrows?'

She laughed. 'Well, maybe the budget version. I'm sure it must be possible to get a Spitfire or Hurricane to fly over, if we can afford it.'

'OK, this is looking pretty adventurous so far,' Stevie said, glancing at her notes. 'We'll leave it there for now, eh? I'll take email addresses and we can start assigning jobs. Good work, everyone.'

Lexie followed the group to the door. She touched Janette's elbow as she prepared to leave.

'Janette, can I have a quick word?'

'Of course. What's up, Lexie?'

'I just wanted to ask about the arrangements for Friday night. Your Sophie's sleepover.'

'Oh yes, she's ever so excited,' Janette said, smiling. 'Connor and Oliver are coming over around five, then I think the plan is takeaway pizza and that card game they love until the wee small hours.' She frowned at Lexie's worried expression. 'There isn't a problem, is there? I'm sorry, I should have checked that he didn't have any food allergies or anything. Sophie tells me off if she thinks I'm making a fuss so I try to take a back seat. Well, they're getting quite grown up now, aren't they?'

'That's what worries me,' Lexie said quietly. 'Sorry, it's probably just mum paranoia. Connor's never stayed over with a girlfriend before, that's all.' She met the older woman's eyes. 'I'm sure you've got it all in hand though, right?'

'Honestly, I understand where you're coming from but there isn't a thing to be concerned about,' Janette said in a soothing tone. 'Graham and I will be there to keep an eye on things. You just relax and enjoy having a night to yourself.'

Chapter Three

When Connor got out of his last lesson on Friday, his mates were outside the art block waiting for him. Crucial and JJ were raining punches into each other as usual, red-faced and giggling, while Oli showed Sophie something on his phone.

'All right, Loser?' Crucial huffed breathlessly from his head-lock under JJ's arm.

Connor grunted and went to see what Oli was showing Sophie.

'Hiya, Con.' Sophie stood on tiptoes to peck his cheek, and he blushed furiously. Did she have to do that when the others were looking? She must know Crucial and JJ would start taking the piss as soon as she was out of earshot. Still, he managed a bashful smile for her.

'Hi guys,' he said. 'What you watching, Ol?'

'Bro, it's fricking awesome.' Oliver passed over the phone so he could see. 'Trailer for *Star Wars: Squadrons*. Kickass gameplay, and the graphics are lit. You are getting it, right?'

'Dunno,' Connor said. 'If Dad sends me some money I might, but I don't want to ask Lexie for any. Things are a bit tight right now.'

'Mmm, I bet.' JJ let Crucial go so he could make an obscene gesture with his thumb and forefingers. 'Lexie always looked good and tight to me. You don't know how lucky you are having that walking around in just her pants, Carson. The least you could do is get us some photos.'

Connor scowled at him. 'That's my stepmum, you twat. Anyway, she doesn't walk round in her pants.'

Crucial shook his head solemnly. 'How can a woman with tits that fine not have enough cash? She should sell her body, she'd make a mint.'

'I've got a fiver.' JJ looked from Crucial to Oli. 'Come on, lads. Surely we can have a whip-round, keep Loser's old mum from the poorhouse?'

Sophie glared at him. 'You're a pig, JJ.'

He grinned. 'Yeah, you love it.'

'Jesus,' she said, rolling her eyes. 'I seriously need to make friends with some girls.'

'What about Crucial?' JJ said, nudging his friend in the ribs.

'I'd better go. My dad'll be waiting.' Sophie squeezed Connor's arm. 'Don't let them wind you up,' she whispered. 'I'll see you tonight.'

'Well?' Crucial said when she'd gone.

'Well what?' Connor asked.

'Well, have you boned her yet? You've been dating two months, you must've got a bit by now.'

Connor flushed crimson. 'Go eff yourself, Crucial.'

'Whoa!' Crucial held up his hands. 'Language, Carson. You kiss your smoking-hot stepmother with that mouth?'

'Course he hasn't boned her,' Oli said. He looked at Connor. 'You haven't, have you?'

'You can all mind your own bloody business,' Connor said, blushing still deeper.

'You're such a simp, Loser,' JJ said, shaking his head.

'I'm not a simp. I just like her, that's all.'

'Yeah, whatever. I reckon she owes you some action, the way you're always running after her. Don't want to die a virgin, do you?'

'I heard they can tell,' Crucial said soberly.

Connor frowned. 'You what?'

'If you die a virgin, they can tell.'

'How can they tell?'

'Dunno, from how pink your dick is or whatever. They can tell if you haven't used it. And they have to put it on your death certificate, so then everyone knows. Like, they *legally* have to.'

'Like hell they do.'

'Seriously. My brother works in a hospital and he told me.'

'Not something I need to worry about then,' JJ observed airily.

'You are so full of shit, JJ,' Oli said. 'We all know you've never even touched a girl.'

'No, you're right, I haven't,' JJ said, nodding sagely. 'I don't touch girls. Only women.'

Oli snorted. 'Yeah, right.'

'I lost it in Year Eight, mate. Keep waiting for one of you virgins to catch me up.'

'In Year Eight you started crying because you accidentally called Mrs Dubrovnik "Mum" in front of our whole class. Give you a pity shag afterwards, did she?'

Connor nudged him. 'Come on, Ol, let's go get the bus.'

They left Crucial and JJ to another game of 'who can punch the hardest?' and headed to the bus stop.

'Well, have you boned her?' Oli said when they were alone. 'I won't tell those guys, promise.'

'Course I haven't,' Connor muttered.

'What have you done?'

'Not much. Just, you know, messing about.'

'Tops and bottoms, or just tops?'

Connor felt his cheeks burning. 'You really promise you won't tell JJ and Crucial?'

'Course not. Best mates, aren't we?'

'Just kissing, that's all,' Connor mumbled, keeping his eyes fixed on the ground. 'I mean, properly, with tongues and everything. Well, sort of properly. We're still practising.'

'Really, tongues?' Oli looked suitably impressed. 'Nice one. You're still going to her birthday thing tonight, aren't you?'

'Course.'

'Cool. Can't wait to play Magic, can you?'

Connor brightened. 'I know, it's going to be awesome.'

He felt so much more relaxed when it was just him, Oli and Sophie, away from the bickering and banter of JJ and Crucial. He hated it when they talked the way they did about Lexie, or wound him up about Soph, but he knew letting them see just how much it got to him would only make them do it more.

'So what's up with your stepmum then?' Oli asked. 'They're not going to start taking your stuff away or anything, are they? They do that if you can't pay your bills.'

Shit. Could they really do that? Connor hadn't thought of that.

'Hope not,' he said, frowning. 'She hasn't said anything to me, but I heard her talking to my nan and I don't think the restaurant's been making that much. Not compared to the one Dad and Uncle Theo used to run anyway.'

'Doesn't your dad send her any money?'

'Some for my food and clothes, and he sends me pocket money when he remembers I'm alive, but nothing to help Lexie. Him and her aren't properly married now. I mean they're not divorced yet, but they're not like real married people any more.'

'How come you don't go live with your dad?'

Connor snorted. 'I'm not living with *him*. He doesn't give a shit about me. He doesn't give a shit about anyone but himself.'

Oliver regarded him for a moment.

'Don't worry about *Squadrons*, Con,' he said at last. 'You can borrow mine when I get it. I'll let you have first go.'

'Really?'

'Course. You'd do the same for me.'

Connor smiled. 'Cheers, Ol. You're a good mate.'

–

When Connor got home, Tonya was sitting at the kitchen table with dozens of sheets of paper spread out in front of her.

'Hi Nana.' He looked at the printed sheets. 'What's all this crap?'

'Hello, sweetheart.' She stood up and crushed him in a hug. 'It's for this damn fool 1940s festival your stepmum's got me involved in. I said I'd go through quotes from entertainment acts we'd like to book so the committee can put in a request for funding to the parish council. Nationalistic rubbish, but I suppose it'll be popular with the inbred heathens around here.'

'What're you doing it for if you think it's rubbish?'

She shrugged. 'Because I'm a cantankerous old bat whose only joy in life is to make life difficult for small-minded morons like Ryan Theakston. And because I care about this family and want that daft restaurant to do well, although I'd appreciate it if you'd keep that under your hat.'

Connor smiled. 'It's all right. Lexie knows already.'

She rested a hand on his cheek, smiling wistfully. 'You look ever so much like your mum, Connor.'

'I know. You tell me every time you come over.'

'Well, I can't help it. The older you get, the more of her I see in you.' She sat back down and started shuffling papers about. 'So. Off out tonight, I hear.'

'Yeah, Lexie's driving me over to Sophie's soon as I've packed my stuff. Where is she anyway?'

Tonya pulled a face. 'On the phone. Guess who to?'

She nodded in the direction of the hall. Connor could hear his stepmum's raised voice coming from behind the door, her words muffled so she sounded like an irate bumblebee.

'Ugh. Not Dad?'

'I'm afraid so.'

Connor opened the door and peeped around it. Lexie was in the hall with the landline phone to her ear, looking seriously pissed off.

'For Christ's sake, Daryl! I'm not asking for much, am I? It is half your house.'

Connor glanced back at Tonya, who shrugged.

'You were the one who left me paying for a lifestyle I never wanted; that you knew was always going to be beyond my means as a single woman,' Lexie snapped. 'God knows I did my best to convince you a house this size for just the three of us was ridiculous, but you were adamant—' Lexie paused, scowling. 'Yes, I know you pay your half of the mortgage, Daryl, but on my earnings I can just barely afford my share. Besides, there's more to keeping a six-bedroom house—' Pause. Scowl. 'So what if you're not living in it? Thanks to you I have to bloody live in it, don't I? And so does Connor. I mean, the council tax alone is ruinous. Even if you were just able to send an extra fifty quid a month towards household expenses—' She paused again, and her brow seemed to knit even tighter. 'You'll think about it, will you? Well how fucking magnanimous of—'

She stopped suddenly when she noticed Connor watching her.

'Connor,' she said, forcing a smile. 'You, er… you heard that, did you?'

He nodded.

'No chance you could pretend I said "flipping"?'

He shook his head.

'All right, I'll put a quid in the swear jar later.' She beckoned him over. 'Here, come talk to your dad.'

'Do I have to?' Connor muttered.

She covered the mouthpiece with her hand. 'Come on, Con. You haven't spoken to him for three weeks.'

Sighing, Connor went to take the phone. Lexie disappeared into the kitchen and closed the door.

'Hi Dad.'

'All right, dude?' his dad said in that falsely jovial tone he always used, as if his son was still five years old. 'How's it hanging?'

'Not bad.'

'School good, is it? I hope you're studying hard.'

'Yeah, fine.'

'You're, er... you're in Year Nine now, right?'

'Ten.'

'Ten?' His dad sounded puzzled. 'I thought Year Nine was fourteen. You are fourteen still, aren't you?'

Connor was glad his dad couldn't see him roll his eyes.

'You turn fourteen in Year Nine,' he said. 'Then you go up to Year Ten. I'm an August birthday so I'm always youngest in the year.'

'Right. So is this your big exam year then?'

'No, that's next year.'

'Ah. Of course. Sorry, Connor, it's a long time since my schooldays.'

'What were you and Lexie arguing about?'

'Oh, just some boring stuff about the house.' Connor could almost hear his dad grin. 'How's the little girlfriend? Sophie, isn't it?'

Typical Dad. He couldn't remember what year Connor was in, but he remembered every tiny detail of his love life.

'She's all right,' Connor said cautiously. 'We're doing a thing for her birthday tonight.'

'Are you indeed? A thing, eh?' his dad said in the suggestive tone that made Connor want to puke. 'Nudge nudge, wink wink, say no more.'

'What?'

'You know, the Monty Python sketch? Nudge nudge, wink wink? Eric Idle and Terry Jones?'

Connor was silent.

'Oh, come on! You seriously don't know that?' Daryl said. 'That's a classic, that is. I thought I raised you better than that, Connor.'

Raised him? That was a laugh. Connor glanced at the kitchen door and squared his shoulders.

'Dad, look. Were you going to send me any money soon?' he demanded in a low voice.

'Why, do you need some?'

'No, but Lexie does. I mean, I think she might.'

'Lexie has made it quite clear she's no longer any concern of mine,' Daryl said, his voice suddenly hard. 'She makes her own way now. That was what she told me she wanted when we separated.'

'I know, but the house isn't just hers, is it? I'm not hers either, Dad. I don't feel right getting money from you to spend on stuff for myself when she's struggling to pay the bills for both of us.'

'Ah. Struggling with the bills, is she? I suppose that means the restaurant's floundering.'

The note of satisfaction in his father's tone made Connor want to swear and slam the phone down, hard. But he forced himself to stay calm.

'I don't think so,' he said. 'But it's expensive managing a whole house, isn't it? Electricity and stuff like that. And there's food, school things, clothes…'

'I send her money for everything you need. No one can ever say you're not being provided for.'

'But I won't be provided for if we can't afford to pay the bills, will I? Not if they start taking our stuff or throw us out of the house or whatever.'

'Now come on, don't exaggerate. Things can't be as dire as all that; I'd have heard.'

'All I know is, Lexie's worried. That makes me worried too.'

'Well… all right, let me look into it. I certainly don't want you worrying.' Daryl sighed. 'Look, Connor. I'm glad I got this opportunity to speak to you. There was something I… something on my mind.'

'What is it?' Connor asked warily.

'You know it won't be long until my contract ends. I've been out here fourteen months now – another ten and I'll be home again. It'll soon flash by.'

Connor felt a stab of worry. 'You're not moving back here, are you? Not into our house?'

'No, that wasn't what I meant. I mean, I'll be back in the UK – for good this time – and I'd really like it if you and me… if

26

there was a chance...' He trailed off. 'You do understand, don't you, lad? Why I went? If I'd stayed we would've lost everything. I took the job in Japan for your sake.'

Yeah, right. Like his dad had ever done anything for his sake.

Connor had been thirteen when his dad had announced he'd sold the restaurant in Halifax and was leaving for a job abroad. He well remembered how distraught he'd been when his dad had half-heartedly talked about taking Connor with him and finding him a place at a British school out there. How he'd cried and cried, and Lexie had begged for him to be allowed to stay behind with her – and how his dad, with an all-too-obvious expression of relief, had agreed with barely an objection raised. For the sake of Connor's education, he'd said. Certainly not because he wanted an excuse to get his son out of his sight.

'If you say so,' Connor said, as evenly as he could manage. 'I don't want to move in with you, though. I like it with Lexie.'

'No.' Daryl sighed. 'No, I wouldn't have expected that. But I do want me and you to... I love you, son. I hope you know that.'

Connor didn't know why, but hearing those words from his father made him feel... not good. Not like you were supposed to feel when your dad told you he loved you. All he felt was angry, and hurt; almost like he'd been punched. When was the last time his dad had said that to him? When he was four? Five? Before his mum...

'OK.' Connor was silent for a moment, scowling at the little leather address book that lived by the phone. 'So will you send Lexie more money? I know you send her some for my stuff but it's not enough. She says I grow out of clothes as fast as she buys them.'

'Why, how tall are you now?'

'I'm nearly six foot, Dad.'

'Are you?' Daryl fell silent for a moment. 'Bloody hell.'

'I think you should let her sell the house so we can live somewhere cheaper. She hates it here anyway. Everyone in the village thinks the new estate's an eyesore and it should never have been built.'

'You think that, do you?' Daryl said sternly. 'You seem to have an awful lot of opinions these days, young man.'

There was a time when a comment like that from his father would have made Connor instinctively shut up and shrink back into himself. But then he thought about Lexie and everything she'd had to deal with since his dad had left, and he pulled himself up tall.

'Yeah, I do,' he said stoutly. 'Good ones that I've thought about. Lexie told me I shouldn't ever let people make me feel ashamed of being able to think for myself.'

'I bet she bloody did.' His dad sounded angry now; ready, as always, to fly off the handle at the slightest provocation. 'She's brainwashed you, hasn't she? Turned you against me. Fuck, I knew it! I knew I should never have given in when you asked to stay with her.'

'She hasn't done anything to me,' Connor said urgently. 'She never told me to say this stuff – she doesn't know I know anything about it. Don't send me any more money, Dad, please: I don't want it. Send it to Lexie. She won't take it from me, but she'll take it from you.'

'Well, for your sake I'll see what I can afford,' Daryl said. 'And perhaps you might like to think about how you speak to your father, Connor Carson.'

'Fine,' Connor said. 'Bye then.'

Connor didn't wait for his dad to reply before hanging up.

Chapter Four

'I took the liberty of helping us both to a vodka and orange,' Tonya said when Lexie sat down at the kitchen table. 'I thought you could probably use one.'

'You're not wrong.' Lexie took a grateful gulp of the drink. 'Thanks, pseudo-Mum.'

'How's my erstwhile son-in-law then?'

'He's an utter, utter prick. No offence.'

'None taken. What was he calling for? To talk to Connor?'

'Are you kidding? When does he ever call to talk to Connor? I asked him to ring.' Lexie glanced resentfully around the large kitchen with its faux-rustic aesthetic. 'I was hoping he might agree to contribute something extra to this ridiculous house. He seems to think that as long as he covers his share of the mortgage, the rest of the running costs are nothing to do with him.'

'Why don't you put it on the market? The two of you are going to have to sell it at some point.'

'Daryl won't have it. He's obsessed with bloody property price trends. Says we need to wait till we're at the peak of the curve so we can release maximum value from it.'

'Sounds like Daryl.' Tonya took a thoughtful gulp of her drink. 'You know, when my daughter first brought that boy home I was quite impressed. Elise was always such a strait-laced child, I was sure she'd end up marrying some dull bank-manager type and I'd have to spend every Christmas Day pretending I voted Tory and watching my language. When she turned up with Daryl Carson, with his earring and his green hair and his jacket with the Ban the Bomb patch, I was pleasantly surprised.'

'How old was he?'

'Sixteen when I met him. She invited him, Theo and a few other school pals over for a post-exam party, but it was Daryl she couldn't keep her eyes off. I knew I was destined to have him for a son-in-law that day, young as they were.'

Lexie smiled. 'I bet you were so disappointed when he ditched the green hair and went into restaurant management.'

'Well, that was my dad's fault. He offered him a foot in the door in the hospitality business.'

'And the next thing you know, his piercing's healed up and he's a leading light in the local Rotary Club.'

'Yes.' Tonya stared into her glass. 'And yet he never was that way while Elise was alive. It was only after she died that he threw himself into work. He'd been a grafter before but it was when he lost Elise that he became…'

'Career-driven?'

'Obsessed.' She sighed. 'I know he can be a hard man to get on with, but you have to feel sorry for him. Elise left a big hole in his life. For me too, but for him… a widower at twenty-six, a single dad. Thank God he found you.'

Lexie smiled. 'You know, when he first brought me to be introduced to you I was scared stiff. I was sure you'd resent me for taking your daughter's place in his life, and Connor's. Instead you gave me a big hug then went out of your way to get me squiffy.'

Tonya laughed. 'Well, some things never change. Cheers, m'dear.' They clinked glasses.

'Why were you so nice to me?'

She shrugged. 'I could see you were good for him. For both of them.'

'Not for Daryl,' Lexie said. 'I was too young, then, to under-stand why it couldn't ever work between us. Now when he calls, he's like a stranger. All we do is fight.'

'You loved him once though.'

'I thought so. I mean, I did, it was real, but...' She paused. 'I loved him, but I wonder if I ever really knew him. The person he was underneath.'

'Why did you fall for him?'

'I can tell you why I unfell for him. Connor. The way Daryl pushed him away all the time.'

'That wasn't what I asked.'

Lexie shrugged. 'Well, he was handsome, successful, steady – the sort of thing that feels like it matters when you're twenty-three. He could be fun, and very sweet at times. Our second date, he turned up with my passport, a packed suitcase and two tickets to Venice – he'd bribed my housemate to help him surprise me. And knowing how he'd lost his wife... I couldn't help melting.' She sighed. 'Where did it all go wrong, Ton? I never thought we'd spend all our time yelling at each other.'

'I did wonder, in the early days, if you'd cope. Daryl was barely there, and you were very young to manage Connor alone.'

She smiled. 'Yes, Connor. The one good thing that did come out of my doomed marriage. Even on his sulkiest teenager days, I've never regretted that part of it.'

'You sure?' Tonya said, lifting an eyebrow. 'I know you always wanted a baby of your own. Wasn't there even a little part of you that thought Daryl moving abroad was your chance to break free of the Carson family and start afresh?'

'Not even a flicker,' Lexie said firmly. 'Daryl's welcome to sod off halfway round the world for my money, but I'll never regret being Connor's stepmum. I've not done much in my life I can be proud of, but I'm proud of him.'

'You haven't given up on a family of your own though, have you?'

'Connor is a family of my own.' She fell into thoughtful silence. 'I would like to meet someone else though. I'd still love to have a baby.' She glanced up at Tonya. 'But whatever happens,

I won't walk away from Connor. Even if it means I can't have those things until later in life – even if it means I can never have them. He's just as much my kid as Daryl's.'

Tonya smiled. 'I don't know why I asked when I already knew the answer.' She stood up and rested a hand on Lexie's shoulder. 'Well done,' she said quietly. 'On behalf of my Elise. I know she'd be grateful for all you've done for her boy.'

Lexie dipped her head for a moment.

'Thank you,' she whispered. 'I know I'm not perfect but I've done my best. Knowing you believe in me… it helps.'

'Let's talk about happier subjects, eh?' Tonya gave her shoulder a rub and sat back down. 'So what are you doing tonight while Connor's off losing his innocence?'

Lexie winced. 'Ugh, don't even joke. I'm worried enough as it is.'

'Oh, let him enjoy himself. And you go enjoy yourself. Have you got plans?'

'Yeah, Theo's coming over. We'll probably watch a film or something.'

'Theo? I'd have thought you'd be sick of the sight of him after seeing him at work every day. Besides, he was Daryl's friend, not yours.'

'Not since we took over the restaurant. Honestly, Ton, I don't know how I'd have coped without him this past year. He's the best friend I've got these days.'

'Haven't you got other friends you can go out on the town with? You're still young, Lexie. You'll only end up talking business with Theo.'

'No I won't. We talk about lots of things.' Lexie finished the last of her drink. 'I dunno, it feels like hard work when I get together with my old mates now – ever since me and Daryl separated. Half of them are still single, and the ones who've got families, their kids are in nursery or primary school. And there's me with a kid of fourteen that I've inherited from my not-quite-ex-husband… I feel like they're not sure how to talk to me any more. Like I'm some sort of freak.'

'Oh, that's your imagination.'

'Perhaps. Still, I find it difficult to join in the conversation. Our worlds are just so different.' She stood to put her glass in the dishwasher. 'I know exactly what they think. They think Daryl's walked out on me and lumbered me with his kid, and I'm too much of a pushover to walk away. They always did think I was a mug to get involved with a single dad at twenty-three. Maybe I am imagining the pitying looks, but they still hurt.'

'What about Connor's friends' parents?'

'We get on all right, but they're all so much older than me.' Lexie sighed. 'I don't know where I fit any more, Ton. I'm starting to feel seriously old before my time.'

They heard the front door open, and the words 'Honey, I'm home!' rang through the house.

'Theo,' Lexie said, smiling. 'He never knocks.'

A second later, the man himself appeared.

'Evening, ladies,' he said. 'As you were. No need to stop talking about me.'

Lexie smiled at him. 'I'd like to say that's your ego, but by sheer coincidence we actually were just talking about you. I was hatching a plan to lure you to the pub after your chat with Connor.'

'Well, that sounds like the cue for me to love and leave the pair of you,' Tonya said, standing up. 'I've got packing to do.'

'Not another cruise?' Theo said. 'Ton, you really ought to stop watching those *Miss Marple* repeats on ITV3. You're a sucker for the Saga ads.'

'Listen, young man, how I choose to enjoy my retirement is my own business.'

'I bet they're full of octogenarian swingers and champagne lush army majors, aren't they?'

She grinned. 'Wouldn't you like to know?'

'No, actually.'

'What's the chat with Connor in aid of then, Theo?'

'Birds, bees, that sort of thing,' Lexie told her. 'I thought he'd appreciate some fatherly advice before he spends the night at Sophie's. Well, godfatherly advice.'

'I still can't believe I agreed to do this,' Theo muttered. 'Where is the boy, then?'

'In the hall, talking to his dad.'

Theo's brow darkened. 'So Daryl's remembered he's got a son, has he? I guess Neptune must be in retrograde or something.'

'Actually, no. I asked him to call me about the house.' Lexie stood up and kissed him on the cheek. 'Thanks for doing this, love. I've got spag bol and a bottle of red for afterwards as your reward.'

'All right, I'm going,' Theo said. 'But it'd better be a bloody good red wine, that's all. And you owe me a pint at the pub as well.'

Chapter Five

Friday was Theo's day off, and he'd come straight from the gym to catch Connor before Lexie drove him to his girlfriend's. The thought of the ordeal ahead wasn't a happy one, but a promise was a promise, after all. Besides, Lexie was right: it was hard luck on the kid not having his dad around to help him through the more excruciating aspects of puberty. Theo knew from experience what that felt like, growing up with just his mum. At Connor's age, he'd often secretly wished he had someone – maybe an uncle or a grandad – he could talk to. But the only male presence in his life back then had been his mum's boyfriend of the moment, and he tried not to get too attached. They never stayed long enough to make it worth his while.

Anyway, as painful as it was no doubt going to be, Theo was Connor's godfather and it was time he stepped up. He girded his loins – well, it was really more of a buttock-clench, since he wasn't exactly sure how loins were meant to be girded – and stepped out into the hall.

Connor was just hanging up the phone, face like a thunder-cloud. Since Theo knew that this was the habitual expression of the species *teenageus boyus*, he tried not to take it personally.

'All right, mate?' he said with a friendly grin. 'So, I hear you've got a sizzling hot date tonight.'

'Um, well, I'm staying at Sophie's.' Connor summoned a smile. 'Hi, Uncle Theo. Sorry about *Spider-Man*. We can watch it next week.'

'Don't worry about it.' Theo nodded to the stairs. 'You got five minutes? I wanted a quick word in private.'

'Now? I need to pack my stuff.'

'It won't take long.'

'All right.' Looking puzzled, Connor led Theo up to his bedroom.

'Um, pull up a beanbag,' Theo said, gesturing to the one in the corner.

Connor flopped down, his long, skinny legs stretching out in front of him like a knock-kneed spider not sure how to arrange its limbs. Theo perched on the edge of his godson's gaming chair, trying to pretend he hadn't noticed the mess.

Christ, or the smell, he thought, wrinkling his nose. Dirty mugs – some sporting an impressive coating of mould – littered the place among unwashed underpants, discarded socks that looked as though rigor mortis had long since set in, well-thumbed comic books and copies of *SFX* magazine, plus God knew what other crap.

Teenagers were disgusting. Had he been this bad when he was Connor's age? He made a mental note to take his mum some flowers the next time he went to visit.

'So... have you decided what you're wearing to the 1940s fest?' he asked. 'I know you love an excuse to dress up.'

'Jesus, I don't have to go to that thing, do I?'

'Course you do. You're going to look adorable in a little evacuee costume. Short trousers, Fair Isle tank top, a pair of woollen knee socks...'

'That'd better be a joke, Theo.'

He smiled. 'Yeah, it was a joke. We'll get you a nice, sexy GI uniform, eh? You can pretend you're pre-Captain America Steve Rogers.'

'Why did you want to talk to me in private about 1940s costumes?'

'I didn't. That was just to break the ice.' Theo reached up to rub his neck. 'Look, er... son. We've known each other a long time, right? Since one of us was born, in fact.'

'Well, yeah.' Connor frowned. 'Shit, you're not dying, are you?'

36

'No, but if the ground wanted to open up and swallow me then I wouldn't complain,' Theo muttered. He looked at Connor, who was combing his fingers through his too-long brown curls. 'Lexie asked if, um… if I might have a word with you. Man to man.'

'Man to man? Oh God.' Connor groaned. 'Please say we don't have to do this.'

'Look, I'm not going to start asking questions about your balls or anything,' Theo reassured him. 'Your stepmum just thought you might like to have someone to talk to who knew about stuff. You know, boy stuff. I mean, man stuff.'

'Uncle Theo, it's fine. I know how it all works. I've known since I was five.'

Theo blinked. 'Have you?'

'Yeah, my nan got me a book. With cartoons and that.'

'Right,' Theo said. 'To be honest, it wasn't really the technical side of things I was expecting to have to speak to you about. I just thought you might have, er, questions. About Sophie.'

Connor frowned. 'Questions about Soph?'

'Yeah, things you might be worried about. Sex stuff, you know?' Theo glanced at the cover of a gaming magazine on Connor's bed, which bore a lurid illustration of a generously bosomed female elf wearing the skimpiest of armoured bikinis. 'Then again, maybe I should be the one asking you for tips.'

Connor flushed. 'Please, Theo. Please can we not do this? I'll pay you actual money to not do this.'

Theo sighed. 'Look, Con. You can trust me when I say I feel as awkward about this conversation as you do, but sex is really nothing to be embarrassed about. Pretty much everyone does it – or will do it someday, in your case. I just want you to feel you've got someone you can talk to, OK? Maybe not right at this moment, but if you ever feel you need advice. I know you're not going to want to talk to Lexie or Tonya about that stuff, and your friends… well, it might be a long time since I was fourteen, but I do remember that I was full of bullshit, and so were all my mates. It goes with the territory for lads your age.'

Connor blinked. 'Does it?'

'Yep. Plus everyone's got that one knobhead mate who claims he's really sexually experienced but in reality has never had a sniff. Who's your one?'

'What?'

'Come on, I know you've got one. Which of your friends reckons he's had sex with loads of girls?'

'Oh. JJ,' Connor said. 'So you had a mate like that at school too?'

Theo nodded. 'I told you, everyone does.'

'Who was yours?'

'You know him actually,' he said, smiling. 'Daryl Carson.'

Connor raised his eyebrows. 'Dad?'

'Yeah, till he started going out with your mum in Year Eleven. And he was full of it as well, just like your friend JJ. I can guarantee you the lad's still a virgin, as are all the boys you know, no matter what bollocks they come out with.'

Connor's blush was still a fixture, but his lips twitched with a smile.

'Thanks, Theo.'

'No problem. So, er, was there anything you wanted to ask me?'

'Not really. I've got the internet.'

Theo laughed. 'And I'm sure your search history makes for a fascinating read.' He reached over to clap Connor on the shoulder. 'You know where I am if you need me, OK? Just on the end of the phone.'

'Yeah. Cheers.'

Theo made as if to go, then, in his best Columbo impersonation, stopped at the door and turned back.

'Oh, by the way. There was one more thing.' He took a blue, cellophane-wrapped box from his jacket pocket. 'I'm sure you won't need these for a while yet, but it's better to be safe than sorry, isn't it? Just tuck a couple in your wallet, then whenever the time comes – I mean, many, many years from now, when you're physically, emotionally and legally ready – you'll know you're prepared.'

He tossed Connor the box, and the boy's eyes widened.

'You know how to put one of these on, right?' Theo asked. 'You've learnt about it at school?'

'Yeah, I know.' Connor's face was now roughly the colour of an over-ripe pomegranate. 'Bloody hell, Theo!'

'Because I could show you. There's probably a courgette in the fridge I could—'

'Jesus Christ, please no.' Connor buried his face in his hands. 'This is it. I am officially dead. This moment has literally just ended my life.'

'All right,' Theo said, holding his hands up. 'I get the message. Awkward conversation over, never to be mentioned again. But if you do find things with Sophie are getting a bit heavier than anticipated—'

'Oh *God*!' Connor wailed.

'—then just make sure you've got something on you. I'm sure I don't need to tell you about the dangers of unplanned pregnancies, STDs, et cetera. Be prepared, that's all I'm saying. You were a boy scout, it ought to come naturally to you.'

'Please, Theo. If you really care about me, just go, now, before I die of embarrassment right here on this beanbag.'

Theo smiled. 'Well, I tried.' He patted Connor on the shoulder. 'Just look after yourself, kiddo. I've only got one godson; you can hardly blame me for wanting to keep him safe.'

–

Lexie was stirring bolognese sauce on the hob when Theo, looking mildly traumatised, entered the kitchen.

'So, how did it go?' she asked.

'I think there was mutual unspoken agreement that we would never, ever speak of this day again. Oh, and Connor owes your swear jar about six weeks' pocket money.'

'That bad, eh?'

'Let's just say it'll be at least a week until my toes uncurl.' He managed a smile. 'Still, I think I got the message across. I told the lad he knows where I am if he needs someone to confide in.'

'Thanks, Teddy. I appreciate you stepping out of your comfort zone to do this for him.' Lexie squeezed his elbow. 'You dish up while I drive Con over to Sophie's. I won't be ten minutes.'

–

Lexie dropped Connor off outside the Cavendishes' place in the neighbouring village of Morton just before six. Sophie must have heard them pull up, since she opened the door before he'd even raised his fist to knock.

'Con! Yay, you're here! Thanks for coming, sweetie.'

Connor blinked. Sweetie? Did they sweetie now? They'd never sweetied before.

Sophie took his hand to pull him into the house and kissed him on the lips, but Connor moved away.

'Aren't your mum and dad here?'

'Yeah, but they're out in the summer house so no need to worry about them. Ol isn't here yet either, which means I get you all to myself for a bit.' She tugged on his hand. 'Here, come up to my room. I want to show you something.'

He flushed. 'Um, OK.'

'Well, what do you think?' she said when he'd followed her into her bedroom. She gestured to a scale model of the Millennium Falcon on her desk. 'I got the kit for my birthday. It's taken me ages to build it.'

'Whoa!' Connor ran a reverent finger over the body. 'Serious collectible, Soph.'

'I know, right? Oh, and guess what else I got?'

'What?'

She took two tickets from a drawer and waved them at him. 'Ta-da! Leeds Comic Con tickets, for me and you. Just us, none of the others.' She flushed. 'I thought it'd be romantic. You know, for our eight-month anniversary in October.'

'You're not serious.' He took the tickets from her and stared at them. 'Oh my God, I can't believe your parents got these for us! I'll have to bring your mum a fruit basket or something.'

She laughed at his excitement. 'So who do you think you'll go as?'

'Boba Fett,' he answered immediately.

'Again?'

'Course. Why be anyone else when you can be Boba Fett?'

She smiled. 'And this, Connor Carson, is why I love you.'

His cheeks heated as he wondered whether she meant it. Probably not. Girls said stuff like that all the time, didn't they?

'Um, thanks,' he said.

'I love saying your full name. It makes you sound like a superhero.'

'What makes you think I'm not?'

Sophie laughed. 'You seriously think you can smuggle a *Donnie Darko* line past me without me noticing? Nice try, Con.'

'I'd be disappointed if I could,' he said, smiling. 'So what will you wear?'

Sophie shrugged. 'I thought maybe She-Hulk. I'm in a Marvel sort of mood.'

Connor nodded his approval. 'Nice. You know, Soph, I never knew girls could be cool until I met you.'

'Well, I never knew boys could be sweet until I met you.'

She took his hand and led him to her bed. They sat down, and she lifted her lips up to his.

Connor closed his eyes and opened his mouth a bit, trying to remember the YouTube videos he'd been watching to help him improve his kissing technique. He was definitely getting better:

41

there was hardly ever any escaping saliva now, and Sophie seemed to like it – at least, the noises she made suggested she did. Connor enjoyed the noises, although they frightened him a bit too. He was hoping Sophie wouldn't want to move too quickly to the next stage. In spite of JJ and Crucial's teasing, he'd much prefer to take things slow. He really liked Sophie Cavendish, who was pretty and interesting, and made him laugh, and liked all the same things he liked, and he couldn't help worrying she might go off him if he wasn't very good at whatever the next bit was. He was only just getting the hang of this bit.

She was making the noises again. He could do without that right now, to be honest. Oli would be here any minute, and Mr and Mrs Cavendish. He didn't want to be in the sort of state those breathless little moans and sighs tended to get him into.

One of her hands massaged his back, and Connor, thinking he ought to show a similar level of enthusiasm, wrapped one of his arms around her so he could rub his hand up and down her spine a bit.

She seemed to like that. More noises. God…

Apart from the issues of excess drool and when to break for air, what to do with your tongue was the most awkward part of the business. No amount of studying snogging on YouTube, practising how wide to open your mouth and how to move your head around, could help Connor with that. Did you shove the whole of it right in, like, a full tonsil excavation? Or sort of dart it in and out like a snake? Spiral it round and round like a cement mixer, maybe? Or was it supposed to be kind of the tongue version of a thumb war – like he should sort of scoop hers up and wrestle with it a bit? He tried a few different things, paying close attention to the noises Sophie made in response, but that was no help. She seemed to like all of it. Perhaps he should've asked Uncle Theo for a bit of advice after all. Theo had always had loads of girlfriends and…

Shit! Her hand was sliding over his jeans. Up his thigh, not stopping, not… Connor put his own hand over it to halt its progress.

Sophie pulled her lips away from his.

'What's up?' she whispered. Her eyes looked huge after the kiss, and sort of wet, like Ariel the mermaid or something.

'Oli's going to be here soon.'

'I know,' she said, rolling her eyes. 'Mum wouldn't let you stay over on your own so I had to invite him to keep it respectable. You want me to though, right?'

'Yeah, course. Course I do. I just think… we'd better not get carried away.'

'I guess not.' She kissed him again: just a little peck this time. 'I love how you're so sensible, Connor. You don't push for it like the others do.'

'Um, cheers,' Connor said, although he wasn't sure 'sensible' sounded like much of a compliment. Also… others? What others? He didn't know Sophie had had boyfriends before him. Not that he minded, but it worried him to think she might be comparing him to other, better kissers.

Was she even still a virgin? God, he didn't want to think about that. The idea she might have so much more experience than him was the one thing guaranteed to get him stressing out even more than he was already during their make-out sessions.

She smiled provocatively. 'Anyway, maybe I can get you alone later. It is my birthday party.'

'Yeah.' He forced a smile. 'That'd be… um, nice.'

Chapter Six

'What do you suppose he's up to now?' Lexie asked Theo as they waited at the bar of the Highwayman's Drop.

'Look, relax, can you? Connor's fine.'

'You don't know that. God only knows what that little vixen's doing to him, the poor wee innocent.'

Theo laughed. 'Sophie? She's another one of these cosplay geeks, isn't she?'

'Exactly. She'll be there in her PVC Harley Quinn catsuit, bearing down on my little frightened Connor with a gleam in her eye and a cat o' nine tails in one hand. The experienced older woman. I've seen *The Graduate*.'

'Lex, she's fifteen and into role-play gaming. Those kids have a very different idea of the role of a Dungeon Master than you do, trust me.'

'All right, so I've become a worst-case-scenario panicky mum lady. Don't judge me.' She pulled out her phone. 'I'll just give Janette Cavendish a quick ring, check they're OK.'

Theo took the phone from her and tucked it into his pocket. 'Nope. Confiscated. You'll have a large pinot, relax and enjoy a night's holiday from being mum to a teenage boy. Which, as you're fond of reminding me, you're really far too young to be.'

'God, am I ever,' Lexie said, sighing.

'Hiya,' Brooke said as she approached to take their order. 'Did I just hear you two talking 1940s costumes?'

'Er, no,' Lexie said. 'Different costume conversation.'

'What can I get you both then?'

'Large house white and a pint of Best please.' Lexie summoned a smile. 'So what do you think you'll wear to the festival?'

'Depends how much effort I can be bothered to put in. I quite fancy going as a Wren, but I'll probably leave it till the last minute and end up wearing my mum's mac and pretending I'm in the French Resistance. How about you guys?'

'That's one thing we don't need to worry about. We can just wear our work gear.' Theo grinned as he watched her pour his pint. 'So, any clues as to what might be going on under the long mac, Brooke? Please say it involves suspenders.'

Brooke grinned back. 'Who says it involves anything at all?'

Theo ran a finger under his collar. 'Yikes. Better put some ice in that pint.'

Lexie nudged him. 'You never let up, do you?'

'Have to keep my arm in, love.' He nodded to an empty table. 'You grab us a seat. I'll get these.'

'I thought I owed you a pint.'

'I'll let you have a stay of execution on owed drinks until Daryl finally manages to crowbar his wallet open.' He patted her arm. 'Tonight's on me, Lex. You need a break.'

She smiled at him. 'Thanks, Theo.'

'I'd advise the snug,' Brooke told her in a low voice. 'It's Friday. That means Ryan Theakston's going to be in later looking for someone to bore rigid with tales of his military exploits at that bloody re-enactment group.'

'Right. Thanks for the tip.'

Lexie went to claim a table, leaving Theo to chat up Brooke. It made her smile. She'd been that girl once herself, many years ago.

At thirty-three, Theo was still every inch the handsome, irresponsible charmer he had been the night she'd met him seven years ago, when, with his mate Daryl, he'd approached her in the Leeds casino she'd been working at to see if she might fall for his lines. Lexie, young as she'd been then, had still been wise enough to look past this obviously inveterate flirt to his steadier friend.

Funny how things turned out. In the end it had been flighty Theo who'd been there when she'd most needed someone to lean on, and sensible Daryl who'd let her down. Let them all down.

It seemed strange to remember that just a few years ago it would've been the three of them heading out to the pub, usually on a Tuesday night when the restaurant Daryl and Theo ran together was closed and Connor – still a whispering, pale little lad with fringe in his eyes – was staying over with his nana. If only Lexie could have seen what was looming on the horizon…

Looking back, she was irritated with herself for not spotting the signs that her marriage was destined to fail before it had even begun. Yes, she'd been young and in love, but she ought to have known better. She'd been flattered, then, by the way Daryl had paraded her around Chamber of Commerce and Rotary functions, proudly introducing her to his business contacts as 'my future wife'. She'd been proud of the admiring glances he'd attracted; how he'd been hailed as some sort of whizz-kid restaurateur, little realising just why Daryl threw himself into his work with such vigour.

Above all, she'd glowed with pleasure when he'd compli- mented her on the relationship she was building with Connor. Lexie had been wary when, on their first date, Daryl had revealed he was the father of a seven-year-old boy. That he was a widower had been intimidating enough, and when Lexie had discovered he was a single dad into the bargain, she'd almost called time on the whole thing. Every one of her friends had advised her to ditch him before she got in any deeper.

Nevertheless, a second date followed the first, and then a third. Eventually Lexie was introduced to her boyfriend's young son – a shy little soul, quietly grieving for the mother he'd lost far too young, desperate for love – and an instinct she didn't even know she possessed had taken over. She'd watched

46

Connor's eyes follow his father – the father whose face filled with pain every time he caught sight of the boy – and her heart had melted. In the end she didn't know which part of the package she was marrying into: whether it was Daryl's wife she wanted to be, or Connor's mum. She only knew she was past the point where she could walk away.

It was only after they were married that things started to niggle. Little things, at first. At Daryl's request, Lexie gave up her croupier job so she could spend her nights at home with him and Connor. She wanted another job; a daytime job that wouldn't take her away from her new family, but Daryl wouldn't hear of it. Connor needed her at home, he said, and besides, they didn't need the extra income. Then she worried about his relationship with Connor, and begged him to take more of an interest in the boy's hobbies. Daryl made a token effort to reconnect with his son but he soon grew distant again, that same look of pain in his eyes.

The only time Daryl ever acknowledged Lexie's needs was when she told him she'd like to move house. She didn't feel right living with him in the home he'd shared with his first wife, his teenage sweetheart Elise, who'd died just over a year before they met. Daryl was enthusiastic about that idea, and Lexie had been pleased that she still had some influence with him. However, he quickly took over all the arrangements and Lexie found herself shut out of the decision-making entirely. The next thing she knew, they were in a six-bedroom new-build on the outskirts of Leyholme that felt far too large for their little family. Daryl had said they needed it – someone of his status and ambition needed a home that looked a bit imposing – and after all, he'd said, with a cheeky squeeze of her bottom, who knew that they might not fill the empty rooms before long?

And that had been the real clincher. The baby. The baby that Lexie had been so keen to try for, and that Daryl had continually made excuses to put off.

At first, timing was the issue. The business was still growing. They needed a decent nest egg first: something they could draw on if lean times should come. Then it was Lexie herself. She was young – nearly four years younger than Daryl. She didn't want to ruin her figure just yet, did she? Give up her best years to dirty nappies and midnight feeds? She had plenty of time to have a baby – it was a foolish woman who had children before thirty, in his opinion. Of course, it had been different for him and Elise: they'd been in love since they were kids, so when Elise accidentally fell pregnant at nineteen, marrying and starting a family hadn't really been a big deal. They were going to do it anyway; finding out Connor was on the way had just brought it forward a bit. There was a period during her marriage when Lexie had felt that if she heard the phrase 'things were different with Elise' one more time, she'd start googling undetectable poisons.

And then, finally, he told her he was ready to start trying – just in time for Lexie to realise that Daryl Carson was the last man she ought to have a child with. His strained relationship with the son he already had was enough to make her see that. Besides, by then Lexie knew in her heart that Daryl didn't really want another child. All he wanted was to try to prevent something he ought to have realised was inevitable – the end of their marriage.

The trouble with Daryl was that he hadn't wanted a wife at all: not really. Not in the sense of a companion and friend to share his life with – that place had been occupied by Elise, and it never could be filled by anyone else. All he'd wanted was a trophy, and a tool; someone young, fun and attractive he could show off at networking events, who could accessorise his big house, impress his business associates, and bring up his son.

Lexie had known her marriage was over long before it had officially been pronounced dead. It had been Connor who'd kept her from leaving, although in the end she and Daryl were as good as strangers living under the same roof. She no longer relished being her husband's wife but she still loved being Connor's stepmum, and her fear of losing him had kept her with

48

Daryl long after she ought to have called time on the marriage. The best thing Daryl ever did for the boy was to agree to Lexie's pleas that he should stay in England with her when his dad was offered a two-year contract working for a restaurant chain out in Japan. Uprooting Connor from the life he knew to live in a strange country with an indifferent father would have been the worst thing that could have happened.

And then there was Theo, the one person who had even more reason to resent Daryl Carson than she did. Lexie was actually angrier with Daryl for the way he'd treated his old friend and business partner than she was on her own behalf. Seriously, who did something like that? Concealing the state of the finances in that cold, calculated way; preparing his own exit strategy via a friend with contacts in Japan, then casually announcing weeks before he was due to leave that the business was in its death throes and he'd sold his share for less than half what it ought to have been worth? Given no opportunity to buy his partner out, Theo had been forced to sell his half for a pittance, only barely scraping enough from the ashes of his hard work and dreams to invest in a modest new venture.

But despite Daryl's betrayal, Theo's loyalty to his former friend's family had never wavered. They were all SODs together, he liked to say – Survivors Of Daryl. Lexie didn't know what she would have done without Theo's support and friendship. He was always there to offer a shoulder to cry on and a loan if she needed it, although he was hardly flush with cash himself. And then finally, when she'd been struggling to get a job with a CV that, thanks to Daryl, contained far more gaps than skills, he'd saved her bacon by offering to help her get a business loan so she could go into partnership with him at the little cafe-restaurant they eventually named the Blue Parrot. It was only after Daryl had gone that Lexie realised there was a lot more to Theo Blake than a knicker-dropping grin and a flirty one-liner.

'Tuppence for them?' Theo said as he came over with the drinks.

49

She smiled. 'Just thinking how lucky I am to have a friend like you.'

'I should say you are, after what I went through tonight. I wish I had a daughter I could use to get my own back.' He paused. 'On second thoughts, I really don't.'

'You'll settle down one day.'

'Not if I have anything to do with it.' He sighed as he took a seat opposite her. 'Mind you, I'm not sure the universe isn't trying to send me some sort of message. I'm going through a dry period at the moment.'

'Yeah?' She glanced at the barmaid. 'Brooke Padgett seemed keen to flutter her eyelashes at you.'

'Just a bit of polite social flirting. Brooke's not interested, she's turned me down before.'

Lexie raised her eyebrows. 'That must've been a new experience for you.'

He didn't smile. 'Dunno, Lex. I'm starting to feel like my age is catching up with me.'

'You're not genuinely thinking about finding some poor, unfortunate girl to settle down with?'

'God, no. Me with a wife and family? Seriously, can you imagine?'

'I know, the poor sods.'

'I mean, maybe if I met someone who was on the same page as me when it came to kids. I couldn't compromise on that.' He took a sip of beer. 'Even then, though, I'm not sure she really exists, this perfect woman.'

'Bit harsh on our kind, isn't it?'

'I don't mean in general, I mean for me personally,' he said. 'I've been on a lot of dates, Lex. I've been out with women who are funny, warm, beautiful, sexy, exciting. Women who share my interests, who make me laugh. Every one of my ideal qualities in a partner, but never the whole lot in one package.'

'Bloody hell, Teddy. I never realised you had such high standards.'

He gestured down his body. 'Can't take all this out of circulation for just anyone, can I?'

'So that's the reason you shag around, is it? You're actually a closet romantic eternally searching for your soulmate? I knew you were a man of hidden depths.'

'Well, no, generally I'm just randy,' he said, smiling. 'I'm not kidding though: I genuinely don't think my perfect person exists. If she did, I'd have met her by now. And if she did, the chances of someone like her wanting to be with someone like me are slim to none. So why brood on it?'

'There's not a single person you dated where you thought "hmm, maybe this could work"? No one you wanted to get closer to?'

'Nope,' Theo said. 'Go on, love, say it. I'm a heartless, shrivelled husk of a man destined to die alone.'

She smiled. 'Well, perhaps, but I'm fond of you. Maybe we can share a sofa at the old folks' home, eh? My chances of meeting Mr Right are looking pretty slim these days too.'

'I think I gave up on the whole "ideal partner" thing before I hit puberty. Real life just isn't that Disney.' Theo fell silent. 'I do feel like I'm getting a bit old for playing the field though. Casual dating isn't nearly as much fun as it used to be.'

'Is this Theo Blake I hear talking?'

'I know. Never thought you'd see the day, right?' he said, smiling. 'Ignore me, I'll be back to my old self soon enough. Just having a brief attack of existentialism; probably one of those twenty-four-hour bugs.'

Lexie took a long draught of her wine.

'I've missed this,' she said with a deep sigh. 'Hanging out at the pub, setting the world to rights. Why ever did we stop doing regular pub nights? We've hardly been out for a drink the past two years.'

'Daryl, I guess. When you guys started having problems, it all got a bit awkward. Then there was Connor to keep you busy, and the restaurant...' Theo shrugged. 'Suppose we just got out of the habit.'

'Suppose so.' She scowled. 'Trust it to be Daryl's fault.'

'Oh, forget him. We're here now.'

'Tonya thinks I ought to be sick of you. She can't understand why I don't go hang out with my other friends when I see you all day at work.'

'Well, do you want to? I promise I wouldn't cry. Much.'

'No.' She glanced over his shoulder at the tables of people enjoying their Friday night drinks. 'Funnily enough, not at all. All my old friends want to talk about now is kids where they've got them, or relationships where they haven't. I feel a right bloody lemon, sitting there with nothing to contribute but tales of Connor's teenage angst. It feels like you're the only one of my mates who gets me these days.'

'I suppose that's a compliment,' he said, smiling. 'Let's just have a nice night, shall we? It's not often you're freed from parent duty to go out and enjoy yourself.'

'God, yes.' Her eyes sparkled. 'Hey, we could go clubbing.'

'Oh please, no. I'm far too old for clubbing. I'd probably do my hip in trying to show the kids how to moonwalk.'

'Ah, I bet we could teach them a thing or two.'

'I've met my quota for embarrassing interactions with young people today, thank you. No clubbing.' He sipped his beer. 'So how about you, then? Any hot dates lined up? Sounds like you're stuck in a bit of a dry patch yourself.'

She shrugged. 'I'm a married woman, aren't I?'

'Only on paper. I don't see why you shouldn't get yourself out there. You can bet your arse Daryl has been.'

It was testament to the complete obliteration of the feelings Lexie had once had for her husband that the idea of him with someone else didn't produce even a flicker of jealousy.

'I know,' she said. 'I wish we didn't have to wait so long to file for divorce. It seems daft to have to wait two years when you know it's definitely over.'

'So why don't you start dating again? Just because you still have to be married to Daryl for another year doesn't mean you need to live in celibate misery the whole time.'

'Because of Connor, I suppose. After all the upheaval he's had in his life so far – his mum dying, then me moving in, the new house, his dad leaving – he needs a bit of stability. There'll be plenty of time for me to think about meeting someone when he's gone to uni.'

'It's four years till he'll be off to uni. That's a long time to go without sex.'

'For you, maybe,' she said, smiling. 'I can sort myself out, don't worry. Dating's one more hassle I don't need with everything else I've got on my plate.'

'Don't you miss being with someone? It's not all about the sex.'

'Says the man who's shagged his way round most of the county.'

'That wasn't all about the sex either. You still have to have that connection, even if it's only a one-night thing. Otherwise we'd all just be sorting ourselves out.' He glanced up. 'You don't fancy elaborating on that? Because I could stand to hear a few more details.'

'No.'

He smiled. 'Still, you know what I mean. Sex might not always be an act of love, but it always has to be an act of trust. There is a bonding process involved, even with casual hook-ups. You're letting someone have intimate access to your body: that's never a minor thing.'

'Blokeish privilege, that sort of talk,' she told him. 'It's always been easier for you lot to have casual sex. I don't just mean because there's never been the same stigma, or because you haven't got the baby-carrying bits. You don't have to make yourselves vulnerable the same way we do.'

'Well, maybe you're right.'

Lexie picked up a beer mat and thoughtfully peeled off a few strips. 'It's a nice idea in principle. I did have the odd one-night stand before I met Daryl. Still, I don't think I could do what you do.'

'I can't help feeling we overcomplicate sex in this country,' Theo said. 'I mean, boil it right down and it's just another hobby, isn't it? As long as you take the necessary precautions and you've both got the same agenda. I might have casual sex, but only with women who are looking for casual sex. Honesty's the key. That way no one gets hurt.'

She snorted. 'Right. And did you discuss all these deep ethical convictions with that poor cow who had your name tattooed onto her right bumcheek? She seemed to think you were in it for the long haul.'

'Hey, that wasn't my fault. It was her who neglected to mention that she was insane.'

'Yeah, and what about Regina?'

'Which one was she?'

'The one who tried to convince you to go and meet her parents. In Papua New Guinea.'

'That wasn't my fault either.'

Lexie smiled. 'Course not.'

'I'm right though, aren't I?'

'About what?'

'Sex. We're talking healthy exercise, stress-relieving endorphins, and it's better for our livers and waistlines than the other great British pastime.' Theo toasted her with his pint before taking a sip. 'If we could just get over our hang-ups, we could all be having a lot more of it. Maybe even make it our official national sport. Like cricket, except you're less dependent on the weather and in this game everyone's a winner.'

'I hope this isn't the same talk you gave Connor, Theo.'

'No, don't worry. He got the kid-friendly version, which is "don't do it, and if you absolutely have to do it, make sure you do it safely".' Theo swallowed the last of his beer. 'I'll tell you what's really depressing. That boy's got a better love life than either of us these days.'

'Oh God, don't. I'd just about managed to stop worrying.' She stood up. 'I'll get another round in.'

Chapter Seven

The next morning, Lexie realised why her party-going days were long since over. If even one drink in the pub – well, all right, two large wines, plus the one she'd had with her spaghetti bolognese beforehand – was enough to make her feel there were herds of bison galloping over her optic nerves, then how had she thought she could manage a night at a club? She was glad Theo had talked her out of it.

As it was, she felt just human enough to roll out of bed and make herself semi-presentable before Connor was likely to want picking up from Sophie's.

'Morning,' she said, as brightly as she could manage, when he wandered into the kitchen at around ten. 'I was just about to call and see if you wanted a lift.'

Connor looked at her through narrowed eyes. 'You went out last night, didn't you? Your eyes are all red.'

She grimaced. 'All right, maybe. Just to the pub with Theo. Did Sophie's dad drive you home or did you get the bus?'

'Neither, I walked.'

'Walked?' she said, frowning. 'From Morton?'

'Yeah. It's not that far, is it? I'm not a little kid, I can walk if I want.'

'But you never walk anywhere. You're lazy as sin, Con.'

'Well, this morning I felt like going for a walk.'

He was avoiding meeting her eyes, staring down at the floor tiles. Lexie's brow furrowed.

'You're OK, aren't you?' she said. 'Everything's all right?'

'Yeah, fine,' he muttered.

But Lexie had been playing mum to Connor for too long now not to know when something was bothering him. This wasn't just general teen sullenness; he was upset about something.

She went to put an arm around his shoulders. Or at least, as close as she could get to his shoulders since his last growth spurt, which was around the middle of his back.

'What's up, my love?' she said, giving him a squeeze. 'You didn't fall out with Sophie, did you?'

'No.'

'Then what's wrong? Didn't you have a nice time at the sleepover?'

He shrugged. ''S'all right.'

'Did you play your game?'

'Yeah.'

'And was it as good as you hoped?'

He shrugged again, grunting something inaudible in reply.

'So… there's nothing you want to talk to me about?' Lexie tried. 'Nothing that might've happened with Sophie or… or anything?'

He turned his flushed cheeks away, shaking his head so that his long curls bounced.

Lexie studied him for a moment.

'Well, OK. You know where I am if you change your mind,' she said at last, realising it was useless to press him if he didn't want to open up about whatever was bothering him. 'You want breakfast?'

'No thanks. Not hungry.'

'Oh, guess what? Dad transferred us some money, it showed up in my account this morning. I can get you a new school blazer now.'

'Right.'

She squinted at him. 'You wouldn't happen to know why we're suddenly richer, would you? Your father didn't sound too keen on parting with any cash when I spoke to him yesterday.'

Connor shook his head again, still avoiding eye contact. 'I'm going up to my room.'

'All right. If you're hungry later, there's a fresh loaf in the bread bin and peanut butter in the cupboard. Make sure you have some fruit with it, won't you?'

'Yeah, fine.'

He slouched off to his bedroom looking thoroughly miserable, even by teenager standards. Lexie sighed as she watched him go, feeling once again that the boy she'd come to love as a son was getting further and further from her reach.

–

It was a Wednesday morning two weeks later when Connor went down to the kitchen to grab a cereal bar he could eat on his way to school.

He'd got into the habit of coming down later now, instead of sitting with Lexie for breakfast. She'd finally stopped asking what was wrong every five minutes, but she was still watching him closely. He couldn't stand that: the concern in her eyes every time he caught her looking at him. It made him feel like total crap when she worried about him.

He was hoping she'd have gone back upstairs to get ready for work, but she was still in the kitchen, drinking her morning coffee while she gazed with unseeing eyes at the paper. She looked up when he came in – the worried look again – and he felt his stomach clench with guilt.

'Morning,' she said.

He grunted.

'Have you got time for some toast before you run away? I can put some in for you.'

'I need to go for the bus. I'll take a Special K bar.'

'All right, but take a banana as well.' She stood up to fetch one for him.

'Don't bother,' he said, striding to the fruit bowl. 'I can get it.'

'So… everything all right at school?'

He nodded, stuffing the banana and cereal bar into the pocket of his hoodie.

'And Sophie's OK? She hasn't been round in a while.'

'She's fine.'

Lexie sighed. 'Con, talk to me, please. I can't live with someone who only speaks in monosyllables. What's wrong?'

Connor scowled. 'Nothing. I told you, nothing's wrong. Just drop it, Lexie, OK?'

She sighed again. 'All right. Well, don't forget I'm on the teatime shift today so I won't be in when you get home. There's a beef stew in the slow cooker.'

'Right. Bye then.'

'Hang on.' She opened one of the kitchen drawers and took out a gift-wrapped package. 'I got you something.'

He stared at it. 'What for? It's not my birthday for ages.'

'I know, but I can tell you've been having a difficult time lately, and… well, I thought you deserved a little present out of the extra your dad sent. There's so rarely any spare cash for me to treat you with.'

Connor tore open the wrapping and blinked at the long-desired *Star Wars: Squadrons* game.

'It is the one you wanted, isn't it?' Lexie said, smiling nervously. 'The one all your friends have been talking about?'

'Um, yeah. Thanks.'

'Why don't you ask Oliver and Sophie over this weekend and you can have a bit of a gaming party? I'll get some snacks in.'

Connor scowled. 'Why do you keep on about them all the time? I said I don't want to see them, all right? God!'

Lexie's face crumpled.

'OK,' she said quietly. 'I just thought it would be nice for you.'

Connor looked at the game in his hand, then at Lexie, registering the hurt in her eyes.

'Sorry,' he said in a softer voice. 'That was a douchey thing to say. Sorry, Lexie.'

'Oh, well, never mind,' she said, smiling a little sadly as she patted his elbow. 'I know you've been having a rough time.'

'It was nice of you to get the game for me.' Connor hesitated, then bent down to peck her cheek. 'Thanks.'

She smiled properly then, the warmth of it lighting up her face and crinkling the corners of her eyes, and for just a moment Connor felt happy at having made her happy. Then the gloom that had been a permanent fixture since the night of Sophie's sleepover set in again.

'I've got to go,' he said.

'Connor!' Lexie called after him. 'Remember that if you ever want to talk—'

'Yeah, yeah, I know.'

He made his way through the sleepy village streets, fragrant with recent rainfall and spring blossom, taking the route to the bus stop that he knew was least likely to mean he'd end up bumping into Oli. However, when the bus stop came into view he saw that Sophie was there, looking around her anxiously.

Shit! What was she doing here? Her dad usually drove her to school, and anyway, she lived a couple of miles away in the next village. Was she there deliberately to catch him?

He was about to turn and head for a different stop when she called to him.

'Connor!'

Connor tried to pretend he hadn't heard and strode off in the opposite direction, but she was soon jogging up to his side.

'Connor, wait, please!' she panted.

He scowled at the ground. 'Leave me alone.'

'Not until you tell me what's going on. You avoid me at school, you ignore my WhatsApps... why are you ghosting me, Con? Have you gone off me or what?'

His scowl relaxed slightly. 'No.'

'Then what is it? Didn't you enjoy yourself that night? You told me you liked it.'

'I... did.' His scowl deepened again, and he turned his face away. 'I can't do this.'

'Please, Con, talk to me. Tell me what I did wrong.'

'I... I said I can't do this, right? Just leave me the fuck alone, Sophie, can you? Please.'

He strode off. Sophie watched him go, her eyes filled with hurt, puzzled tears.

–

Theo nudged Lexie, who was leaning against the Blue Parrot's mahogany bar, staring vacantly at her reflection in the illuminated mirror that backed the spirit optics.

'Are you going to take Nell and Xander's order or what? They pointedly closed their menus five minutes ago.'

'Hmm?' She roused herself. 'Oh, sorry. Yes.'

She wove through the little tables with their floral tablecloths and wine-bottle candlesticks to where the headteacher of Leyholme Primary School was sitting with his wife, who taught the Reception class.

'Afternoon,' she said, summoning a smile.

Nell and Xander were a pleasant couple of around her age who lived in that adorable farmhouse on top of the moors, Humblebee Farm. It had been little more than a wreck when Lexie had first moved to the village to be with Daryl, but Nell had worked hard to transform it into a cosy nest since she'd taken up residence. Lexie always envied her the place when she compared it to her own faceless detached on the much-maligned new-build estate that sat on the outskirts of the village.

Xander had been Connor's Year Three teacher back when Lexie first started seeing Daryl. He and his new wife Nell – Stevie Madeleine's eldest daughter – were regulars at the Parrot and Lexie had come to know them quite well.

'Hi Lexie,' Nell said. 'Everything going OK with the festival plans? My mum's volunteered us to help on the day, you'll be pleased to know. We tried to object but she started jabbing her finger like Lord Kitchener and muttering ominously about how our village needed us.'

'Stevie gets a bit into these things,' Xander said, smiling. 'Suddenly I had this vision of my guilt-stricken face while some future offspring asked me what Daddy did during the great Leyholme 1940s Festival.'

Lexie laughed. 'Yeah, things're going pretty well. The parish council approved our grant, so Janette's started booking in the entertainment. We might even manage to arrange a flypast.'

'The kids'll love that.'

'Well, what can I get you both?' Lexie asked, taking out her notepad.

'Is it weird that I'm fancying the pease pudding with saveloys?' Nell said. 'It's not like me to go for the stomach-lining stuff. I think this might be my first official pregnancy craving.'

'Yes, Carmel in the post office told me you were expecting a little one in the autumn,' Lexie said, smiling. 'Congratulations, you two.'

'I suppose we ought to have kept it secret until after my first scan, but who can keep anything quiet here? Carmel probably knew before I did.'

'Well, as an honorary mum of one I feel qualified to state that your life will never be the same again. Your little sister must be excited, is she?'

'God, isn't she just? And my mum isn't much better than Milly.'

'How is Connor, Lexie?' Xander asked. 'School OK? He was always a bright lad.'

'Oh, I don't know,' Lexie said, sighing. 'He seems to have caught a serious case of Teenager recently. He doesn't tell me anything any more, about school or anything else.'

Xander frowned. 'I hope he's all right.'

'I'm sure he is.' Lexie summoned a smile. 'You know what they get like. There must be a period of about five years where their only form of communication is a grunt.'

But in her heart of hearts, Lexie didn't believe Connor was all right at all. She'd been worrying herself sick about him ever since she'd ventured into his room that morning to clear out some of his dirty cups.

She delivered Nell and Xander's food order to the cook then went back to the bar, where Theo was preparing a tray of drinks.

'Are you going to tell me what's up then?' he asked while he pulled a pint of John Smith's. 'You've been staring at the walls like a stoned zombie all morning.'

'Connor. What else?'

'Still quiet, is he?'

She nodded gloomily. 'I bought him this PC game he wanted, hoping it might cheer him up a bit, but when I suggested inviting his friends over to play it he bit my head off. He never mentions Sophie now, he just shuts himself up in his room.'

'They've probably had a lovers' tiff. First girlfriend, there's bound to be teething troubles.'

'That's what I thought. But then I went into his room to get some of the cups he likes to collect in there and I found...' She lowered her voice. 'I found a packet of condoms, Theo. Under his bed.'

'Well, yeah. I bought them for him.'

She frowned. 'You did what?'

'I bought them. I brought them over when I came round to have my manly talk with him.'

Lexie glared at him. 'Bloody hell, Theo! I'm worried enough about the idea he might start having sex before he's old enough; I could do without his godfather giving it his full endorsement.'

He held his hands up. 'Hey, you said you wanted me to do the safe sex talk and I did it.'

'I meant "safe sex" as in the sort that's one hundred per cent safe because you're not actually having it. I thought you were going to try to talk him out of it.'

'I did. I just thought that on the off-chance he was going to do it anyway, he ought to have what he needs to do it safely. I don't think you fancy becoming a glamorous granny in your early thirties, do you? Don't worry, Lexie, he won't have actually used them.'

'Yeah? Then how do you account for the fact they were open? Two had been taken out, I counted.'

'Had they?' Theo frowned for a moment. 'Oh, I know. I told him to slip a couple in his wallet so he'd be prepared.'

'*What?*' She shook her head. 'Last time I trust you to help me parent.'

'Come on, stop worrying. He won't have done anything with them. Not Connor.'

'Then why's he been acting so strangely?'

'Because he's a kid. They're strange beasts, that's what they do.'

'I'll tell you what I think.' She gazed morosely at a poster of a sexy blonde woman surrounded by men in uniform bearing the slogan *Keep mum – she's not so dumb!* 'I think he might've let things go too far with Sophie and now he's terrified of the consequences.'

'If he remembered the condoms, you'd hope there wouldn't be any consequences. Other than emotional ones, I suppose.'

'And legal ones,' she whispered. 'They're underage, Theo.'

'The age of consent exists mainly to protect children from older people who might take advantage of them. They won't prosecute a couple of kids for sleeping together before they turn sixteen.'

'But Connor might not know that. He's obviously worrying himself to death about something. He probably thinks the cops are going to turn up and haul him off to jail. Either that or he's just been traumatised by the whole experience, the poor lamb.' She sighed. 'I wish I knew how to get him to talk to me.'

The phone behind the bar rang, and Theo went to answer it.

'Blue Parrot?' He frowned. 'Alexis Whittle? Yes, she works here. Hang on, I'll put her on.'

He passed her the handset. 'For you. I think it might be the school.'

With a growing sense of trepidation, Lexie put the phone to her ear.

'Hello?' Her eyes widened. 'He's done what? *What?* Oh my God! Oh, I am so sorry. I don't know why he… yes, of course, I'll fetch him at once.'

'Shit, what is it?' Theo said when she'd hung up. 'That didn't sound good.'

'It's Connor,' she said in a low voice. 'He's been given a three-day suspension for fighting at school.'

Chapter Eight

'Um, hi,' Lexie said to the receptionist at Ravenswood Secondary School. 'Alexis Whittle. I was called in to pick up my stepson.' Her cheeks burned with mortification. 'He's been given a suspension.'

'What year group is your stepson in, Mrs Whittle?'

'Ten. Connor Carson.'

The woman made a telephone call, and soon Mr Walters, Connor's head of year, appeared in reception.

'Ms Whittle,' he said with a warm smile. 'Thank you for coming in at such short notice. Please, step into my office.'

She followed him to his office and he gestured to a seat at his desk before taking the one across from her.

'Mr Walters, I'm so sorry,' she said. 'I don't know what could have got into him. Connor's never been in any sort of trouble like this before.'

'I must admit, I was surprised myself. Connor's behaviour in school has generally been exemplary, apart from the usual horseplay you might expect among groups of boys.'

'What happened?'

'A fist-fight seems to have broken out between Connor and another pupil in the queue for the canteen. I was reluctant to exclude him, but he bruised the boy's eye rather badly so I'm afraid this was more than just messing about. School policy is very clear on the punishment for fighting.'

'Yes. Yes, I understand that.' Suddenly Lexie was hit by an overwhelming urge to cry, and she lowered her head while she fought it back.

'Would you like to take a moment?' Mr Walters asked.

'No.' She took a deep breath. 'No, I... I'm OK. Sorry.'

'Is there anything we as a school ought to be aware of? Any problems at home?'

Lexie shook her head. 'Nothing's changed, if that's what you mean. His dad and I are still separated. Daryl's going to be working out in Japan for another nine months and Connor lives with me. That's the same home situation as he's been in for over a year now.'

'That must be hard for you,' he said quietly.

'I get by, mostly. But it is a difficult age, and... well, I suppose most of your Year Ten mums are a fair bit older than I am,' she said, smiling weakly. 'I do feel out of my depth with him at times.'

'Connor's mother is...' He checked his notes. 'Oh yes, of course. No longer with us. So you've adopted him?'

'No, not officially, but I do have parental responsibility for him along with his father. I mean, if there's anything I need to sign or... anything.'

'Could his mother's death be influencing his behaviour? To lose a parent at such a young age is likely to have far-reaching emotional consequences long afterwards.'

'I'd considered that myself,' Lexie said. 'Connor hasn't mentioned his mum to me though. If he's been dwelling on her death, I can't think what might have triggered it.'

'No new partner for you, anything like that?'

'No, nothing different at all. But Connor has been behaving strangely for a couple of weeks.'

Mr Walters frowned. 'In what way?'

'He's been very quiet, and he seems to have stopped seeing his friends completely outside school. I've tried to get him to talk to me, but he's adamant everything is fine. I thought he might have fallen out with his girlfriend.'

'Ah. There's a girlfriend in the equation, is there?' Mr Walters said. 'Well, that might account for it.'

'Who was the student he was fighting with? Are you allowed to tell me?'

Mr Walters glanced down at an incident report. 'A boy named Daniel Anderson.'

She frowned. 'Crucial?'

'Pardon?'

'Oh, sorry. Crucial: that's what the other boys call him. No one seems to remember why.' Lexie shook her head. 'That doesn't sound right. Daniel's a friend of Connor's.'

'According to this report, it was an incident of name-calling that caused Connor to start the fight. The other boy will of course be disciplined too, but Connor's admitted it was he who was the instigator.'

Again, that didn't sound right to Lexie. Those boys were always calling each other names and play-fighting, it was part of how they bonded. Why should Connor suddenly fly into a rage?

'This isn't like him at all,' she said to Mr Walters. 'Really, I can't understand it. Connor's always been a very gentle boy.'

Mr Walters stood up. 'Well, I think that a heart-to-heart might be in order when you get him home. He clearly has some issues he'd benefit from talking about.'

–

Connor didn't speak a word on the drive home. He just sat in the passenger seat, hugging his rucksack. Lexie didn't say anything either. She wasn't sure what to say. Half of her just wanted to give the boy a big hug, while the other half was in favour of grounding him for the rest of his natural life.

'I'm going to my room,' he muttered when they got back to the house.

'You're doing no such thing,' she told him. 'Living room. Now.'

'I don't want to talk about it, Lexie.'

'What you want and what's going to happen are two very different things, young man. Do as you're told.'

He glared at her for a moment, then threw down his schoolbag and stomped into the living room.

Lexie followed him in and pointed to the sofa. 'Sit down.'

He flung himself down, and she took a seat in the armchair.

'So are you going to tell me you're not angry, you're just disappointed?' he said.

'You're right, Connor, I'm not angry. Bloody furious is what I am! Now do you want to explain yourself?'

He shrugged. 'Crucial was being a dick.'

'Crucial's always being a dick. That's no reason to give him a black eye.'

He shrugged again.

Lexie sighed. 'Con, I genuinely just want to help. Can you at least give me a clue? I won't punish you if you can explain.'

'Fuck, Lexie, just ground me and get it over with. You're not my mum.'

Lexie recoiled as if she'd been slapped.

It was perfectly true: she wasn't his mum. She often prefaced some parental act by mentioning that fact. But never, in all the years she'd been responsible for him, had Connor ever thrown it in her face like that. She'd anticipated that 'you're not my real mum' might make an appearance sometime in the teen years, but still, she was surprised by how much it hurt.

'No. I'm not,' she said quietly. 'You know I care about you as much as if I was though. When you're unhappy, I want to fix it.'

'Well you can't.' Connor looked like he was struggling to hold back tears. 'I'm not a little kid any more. You can't stick on a plaster, give me a hug and make it all OK.'

'Don't I know it,' Lexie muttered.

'Can I please just go to my room?'

She sighed. 'Yes, go. You might as well.'

'Am I grounded or what?'

'Of course you're bloody grounded. I'm taking away your Wi-Fi privileges too. You can have them back on Friday, if you manage to avoid punching anyone until then.'

'Fine. I don't care.' His face working feverishly as he fought to hold off tears, Connor stomped off upstairs.

When he was gone, Lexie, too, found herself overcome by tears.

She'd lost him, hadn't she? This time, she'd really lost him. What was it? Sex? Drugs? Self-harm? Bullying?

'Oh... God.' She gave a wet laugh and wiped her eyes. 'All right, Lexie. Crying's no good to you. Bloody well fix it.'

She took out her phone and pulled up Janette Cavendish's number.

'Janette, hi, it's Lexie,' she said when Sophie's mum answered. 'Have you got five minutes?'

'Of course. Is it about the festival?'

'No, it's about Connor. The sleepover two weeks ago.'

'Oh. Yes. I've been meaning to call you about that actually.'

Sophie's mother sounded faintly guilty, and Lexie felt a surge of worry.

'Why, is there something I need to know?' she asked. 'I hope Connor didn't do anything wrong.'

'There was something, yes.' She sighed. 'I'm so sorry, Lexie. Sophie's always been such a good girl; I can't think where she got it from.'

Lexie's stomach lurched. Oh God. Drugs, was it drugs? Was it one of the really bad ones – heroin, cocaine, meth? *Please, please don't let it be that...*

'Where she got what, Janette?' she asked, trying to keep her voice steady.

'The vodka. I found her and the boys passing a bottle between them. I took it away from them at once, of course. I'm sorry, I ought to have told you as soon as it happened.'

'Vodka?' OK, not meth then. Lexie let herself breathe.

'I really am so sorry,' Janette said. 'Trust me, it won't happen again. It's a case of once burned, twice shy as far as me and her dad are concerned.'

'There wasn't anything else? I wondered if Connor and Sophie had had some sort of falling out.'

'Yes, I wondered that myself. Sophie's been ever so upset. She says Connor's ignoring all her messages.'

'You wouldn't know why, would you? I can't get a word out of him.'

'I honestly can't think. Sophie tells me they didn't have any sort of row; he just stopped speaking to her. They seemed perfectly happy at the sleepover.'

'They didn't... look, I'm sorry to have to ask, but I need to know. They definitely kept to their own rooms all night, didn't they?'

'Oh yes, you don't need to worry about that. Her dad and I were very vigilant in that respect.'

Lexie breathed a sigh of relief. 'Well, that's one weight off my mind anyway. Thanks, Janette.'

When she'd ended the call, she rang the Fosters and spoke to Oliver's dad. All she could discover from him was that Oliver, too, seemed to be getting the silent treatment from Connor. Lexie hung up feeling she was still none the wiser.

She went up to Connor's room and knocked softly on the door.

'Con? Can I come in, love?'

'No.'

'Well, do you want to come down and have some dinner then?'

'I'm not hungry.'

'I, um... I spoke to Sophie's mum. She told me about the vodka.'

'Right. So ground me a bit more then. I only had a few mouthfuls.'

'I'm not going to ground you. I just want to know what's bothering you.'

'Nothing. I'm fine. Just leave me alone.'

Sighing, she went back downstairs and slumped on the sofa. Tears pricked her eyes again.

She ought to go back to work, but she felt completely wiped out. Parenting today felt as draining as a nasty dose of the flu. Besides, she didn't want to leave Connor alone. She was starting to seriously worry he might be clinically depressed or something.

Lexie took out her phone and dialled the restaurant.

'Blue Parrot?'

'Theo, hi. It's me.'

'Lex? You sound awful. Is Connor OK?'

'No. No, I don't think he is.' Unable to stop herself, she burst into tears again. 'Theo, I don't know what to do. I can't get through to him at all. I'm terrified he's addicted to something or cutting himself or Christ knows what.'

'Hey,' he said gently. 'Now, don't be upset. It'll be nothing more than a fall-out with his girlfriend, you'll see.'

'It's more than that, I know it. Look, can you ask Charlene if she'd cover my shift this afternoon? I'll do hers on Saturday. I really don't want to leave him alone at the moment.'

'Of course. Don't worry about us, we'll manage.' He paused, listening to her soft sobs down the line. 'Are you going to be OK, Lex?'

'I'll be fine.' She wiped her eyes on her sleeve. 'I just wish I knew where to go from here.'

Chapter Nine

Charlene – one of two other servers who worked part-time at the Blue Parrot – was happy to cover Lexie's shift, but Theo found himself struggling to focus that afternoon in the restaurant. All he could think about was Lexie, and Connor.

She'd sounded so upset. He could still hear her voice, choked with sobs. While he'd done his best to reassure her it was probably nothing serious, Theo couldn't help worrying too. Surely Connor couldn't have got himself into anything dangerous? He was hardly the type to dabble with drugs – Theo would be surprised if the boy had ever so much as puffed on an illicit cigarette, let alone anything stronger. Then again, he'd never been the type to get into fights before either.

Poor old Lex. She had so much to deal with nowadays. He felt a too-familiar surge of anger towards the man he'd once believed to be his best friend as he thought about how Daryl had walked out on his family, leaving his young wife to raise his son alone. Theo was hardly a shining example of responsible adulthood, but if – God and all his angels forbid – he ever found himself unlucky enough to have a baby on the way, you could be damn sure he'd step up to the plate.

'Parcel for you, Theo,' Charlene said, pulling him out of his thoughts.

He took the package from her. 'Oh. Thanks.'

'Anything exciting?'

'Just my costume for the 1940s fest.' He glanced down at the hairy vintage suit he wore for work. 'I was going to wear this thing, but then I decided something with a bit more sex appeal wouldn't go amiss for a day. Hope it fits.'

Charlene glanced around the handful of customers. 'Go try it on if you want. I can manage here.'

'Yeah, all right.'

He nipped upstairs to his flat above the restaurant and put on the costume, a slate-grey RAF officer's uniform with matching peaked cap.

'What do you think then?' he asked Charlene when he went back down, gesturing to the uniform.

She nodded. 'Suits you, boss. Very suave.'

'Thanks.' He glanced around the thin smattering of customers. 'Charl, do you think you could deal with this lot till closing time? I feel like I ought to go check on Lexie. She didn't sound well at all when I spoke to her earlier.'

Not wanting to reveal anything personal, he'd told Charlene a bad migraine was the reason Lexie wanted to exchange shifts.

'Yes, I can cope for the last hour,' Charlene said. 'You go; tell her to get well soon from me. I've got my keys to lock up.'

'Right. I'll just go change.'

'No, leave it on,' Charlene said, smiling. 'I'd say that's just the thing to cheer her up. It'll give her a laugh if nothing else.'

–

When Lexie opened the door to him, Theo could almost believe his own cover story. His friend certainly didn't look well. She was very pale, her eyes puffy and streaked with mascara.

'Did somebody here order a strippergram?' he said, gesturing to his uniform.

She summoned a weak smile. 'Silly bugger. Why aren't you at work?'

'It was quiet so I knocked off early. I was worried about you.'

'You didn't need to come in fancy dress. I mean, not that it doesn't look good on you.'

'Charlene thought a bit of sexy role play might cheer you up.' He took in her white face and red, swollen eyes. 'Lex, you look terrible. Here, let me in.'

As soon as the door had closed, he folded her in a hug. She let out a muffled sob against his chest.

'Oh God, I'm sorry,' she whispered. 'I'm pathetic, aren't I? Sitting here crying my eyes out because I'm too crap a mum to know what to do for the best.'

'You're not pathetic and you're not a crap mum. None of this is your fault, Lexie.'

'Here, come into the kitchen and have a drink while I feel sorry for myself all over you.'

She led him to the kitchen and poured them each a glass of wine.

'What am I going to do, Theo?' she asked when they were sitting down. 'All the years I've been looking after that boy, I've never felt so utterly lost and helpless. He even told me I wasn't his mum. He's never said that to me before.'

'Has he come down from his room since you fetched him from school?'

'No, not even to eat. So now I've had to add "potential anorexia" to the list of things that might be wrong.'

'What happened, Lex?'

She shook her head. 'That's what I can't understand. He started this fight after one of his mates insulted him. Thing is, this kid Crucial's king of the wind-up merchants; he always has been. They've been friends for years and it's never come to serious blows before.'

'Have you told Daryl?'

'I texted and asked him to call me whenever time zones allow. I'd rather speak to him in person.' She sighed. 'He's going to make such a stink about it though, and that's the last thing Connor needs right now. If his dad has a go at him, he's going to close up even more.'

'Do you think it'd help if I talked to the boy?'

'Possibly, but I wouldn't try today. He's just a lanky pillar of sulk right now. If either of us badger him any more now, he's only going to put up more barriers.'

'So when do you think I should try?'

'The weekend? I reckon the best thing would be to work it in casually. Maybe you could take him to the football or something, do some male bonding.'

Theo smiled. 'Except he hates football.'

'Well, the cinema then. Somewhere you can make it seem spontaneous rather than looking like I put you up to it.'

'Right. Leave it with me.'

She smiled weakly at him. 'You know, Theo, I honestly don't know what the pair of us would do without you. Why are you always looking out for us? After the way Daryl did the dirty on you, you'd be within your rights never to want to clap eyes on anything connected with him ever again.'

He swirled his wine. 'Maybe that is why. I couldn't help feeling sort of responsible for you both when he left you up shit creek like that. You'd never have met him if it hadn't been for me.'

'I know. Possibly the best and worst thing that ever happened to me,' Lexie said, smiling.

He quirked an eyebrow. 'Best?'

'Oh, not for Daryl's sake. For Connor's.' She dipped her head to meet his eyes. 'And yours. I gained and lost a pretty crap husband, but I got a bloody brilliant son out of it, and an awesome best friend. Two things that make me feel my doomed marriage was worth it.'

He smiled. 'We nearly fell out over you, you know. Me and Daryl.'

'Did you?'

'Yep. I think I had a right to be pissed off, given I'd seen you first. I took great issue with him swiping the sexy young croupier I'd called dibs on from right under my nose.' He looked at her. 'Why did you go for him and not me?'

She laughed. 'Are you kidding?'

'Honestly, I genuinely want to know. Was it the sharp suit? I wasn't a bad-looking lad, was I, even if I was a bit of a scruffbag?'

'You know you weren't,' she said, smiling. 'You just weren't a good investment, Theo. I wanted a steady boyfriend, not a roll in the hay – as fun as I'm sure it would've been.'

'You bet your ass it would.'

Her eyes clouded with nostalgia. 'I tell you what though, those were the days. I felt so glamorous in that job, dealing cards in my little black dress like a Bond girl.' She glanced down at her current outfit of faded grey jogging bottoms and baggy *High School Musical* T-shirt. 'Ugh. And now look at me.'

'Give over, you look great.' He reached over to remove a false eyelash that had fallen off and stuck to her cheek. 'I mean, maybe not right now, but generally. You know, I quite fancy you in your waitress gear.'

'Well, thanks. At least someone does.' She ran a finger over the eagle motif on the front of his RAF uniform. 'You're looking pretty hot tonight yourself. I ought to dress you up more often.'

'Here.' He went to fetch the wine. 'Have a bit more of this and I'll order us a takeaway. I'm not leaving tonight until I've managed to cheer you up. Two shoulders available for crying on and all the hugs you want on tap.'

She smiled. 'Cheers, mate.'

'Hey. That's what friends are for, isn't it?'

–

Theo's phone alarm went off at seven a.m. as usual. He fumbled blindly for it, then blinked his eyes open when he met a wall of warm, naked flesh where his bedside table ought to have been.

What? Who...

'Oh *shit*,' he whispered.

'Wur?' Lexie mumbled as the phone alarm intruded into her dreams. Theo reached over her to turn it off, hoping it wasn't loud enough for Connor to have heard.

'Theo,' Lexie muttered. 'What are you doing in my room?'

'If you really can't remember then honestly, I feel pretty insulted.'

'Oh God.' She groaned deeply. 'What the fuck did we do?'

'The second bottle of wine was a bad idea.' He glanced at the floor, strewn with the clothes they'd torn from each other when they'd fallen in here the night before. 'Really, really bad idea.'

She peeped under the duvet at their two naked bodies and groaned again. 'What were we thinking? Oh my God oh my God oh my *God*!'

'Lexie, it's fine,' he said soothingly, drawing her into his arms.

'No. Don't do that. Don't hold me.' She wriggled free. 'This is bad, Theo.'

'Why is it bad? We're adults, aren't we?'

'Because we're mates!' she hissed. 'And despite your theories to the contrary, sex isn't like bloody cricket.'

'Can't it be? You're right, we are mates; good mates. I think we can handle this. It's one shag, Lexie.' He grinned. 'Besides, you didn't think it was all that bad last night.'

'Stop it,' she said, scowling. 'This was a stupid, stupid thing to do. Christ, and with a kid in the house! I'm a bad parent, that's all there is to it.'

'Oh, he didn't hear anything. He's on the other side of the house. Anyway, we were reasonably sneaky, despite the wine.'

'Jesus, how could I have let this happen?' She looked at his bare chest and winced. 'It's your fault. You and your RAF uniform.'

He swung his legs out of bed and bent down to retrieve his boxers. 'Well, you can beat yourself up about it if you want. I'm not going to. Two mature adults who like and respect each other had some safe, healthy, and, I might with all modesty add, bloody enjoyable sex. It's hardly the crime of the century.'

'It can't happen again.'

'All right. Shame though, I had a great time.'

For the first time since they'd woken up, her lips twitched with a smile. 'I won't deny it was fun. You've no idea how long it's been for me.'

'I thought you could sort yourself out.'

'Well, yes, but that's not quite the same.'

He glanced at the uniform strewn across the floor. 'So we've got a bit of a problem here. I'm going to look pretty conspicuous sneaking out dressed as a World War II flying officer.'

'Borrow something of Daryl's,' she said, nodding to the wardrobe.

'Right.'

He helped himself to a pair of Daryl's jeans and an old Nirvana T-shirt. It was a bit tight on him but it'd do until he got home.

'This won't change anything, Lexie,' he said, while he got dressed. 'Perhaps it wasn't the wisest move, but we're still friends. It doesn't have to make anything awkward if we don't let it.'

'No, you're right. Let's just go back to normal and forget it ever happened.'

'Forget it? You must be joking. I'm filing it away along with the day I lost my virginity and other cherished memories.' He sat by her on the bed. 'Come on then, give us a hug. Show there's no hard feelings.'

'I suppose I can manage that.'

She sat up and he drew her to him. He was fully clothed now but Lexie was still naked, and as the duvet fell away he got an eyeful of her upper body in all its creamy, bouncy glory. She looked amazing first thing in the morning, her cheeks pink and her blonde hair attractively tangled. Theo tried not to focus on the breasts pressed up against him as he rubbed a comforting hand over her bare back. He couldn't help thinking back to last night, her whispered moans of pleasure as she'd sat astride him and he'd caressed her body with his hands, his lips…

Mentally he gave himself a slap, forcing himself to snap out of it before his own body started responding to the memory. This was supposed to be a friendly hug, for Christ's sake, not foreplay. Hard feelings were about to be the least of his worries.

'Cheered you up pretty well, didn't I?' he whispered.

'Well, yes, I can't deny you took my mind off things.'

'You're welcome.' He kissed her cheek and let her go. 'Please don't beat yourself up about this, Lex. It's the most natural thing in the world. You've been doing enough self-flagellating lately as it is.'

'Perhaps you're right. It was only one night, after all. And I feel a hundred times less stressed out than I did yesterday.'

'See? I told you sex was good for the soul,' he said, grinning. 'I'll see you at work, eh? I'd better sneak out before Connor wakes up.'

Chapter Ten

Theo tiptoed downstairs and crouched down to put his shoes on. He was about to creep out when...

'Uncle Theo? What're you doing here?'

Shit. Connor. Think, Theo...

Casually he removed his shoes again, as if he'd just arrived, then looked up to smile at Connor watching him from the top of the stairs.

'Morning,' he said brightly. 'Let myself in with my emergency key, I hope you don't mind. Just some work stuff I need to talk to your stepmum about. Is she awake?'

'Dunno. Don't think so.'

Theo felt a wave of sympathy when he looked at Connor's puffy eyes. Lexie obviously wasn't the only person in the household who'd spent most of yesterday in tears.

'Well, let her sleep for a bit. I'm in no rush,' he said. 'How are you doing? I heard there was some trouble at school.'

He flushed. 'Yeah. Got into a fight. Um, Theo...'

'Hmm?'

'Theo...' Connor choked on a sob. 'I'm in trouble.'

Theo didn't say anything. He just climbed the stairs and held open the door of Connor's room for him, then followed him inside.

'I told you not so long ago that if you ever wanted to tell me anything, I'd listen without judging,' he said quietly when they were sitting down on beanbag and gaming chair respectively. 'Is there something you want to talk to me about, Con?'

Connor nodded miserably.

'Is it about girls?'

'Sort of,' Connor mumbled. 'You won't tell Lexie, will you?'

'Well, I can't promise that until I know what it is. I won't tell anyone who doesn't need to know to keep you safe.'

Connor was silent. Worrying he might have triggered the boy's defence mechanisms again, Theo tried to think of a prompt that would reopen the dialogue.

'What was your fight at school about?' he asked.

'Ugh. Crucial. He called me gay because I hadn't done it with Soph yet so I punched him.'

Theo frowned. 'Kids still use gay as an insult, do they? I was hoping it might've been consigned to the dustbin of playground insults from the dim and distant past by now.'

'Crucial does. He's such a twat.'

'Is that why you're upset? Has he been bullying you?'

'Don't be stupid, he's only Crucial. He's always been like that.'

'Well, then why so angry with him this time?'

Connor shrugged. 'Dunno.'

Feeling he was losing the boy again, Theo tried a different approach.

'Lexie says you've been quiet since the sleepover,' he said. 'Did something happen with your girlfriend?'

'No,' he mumbled. 'I mean, kind of.'

'Do you want to tell me what it was?'

'Guess so.'

Theo leaned towards him, assuming what he hoped was a sympathetic expression. 'All right, go on. I'm listening.'

Connor hesitated before beginning, picking at a thread on his pyjama bottoms. 'Well… we were in her room on our own for a bit, that night I stayed over. We were kissing and…' He flushed deeply. 'She wanted to, um… to touch me. You know, down there. Only I said I wasn't ready.'

'OK,' Theo said evenly. 'Did she put any pressure on you to go further than you were comfortable with?'

'No, she said it was fine. So we… we did some other stuff instead. Like, top halves, not bottom halves, and that was kind of good.'

Theo felt a wave of relief. If that was all, Lexie had nothing to worry about. That was normal, healthy experimentation for kids their age. It sounded like Connor had been very mature about what he wanted, and if Sophie respected that, it must be quite a strong relationship.

'Then what have you been worrying about?' Theo asked.

'OK, so, Soph had this vodka hidden in her cupboard and we were passing it round while we played Magic – me, her and Oli – till her mum came and took it off us. I think if we hadn't drunk it then it wouldn't have happened maybe, but we went a bit silly after and, um… well, do you know there's this game called Spin the Bottle?'

'I remember it with great fondness.' Theo frowned. 'Is that it? She kissed your friend Oli?'

'No.' He looked up helplessly to meet Theo's eyes. 'I did.'

Theo blinked. 'Oh.'

'Is that all you're going to say about it?'

'Well, no. How did that make you feel?'

Connor's blush deepened. 'I… I actually kind of liked it.'

Theo tried not to let any surprise show in his face.

'And your friend, what about him?' he asked. 'Did he like it too?'

'Dunno. I thought he didn't. Like, he pretended to be into it but it was just messing about for the game, you know? Sophie thought it was hilarious, she was pissing herself laughing at us, and then we stopped and Oli was laughing like a nutter too, like it was all a big joke. So then I laughed as well so they wouldn't think I was the one who'd been into it. But then after me and Ol went to our room…'

'Something happened?'

Connor nodded unhappily. 'We were sitting on his bunkbed talking about *Star Wars*. Oli reckons droids in the *Star Wars* universe ought to be given the same rights as people, you know, because they can make decisions and feel emotion and that, so they're basically people being used as slaves. But I didn't think that would work, because they can still be programmed to do stuff and that overrides their ability to make moral choices.'

'Unless they can break their programming. Then they'd be able to exercise free will.'

'Yeah, but even then though, if they have their memory wiped they can be reset and—' Connor shook his head. 'Anyway, never mind that now. That's when, um... when it happened again.'

'That does sound like a pretty sexy conversation,' Theo said, nodding. 'So you kissed? Nothing else?'

'No, just a kiss. Only I kissed him, and Oli didn't laugh this time. He... he did it back.' Connor hid his face in his hands and let out a sob. 'And now I don't know what to do.'

'You didn't know he might like you like that?'

Connor shook his head. 'I didn't know he liked boys.'

'And you didn't know you did either,' Theo said gently.

'No. I mean, maybe I don't. Or maybe I do. I don't know. I'm still trying to get my head round it.'

'But if you do, you know that's OK, right? And if you don't, well, that's OK too.'

'Yeah, I guess. It's just I really like Soph and... shit, I don't know what to tell her. She'll hate me for cheating, and now I don't know which one of them I *like* like or if Oli'll still want to be friends if I pick Soph over him or... what should I do, Uncle Theo?'

'Have you spoken to either of them about it?'

'No. I've been avoiding them.'

'Well, it sounds to me like you and your friend Oli need to have a talk.'

'God, no! What if he tells the others what happened? Crucial and JJ would slaughter us.'

Theo stood up to rest a hand on his godson's shoulder.

'I'm sure he wouldn't do that,' he said gently. 'He's always been a good, supportive friend, hasn't he? Besides, he'd have just as much to lose as you.'

'Yeah, but… what if he wants me to break up with Soph?'

'Well, you won't know that until you discuss it with him.'

'No. I can't. I'd be too embarrassed.'

'So what's your plan then? Avoid the pair of them until you leave school?'

'It's just hard to know what to say,' Connor muttered.

'I know it is.' Theo gave Connor's shoulder a squeeze. 'But it's something I think you have to do.'

'Maybe.' Connor looked up to smile weakly at him. 'You're so much better than Dad would've been if I'd tried to talk to him about this. He'd never get past me liking a boy like that.'

'Well, luckily for both of us I'm not your dad. You feel better for talking about it?'

'A bit.'

'I'm glad.' He sighed. 'To be honest, Con, I know it sounds mean when you've been upset but I'm kind of relieved.'

Connor blinked. 'Are you?'

'Yeah. Lexie was worried sick you'd got Sophie pregnant or were hooked on smack or something. I know it's a tough situation for you to deal with but I'm glad you're safe.' He patted the lad's shoulder. 'You really ought to tell your stepmum what's been bothering you. She'll understand.'

'But she'll be mad if she knows me and Soph have been doing stuff, won't she? She always seems dead worried about that.'

'I don't think she'll be mad at all. It sounds to me like the two of you have been very mature and sensible. I think she'll be proud of you for handling it so well.'

'Really?'

'Sure thing. I'm certainly proud of you. You're nowhere near as much of an arse as I was at your age.'

'Thanks, Theo,' Connor said, smiling. He looked up. 'I was really horrible to Lexie yesterday. It's just been making me so mad, not knowing what to do. I've been a total douche to everyone.'

'Then perhaps you ought to say sorry to her. You know, she loves you a lot. That's the reason she worries about you.'

'Yeah. I know,' he mumbled.

'Well, I'll leave you to think things over. You really ought to consider talking to your friend. I don't think you'll be able to move on until the pair of you have discussed what happened between you.'

'OK. I'll think about it.'

'You can call me any time, remember. I'll always be ready to listen.'

'Theo?' Connor said as he turned to go.

'Hmm?'

'Did you really come over this morning? I never heard you come in.'

'No, well, I was very quiet. I didn't want to wake you up.'

'You know, my dad's got a Nirvana T-shirt like that.'

'Has he?' Theo ran a finger under the too-tight T-shirt collar. 'He always did have good taste in music.'

'With the same smudge on the sleeve and everything.'

'Is that right? What a weird coincidence.'

Connor smiled. 'It is a bit, isn't it? Bye then.'

–

'Guess who got breakfast in bed this morning?' Lexie asked Theo in the restaurant later.

'Can I have a multiple choice?'

'Nope. It was me. Connor brought it up to me about half an hour after you left.'

'Why did he bring you breakfast in bed?'

'Well, I'm making it a bit grand by calling it breakfast in bed really. It was only a cereal bar and a cup of coffee.' She smiled.

'Still, the thought was there. He apologised for being such a brat yesterday, gave me a hug and now we're the best of friends again.'

'Did he tell you what's been bothering him?'

'No, but he looked more like his old self than since before that accursed sleepover. I don't feel nearly so worried about him today.'

Theo felt an unfamiliar, warm sensation creep into his chest. So his talk with Connor had made a difference. He hadn't really known how best to counsel the boy during their heart-to-heart earlier so he'd just groped his way along as best he could. It was a proud, satisfied feeling that engulfed him, knowing he'd helped the kid navigate the choppy waters of adolescence a little better.

'Did he tell you we bumped into each other this morning?' he asked Lexie.

She grimaced. 'Shit, really? No, he didn't. Does he know then?'

'I tried to cover for us but I don't think I got away with it, unfortunately. Anyway, he didn't seem too horrified. He's really a great kid.'

She looked at him, one eye narrowed. 'He talked to you, didn't he? About what was wrong? That's why he was in a better mood this morning.'

Theo nodded. 'I wasn't sure I'd been much use, but it sounds as though he found it cathartic. I'm glad.'

'Well thank God he talked to someone. So what is wrong then?'

'Well… I'd better not go into the details. I promised him I wouldn't unless I thought he was in danger, which he isn't, and I don't want to betray his trust when he opened up to me. Let's just say it's nothing for you to worry too much about. I mean, he is going through some stuff, but it's not dangerous.'

'So he and Sophie haven't…'

'No. Still at nice, safe second base, at Connor's request. After what he told me today, I think you've got every reason to be proud of him.'

She exhaled through her teeth. 'Jesus, that's such a relief. I won't push, as long as he's safe. Keep an eye on him for me though, eh? He seems to like confiding in you.'

'You know I will.'

She glanced at the kitchen hatch, where Tamara, the cook, had just brought out a plate of corned beef hash. 'That's for Table Eight. I'll take it.'

Theo looked over at the woman sitting at Table Eight, rather ruining the wartime vibe by tapping at a laptop while she waited for her lunch. She was probably in her mid-thirties, curvy and very pretty, with long, braided black hair. Every now and then, she cast a sideways glance in his direction and smiled slightly.

'That's all right,' he said. 'I'll take it to her.'

Lexie shook her head, smiling. 'Come on, Teddy, chatting up the customers again? I sometimes think you only went into the restaurant business because it was a good way to meet women.'

'No. There was the free food as well.' He patted her arm. 'I'm glad you feel better, Lex. Now stop worrying, eh? Everything's going to be all right, I promise.'

Chapter Eleven

Connor was sitting with Crucial at the back of their English class when the dinner bell went, a week after he'd gone back to school. The fight between them had been all but forgotten now, despite the legacy of some yellowish bruising around Crucial's left eye. However, Connor still hadn't summoned the courage to talk to Oli.

'Coming to the canteen, Loser?' Crucial asked.

Connor shook his head. 'I've got sandwiches. I'm going to find somewhere quiet to eat so I can finish off the maths homework.'

'What's with you lately?' Crucial demanded. 'Why're you always disappearing off on your own, are you a closet wanking addict or something? You've gone dead weird, everyone's been talking about it.'

'I'm all right.' Connor slung his rucksack over one shoulder. 'See you in French.'

His favourite spot for avoiding his friends during break times was a wall round the back of the library, technically out of bounds to pupils, that separated the school grounds from a neighbouring churchyard. Overgrown and neglected, it was the perfect place for hiding out.

God, he was sick to death of being on his own though. Theo was right, he really ought to try to fix things with his best mate and his girlfriend – if she was his girlfriend still. The consequence of trying to avoid Oli and Sophie was that he was now seeing more of his other two friends, who, let's face it, were a huge pain in the arse. He missed painting Warhammer figures with Oli, and writing fanfic with Soph. He missed the closeness he and Sophie had started to build, and her arms around him when they kissed. He missed having people to talk to who did more than just tell sex jokes, hit each other and take the piss.

'Um, hi.'

Connor looked up from his sandwich. Oli was standing in front of him, scuffing at the ground.

'Hi Ol.'

'Can I sit with you?'

'If you want.'

Oli sat down beside him on the wall.

'JJ said he thought this was where you'd been hiding at break times,' he said. 'What for, Con?'

Connor shrugged. 'Wanted to be on my own.'

'So... are me and you not mates any more then?'

'Course we are.'

'Only, you never get the bus with me now, and you never message me back or sit with me in class,' he said, fiddling awkwardly with the strap of his rucksack. 'So I thought maybe we weren't. Because... because of what happened that night.'

Connor flushed, kicking his heels back against the wall.

'Freaked you out, didn't I?' Oli muttered.

'No. Well, maybe.'

'You didn't like it?'

'No, I... I sort of did. It was just... surprising.' Connor swallowed down the last of his sandwich. 'So you like boys then?'

'Um, yeah. Do you?'

'Not sure yet. I definitely like girls. I think maybe I like boys too. I'm still working it out. So, like, you always knew?'

'Since I knew I liked anyone. I never did like girls, I just pretended.'

'Why didn't you say anything?'

'JJ and Crucial,' he said gloomily. 'You know what they're like.'

89

Connor nodded. 'Why did we make friends with them again?'

'JJ had *Halo*.'

'Oh yeah, right.' Connor glanced at him and shuffled a bit closer. 'So do you, um… do you like me then? I mean, not just mates sort of like?'

'Dunno,' Oli muttered. 'Think so. How about you?'

Connor shrugged. 'I kind of miss having you around.'

'Right.' Oli stared at his toes. 'That's all?'

'No. I liked it when we kissed too.'

Oli brightened. 'Did you?'

'Yeah, it was nice. Different than with Soph. Not better or worse, but just sort of nice differently.' He gave his friend's shoulder an awkward pat. 'Sorry I went weird on you, Ol. It was… new, and I didn't know what I felt about it.'

'That's OK. So, um, you want to do it again?' Oli asked hopefully.

'Thing is though, I really like Soph too. I mean, she's really cool, you know? It's not fair to cheat on her, and I don't want to break up, I don't think.'

'Oh.' Oli went back to staring at his feet.

'But you're cool as well,' Connor added quickly. 'Look, can we just go back to being mates for a bit? I feel like I need time to get my head around everything, but I don't want to not be mates any more. It's been the worst, not having you to hang with.'

'I know, it's been crap.' Oli smiled. 'You're such a dickhead, Con.'

'Yeah, I know I am. Sorry.'

'So shall we shake hands and make up?'

'I think we should probably hug,' Connor said. 'Friend hug though.'

'All right. Then maybe you can come round and play *Squadrons* this weekend?'

'Yeah, cool, I will.'

Connor put his arms around his best friend for a slightly awkward embrace. They didn't hug as a rule, but this felt like a special circumstance. Besides, they'd already kissed so it seemed a bit daft to go back to the formality of shaking hands.

'Oh my God, I knew it!' a girl's voice whispered.

Connor let Oliver go and looked around. Sophie had appeared round the side of the library and was staring at them, her face white.

'Soph, just, hold on a sec—'

'I knew there had to be something going on between you two! You looked like you enjoyed that kiss a whole lot more than you said you did when we played Spin the Bottle.'

'No, it isn't like that this time! Soph—'

'So this is why you've been ghosting me, is it, Con?' she said in a choked voice. 'So you could sneak up here for a grope with your secret boyfriend every break?'

'What? No! That doesn't make any sense.'

'He honestly hasn't,' Oli said, glancing helplessly at Connor. 'We just kissed a couple of times. Please don't tell Crucial and JJ on us.'

'Oh my God! A *couple* of times?' Sophie stared at Connor. 'So this whole thing, me and you… you needed a fake girlfriend to stop those other two twats taking the piss, right? I should've known you weren't really into me when you said you wanted to take things slow. Boys never want that. God, and I was actually stupid enough to believe you were just sweet and shy!'

'That's not it at all. Please just let me tell you.' Connor stood up to approach her, but she recoiled.

'Stay the fuck away from me, Connor Carson,' she whispered. 'You know you were the first boy I ever let… let touch me? The first boy I really believed I might be in love with?'

He blinked. 'What?'

'I can't believe you'd use me like that. I thought… I thought you cared about me.' She choked on a sob. 'This is over,

Connor. You hear me? You're a total, total dickwad and I never want to see you again as long as I live.'

—

'...so anyway, when my divorce came through I decided it was time to start living life for me, you know?' Francesca paused to take a sip of her wine, holding eye contact while she drank. 'Time to have all the fun I never got to have when I was with Jesse.'

'Sounds like you know what you want out of life.' Theo held up his hand to the waiter and nodded to the wine to indicate they'd like another bottle brought over. 'I really admire that, Francesca.'

She smiled. 'Well, thank you, Theo. So, what's your story?'

Theo shrugged. 'I'm not sure I've got one. I run a 1940s restaurant out in Leyholme, as you know. My romantic history's quite spectacularly uneventful in any department apart from the bedroom. I'm into kickboxing but I'm not very good at it, my favourite band's Queen but I tell people it's Pink Floyd because it sounds cooler, I enjoy the films of Buster Keaton, and generally I just like to have a laugh and not take life too seriously.'

'It certainly sounds like we're on the same page there.' Francesca topped up his wine for him. 'Here's to having a laugh, eh?'

She lifted her drink and Theo clinked his glass against hers.

'To having a laugh,' he said.

This was his first date in ages: the one he'd hoped might mean an end to the recent woman drought in his life – well, aside from that night he'd spent with Lexie, but he wasn't sure he ought to count that. Except the fact was, while Theo was doing his best to respond in kind to the tactful yet obvious body language that told him Francesca was definitely interested in taking this date back to his place, he was struggling to really get into it.

It was bloody annoying actually. Francesca was as close to perfect as you could get for him: sophisticated, attractive, good company – just the sort of girl he liked to go out with. Divorced too. Recent divorcees were Theo's favourite sort of date because they tended to have the same outlook as he did when it came to dating and sex: a bit of fun, no commitment and definitely no strings attached, with no hard feelings when, after perhaps a month or six weeks, either he or the girl decided they wanted to call time on things and move on. If she didn't end it at that stage, Theo always made sure that he did. Any longer than a couple of months and feelings were likely to start creeping in – on the woman's side, obviously, never on his – which was when a bit of fun stopped being quite so fun and people were at risk of getting hurt.

The problem wasn't Francesca. It was Lexie – or rather, the memory of Lexie, that night they'd spent together. Theo couldn't deny it; it had been the best sexual experience he'd had in a long time. No, scratch that: the best sexual experience he'd had *ever*, and Theo had had a lot of sexual experiences with a lot of women who'd been a heady blend of beauty, charm and sex appeal. The way Lexie had trusted him so completely, held nothing back... sex with her had been a different experience from the type he'd previously enjoyed with virtual strangers.

So much so, in fact, that Theo couldn't stop thinking about it. He'd once told Lexie that sex wasn't always an act of love but it was always an act of trust, and who could you trust more implicitly than your best friend? So many times recently he'd caught himself letting his mind wander back to that night, the heat of Lexie's flesh, the scent of her as he'd rocked her against him, face flushed, lips parted and panting, her fingers buried in his hair... it made it bloody difficult to do his job when every time his gaze fell on her, he started thinking about how it would feel to tear her waitress uniform off and make love to her on the bar.

That was what happened when you dropped your guard. For years, while acknowledging that Lexie Whittle was a very attractive woman, Theo had kept her behind an off-limits screen of nothing more than platonic friendship. She'd been his best friend's wife for most of the time he'd known her, and, when she was no longer that, she was herself his best friend, not to mention his business partner. It wasn't appropriate to think about her in that way. But now the screen had been shattered, it seemed there was no way Theo could fix it back in place.

Perhaps part of the problem was that she'd called time on things straight after. To enjoy the best sex you've ever had and then be told immediately afterwards that it was done now, over, never to be enjoyed again, was bound to stoke a certain longing to have the experience repeated.

'…so that was when I retrained as a physiotherapist. It was all I ever wanted to do, so yeah, I don't regret it.' Francesca raised an eyebrow. 'Theo?'

'Hmm?' He glanced up from his wine. 'Oh. Yes. It does sound like a rewarding career. I'd have loved to do something like that myself.'

Appeased, she smiled and continued whatever she'd been talking about. Theo watched her perfectly glossed lips move as she spoke.

Francesca was funny, but she wasn't Lexie funny. Pretty, but not Lexie pretty. Or beautiful, rather. He still remembered the night he'd first seen Lex at the casino, this gorgeous, long-legged croupier in an almost non-existent second skin of a black mini dress, her blonde hair pulled back in a sophisticated twist, expertly dealing cards at the poker table. Lexie had said she felt like a Bond girl in that job, and she'd sure as hell looked like one. No wonder Daryl had been so intent on sweeping her off her feet, taking her to the altar less than eight months later.

Theo remembered how she'd looked on that day too; her wedding day. He'd stood beside Daryl, in his tails and waistcoat, with the ring in his pocket, waiting for his friend's young bride to make an appearance. God, but she'd been stunning – breath-taking even, in a figure-hugging ivory gown that caressed every inch of her. His jaw had almost hit the floor when she'd walked down the aisle towards them. For a moment, just a fleeting moment, he'd half wished he and Daryl could change places.

But the most beautiful he'd ever seen her had been on that night just over a week ago, wearing nothing except her own skin... and his against it.

Daryl never had appreciated just what a gem he'd got in Lexie Whittle. He was proud of her beauty, charmed by her vivacity, grateful for the way she took care of Connor, but he'd never really *seen* her. Even back when Theo and Daryl were still friends, it used to irritate him. The way Daryl constantly compared her to Elise wound him up most of all. Elise had been a lovely girl, but she wasn't Lexie, and Lexie wasn't Elise. If Daryl was so hung up on the wife he'd lost, why find himself a new one? Whoever she was with, Lexie deserved to come first with them.

Francesca was talking about the day Theo had asked her out at the restaurant now: how attracted she'd been to him, how flattered when he'd made the first move. Her voice had sunk to a seductive purr, and she reached out to run a finger over the back of his hand. Theo forced himself to smile, giving all the right responses whenever she left a gap for him to speak, but he was on autopilot; just going through the motions.

What he'd said to Lexie had been true: casual dating wasn't nearly as much fun as it used to be. Maybe he was getting old, or maybe he was just getting bored. Why did he do it? The thrill of the chase? Except he couldn't be bothered to do much chasing, these days. He'd only asked Francesca out because she'd made it easy for him.

The sentimental answer, of course, was that having grown up without a father, watching a string of his mum's boyfriends pass through the house and her poor heart break a little with each failed love affair, he'd had no model of a healthy, committed relationship in his formative years to aspire to. The *X-Factor* tragic backstory angle was bollocks though. The truth, as he well knew, was that sex with attractive women massaged Theo's ego: the poor, fragile, ephemeral thing that it was.

Still, he'd always known he didn't want a kid, and that was something he was happy to lay at his absent father's door. The idea of being a parent horrified him when he thought of all the ways there were for him to fuck life up for a child. Being a godfather was responsibility enough, especially just lately. He really admired Lexie for wanting to give Connor the stability of a steady home life like the one he'd missed out on himself.

Lexie again. Why did his thoughts keep wandering back to her? He realised Francesca was still stroking his fingers and forced himself back into the moment. Lexie had made her views on anything else happening between them quite clear; he didn't know why he was still obsessing over it. Whereas here was a beautiful woman massaging both his hand and his ego with flirtatious touches and that seductive, smoky gaze – someone who was undeniably interested in whatever he might have to offer her tonight.

He looked at the manicured fingers covering his and smiled. 'So do you have a set bedtime, Francesca, or do your parents let you stay out as late as you like?'

She laughed. 'I'm free, single and ready to mingle, if that's what you mean. What did you have in mind?'

'I thought that after we'd eaten, you might like to come back to my place for a nightcap and I'll play you some of my Barry White vinyls. What do you say?'

'I think I'm going to need more to entice me than Barry White,' she said, looking up at him through lowered lashes. 'What else do you have to offer?'

'Oh, I'm sure I can think of something you'd enjoy. How about—'

Their flirting was interrupted by the buzz of his mobile phone, sitting on the table by his wine glass.

It was Lexie. What did she want? She knew he was going out tonight.

'Francesca, I'm so sorry about this,' he said. 'It's my business partner. I have to take it, it might be urgent.'

Francesca didn't look happy at being interrupted just as their flirting was getting interesting, but she nodded.

'Lex, what's up?' Theo said in a low voice. 'I'm in a restaurant.'

'Oh God, sorry, Theo. You're out with Table Eight tonight, aren't you? I forgot you had a date.'

'Well, never mind. Is it urgent?'

'I just wanted to ask if you'd heard from Connor.' He noticed her voice was trembling.

'Connor? No. Isn't he home?'

'No. He goes to youth club after school on Wednesdays, but he should've been back half an hour ago. When I rang the guy who runs it, he said Connor hadn't even turned up.'

'What about his friends, have they seen him?'

'I rang Janette Cavendish and Oliver's parents, but they don't know anything. All I could find out was that he had a big row with Sophie today at school. Theo, I'm worried.'

'Have you called his mobile?'

'I tried, but he's switched it off. Will you let me know if he gets in touch with you?'

'Of course.' He hesitated, looking at Francesca. 'Do you want me to come over?'

'No, no, don't be daft. Enjoy your date. There's nothing you can do here.'

'What will you do?'

'Ring the parents of his other two mates and if they don't know anything, start scouring the streets, I suppose. Shit, Theo, I hope he's OK.'

'I'm sure he is. Look, keep me posted, won't you?'

He hung up and immediately tried Connor's number, but Lexie was right: it was switched off, and the call went straight to voicemail.

'Con, when you get this, can you ring your stepmum or me right away? Please,' he muttered after the beep.

'All done?' Francesca asked, raising an eyebrow.

'Yes.' He smiled at her. 'Sorry about that.'

'Is everything all right?'

'Yes. I mean, it's nothing for you to worry about.'

He was only half concentrating on her, one eye still fixed on his phone. Where was Connor? Should he go back to Leyholme and help look for him? *Oh God, please say he hasn't done anything stupid…*

Chapter Twelve

'…and that's when I knew the marriage was definitely over,' Francesca said as they finished their main courses. 'I mean, in the back of a Volkswagen! If he had to be unfaithful, he could have at least kept it classy.'

She frowned when Theo didn't respond.

'Sorry, Theo, is my life story boring you?'

He looked up from his phone. 'Hmm?'

'Look, do you need to be somewhere else? You've barely said a word since your friend called.'

'Sorry. Sorry. Just worried about something.' He jumped as his phone buzzed again. 'Francesca, I—'

'You need to get that,' she said, looking fed up as she propped her chin on her fist. 'Is it your friend again?'

'No, it's the kid of this guy I hate… look, it's a long story. I'll take it outside.'

He hurried into the foyer of the country hotel they were dining at, where he could talk in private.

'Connor, mate, where the hell are you?' he hissed. 'Lexie's looking for your body in every ditch and disused quarry in the Calder Valley.'

The boy sobbed. 'Can we talk, Uncle Theo?'

He glanced through the open door to where Francesca was fiddling with her phone, looking bored.

'Sure, kiddo,' he said. 'What's up? Are you safe?'

'Yeah. Sophie dumped me.'

'Oh… God.' He sighed. 'I'm sorry, Con. Look, where are you? I'll come and find you.'

'In the park. I didn't dare go home.'

'Why not?'

'Sophie found out about what happened with Oli, that's why she ended it. I thought if she told her mum, she'd ring Lexie about it and then I'd be in all kinds of shit.'

'So you thought you'd sit in the kiddies' playground in the dark and wait to get murdered by some passing psychopath, did you?'

'What, in Leyholme?'

'Well, you never know. Just stay where you are, OK? I'll hop in a taxi and be there in no time.'

When he'd hung up, he asked the receptionist to call him a cab and hurried back to Francesca.

'Sorry, love, I have to go.'

'Mmm. I had a feeling you might say that.'

'Look, it's been fun.' He pecked her cheek and chucked a few twenties down on the table. 'Here, have this on me. I'll call you.'

Once he was inside the taxi, Theo texted Lexie to let her know Connor was safe and he'd be bringing him home shortly. When he arrived at the park, he discovered the boy sitting on a swing with his hood up, pushing himself morosely back and forth.

Theo nodded. 'All right?'

'Hiya.'

He sat down on the swing next to Connor's. 'So you broke up with Sophie then.'

Connor swallowed a sob. 'She broke up with me.'

'What happened, Con?'

'I talked to Oli, like you told me.'

'How did that go?'

'Yeah, all right. He does like me, but he said he was happy we should just be mates and I told him I wanted to see how things worked out with Soph. I don't think he liked that much but he said it was OK. But then she caught us hugging and she wouldn't believe me when I said that's all it was.' He choked back another sob. 'And now she'll tell everyone, JJ and Crucial and everyone at school, and Lexie's going to kill me.'

'She's going to kill you if you don't go home when you're supposed to. Why do you think she's going to kill you for what happened with Oli?'

'She's always gone on at me about how it's important to make good choices and not hurt people, ever since I was little. I hurt Sophie loads, and Oli too. And I cheated on Soph, which is like the worst thing you can do, right? I once heard Lexie tell Dad that if he ever did that to her, she'd castrate him in his sleep with a rusty Swiss army knife.'

Theo blinked. 'Bloody hell, did she say that? She's terrifying.'

'What's castrate mean anyway? Like, murder?'

'Er, no, not quite. I'll tell you when you're older.' He rested a hand on the boy's shoulder. 'It's time to tell her the truth, Connor,' he said gently. 'I promise on my honour as a… godfather that she won't be mad with you.'

'Yeah. S'pose I have to now.' Connor looked up at him. 'Will you stay with me though?'

He frowned. 'Me?'

'I won't feel so scared if you're there.'

'Oh, well… yes, I suppose I can do that.' He patted his shoulder. 'Come on. The sooner we do it, the sooner it's done.'

–

'Connor!' Lexie gasped when she opened the door. She threw herself at him for a hug. 'You bloody little… bastard! Where the hell have you been? Do you know how worried I was?'

'Sorry,' he muttered.

'Get inside, now.' She glanced at Theo. 'Thanks for bringing him home, love. I'm so sorry you had to cut your date short. Don't worry, he's about to be good and grounded for it.'

'Um, Lexie.' Connor glanced at Theo. 'I need to tell you something.'

She frowned. 'OK. What is it?'

'Can Theo come in? I want him to be here when I tell you. It's, um… it's kind of important.'

'Well, yes, of course he can,' she said, looking surprised. 'Let's go in the living room then.'

Connor sat on the sofa, eyes cast down, and Theo took a seat beside him. Not really knowing what his role as moral support was supposed to entail, he gave the boy an encouraging pat on the back.

'It's all right, Con.' He smiled at Lexie. 'You can tell her. I promise it'll all be OK.'

'What is it, Connor?' Lexie said softly. 'You had a row with Sophie, is that it?'

Connor nodded miserably. 'We kind of… we kind of split up. Did you talk to her mum?'

'Yes. She said there'd been an argument. She didn't know what it was about.'

'I thought she might've told you…'

'Told me what?'

'Told you…' He glanced at Theo, who nodded encouragingly. 'It's just, I think I might be kind of bi. Or maybe pan. I'm not sure yet.'

'Oh, sweetheart.' Lexie leaned across to take his hand. 'Is that it? That's what's been bothering you all this time?'

He nodded. 'Theo told me it was OK. I mean, I know it is; you always told me it would be, if I liked boys or girls or both or neither or whatever. But then I did a bad thing to Sophie and I felt really crappy.'

'This is where it gets complicated,' Theo told her.

Lexie frowned. 'All right. Can you tell me the bad thing?'

'I kissed Oli. Behind her back, kind of. He's gay, only I didn't know that then, but anyway, it still happened. So now he likes me, and Soph says she thinks she loves me, but she hates me too for cheating on her and I don't know which one of them I like more but I don't want to lose either of them and I'm terrified

Sophie's going to tell all my mates and everyone at school who might be a dickhead about it and… ugh, it all just blows so badly I don't know what to do.'

He burst into tears, and Lexie went to sit on the arm of the sofa so she could hug him.

'Oh, Connor, sweetie,' she whispered. 'Why didn't you tell me all this before? I've been imagining all sorts of awful things.'

'I thought you'd be mad,' he muttered. 'Cheating's really bad, isn't it?'

'It is bad, but you were going through a confusing time. I think that's something Sophie ought to understand.'

'She doesn't understand at all. She thinks I just pretended to like her so the others wouldn't realise me and Ol were doing stuff. Lexie, she said she…' He choked on a sob. 'She said she never wanted to see me again.'

'She's angry and hurt. That won't last.' Lexie sighed and hugged him tighter. 'Anyway, maybe it's not such a bad thing that you two should take a break. It sounds like you've got a lot of confusing thoughts and feelings spinning about inside you at the moment. Perhaps you ought to take some time to deal with those before you start thinking about dating again. You're very young to have this kind of pressure on you, Connor.'

He sniffed. 'But she won't even talk to me. I still want her to like me, even if we stop being boyfriend and girlfriend.'

'Of course you do.' She kissed the top of his head and released him from the hug. 'Would you like me to speak to her?'

'No. Thanks.' He glanced at Theo. 'I think I have to do it myself.'

She put an arm around him and rubbed his shoulder. 'That's very mature of you, my love. I'm proud of you.'

'Why? I hid things from you and I got excluded and I made a total balls-up of everything.'

'And then you felt bad and you tried to fix it. That's all any of us can do.'

He smiled feebly. 'Cheers, Lexie. Sorry I've been so bratty lately.'

'All forgiven.'

'And I'm sorry I said you weren't my mum. That was a really shitty thing to say to you.' He looked up at her. 'I mean, you totally are really.'

'Aww.' She gave him another squeeze. 'I suppose you'll die of embarrassment if I tell you I love you in front of Theo, but just this once I think I have to.'

'That's all right. I mean, I do too,' he said, blushing furiously under his hoodie. 'Can I eat tea in my room? I'm kind of wiped out.'

'All right. I'll bring you up a baked potato with cheesy beans, how's that?'

'Thanks. Um, am I grounded then?'

'No, I don't think I can find it in my heart to ground you after all that.' She fixed him with a stern frown. 'But no more disappearing acts, OK? I don't think my blood pressure can take another one.'

—

'So that was what was bothering him?' she said to Theo in the kitchen, putting a jacket potato into the microwave. 'He's been stuck in the middle of this love triangle with Sophie and Oliver?'

Theo nodded. 'Sorry. He asked me not to say anything to you.'

'Well, thank God, that's all I can say. I mean, poor little love, obviously, but I was so scared it was something dangerous.'

'I know you were.'

She smiled at him. 'Uncle Theo to the rescue again, eh? You're getting pretty indispensable around here.'

'Ach, I bet you say that to all the boys.'

She patted him on the back. 'Thanks for looking out for him, Teddy. I feel really bad about your date.'

'So you should. Table Eight had made it pretty clear I was on a promise, so that was a solid bit of cockblocking from you and young Connor.'

She laughed. 'You want a drink then?'

'No, thanks. I already had half a bottle in the restaurant. You go ahead though.'

He flinched and looked the other way as she bent over to take the wine out of the fridge, once again forcing himself not to dwell on his memories of what lay underneath those leggings.

'Why don't you give Table Eight a call now?' Lexie asked as she poured herself a glass. 'I'm sure that with a suitably grovelling apology, she'd be happy to pick up where you two left off.'

'No, don't think I'll bother. I wasn't all that into it even before you rang, to be honest. Just couldn't seem to get in the mood.'

'How come?'

'God knows. My mind was wandering all over the place.' He sighed. 'No, not all over the place really. To one particular place.'

'Where was that?'

'You,' he said simply. 'Lex, I can't stop thinking about that night – me and you. I've never enjoyed myself so much in bed with someone.'

She smiled wistfully. 'I must admit, it's been on my mind too. I'd forgotten sex could be like that.'

'It never has been like that for me. I think because we're mates, it just made it so much easier to lower my defences. I mean, knowing each other inside out, not having to feel embarrassed or second-guess ourselves. Not having to pretend we're madly in love, just being able to be completely honest about what we want and what we like…'

'I know.' She sighed as she took a seat opposite him. 'But it can't happen again, as much as I wish it could. We need to stop dwelling on it.'

'Why can't it?' He leaned over the table to take her hand. 'OK, so I had this idea in the taxi over.'

'I know what you're going to say. The answer's no, Theo.'

'No, but hear me out. So, you don't want to date because you're still married to Daryl, and Connor needs a stable home environment, and it's all just a bit complicated at the moment, right?'

'Right.'

'But you'd quite like to have some sex.'

'Well, all right, maybe, but—'

'And I'm a lifelong commitment-phobe with parental abandonment issues who enjoys sex but is getting increasingly bored of hooking up with women I barely know, right?'

'Is that what it says on your Tinder profile?'

'Pretty much. So, what do you say we make it a regular thing? I mean, we'd still just be mates, but mates who sleep together. No need to make it exclusive or anything. Dating-wise, we'd both be free agents. There's no risk of us falling for each other, we know each other too well, so where's the harm?'

'Fuck buddies, you mean.'

'I reckon that sounds a bit utilitarian. "Friends with benefits" sounds nicer to me.'

'Yeah, and what about Connor?'

'What about him?'

'I'm supposed to be a role model for him, Theo. It's a bit rich for me to sit there giving him lectures about the dangers of underage sex while I'm getting my jollies boffing his godfather on evenings and weekends.'

'We'd be discreet. There's no reason Connor needs to know a thing about it.'

'Hmm. There'd be bother if Daryl found out.'

'Oh, fuck Daryl,' he said, scowling. 'We don't owe him anything.'

'I meant he could make life difficult for me. I am legally his wife, and this house belongs to us both. It could affect my position when it comes to the divorce.'

'Well, were you going to ring him up and tell him?'

'No.'

'Neither was I, so there you go. It's just a simple arrangement: meeting each other's physical needs without all the hassle of dating. Sex is fun, orgasms are nice, ergo let's have a few more of them together.'

Lexie fell silent, running a thoughtful finger around the rim of her wine glass while she considered the idea.

'OK, I won't say I'm not seriously tempted,' she said at last. 'But... well, working together, sleeping together. Looking after Connor. I'm really not sure adding a physical element into our relationship is a good idea, Theo. Sex complicates things.'

'No it doesn't, people complicate things,' Theo said. 'Sex is about the most straightforward thing there is, if you don't overthink it.'

'You really believe that?'

'Course I do. It's just good, healthy exercise. Plus like I said before, the endorphins are great for mental wellbeing and stress relief. I mean, that's actual science, Lex. You can't argue with science.'

'But friends don't do that sort of exercise together. Friends take up squash or join a whist club or something.'

'I don't see any reason friends shouldn't enjoy something a bit more stimulating if they want to,' he said with a shrug. 'That sort of arrangement's hardly unheard of, is it?'

'I guess some people are able to make it work for them, yes, but—'

'Lexie, you know me better than anyone. After all these years, are you really going to suddenly fall for me because of a few shags?'

'Well no, of course not.'

'And the same for me, so what's complicated about it? It's social conditioning that makes us believe sex has to go hand in hand with romantic feelings. Trust me, there's nothing more liberating than breaking free of that sort of thinking.'

'OK, now you sound like Tonya,' Lexie said, smiling. 'So you're basically saying regular sex will be no different from going jogging together, are you?'

'Pretty much. Except we'd be naked, obviously.'

She ran her eyes over his body. 'I must admit, that part does sound good.'

'If I really believed it might be a risk to our friendship, I never would've suggested it. I don't want to lose you, Lex.' He gave her hand a squeeze. 'I just thought it could be fun, that's all. We managed it once without any issues, and I think we firmly established then that we're pretty explosive together.'

'We did, didn't we?' Reluctantly, Lexie drew her hand away from his. 'But I can't, Teddy, I'm sorry. I'd like to believe it's that simple, but I still think seeing each other all day at the restaurant, being mates... it could end up making things messy. You're the one non-messy thing I've got to be grateful for in my life, and I really don't want to jeopardise that. Let's keep things how they are, eh?'

He sighed. 'I had a horrible feeling you were going to say that.'

'Do you mind?'

'Of course I don't mind, if that's your decision.' He stood to leave. 'Shame though. We'd have been good together.'

'I know we would.' She smiled up at him. 'Still friends?'

'Always.' He leaned down to give her a peck on the cheek. 'Night, love. See you at work.'

–

When Theo had gone, Lexie went upstairs to take Connor his jacket potato. She found him lying on his bed, staring up at the ceiling.

'All right, my little sunbeam?' she said, ruffling his hair. He smiled at the endearment from his childhood.

'Yeah,' he said. 'Just thinking.'

'About Sophie?'

'About lots of stuff. Mum, mostly.'

Lexie put the food down on his desk and went to sit by him. 'Do you remember much about her?' she said gently.

'Little bits. Like, I remember when she used to take me to see Nana she always bought me a comic and a Milky Way on the way home. And when she brought me cocoa, there was this song she sang. Only I can't remember how it goes now. I wish I could. It feels like I've forgotten her when I can't remember stuff I used to know about her.'

Lexie looked down at him, blinking back tears as she traced the features of the child he'd once been in his face. She knew how that song went. Connor used to hum it to himself all the time when he was a little boy; usually when he felt afraid or upset, missing his mum. Lexie, sensing the tune gave him comfort, had got into the habit of singing it to him at bedtime herself after she moved in with Daryl. She wondered if he remembered when she, too, had sat by his side while he drank his cocoa and sung to him.

'"Oranges and Lemons",' she said quietly. 'It's an old children's rhyme about the church bells of London. Here.' She sang it softly to him, and he smiled.

'Yeah, that's it. Thanks, Lexie.'

'You're welcome, sweetheart.'

'Lexie?'

'Hmm?'

'I'm sorry Dad was such a dick to you. You deserved better than someone like him.'

'Oh, well, I don't know about that. These things are always more complicated than they seem.' She tried to make it her policy never to speak badly of Connor's father in front of him. 'Besides, I got you out of it, didn't I? Have your spud now, sweetie, before it gets late.'

Lexie planted a kiss on his curls before going to her own room. She lay down on the bed, feeling a tear slide down her cheek. She wasn't sure what it had been about that little conversation that had got her all emotional, but there it was.

She rolled over and looked at the empty half of the double bed. Theo wasn't the only one who'd been dwelling on the night they'd spent together. Not only the sex, which had admittedly been pretty amazing, but the feel of someone else's skin against hers as Theo had snuggled into her afterwards, lightly stroking her bare flesh while she fell asleep. That feeling that she was no longer alone and unsupported in this big, scary world; that she had someone by her side who'd be there for her when times were tough.

She couldn't deny she'd been lonely since Daryl had gone. Even after their marriage had broken down and the sex had long since dried up, they'd continued sharing a bed – through habit more than anything – and it had given her comfort of a kind to feel him by her side in the night. The loneliness had been even worse lately than it had when he'd first left. What with worrying about Connor and coping with the pressures of parenthood on her own, it felt so depressing to trudge up to an empty bed night after night. Lexie didn't want the hassle of another relationship, not at this point in her life, but the night she'd spent with Theo had made her realise that she did miss the companionship of a bedmate – a lover. She missed a pair of tender arms around her as she fell, satiated, safe and protected, into sleep. Someone to hold on to in the dark…

After hesitating a moment, she brushed away the tear on her cheek and reached for her phone to send a text.

> I changed my mind. Come in through the kitchen after Connor's asleep, I'll leave the back door open x

Chapter Thirteen

Theo smiled at Lexie as she collected a tray of drinks from him at the bar. She flashed him a wink as she shimmied off with them, deliberately giving her hips a little extra wiggle because she knew it got him going.

Their friends-with-benefits arrangement had been in place for three weeks now, and it was working better than he'd ever hoped. He felt like a teenager again, with the forbidden thrill of sneaking around giving an added zing to their lovemaking. Not that they really needed it. They could supply plenty of zing on their own.

The first time hadn't been a one-off. Lexie was easily the best lover Theo had ever had: uninhibited, fun, daring and beautiful. Theo didn't know if he could ever go back to the type of sex he'd been having before, now. Still, he was optimistic that this was one relationship he could keep going for a good long time: at least until Lex decided she wanted to start dating again.

One of the best things about it was that Theo knew there was no risk of Lexie getting romantically attached to him, as had occasionally happened with lovers in the past, despite his best efforts to guard against it. They had too strong a bond as friends to ever fall for each other: it was just sex, sweet and simple. There was something very pure about that, in an odd sort of way. It seemed strange to him now that this wasn't the way everyone chose to conduct their sex lives.

It was so bloody refreshing, too, not to have to flatter and flirt, pursue and retreat; all those daft games that went with dating. It was actually really relaxing, being able to acknowledge that in this case sex was just that and nothing more. No stress, no overthinking; just good old-fashioned intercourse between people who liked and respected one another.

In the past, sex had always felt like something you had to earn; to bargain for. You followed a set pattern of interaction with the other party – the rules of engagement, if you like – until all barriers were down. You flirted, she demurred. You cooled down, she warmed up. She touched, you responded. Always playing the game; a game Theo had grown increasingly bored of this past year or so. But he didn't need to play any games with Lexie. There was complete frankness and honesty between them, coupled with a thorough knowledge of who the other person was that gave their lovemaking a satisfying simplicity Theo had never before experienced.

It was doing Lexie the world of good too. She looked so young and fresh lately, pink-cheeked and smiling, as she had in the days before she'd moved in with Daryl and the cares of the world had settled on her shoulders. She had something in her life now other than constant worry about Connor and her ever-precarious finances; something simple and joyous that really made her happy.

Knowing she was happy made Theo happy too. His previous relationships, if you could call them that, had always been more or less selfish – although he'd always been careful to select lovers he knew were on the same page as him when it came to intimacy to avoid anyone getting hurt, and of course he'd done his best to ensure they had a pleasurable experience in bed, Theo enjoyed sex and he'd been thinking of himself first and foremost when he sought it out. Now, for the first time, he felt like he wasn't only doing something to make himself feel good; he was making his friend happy too, improving her quality of life both in and out of the bedroom. Lexie, to him, had never looked more beautiful than she had these last few weeks. Particularly when she had no clothes on.

Not that there wasn't a physical cost to all those quality orgasms, he thought, stifling a yawn. Hiding what they'd been up to from Connor meant late nights creeping into the house after the boy was asleep, and early mornings sneaking out before he got up for school. It was worth it though. Oh God, was it worth it…

Lexie was smiling at him from across the restaurant, where she was chatting with Claire, the other waitress sharing her shift today. He smiled back, then took the accounts book from under the bar and headed over to them.

'Claire, do you think you could cope on your own for half an hour?' he said, flashing her a dazzling smile. 'Lexie and I could do with going over the figures for the extra staff and catering we'll be getting in for the festival. Might as well get it over with now while it's quiet.'

Lexie groaned – slightly too hammily, Theo thought. 'Oh God, do we have to?'

'I'm afraid so.'

She sighed. 'Well, it's a boring job but it has to be done, I suppose. Will you miss us if we pop up to the flat for a quick meeting, Claire?'

'No, that's OK,' Claire said. 'If it gets busy I'll fetch you.'

'You'd best not leave the restaurant unattended,' Theo said, casually flicking through the accounts book. 'Just send me a text if you need us and we'll jog back down, all right?'

'Will do, boss. I mean, bosses.'

As soon as they were out of sight Theo was pulling off his tie, Lexie untying her apron. Immediately the door closed on Theo's apartment, he pulled Lexie to him for a deep kiss, his fingers seeking out the buttons at the front of her dress.

She laughed breathlessly. 'I thought you wanted to go over some figures.'

'Just one. It's under this bloody thing.' He looked down at her dress. 'Who chose these uniforms anyway? There must be a hundred buttons on this bastard.'

'Um, you did?'

'Well next time, remind me to pick the kind with Velcro.'

He finally got enough buttons undone to push the thing down her body, and Lexie stepped back to let him see her.

'What do you think?' she said, gesturing to the suspender belt and seamed stockings she was wearing over her underwear. 'I'm method 1940s-waitressing today. Consider it payback for the RAF uniform.'

Theo let out a low whistle. 'Bloody hell, Lex. You look like a Victoria's Secret model.'

'You approve then?'

In answer he picked her up, her limbs twining around him, and carried her into the bedroom.

'You…' He laid her on the bed and ran his hand up the inside of one silky-smooth stockinged leg. '…are a tease. I can't believe you've been wearing that gear all day and I never knew.'

He took off her bra and she moaned softly as he brought his lips down to caress a nipple.

'What would you have done if you did?' she asked.

'Well, it wouldn't have been very professional. I'm not sure I could've been patient enough not to just hoist you up and go for it right there on the bar.' He bit his lip as she stripped him of his shirt and ran her hands over his bare chest. 'Christ, you're sexy.'

'Back at you, mate.'

He glanced at her left hand as it glided over his chest. 'How come you still wear those, Lex?'

She held up her hand to look at the wedding and engagement rings on her third finger. 'Sorry, are they digging in you?'

'No. I just wondered, that's all.'

She laughed. 'What, you want to talk about that now?'

He slid down her body to draw his tongue over the skin of her tummy, his fingertips trailing lightly over her inner thigh. 'No, not really.'

'That feels good, Theo,' she whispered. 'If you really want to know, I wear them to avoid unwanted advances from men.'

'Take them off for me.'

'Why?'

'Because if you don't, I won't do that thing you like,' he whispered, flicking his tongue under the waistband of her knickers.

She smiled and twisted them off her finger. 'All right, if you're going to fight dirty.'

'That's the stuff.' He unhooked the suspenders so he could slide her knickers off. 'Something else you don't need to be wearing at the moment.'

'We haven't got long. We'd better call that it for foreplay.'

'I love it when you go all practical on me.'

'Good.' She unzipped his fly. 'Come on, before they realise what we're up to.'

—

'Thanks for that,' Theo said breathlessly as they dressed again afterwards.

'You too.' Lexie lifted her hips while she wriggled back into her pants. 'What we lacked in time I'd say you more than made up for in effort.'

He glanced down at her legs as she hooked her stockings up again. 'You know, I'm going to really struggle to focus knowing you've got those suspenders on.'

'You want me to leave them off, go the full Nora Batty?'

'Mmm.' He nuzzled into her neck. 'Would you chase me around with a broom?'

'No. There is such a thing as too sexy, Theo.' She batted him away. 'Now get off me and get dressed, naughty sex person.'

He sighed as he buttoned up his shirt. 'It's no good, Lex. Suspenders or no suspenders: I fancy you whatever you're wearing. I'm destined to be hot under the collar the rest of my working life.'

She smiled. 'Good. Turns me on when I know you're having impure thoughts about me in the workplace.'

'Vixen.' He finished dressing and leaned across the bed to kiss her ear. 'Shall I come round tonight?'

'No, leave it till tomorrow. You must be knackered after doing it every day for three weeks straight.'

'Sometimes twice.'

'All right, no need to show off. I was there, you know.'

'Yes, I remember,' he whispered, nibbling her earlobe. 'It wouldn't have been nearly so much fun on my own.'

She pushed his face away from her, smiling. 'You'd better cut that out, before we end up going for the double again. Catch up on some sleep tonight, eh? Connor's staying at Oliver's house tomorrow so you can come over early and we'll make a night of it.'

'What, you mean we'll have time for a full round of foreplay? That'll be a novelty.'

'We could even have dinner together. It's good for us to occasionally remember to have a conversation between shags.'

'I'll look forward to it,' Theo said, standing up and chucking her dress to her. 'So Con's staying at Oli's, is he? Aren't you worried about him going to another potentially traumatic slee-pover?'

'This one ought to be pretty innocent.' She slid her rings back on. 'Their other two friends are going as well. They're planning to play Dungeons and Dragons all night so I doubt it's going to get too erotically charged.'

'Sophie going too?'

She shook her head. 'No, she's still not speaking to him. He's pining away for her, poor little pup. Mind you, he seems better than he was – sad about it but in a healthy sort of way, if that makes sense.'

'That's good, I suppose.' He squeezed her hand. 'Let's go back down, before Claire gets suspicious. We'll pick this up tomorrow.'

–

'Here I am, yours to do as you like with!' Theo called when he walked into Lexie's place the following evening, clutching some flowers and a bottle of chilled champagne. 'I thought we might—'

He stopped short when he reached the kitchen. Connor was there, sitting at the table with his chin on his fists while Lexie cooked.

'Oh. Hi, Con.'

'Hiya Theo.'

'Sorry,' Lexie mouthed from behind Connor.

'What's up, kiddo?' Theo asked, sitting down at the table. 'I thought you were going out tonight.'

'I did, but Oli threw up so his mum said we'd all better go home in case he had a bug. I reckon he probably just ate too much. His mum's always fussing.' He frowned at the flowers and bubbly. 'What're these for?'

'Well they weren't for you,' Theo said, smiling. 'The flowers are for Lexie and the champagne was for both of us. We're celebrating.'

Lexie raised her eyebrows. 'Are we?'

'Yes,' he said, giving her a pointed look. 'You know, the profits? Up ten per cent on this time six months ago, and we've got the big festival to come yet. The Blue Parrot's on the up, you guys. This time next year, we'll be millionaires.'

'Sorry,' Connor said. 'I guess you didn't expect to find me here, right?'

'I didn't, but that doesn't mean you're not welcome. You probably deserve to toast the place as much as anyone.' He glanced at Lexie. 'He can have a glass with us, can't he? I reckon he's old enough.'

She smiled. 'All right, just a small one.'

Theo stood up and went to fetch some flutes from the cupboard next to Lexie.

'Sorry,' she said in an undertone. 'I did text.'

'Didn't see it. Never mind.'

He poured two glasses of champagne for himself and Lexie, and a half glass for Connor.

'Well, to us lot, I suppose,' he said, raising his glass. 'May the odds be ever in our favour.'

Lexie laughed. 'What sort of toast is that?'

'The best sodding toast I can come up with off the top of my head, that's what sort.' He glanced at Connor and grimaced. 'Sorry, I forgot about the household swear jar. Smegging, I meant to say. How much did that just cost me? Sodding isn't really a proper swear.'

'That's all right, we don't charge for minor infractions,' Lexie said. 'I reserved a few of the more socially acceptable profanities for the sake of my sanity.'

Connor took a sip of his champagne and pulled a face. 'Eurgh. How do you old people drink this crap?'

'Crap? How dare you, child,' Theo said, flicking his ear. 'That's good stuff, that is. None of your seven-quid-a-bottle prosecco.'

'What's smegging mean anyway?'

Theo stared at him. 'You're yanking my chain.'

'Eh?'

'Seriously. You are actually kidding?' He turned to Lexie. 'He is kidding? I mean, you're not genuinely telling me he's got notepads full of fanfic for *Stargate*, *Firefly* and pretty much every other sci-fi show ever made spilling off the shelves in his room but he's never seen *Red Dwarf*?'

Lexie smiled. 'You're a real closet geek, aren't you?'

'Well that's better than being a failure as a parent, which I've just discovered you are. All this time, you've let the boy fritter his life away on inferior science fiction while a classic, a *classic*, was right there for the watching. Lexie Whittle, I'm appalled.'

'You going to call social services on me?'

'No, although I'd be within my rights. I'm going to do what any self-respecting godfather would and fix the situation.' He turned to Connor. 'Come on, lad, in the living room.'

Connor blinked at him. 'What for?'

'For the benefit of your education. Me, you and your mum are having a TV night. I've got series one to six I can stream and I'm not leaving until we've watched at least the first two.'

–

Four hours later, Connor had dozed off next to Theo on the sofa while Lexie sat in the armchair, gazing placidly at the pair of them.

'Sorry,' she whispered to Theo. 'Not exactly the passionate evening I promised you, was it?'

'Oh, don't worry about it.' He glanced at Connor. 'Actually, I really enjoyed myself – I mean, a very different kind of enjoying myself than anticipated, but this was fun tonight. It's like you see things you've watched a thousand times through new eyes when you introduce a kid to them. I swear, when he laughed at the jokes I felt as proud as if I'd written them myself.'

'He likes spending time with you. I never realised how much he missed having an adult male influence in his life until recently. Daryl might not have been the world's greatest dad but he was better than nothing, I guess.'

'Well, I like spending time with him.' Theo leaned back and sighed. 'You know, for years I told myself it hadn't affected me, growing up without a dad. But when I spend time with Connor... I don't know. There's some part of me that almost seems to be trying to compensate for that gap in my life by filling the gap in his.' He looked at the sleeping boy and smiled. 'When I feel like he looks up to me, it makes me... makes me think better of myself, I suppose. Makes me want to be that man he thinks I am.'

Lexie smiled too. 'Welcome to my world. I know that feeling well.'

'You don't think he suspects anything, do you?'

She raised a finger to her lips.

'Hasn't got a clue,' she whispered. 'But we need to be careful, Theo. We can't risk him finding out.'

–

'No, he doesn't *look* like a cat. Well, apart from his teeth. He just *is* a cat.'

Oli blinked. 'He's a cat who doesn't look like a cat?'

'Yeah,' Connor said. 'Like, he evolved from cats like we evolved from apes, right? So he basically just looks like an ordinary man, only he dresses like Vegas Elvis and is kind of… dunno, just catty.'

'Sounds weird.'

'No, it's dead good, promise.'

'And it's like *Original Series* old?'

'*Next Generation* old. This isn't like *Star Trek* though. It's well funny, you should watch it. Theo says *Red Dwarf* series one to six are classics of the genre. I've only watched the first three so far but I'm going to binge the rest this weekend.' He caught sight of a group of girls walking towards them from the canteen. 'Look. Sophie.'

'Don't bother, bro. You know she won't talk to you.'

'Soph!' Connor called. But she blanked him, making a show of laughing loudly at something one of her new girlfriends said as she passed.

'Told you,' Oli said.

Connor kicked glumly at the ground. 'Can you believe she ditched us for a load of girls?'

'Well, she is a girl.'

'Yeah, but that lot don't like any cool stuff. All they care about is TikTok and K-Pop bands and all that boring stuff.'

'You ever going to give up on her, Con?'

'No. I like her, don't I? Anyway, she can't totally hate us. I mean…' He flushed. 'Well, she never told anyone about what happened. Seems like if she really wanted to get her own back, she'd have spread it all over school.'

'All right,' Oli said cautiously. 'But then why's she not talking to us?'

'She's still pissed off, I guess.' Connor sighed. 'I miss her, Ol. I don't know if I want us to get back together, not right now, but I wish we could be mates again.'

'Me too,' Oli said, nodding. 'You've still got us though. I mean, you've got me.'

'Yeah.' Connor smiled. 'S'pose so.'

'So you going to CalderCon in the holidays?'

Connor felt a wave of sadness when he remembered the much bigger convention Sophie had invited him to in Leeds this autumn, to celebrate what would've been their eight-month anniversary. She'd go with someone else now: one of her new girly mates maybe, or even a new boyfriend.

'Dunno,' he said. 'Not sure I can be bothered this year.'

'Come on, it'll be a laugh,' Oli said, nudging him. 'It's your birthday weekend, you have to do something good. You should ask your stepmum if she'll take us again.'

'Maybe.' He brightened. 'Or I could ask Theo.'

'Your uncle?'

'Yeah – well, kind of. He's my godfather. He likes sci-fi, plus he's pretty fun for someone old. Like, cooler than a dad but sort of grown up as well when you need to talk to someone about stuff. I bet he'd even dress up.'

'Will your stepmum mind you asking him?'

'Nah, she'll just be glad she doesn't have to go. Anyway, Lexie and him have got a thing going on so I guess she'd trust him.'

'What sort of thing?'

'You know, a *thing*,' Connor whispered, waggling his eyebrows.

'Oh.' Oli nodded knowledgeably. 'That sort of a thing.'

'Yeah. They think I don't know but they're crap at keeping it secret. I can hear him crashing about in the kitchen when he trips over something sneaking in.'

'Are you bothered? I guess you want her to get back with your dad, don't you?'

'No way. Theo makes her happy. Dad never did that.'

'Yeah, but if she gets with him then your dad might not let you live with her any more. I mean, she's not your real mum, is she?'

Connor was silent for a moment, frowning. He hadn't considered what might happen if his dad found out about Theo and Lexie.

'I guess my dad wouldn't like it much,' he admitted. 'Theo and him were best mates till they fell out. But it's Dad's fault. If he'd been nicer to Lexie then maybe they'd still be together. It's not fair if he treats her like shit for years then tells her she can't have new boyfriends after they've broken up.'

'You think he'd make you go live with him if he found out?'

'He can't make me if I don't want to. That's kidnap or something.' Connor slung his bag over his shoulder. 'Come on, let's go see if Crucial and JJ want to play D&D for a bit before the bell goes.'

Chapter Fourteen

'Oh God, Theo…' Lexie threw her head back as she rocked her body against his. She gripped his arms, her fingers digging hard into his skin.

'Now, Lex?' he whispered.

'Yes… yes, now…'

He thrust deeper, and Lexie cried out as the familiar waves of pleasure washed over her. Seconds later Theo joined her, clasping her tight against him as his climax pulsed through her body to join the dying embers of her own, and the two of them collapsed – panting, exhausted and satisfied – back into bed.

'Bloody hell.' She laughed breathlessly, pushing sweat-drenched hair out of her eyes, while Theo dealt with the spent condom. 'You know, since we started this I've been almost grateful for this daft house. At least Connor's bedroom is far enough away that we don't have to be completely quiet.'

'Me too,' Theo said, joining her in bed again. 'Making you scream is my favourite part.'

She smiled. 'I don't scream.'

'You can if you want to, though. I wouldn't object.'

'No, sorry. That would definitely be pushing our luck.' She leaned over him to plant a soft kiss on his lips. 'Thanks, love. That was amazing, as usual.'

'In the top five, definitely,' he said, nodding. 'Did you come twice then?'

'Yep.'

'Thought so. In that case, I'll upgrade it to top three.' He drew her into his arms and kissed her forehead. 'You're some girl, Lexie Whittle.'

'Ta.' She yawned. 'We should really knock it on the head for a night and go to the pub or something. We don't want to forget how to do the non-benefitty friend stuff. One day we'll need to stop all this, and then we'll have to remember how to make do with the hobbies we had before.'

'Well, we won't have to stop for a while, I hope.'

He leaned up on his elbow and stroked her hair away from her face, smiling as he looked down at her.

'What are you thinking about?' she asked, lazily tracing shapes on his chest with the tip of her finger. 'You've got a funny look on your face.'

'I'm thinking that out of all the women I've been to bed with, you're far and away the most beautiful.'

She smiled. 'Sweet.'

'Tell me something about you, Lex,' he said softly.

'What do you want to know?'

He shrugged. 'Anything. Something I don't know already.'

'A secret, you mean?'

'Yeah. A secret. Something you never told anyone, not even Daryl.'

'Well…' She thought for a moment. 'All right, you know Simon Cowell?'

'Not personally. I sometimes think about him to delay orgasm. What about Simon Cowell?'

'I met him once. He came into the casino and I got him to autograph a playing card for me. How's that?'

He shook his head. 'That's not a secret, it's an anecdote. Something about you, Lex.'

She shrugged. 'I never told you I used to get bullied at school.'

He raised his eyebrows. 'You? I'd have thought you'd be one of those dead popular girls us lads were all completely intimidated by.'

'Nope, I was short and dumpy with braces. Then one day sometime in Year Eleven, the puppy fat disappeared, the braces came off and suddenly there were all these boys staring at me.'

He ran a hand over the curve of her breast and down to her hip. 'I bet there were, lucky sods. Did the bullying stop then?'

'Mostly, except for this one group of girls. They hated me when they thought I was ugly, and then they seemed to hate me even more when they thought I wasn't. This bunch of well-off Pony Club types who looked down on me because my family lived on a council estate. Honestly, they made my life miserable for so long.' She sighed. 'Some kids just can't accept anyone different, and the only response they have is cruelty. It makes me worry for Connor if he decides he wants to come out at school. Not that he shouldn't feel he can, but let's face it, teens can be dicks.'

'I don't think things are anywhere near as bad as in our day when it comes to homophobia in schools. Times have changed, thank Christ. I'm sure there'll already be kids at his school who identify as something other than straight.'

'But there'll still be a few twats, I bet. As long as there are bigoted parents, there'll be bigoted kids. His mates JJ and Crucial are hardly bastions of tolerance, for a start.'

'Connor'll be OK in the end.'

'How do you know?'

'Because he's got you for a mum,' Theo said, giving her a squeeze. 'When he realised he was bi he never let it faze him, did he? Because you'd been telling him since he was little that whatever he discovered about himself, it'd be no big deal. You never assumed his sexuality so he never felt it wasn't OK to question what it was. I bet he wouldn't have had nearly such a healthy reaction if Daryl had brought him up alone.'

She smiled and leaned over to kiss him.

'Thanks, Theo,' she whispered. 'I needed to hear that.'

He lifted her hand to his lips. 'Rings're gone, I see.'

'Yeah. After you pointed it out, it made me think, why am I still wearing them? They're hidden away in the drawer now, out of sight and out of mind, like the husband who gave them to me.' She rolled onto her side to face him. 'So, your turn.'

'My turn to what?'

'I told you my most humiliating secret. Now it's your go.'

'Well…' He grimaced. 'Really, my *most* humiliating secret?'

'Only fair, Teddy.'

'OK, but first you have to swear this is governed by the sacred rules of pillow talk and will go no further than these four walls.'

'All right, I swear. Go on.'

'What's my name?'

'Er, Theo,' she said, frowning. 'Why, did you forget? Or is this a kinky "say my name, bitch" type thing?'

'No, I mean, what's my name short for?'

'Well, Theodore. Isn't it?'

He shook his head. 'Oh God, it's so much worse than Theodore. That lass who had it tattooed on her arse doesn't realise what a lucky escape she had.'

'Nothing else goes with Theo though, does it?'

'One thing does,' he muttered darkly. 'Did I ever tell you my dad was a history professor?'

'You mentioned it. Wasn't your mum one of his students?'

'No, she was working at the university, but she was the same age as his students. I guess that'd appeal to the dirty old bugger – since she wasn't one of the undergrads, he could sleep with her without risking his job. Anyway, not content with knocking her up when she was twenty and then sashaying out of both our lives and back to his wife shortly after I was born – abandoning me like the mid-life-crisis baby I so obviously was – he thought he'd add insult to injury and name me after some obscure Byzantine emperor he'd written a thesis on.'

'So what is your name short for?'

He grimaced. 'Theophilos.'

Her eyes widened, and she clamped a hand to her mouth. 'No way!'

'If you dare tell anyone that then I love you, Lex, but you're dead meat.'

She tried to restrain herself but she couldn't help it. She burst out laughing.

He poked her. 'You're rotten, you are.'

With a Herculean effort, she managed to suppress the gales of laughter. 'Oh God, I'm sorry. That is fucking hilarious though. I'm so calling you that forever, Theophilos Blake.'

'You just dare.'

'What's your middle name, have you got one?'

'Timothy.'

'Oh man, what! Seriously, this is the best day of my entire life.' She forced her face into a sober expression. 'You know, you're actually my first Theophilos.'

'I'm warning you, Lex. One more and you're in for a truly merciless tickling.'

'Sorry. I'm sorry.' She snorted. 'I just can't believe I'm actually shagging a Theophilos. A Theophilos Timothy at that. I mean, talk about one for the bucket list.'

'Right, that's it.' He rolled over her and she squeaked as he pinned her arms with one hand so he could tickle her.

'Geroff, Theo!'

'Nope. Not until you scream for clemency and then some.'

Their play was interrupted by the shrill ring of the landline phone in the hall. Theo rolled off her.

'Who's ringing you at this time?'

'Ugh. Daryl,' she said, rolling her eyes. 'He's the only one who ever calls on that phone. Ignore it.'

'Connor won't get it, will he?'

'Not when he knows it's likely to be his dad. Anyway, he regards the landline with the same suspicion he would a fax machine/Betamax combo plugged into a dial-up modem.'

They waited for the phone to stop ringing. No sooner had the noise ceased, however, than Lexie's mobile started buzzing.

'Him again?' Theo asked as she glanced at the screen.

She nodded. 'Suppose I'd better get it. It must be urgent if he's calling me on the roaming rate.'

Lexie swiped to answer.

'What is it?' She cast a look at Theo. 'I was just in the middle of something.'

'What the hell's this about Connor getting suspended?' her husband demanded.

She frowned. 'Who told you that?'

'I got a letter from his head of year. I am his father, in case you'd forgotten. Were you planning to tell me or what?'

'I tried to. I sent you a message asking you to ring me weeks ago.'

'I've been busy with work stuff. Why didn't you just email?'

'Because I wanted to talk before you started on Connor about it. Anyway, it's fine, Daz. I dealt with it.'

'What the fuck are you playing at, Lexie?' he exploded. 'You know stuff like that goes on his permanent record, right?'

'What am *I* playing it? I didn't put him up to it.'

'You're clearly doing a pretty poor job of keeping him out of trouble. This could affect his chances of getting into a decent uni, Lex! Did you even think about that?'

'It wasn't the first thing on my mind, no. I was more concerned with making sure he was OK.'

Daryl ignored her. 'I let him stay with you because you convinced me it was a bad idea to pull him out of school, but you know, I'm really starting to wonder if I made the right call.'

'You let him stay because you didn't want him with you,' Lexie snapped. 'He could sense it, even when he was a little boy, the way you wished him out of your life.'

'You're not his mother, Lexie. Who the hell are you to tell me how I ought to bring up my son?'

'The person who actually did bring up your son,' she said in a low voice.

'You had no right to keep something like this from me. I should have been told as soon as it happened. What did he get suspended for anyway?'

She took a deep breath, forcing herself to calm down and not throw the phone at the wall.

'Fighting,' she said. 'Just kids letting off steam that ended up going a bit too far, that's all. Not exactly laudable, but I doubt it'll affect his life chances significantly.'

'Hmm. Well, that's not so bad. Did he win?'

She shook her head. 'Did he *win*? Seriously?'

She felt Theo's hand slip into hers and squeezed it gratefully.

'He gave the other lad a black eye,' she said. 'That's certainly not something you ought to be proud of him for, Daryl. Anyway, he was going through some difficult stuff at the time, and he's been punished for it and apologised to the boy involved, so there's no need to make a fuss. We've all moved on.'

'Stuff? What sort of stuff?'

'Well, that's not for me to say. It's personal.'

'Personal!' Daryl snapped. 'Christ, Lexie! You've actually managed to forget whose son he is, haven't you?'

'He might be your son, mate, but he's his own person. It's up to him if he chooses to tell you what's happening in his life. Perhaps if you rang him more than once a month, you might find out the sort of young man your son is becoming.'

'You think I don't care about him?'

She willed herself calmer.

'No, of course I don't think that,' she said in a softer tone. 'I know why it's hard for you, Daz, and I understand, I do, but if you don't make more of an effort to be part of his life then you're going to wake up one day and find your son's grown up into a stranger who doesn't want to know you. Can you at least try to build a better relationship with him? For his sake and your own.'

'All right, put him on now then.'

She shook her head. 'Daryl, it's midnight. He's got school in the morning. Did you forget we're in a different time zone again?'

'OK, then I'll call tomorrow. Five o'clock your time.'

'Right, good. I'll make sure he's in for you.'

'I'm warning you though, Lex. If you can't demonstrate you can take proper care of him, I will bring him out here where I can look after him myself.'

'You wouldn't dare,' she said in a low voice.

'I would, and I have every right to. He's my son – don't you ever forget that. Goodbye.'

'Ugh!' Lexie slammed the phone down, swore loudly at it then burst into tears.

'Hey.' Theo drew her to him and hushed her gently. 'Don't let him get to you, love. You know what he's like when he throws one of his temper tantrums. There's no reasoning with him.'

'I just can't believe he's got the nerve to play the concerned father card, after everything he's done. Honestly, Theo, you don't know how lucky you were growing up without a dad. Better none at all than one like Daryl.'

She felt him tense, and looked up into his face.

'Sorry,' she said gently. 'I didn't mean that the way it sounded. I guess it must've been tough.'

'No, it wasn't… look, never mind about me. Here, lie down and have a cuddle.'

They sank back into bed and he wrapped his body around hers. She burrowed into his arms and let out a deep sigh.

'Could you hear what he was saying?' she asked.

'I heard him say he'd take Connor.'

'He couldn't really do it, could he? I never legally adopted Con. I'm not sure what my rights would be if Daryl tried it.'

'He won't,' Theo said firmly. 'You were right; he's been wishing his son away ever since he lost Elise. He was just angry and set on hurting you – all talk, no substance.'

She gave him a squeeze. 'Did you miss having a dad very much when you were a kid?'

He shrugged. 'I tried to convince myself I didn't. I did secretly envy those of my mates whose dads took them out to the football and played games with them or whatever, but there were just as many with dads who were proper arseholes. From everything my mum told me about him, mine definitely fell into the latter category. He wasn't worth my tears.'

'What's your mum like?'

'Oh, she's very sweet. Sort of childlike. I wasn't all that old when I started feeling as if I was the one who needed to look after her, you know?' He smiled. 'But she loved me to bits, and she worked hard to give me everything she thought I needed. Best mum in the world, even if she wasn't doing it by the book.'

Lexie smiled too. 'That sounds familiar. I mean the not doing it by the book part, not the best mum in the world part.'

'I reckon Connor would agree with both parts.' He looked down at her. 'I'll have to take you to meet her sometime.'

'Seriously, meeting the parents?' she said, laughing.

'Not like that. I just think you'd be interested to get to know her. She lives with my stepdad over in Hebden Bridge.'

'Are you close to your stepdad?'

He shook his head. 'I'd grown up and left home by the time they met. We get on well, but we're more like mates than family.'

'So you never had any sort of man in your life when you were a kid?'

'There was this one guy,' he said, his eyes growing distant. 'Matt. He went out with my mum for a while. She had a lot of boyfriends – she was a romantic at heart, always hoping she'd meet The One, but she wasn't mature enough really to make a go of a relationship. Matt lasted a bit longer than the others though – I think he might have really loved her. For her sake he made a real effort with me, finding out what I was into, who my mates were, taking me out on my bike and for kickabouts in the park. God, I thought he was the mutt's nuts, that guy. I'd never had that kind of attention before.' He smiled wistfully. 'But then him and Mum broke up, and that was the last I ever saw of Matt. I didn't let myself get too close to her lovers after that. I knew they wouldn't be around long, and it'd only end up with me getting hurt as well as her.'

'Poor little boy.' The maternal part of Lexie's heart ached for him, and she lifted his hand to her lips. 'That's the reason I don't want to date while Con's at home. I do believe lads his age benefit from having a man they can respect and learn from in their world, but it needs to be someone who's a fixture, not a flash in the pan.' She smiled. 'Thank goodness he's got such a bloody awesome godfather, eh?'

'I'll never let him down, Lex. If I can promise you one thing, it's that.'

Chapter Fifteen

Theo's alarm went off at the ungodly hour of five a.m., giving him plenty of time to clear out of the house before Connor got up for school. He yawned and swung his legs out of bed to begin the hunt for his clothes.

'Fetch us up a coffee before you go, would you?' Lexie mumbled. 'I can't function on four hours' sleep unless someone pours caffeine into me.'

'What if Con catches me?'

'At five a.m., are you kidding? He can't even think about dragging himself out of bed until he's hit snooze on his alarm at least six times and had me threatening to batter the door down if he doesn't emerge from his pit within the next ten minutes. Connor doesn't know there is a five o'clock this side of the day.'

Theo smiled. 'All right, since I do feel responsible for keeping you up all night. Back in five.'

He pulled on her dressing gown – a short, fluffy thing with Minions on it that Connor had got her as a gag gift – and crept downstairs to the kitchen. He was just about to flick on the kettle when he heard a noise on the stairs.

Connor! Shit. Trust this to be the day the kid decided to experiment with early rising. Theo glanced around for an escape route but the back door was locked, with the key nowhere in evidence. Seeing only one other option, he dived into the pantry and pulled the door closed.

Oh, well this was nice and snug. The tiny pantry was definitely not designed to accommodate a six-foot-two man in a Minions dressing gown who, he now realised as a shelf of tins wedged itself intimately up against his bare backside, had forgotten to pull on a pair of pants before coming down. He held his breath, trying not to make a sound as Connor came in.

God, please say he'd just come to get a snack he could take up to his room…

Theo watched the boy through the crack of the door. For one horrible moment he thought Connor was going to come into the pantry, but while he seemed to hover in front of the door for what felt like a mini lifetime, Connor eventually changed his mind and opened one of the cupboards to get a cereal bar.

Theo crossed his fingers, toes and other extremities, hoping Connor would take the snack upstairs, but no. Instead the boy sat down at the table, produced his phone and started tapping away while he ate his cereal bar at a very leisurely pace. Theo was sure his bum was starting to get a Heinz-beans-shaped bruise across one cheek.

Finally Connor finished his snack and stood up. He turned towards the pantry.

'You know, you can come out if you want, Theo.'

Theo blinked and opened the door.

'All right, smartarse, did you know I was in there this whole time?'

'Yep.'

'Then why didn't you say anything?'

Connor grinned. 'Well, it was funny, wasn't it? Why're you wearing Lexie's dressing gown?'

'I, er… I just popped over to… borrow… some…' His eyes roved wildly around the kitchen.

'Some clothes?' Connor nodded to the dressing gown. 'I can see all your junk, you know.'

'Shit.' Theo hastily readjusted the thing. It really didn't fit him.

'It's fine, Theo. I know already.'

'What do you know?'

'About you and Lexie.' Connor sat back down and started scrolling through his phone again.

'What about me and Lexie?'

'Theo, come on. I just caught you with your dick hanging out, hiding in the pantry wearing my stepmum's dressing gown. I'm fourteen, not thick.'

Theo sighed and sat down too. 'All right, it's a fair cop. How long have you known then?'

'Er, since the beginning, obviously.'

Theo frowned. 'You what?'

'You guys are crap at keeping things secret. I can hear you tripping over stuff when you sneak in.'

Theo flinched. 'Bollocks. You're not going to beat me up, are you? I understand you've got quite an impressive right hook.'

'Nah, it's fine. Lexie's been dead happy lately. I reckon she deserves that.'

Theo smiled. 'No arguments here.'

'And you're all right. I'd rather it was you than someone else.' He pulled a face. 'Especially not my dad.'

'Thanks, kiddo.' Theo slapped him on the shoulder. 'You're not so bad yourself, by the way.'

'Uncle Theo, can I ask you something?'

'That depends what it is,' Theo said cautiously. 'Is it about Lexie and me?'

'No. I just wondered, um, if you'd take me and my mate Oli to CalderCon for my birthday. Lexie normally takes us but she's not really into it.' He flushed. 'I thought you might like it though. There's loads of sci-fi stuff, and people from films and that, and cool costumes. I always go as Boba Fett.'

Theo nodded. 'Good choice.'

'I thought, um, maybe you could go as one of the *Red Dwarf* guys or something,' he said, avoiding eye contact. 'I mean, if you wanted to. You don't have to.'

'That sounds really good actually,' Theo lied. 'I'd love to go.'

Connor beamed. 'Sweet, I'll tell Ol.'

Theo stood up to go and enlighten Lexie about this latest development, but he stopped at the kitchen door. He couldn't help thinking about Matt, the boyfriend of his mum's he'd got so close to, and the hole in his life when Matt was no longer around.

'Con, me and Lexie… you know it's nothing serious, right?' he said. 'We're really just good friends, that's all, same as before. We're not going to get married or anything.'

'Sure, I know that,' Connor said with a shrug, his eyes still fixed on his phone. 'I'm not fussed what you do.'

'Right. Just so we're clear. I'd hate you to… well, never mind.'

–

'What, no coffee?' Lexie muttered when Theo came back in. 'Is the milk off?'

'We've been rumbled, Lex.' He took off her dressing gown and chucked it to her. 'Here, get your clothes on. You need to talk to the kid.'

She blinked, still half asleep. 'What? Who's rumbled? What's a rumble?'

'Connor knows.'

'Shit!' She sat up, fully awake now. 'How does he know?'

'He's a perceptive little sod, it turns out.' He bent down to pick up his boxers. 'Apparently we're not as sneaky as we think we are. Plus if he didn't know before, then I think discovering me hiding in the pantry with my willy hanging out just now definitely put him onto us.'

'What did he say?'

'Not much. Just exploited the situation to get me to agree to take him to CalderCon.' He pulled on his pants and started struggling into his jeans. 'Look, I'd better go. You ought to have a talk with him, explain… Christ, I don't know. Explain something.'

136

'But... explain how? What am I even explaining?' Lexie said, feeling dazed. 'That sometimes grown-ups get randy and have meaningless sex with their mates? What kind of example is that for him?' She groaned. 'Oh God. I'm—'

'Oh, no. Don't start again with that "I'm a terrible mother" business.' He put on his T-shirt. 'Connor's nearly fifteen, Lex, I'm sure he can deal. Just be as honest as you can, explain it to him in teen-friendly terms, and... well, call me after and tell me how it went.'

'Can't you stay and explain it with me?'

'Nope, sorry. You're the parent.'

'Coward.'

'Absolutely.' He kissed her on the forehead. 'Good luck.'

When he'd gone, Lexie got dressed and, with some trepidation, sought out Connor in the kitchen.

'Yeah, I'm just doing it,' he said when he heard her come in, not looking up from his phone.

'What are you just doing?'

'Putting my uniform on.'

She smiled. 'Your ability to lie like I can't see you sitting there in your pyjamas never ceases to impress me.' She took a seat opposite him. 'So... I think we need to talk, don't we?'

'About what?'

'Well, you know. The thing.' She frowned. 'You do know about the thing, don't you? I was told on good authority that you did.'

'What, the you and Theo thing?'

'Er, yeah.'

He shrugged. 'Yeah, I know. What do we have to talk about it for? I don't want to think about your rancid old-people boning.'

Lexie decided to ignore that comment. 'Look, Connor. The thing is, when you're single as an adult, you, um... well, it can get lonely sometimes. So even though there are times when you don't really want to be dating – when you're about to get

137

divorced, for example – you still kind of feel that you'd like to be with someone. Not like a boyfriend, more like a… friend. A special friend that you… do special friend things with. Do you understand?'

'I understand that you're talking to me like I'm five and I just asked where babies come from.'

She smiled. 'All right, a friend that you sleep with, then. Do you know what I mean?'

'Yeah, I know what you mean. I just don't get how that's different from a boyfriend.'

'Well, the main difference is that a boyfriend is someone you're exclusive with. Someone you have a future with. Whereas Theo and me, we're really just good friends.'

'If you like him, that doesn't sound different to a boyfriend to me. You should just tell him you want to be exclusive.'

'Your Uncle Theo's… not an exclusive sort of man,' Lexie said, feeling out of her depth.

'He might be if you asked him.'

'It isn't only that, Connor. Sometimes people like each other – I mean, they really like each other, so that they're best friends – but they know they're always going to want different things in life. A different future.'

'What sort of different things?'

'Well, a family is something I… that I thought I might want one day,' she said, flushing slightly. 'I mean, a bigger family.'

Connor finally put his phone down and looked at her. 'You mean another kid?'

'Yes. I always hoped me and your dad… well, that didn't work out, but if I meet the right person then one day I hope it'll happen. That isn't something Theo would ever want, I know that, but it's a dream I haven't given up on.'

'I didn't know you wanted to have a baby.'

'I suppose I felt awkward talking about it with you. I didn't want you to feel that it meant I didn't see you as mine, especially when you were younger. But now you're nearly an adult, I think you're mature enough to understand that at my age it's a normal thing to want. How would you feel about it?'

Connor was silent for a moment, frowning.

'I think it'd be awesome,' he said at last. 'I always wanted a little brother or sister when I was a kid. It'd be even cooler now.'

'Why?'

'Because then we could go as Mando and the Child to the next CalderCon.'

Lexie laughed. 'Sorry, Con, but I'm not procreating around your cosplay schedule.'

He shrugged. 'Well, it'd be awesome whenever. Seriously though, it'd be good if you hurried up. The new *Mandalorian* season's going to be huge this year.'

He glanced up to grin at her, and she smiled back, feeling a wave of relief. She hadn't realised just how worried she'd been about Connor's reaction to the idea of a potential new baby until this moment.

'So do you understand?' she asked. 'Me and Theo... we like each other, very much, but we're just friends. That's all. One day when I'm divorced from your dad I definitely want to start dating again, and hopefully meet someone I feel I could spend my life with, but that isn't what this is.'

Connor shrugged. 'Whatever. I'm not really fussed what you guys do.' He picked up his phone to resume whatever he'd been doing, paused, then put it down again. 'Lexie?'

'Yes, sweetie?'

'I know Dad was a real tool to you.'

'Oh, that's—'

'Don't say it's not fair. It's totally fair, and I'm too old now for you to have to keep pretending he wasn't a prick.' He took a deep breath. 'And I think... I think you deserved someone better. You were always dead nice and... and I know I'm a brat sometimes, but that doesn't mean I'm not grateful that you brought me up when Dad didn't give a crap about me. Otherwise I think I'd be a total mess now, after what happened to Mum.' Connor's features twitched as he spoke, as though the words he wanted to say were a struggle for him to formulate. 'So you should do whatever you want, that's what I think. You should do what makes you happiest. I want you to be happy more than… more than anything. I know I never say it, but…' He paused, his cheeks crimson. 'Well, I love you and all that.'

'Awww.' Lexie stood up to go and give him a hug. 'I love you too, sweetheart. Thank you.'

'All right, get off me now,' he mumbled, wiggling out of the embrace. 'It's fine, all right? You and Theo need to stop worrying about me. As long as you're happy, I don't care what you do.'

'Well, I think you've earned yourself bacon butties for breakfast for that.' She planted a kiss on his curls before going to turn on the hob. 'And Connor: you know you can't say anything to your dad about this, don't you?'

'Well yeah, obviously,' Connor said, rolling his eyes. 'I won't say anything. Promise.'

Chapter Sixteen

'All right, Theophilos?' Lexie said when Theo answered his phone to her one Friday lunchtime some weeks later.

'I'm refusing to answer to that name even if this is a booty call.'

Lexie swallowed the last mouthful of her Caesar salad. 'Are you free this afternoon?'

'I was planning on going to the gym, but I could be up for a bit of afternoon delight instead,' Theo said. 'I'll get a better workout with you anyway.'

She smiled. 'I was actually going to request your services in a friends-without-the-benefits capacity. Connor's birthday's only a month away so I was planning to go out present-hunting. I could use an undercover geek to give me some advice.'

'Yeah, all right. I'll pick you up in an hour and we'll drive into town.'

'And then I'm sure there'll be time before he's home from school for me to show you my appreciation for the favour.'

'Oh? Well in that case, I'll pick you up in fifteen minutes. See you in a bit, Lex.'

–

'So,' Theo said when they were wandering through Halifax together. 'Which den of geekery shall we start in? Games Workshop? Forbidden Planet? Or we could try our luck in Bilbo's Hobbit Hole.'

Lexie snorted. 'I'm sorry, in what?'

'Bilbo's Hobbit Hole. It's an independent comic book shop.'

'That sounds so dirty, Theo.'

'Probably deserves a band name klaxon, right?'

'No, sorry, you can't have a klaxon for that. You only quoted it, you didn't make it up.'

'I swear you change the rules every week,' he said. 'So, where to?'

'Let's start in Bilbo's Glory Hole, see what they've got in the way of merch. I want to get Con some T-shirts from his dad.'

Theo frowned. 'What, you're shopping for Daryl's presents as well?'

'Yeah, he transferred over some cash and told me to get whatever I thought Connor would like and stick his name on it.'

'Huh. Classic Daryl parenting.'

'I know. Anyway, some new weekend clothes are a must. The T-shirts I bought him three months ago already look like crop tops on him. Seriously, I really hope he's done growing now before he wears me out of house and home.'

She tucked her arm through Theo's and they walked around the corner to the comic book shop.

'Here, let me get that for you.' Theo darted ahead to open the door.

She laughed. 'Oh, I'm sorry. Are you suddenly from the past?'

'Whoops,' he said, grimacing. 'Forgot I was only out with you. Women tend to like it when I do the chivalry thing on dates. Force of habit.'

'Force of hobbit.'

'God, please no more with the hobbit gags,' he said, rolling his eyes. 'Here, is this better?' He went inside and pointedly closed the door in her face.

'Much,' she said when she opened it. She looked around the dimly lit room. 'So, where do we start?'

Theo wandered over to an illuminated glass cabinet and gazed in at the contents.

'Look, Lex,' he said in a low voice. 'Vintage collectibles. Here, check out the Pokémon figures. I had a bucketload of these when I was a kid.' He glanced at the price tags and whistled. 'Bloody hell. Wish I'd hung on to Charizard if that's the going rate for him.'

'Can we go find the clothes?' Lexie said.

Theo's gaze had drifted to a model of Starbug from *Red Dwarf* on the shelf above, still in its original box.

'I'm going to get Con that,' he announced.

She shook her head. 'No, Theo, it's too extravagant for a non-parent present. Get him a comic or something.'

'No, I want to get him that. It's still in the box, Lex. Do you know how exciting that is to kids like Connor? Anyway, *Red Dwarf*'s our thing now.'

She couldn't talk him out of it, and when they made their way upstairs to where the branded clothing lived, Theo was proudly carrying a paper bag containing his purchase.

'I don't suppose they sell costumes in here, do they?' he said, glancing around. 'When Connor looked at me with those big Bambi eyes, I just didn't have the heart to tell him I wouldn't dress up for CalderCon. Mind you, the fact he'd just found me hiding half-naked in the pantry with a tin of beans wedged up my arse might've had something to do with it as well.'

'No. You'll have to hit up eBay.' Lexie grinned. 'Can't wait to see what you find. You two are going to look so adorable together.'

'It's not too late to get yourself a Seven of Nine latex catsuit if you fancy joining us. I can buy you a ticket and some invisible underwear.'

'I'll be washing my hair, sorry.'

Theo pulled a T-shirt from one of the racks, bearing in a *Star Wars* font the legend: *A Jedi in the streets, a Sith between the sheets*. 'Ha! Get Con this, I double-dare you.'

'I don't think so, do you? Get it for yourself, sex maniac.'

In the end they bought a couple of Marvel-branded T-shirts and a Flash hoodie as Daryl's gifts and left to see what they could find in Games Workshop.

'Thanks for coming shopping with me, Teddy,' Lexie said, tucking her arm through his. 'You know, it's fun to do something other than... well, it.'

'We are still having a bit of "it" later though, right?'

'You bet we are.'

A woman in a smart skirt suit that looked far too glam for a Halifax shopping trip was walking towards them. She seemed to recognise Lexie, her eyebrows raising in surprise – at least, as far as they could through the Botox – before she lifted her hand to wave.

Lexie groaned as she waved back. 'Oh God,' she muttered to Theo. 'Just my sodding luck we'd bump into her.'

'Who is it?'

'Allegra Schofield, this girl I went to school with. You remember I told you there was a gang who bullied me?'

Theo frowned. 'Oh. She's one of them, is she?'

'Yeah, the main one. She was the ringleader of this group of well-off, popular girls – you know the sort. Bunch of spoilt, entitled brats who thought they were better than the rest of us. We're all grown up and civilised now, Facebook friends and everything, but she's still the most insufferably smug cow. One of those who stages elaborate Instagram pictures of her Stepford-perfect offspring and takes a daily photo of her sourdough starter. Some days I lose track of which is the starter and which is one of her pasty-faced kids.' She fixed her face into a smile as the woman approached them. 'Allegra, hi.'

'Jan, darling!' Allegra leaned forward to air-kiss her on each cheek then fixed on an expression of faux sympathy. 'And how are you, you poor love? Is Daryl still away?'

'He certainly is, thank Christ,' Lexie said brightly. 'How are Jake and Araminta?'

'Oh, they're little dears, although I do find I want to murder them on a daily basis,' Allegra said, trilling a laugh. 'Minty was just accepted for a place at St Augusta's – you know, the independent primary school? Her father and I are ecstatic. It's ever so competitive there.'

'I'm glad to hear it. And how's the sourdough starter?'

'Er, coming along, thank you,' Allegra said, looking slightly bemused. Theo willed back a smile.

Allegra did that awful face thing again, half sympathy and half sneer. 'Such a shame you and Daryl never had a little one to comfort you now you're all alone. If I didn't have Jake and Minty, I know my life would just feel empty.'

'Well, there are other things I like to think give my life meaning,' Lexie said. 'Besides, I've got Connor.'

'Yes, but it isn't the same when they're not your own, is it? Still, I suppose you have work to keep you from brooding on your failed marriage.'

Theo noted how she emphasised the word 'failed', as if Lexie was wholly responsible for Daryl walking out on her.

'What is it you do now?' Allegra asked. 'Waitressing?'

'Well, yes, in my own restaurant,' Lexie said.

'Ah, of course. That bizarre little war place, I've seen it in your photos.' She looked at Theo with obvious interest. 'And who might this be?'

Allegra was simpering now she'd turned to him, her chest thrust out ever so slightly as she inclined towards him. Theo, a seasoned expert in interpreting those sorts of signals from women, tried to hide his irritation as he smiled his most charming smile for her.

'Oh, this is Theo,' Lexie said. 'He's just—'

'I'm her boyfriend,' Theo said, holding out a hand for Allegra to shake. 'Nice to meet you, Allegra. Any friend of Lexie's is a friend of mine.'

'A new boyfriend already!' Allegra said. 'You certainly don't waste any time, Jan. When did your divorce come through?'

'Er, it didn't,' Lexie said, shooting Theo a look. 'Daryl and me are still waiting for our required separation period to be up.'

'Well, nothing like lining up the next one while you're waiting, I suppose.' She let go of Theo's hand, which she'd held on to rather longer than was necessary. 'I'd better get on. It's been wonderful to catch up though. Listen, are the two of you busy tomorrow evening?'

'Yes,' Lexie said.

'That's a shame. A few of us Kingsway survivors and our plus-ones were planning a little get-together over in Hebden Bridge, sort of a reunion. It would've been lovely to have you along, Jan. And Theo too, of course.'

'Well we're busy, so…'

'But it's nothing we couldn't put off,' Theo said with another charm-dripping smile. 'We'd love to go, wouldn't we, Lex? We can always do that thing we were going to do another day.'

She glared at him. 'Yes. Thanks for reminding me, Theo. Actually I think that thing we were going to do might be put off for a good while.'

'Excellent. I'll send you the event link on Facebook.' Allegra did the air-kiss thing again. 'See you both tomorrow.'

'What the hell did you tell her you were my boyfriend for?' Lexie hissed when she'd gone.

'Well, because she was being all sneery and condescending at you and it was pissing me off. Besides, she fancied me. I wanted her to think you had life all sewn up.'

She snorted. 'Oh, right. With a fine piece of eye candy like you on my arm, you mean?'

'I'm far too modest to phrase it like that. But yes.'

'Did you have to agree to this bloody school reunion?' Lexie asked as they carried on walking.

He shrugged. 'It'll be good for you. You ought to face them and show them up for being a bunch of up-themselves wankers. I hate to think of them sneering behind your back when you could turn up like Scarlett O'Hara in a tarty red dress and have a roomful of jaws hit the floor.'

'You might've asked if that was what I wanted first.'

He guided her arm through his again. 'Oh come on, you'll enjoy it. Neither of us are on the teatime shift tomorrow; we can make an afternoon of it. Have a meal in one of the pubs, drop in on my mum. You were the one who said we ought to do more mate stuff together instead of just shagging all the time. Besides, I want to meet these bellends you went to school with.'

'All right, fine. I'll have to check Connor's going to be OK on his own though.'

'He's nearly fifteen, Lex. He's not going to start playing with matches and running with scissors the second you leave him alone for a night.' He glanced sideways at her. 'What was all that Jan business, by the way?'

She flushed. 'Oh. That. It's an old nickname from school.'

'Where does it come from?'

'*Grease*. You remember Jan, from the Pink Ladies? She was the chubby one with buck teeth. Allegra used to say I looked like her during my braces and puppy fat phase, and even when they were long gone she refused to stop using it. I wish she'd bloody give over with it now, it's been sixteen years. Sort of spoils the all-friends-now vibe she tries so hard to push whenever I see her.'

'It was a bit *Mean Girls*, your school, wasn't it?'

She snorted. 'Try *Heathers*. That place was murder.'

He squeezed her arm. 'Well, sod the lot of them, love. Tomorrow night we're going to march into this reunion and by the time we leave, every stinking one of them will wish they could be Lexie Whittle.'

Chapter Seventeen

By the time they got back to Lexie's place, they were fully laden with bags of comic books, superhero merch and video games, ready for Connor's fifteenth birthday the following month. As soon as Lexie had unlocked the door, Theo guided her inside and pressed her up against the wall for a deep kiss.

'I've been dying to do that all afternoon,' he whispered.

'Just that?'

'No. Not just that. Come on, let's go upstairs.'

Lexie jumped at the sound of a throat clearing behind them.

'Having fun?' Tonya asked.

She wriggled out of Theo's arms.

'What the hell are you doing here?' she demanded. 'I thought you were on a cruise.'

'I got back this morning. What, are you not pleased to see me?'

Lexie shook her head. 'Seriously, why are people always just walking into my house? I need to stop giving you all emergency keys.'

'I brought this to show you,' Tonya said, waggling a rolled-up banner at them. 'Made it for us while I was out on the open seas. For the procession.' She unfurled it to unveil the embroidered slogan *GIVE PEACE A CHANCE* with a white dove motif.

'How many times, Ton? It's a forties festival, not a sixties festival. You're not re-enacting a CND march.'

'It's just as appropriate for the Second World War as the Cold War. Wherever there's fighting, there are people campaigning for peace. Plus I just adore seeing Ryan's face go that lovely shade of puce.' She glanced at Theo, who was looking a bit dazed. 'Well, Lexie, I was going to invite you out for afternoon tea, but it looks like you've made more energetic plans.'

'You'd better go, Teddy,' Lexie said in a low voice. 'Me and her ought to talk. Call me later, all right?'

'Right. OK.' He leaned forward to kiss her cheek, then clocked Tonya's grin and thought better of it. 'See you then, ladies.'

'Excellent,' Tonya said when he'd gone. 'Now we can have a lovely girly afternoon. I'm just desperate to take you to this little tearoom I've discovered. We'll get a taxi.'

'It's all right, I can drive us.'

'Absolutely not. I want you completely relaxed, so no driving today.'

–

Lexie frowned when the taxi dropped them off at their destination.

'Ton?'

'Hmm?'

'Are you sure this is a tearoom?'

'Of course, my love.'

'Only it says "cocktail bar" on the sign.'

'Well, yes, but they do teas as well. There's a lovely iced version, I think it's from Long Island. Come on, my treat.'

Lexie shook her head as they entered and approached the bar. 'I should've known to be suspicious when you insisted on the taxi.' She hopped up onto a stool. 'Actually, no. I should've known to be suspicious when it was you who suggested it.'

'Yes you should. I'm disappointed in you, Lexie.' Tonya picked up a menu. 'Oooh, fish bowls! Shall we?'

'Tonya, honestly, I can't. I have to make Connor's tea, I can't go back home shit-faced from day-drinking.'

'Oh, just give him a fish-finger sandwich or something.'

Lexie was eventually able to negotiate for the least alcoholic drink on the menu, some sort of tropical mimosa, while Tonya ordered herself a large mojito.

'Go on then, out with it,' Lexie said when they'd both been served.

'Out with what, darling?'

'Aren't you going to interrogate me about what's going on with Theo?'

'Oh, that. No, I already knew about that.'

Lexie blinked. 'Did you? How?'

Tonya shrugged. 'It's obvious to anyone who isn't blind that you're sleeping together. I've known for ages.'

'I don't know why we don't just start publishing a bloody newsletter,' Lexie muttered.

'Just casual, I'm assuming?'

'Yes. Nothing serious, just… well, you know. You don't mind, do you?'

'We all have an itch to scratch sometimes.' She took a dainty draw on her mojito that nevertheless managed to drain half the glass in one go. 'Does Connor know?'

'Yes, he knows. He's been very mature about it actually. I was impressed.' Lexie sipped her cocktail, which was actually just a fancier-sounding Buck's Fizz: champagne and fruit juice.

'Well if it's all right by him, I don't see why it shouldn't be all right by me. I certainly don't think you owe his father anything.' She glanced at Lexie's worried face and smiled. 'Oh, I know what you're thinking. Don't worry, he'll never hear it from me.'

Lexie exhaled with relief. 'Thanks, Ton. Not that I think it's any of Daryl's business who I go to bed with now, but it'd only spell trouble for us all if he found out.'

'Be careful, Lexie. You know how gossip can spread.' Tonya reached into her handbag. 'Here, this is for you. Just don't tell anyone on the committee you got it from me, all right?'

Lexie opened up the bunting Tonya handed her: a long string of triangular Union Jacks.

'Awww,' she said, smiling. 'It's a nationalistic celebration of Empire. Thanks, Ton.'

'You're welcome, honey. Seriously, though, don't tell anyone I made it. I'd never live it down at my yoga group.' She finished her cocktail and gestured to the barman to bring the same again. 'Another?'

'No, thanks. I've got loads left.'

'Well, and how have the festival plans been progressing in my absence? Are we nearly there?'

'Yes, pretty much. Ryan's sorted out the road closure for our procession, Janette's booked us a brass band and a Spitfire to do a flyover, and Stevie's been running about like a blue-arsed fly press-ganging all the village groups into running stalls and things.'

'And the restaurant?'

'Oh, the Parrot's going all out. Special VE Day menu, a jazz singer, extra waiting staff, ads in all the papers. We're having a marquee cafe down in the park as well as the restaurant itself, run jointly with Brooke from the pub.' She sucked meditatively on her straw. 'I just hope we get the crowds. Theo and me have invested a lot in this event being a success. We stand to lose a bomb if it fails, and we really can't afford that. I can't afford it.'

'I have every faith in you both.' Tonya twisted her barstool to examine her. 'You look very well. I suppose we've got young Theo to thank for that.'

Lexie smiled slightly. 'I must confess, it's been fun. It's so long since I did anything just for myself. I feel like a proper young person again now – my own person, not just someone's mum.'

'Definitely just casual? You told me you two had been getting closer since Daryl left.'

'It is casual, but… I suppose because we're mates as well, it's like the best of both worlds. Dating without the dates. The physical side of it's great, but it's nice to feel I've got that companionship, emotionally.'

Tonya was silent for a moment, scrutinising her face.

'You ought to be careful, Lexie,' she said at last.

'Oh, don't worry about that. We're not stupid.'

'I don't mean that kind of careful. I mean in terms of protecting your feelings.'

Lexie raised an eyebrow. 'Really? The Mother Superior of the Free Love movement's warning me about feelings?'

Tonya shrugged. 'They're not the same as one-off sex, those sorts of no-strings relationships. It's all fun and games at the start – trust me, I've had my share – but it's easy for emotions to start creeping in after a time.'

'You mean you fell for someone?'

She shook her head. 'He fell for me. I met him on holiday shortly after Elise died, at a time when my feelings were a little all over the place, to say the least. I felt terrible when I couldn't reciprocate, but that's the way it happens sometimes. It's easy to convince yourself you can keep things purely physical, but a friendship with sex in the mix nearly always ends up being more than the sum of its parts.'

'Not for us.'

Tonya squinted at her. 'You sound awfully sure.'

'I am sure.'

'Why? Theo Blake's a handsome lad, and you're fond of him. You know you're sexually compatible. Who says it couldn't turn into more?'

'Because I wouldn't let it turn into more. For now the friends-with-benefits arrangement is giving us everything we need, but I know Theo doesn't want what I want – a baby, a family life. Knowing he doesn't want those things makes it easy for me to maintain a sort of detachment. Same for him, I suppose – although it was always going to be easy for him. He's had plenty of fuck buddies in his time but I've never known him fall for anyone.'

'How do you know he doesn't want a baby?'

'He told me. Multiple times. Honestly, you should hear him on the subject. He talks about having a kid like it's the most horrific thing imaginable.'

'He likes children though, doesn't he? He's always been good with Connor.'

'Yeah, he's great with other people's, but that's very different from being responsible for one as a parent. I think Theo Blake is just one of life's uncles.'

'Why though?'

'I suppose not everyone has that parental instinct. Still, the way he talks about having kids… it almost sounds like some sort of phobia.' Lexie shrugged. 'I guess that's just how it is for some people. It's not for me to judge Theo's life choices just because they're not the same as mine. I certainly wouldn't appreciate it if people started lecturing me on what I ought to do with my reproductive system.'

'You wish his choices could be different though,' Tonya said quietly. 'Don't you?'

'I… no,' Lexie said, feeling her cheeks heat slightly. 'What's the point in wishing? Things are how they are.' She finished her drink. 'Anyway, it's fine, Ton. It's just a bit of fun, then when we're both ready to move on, we will. At this point in my life, it's the perfect arrangement.'

Tonya didn't say anything, but she kept her eyes fixed on Lexie's face while she knocked back the dregs of her second mojito.

–

'You're really sure I look OK in this?' Lexie said, brushing down her blue satin cocktail dress.

'You look great, Lex,' Theo called from the en suite. 'Honestly, you'll be the biggest knockout in the room. Just relax.'

When Allegra had said they were planning a small unofficial Kingsway reunion, Lexie had been dim enough to take her at face value. Of course, Allegra Schofield had never had just the one face. When the event link popped into her Facebook notifications, she discovered that what she'd expected would be a few of them congregating at the bar of a country pub somewhere was actually a proper swanky do in the function room of a smart hotel, with at least forty people going. Perhaps it was the paranoia Allegra had nurtured in her during their schooldays, but Lexie couldn't help suspecting the invitation was less an olive branch than an attempt to humiliate her.

Allegra had always enjoyed sneering at Lexie's working-class credentials. Kingsway had been a mixed bag in that respect, with a catchment area hoovering up kids from all sorts of different backgrounds in and around Halifax, yet it was Lexie the well-off girls had chosen to single out. Was Allegra hoping to show her up in front of the sort of people who'd always believed themselves to be a cut above her at school? Or was it her intention to embarrass Lexie in front of Theo? Allegra had obviously found him attractive, and she hadn't extended the invitation until Theo had announced that the two of them were an item. Perhaps she was keen to show him just what a total Jan his supposed new girlfriend really was.

Lexie readjusted the dress, trying to give her boobs a bit more room to breathe. The fabric was very tight around the chest, especially as it was right before her period, when her breasts were at their most swollen and tender. She'd have to remind Theo to be gentle with them when they made love later. One of her favourite things about going to bed with her best friend was the freedom to be completely frank about things like that, never having to hide her natural bodily functions in embarrassment as she had with boyfriends in the past. With Theo, she didn't need to be any sort of unrealistic ideal. She could just be herself.

'We're going to see your mum before the party though,' she called to him. 'I don't want her to think I'm some harlot in my slinky dress, do I?'

'You don't look like a harlot.' Theo came in from the bathroom. 'You look sexy and sophisticated, because you are. Anyway, she won't notice. She never notices stuff like that.'

Lexie stared at him.

'What?' he said, glancing down at the dinner suit he'd put on. 'Looks all right, doesn't it? It's been a while since I had any reason to give it an airing.'

'It looks…' She approached him and ran her fingers over his chest. 'Wow, Theo. You're hot stuff.'

'Aren't I always?'

'Well, obviously, but usually more of an earthy hot stuff. I've never seen you all gelled and shiny before.'

He did look handsome as sin in black tie, with his usually tousled sandy hair smartly styled and his broad shoulders emphasised by the cut of the suit. Lexie turned to look in the mirror again, but found that her eyes wouldn't stop straying to the man at her shoulder.

'God, Theo, I'm seriously dreading tonight,' she whispered.

'You'll be fine. Better than fine. You'll be the belle of the ball.' Theo presented her with his arm. 'Come on, tiger. Let's go get 'em.'

—

Connor was at the kitchen table when they went in, glued to his smartphone as usual while he picked absently at a bunch of grapes.

'You two look fancy,' he said when he'd torn his eyes from his phone. 'Where are you going on your date? Prom?'

'It's not a date,' Lexie said. 'We're going to some posh party with people I hated at school.'

'What for?'

She glanced at Theo. 'Because, despite his conspicuous lack of a psychology doctorate, your bloody godfather seems to think I have to go bury the demons of my past or something.'

'Ignore her, Con,' Theo said. 'She's going to have a great time.'

'Now, have you got everything you need before we go?' Lexie said. 'There's chilli in the fridge, and I've left a list of emergency numbers next to the phone. If anyone you don't know knocks at the door then don't answer it, and if your dad rings and starts badgering you about that suspension—'

'—tell him to eff off, I know.'

She smiled. 'Well, maybe tell him to call back later so I can tell him to eff off. Now, we've both got our phones in case you need us so—'

He laughed. 'Lexie, I'm fourteen, not three. Just go and have fun or be miserable or whatever you're doing at this party.'

'Right.' She went to plant a kiss on his curls and he grimaced, shaking her away. 'I'll be back before midnight. Make sure the house is still standing, eh?'

Chapter Eighteen

Theo's mum lived in the small upstairs flat of a terraced house high on the hills that circled the pretty town of Hebden Bridge. She beamed when she answered the door, and Theo bent to give her a bear-like hug.

'Hiya, Mum.' He gestured to Lexie, standing awkwardly at his side. 'This is Lexie, the friend I told you about. Lexie, this is my mum, Candy Stratford.'

'Pleased to meet you, Mrs Stratford.' Lexie held out a hand, but Candy put her arms around her for a warm hug instead.

'Hello, love,' she said. 'Here, come in and we'll have some tea and a little cake each, shall we? We always have vanilla slices on Wednesdays.'

'It's Saturday, Mum,' Theo said as she ushered them inside.

'Oh. Yes. I suppose it must be,' Candy said absently. 'Well, then we'll have fondant fancies, which is just as nice. Come and sit down, you two. Don't mind the dogs, they're big softies.'

As soon as they'd entered the house a terrible din had arisen, the air shaking with barks. Several mongrels of unidentified heritage came bounding towards them, and Candy rebuffed them expertly. In the living room, she brushed a couple more hounds from an ancient-looking sofa and gestured for her guests to take a seat.

'Um, thank you,' Lexie said, sitting down somewhat gingerly beside Theo as she tried not to get dog hair on her dress.

Candy's place was small and very bare, with a distinctly doggy smell hanging around and furnishings that looked like they must've seen better days shortly after the war. The only ornaments were a carriage clock and a souvenir seashell from Blackpool on the mantelpiece, and a framed print of Durdle Door hanging on one wall.

It wasn't at all what Lexie had been expecting. For some reason – perhaps because she knew his dad had been a university professor – she'd always imagined Theo as having had quite a comfortable childhood, but Candy seemed to live almost in poverty.

'Where's Graham?' Theo asked his mum.

'He just popped out for a paper. Now then, what was I doing? Oh yes.' She bustled over to the kettle in her open-plan kitchen and flicked it on, then took a packet of fondant fancies from one of the cupboards. Lexie noticed that her hands shook constantly as she made the tea. 'I do love to have visitors. It's the perfect excuse to indulge, isn't it?'

'How are you, Mum?' Theo asked, and Lexie noticed a gentleness in his voice quite unlike his usual half-teasing tone. 'Do you need anything? Money, help in the house, anything like that?'

'Oh, no, not really. Although…' She took a pile of unopened letters from a drawer. 'There were these. Do I need to do anything with them, do you think?'

Theo frowned as he took them from her. 'These are bills, Mum. Did you show them to Graham?'

'No, I don't like to keep bothering him. He has so much to worry about since he got laid off.'

Theo stood up to put an arm around her shoulders.

'Mum, you really need to show these to him or me as soon as they come,' he said gently. 'You remember when they turned off the electricity? Here, I'll take them back with me and make sure they get paid.'

'Well, just take what money you need out of the biscuit barrel as usual,' she said, staring with unfocused eyes into the distance. She roused herself to smile at him. 'Thank you, sweetheart.'

He gave her a squeeze and shooed a few dogs out of his way so he could sit down by Lexie again.

Lexie watched Candy as she brought over the tea tray. Although she had the shuffling gait you might associate with someone very elderly, Theo's mother was relatively young still: a petite woman in her mid-fifties, very pretty. She had her son's fine green eyes, only hers held a sort of vacant innocence that suggested she wasn't quite on the same plane as everyone else in the room. She smiled warmly at Lexie as she handed over a mug of tea.

'There you go, Alison. One sugar, the way you like it.'

'Who's Alison?' Lexie whispered to Theo.

'Her niece. Don't say anything.'

'Oh! Theo,' Candy exclaimed suddenly, clapping her hands. 'Guess what? We've had the television people in town again.'

'Which television people were they this time?' he asked.

'The ones who do that programme... oh, you know. It's like *Pride and Prejudice*, only with lesbians. Her off *Corrie* was in it. They were here filming.' She nodded at Lexie, as if she'd attempted to deny it. 'Yes, they were, I promise you. We get all the television people here. We've had the ones for that policewoman programme, you know, with her from *Corrie* – not that one, the other one, Raquel as was – and all sorts.' She let out a little giggle. 'We're like the Hollywood of the North, Graham says. He says a lot of clever things like that.'

Theo smiled. 'That's great, Mum. Maybe you'll be talent-spotted, eh? You could be the next Kim Basinger.'

She blushed and giggled again. 'Oh, Theo. You're a daft sausage.' She frowned. 'Now, what was my other bit of news for you? I can't quite... oh yes, I know. Your father. He passed away on Monday.'

Theo's head jerked up, tea sloshing over his smart suit.

'What?' he whispered.

'Well, he was seventy-nine, you know. I don't imagine you'd call that a good innings these days, but it's not too bad, is it? Not considering those cigarillo things he used to smoke. Anyway, I suppose I'd better send some flowers from us. I know he doesn't really deserve them, but you shouldn't wish ill to the dead.'

Lexie could feel Theo trembling against her, his face ashen. She took his hand and held it tightly. Candy, oblivious to the way her son's face worked with strong emotion, had already drifted back to talking about the film crew who'd been in the area, excitedly listing the celebrities she'd seen out and about, the costumes and set dressings that had transformed the town.

Theo had just about managed to compose himself by the time his stepfather returned.

'Theo!' The man beamed as he strode in and grasped his stepson by the hand. 'Well well, this is a nice surprise.' He raised his eyebrows when he spotted Lexie. 'Oh. You brought a girlfriend to meet your mam, did you? That's a new one, lad.'

'No.' Theo forced a smile. 'It's only Lexie – you remember, my partner at the Blue Parrot. Actually, we just dropped in for a cuppa on the way to a function so we can't stop.'

'Ah, well, that's a shame. I'll see you both out then.'

Theo stood up and gave his mum a big hug.

'Look after yourself, sweetheart,' he whispered. 'Ring me if you need anything, OK? I'll come for a longer visit next week and we'll go out for dinner.'

'Yes, yes. Don't fuss at me so, Theo, it gets me all in a fluster. Now you and Alison go have a nice time at the wedding.'

'Thank you. We will.'

Graham walked Theo and Lexie to the door.

'How's she doing?' Theo asked him in a low voice.

'She phases in and out,' he said soberly. 'She seems happy enough though, even on days like today when she's not so lucid. As long as she's happy, I'm happy.'

'She's been hiding bills again.'

Graham groaned. 'Has she?'

'Don't worry, I've got them here,' Theo said, patting his pocket. 'I'll sort them out. You need any more money sending?'

'No, no, we're fine. I feel bad enough about what you send already.'

'Graham, come on. The truth.'

Graham sighed. 'Well, we have been struggling since I got laid off. Who wants to employ a fifty-eight-year-old brickie with a bad back, right? I'm not at pension age but it feels like I'm on the scrapheap, all the same.'

'I'll increase the direct debit, soon as I get home.'

'You've no cause to do that, Theo.'

'Yes I have. I don't want you two struggling. Mum's my responsibility.' He wrung Graham's hand. 'Look after her for me, eh?'

The older man smiled sadly. 'You can count on me for that, at least. Long as I'm still here.'

As soon as they were back in the car, the tears Theo had been struggling to hold back started to fall. Lexie pulled him to her for a hug. He sobbed against her, his whole body shaking.

'What are you feeling?' she whispered. 'Tell me.'

He laughed through his tears. 'It's ridiculous, isn't it? Someone who's a complete stranger to me dies: a person I can't even remember, that I've got every reason to despise. Someone I promised myself a long time ago I'd never shed a tear for. And yet...' He choked on a sob. '...here we are.'

'He was your father, Theo. No matter what he did, it's natural you'd feel something. Grief, anger, sadness, guilt – it's all right, all of it.'

'It's not all right!' he exploded, slamming his fist into the side of the driver's seat. 'He doesn't deserve it. That bastard doesn't deserve to have me feel a single fucking *thing* for him. And I hate myself because...' He laughed wetly. 'Because I still do,' he whispered.

'It's not about what he deserves,' Lexie said quietly. 'This is about you. What you need to feel to be able to deal with this.'

'I don't think I'm even crying for him, really. Not the reality of him. More for what might've been – or what ought to have been. The father–son relationship I couldn't quite talk myself out of wanting.'

Lexie held him until his sobs subsided.

'Has your mum always been that way?' she asked.

Theo took out a tissue to wipe his eyes. 'She has her ups and downs. That's my dad's fault as well. She couldn't quite cope with life after he broke her heart; her mental health's been fragile ever since. He went back to his wife and left her holding the baby – put it all behind him, as if me and her had never happened. But Mum couldn't brush it aside that easily, not when she had me as a reminder. She'd built this castle in the air for them… she just craved love. She still does – every time I visit she's fostering another rescue dog. Jack Chamberlain was old enough to be her father and he took advantage of the way she was.'

'That's your dad? I never heard his name before.'

'I try not to say it. It tends to stick in my throat.' He sighed. 'My mum's like a kid, Lex. I love her to pieces, but she gives me so many sleepless nights. She's just… in her own world, more and more. It gets harder to break through every time I see her.'

'Oh, sweetheart,' Lexie whispered, stroking his cheek. 'I had no idea.'

He wrapped his arms around her and rested his head against hers.

'I'm so glad you were here today. I don't think I could've done this on my own.'

'Why did you want me here? You seemed keen to show me this part of your life.'

'I suppose… I wanted you to understand what it was like when I was growing up, trying to look after Mum and hide the way she was from other people because I was terrified someone would come to take me away from her. Why I am the way I am.'

'Why did you want me to understand that?'

'Because I'm ashamed of the sort of man I turned out to be, I guess. For some reason it felt important to have you know where I come from.'

'Well I'm not ashamed of the man you turned out to be. I'm proud of him.'

'Why? I'm really a pretty poor excuse for a human being. I can introduce you to any number of women who'll back me up on that.'

'Not this woman,' she said firmly. 'I think you're kind, and caring, and principled; even sort of noble at times. You're a wonderful godfather to Connor, you look after your mum, and you're the best friend I've ever had. What you are, you are despite where you came from, not because of it. And I absolutely refuse to hear a word said against you.'

He smiled and kissed her forehead. 'Lexie Whittle, you're the best person I know. Promise me you won't ever be out of my life.'

'Cross my heart.' She gave him a squeeze. 'Come on, let's go home. You're obviously not in the mood for a party, and I never was. We'll snuggle up on the sofa with the boy and watch a film instead.'

'No.' He leaned back to look into her face. 'I really think you need to do this, Lex. It obviously still haunts you, how these bullies made you feel. You ought to try and exorcise that.'

She grimaced. 'I'm really not a fan of this sort of therapy, Teddy.'

'It'll be better than you think, I promise.'

'Honestly, we don't have to go, not when you're upset. I can do my exorcism another time.'

'I'm fine. I want to do this with you, Lexie. You helped me with a few of my demons today, now it's my turn.' He gave her a kiss and started the engine. 'Let's go.'

Chapter Nineteen

Lexie wasn't surprised to discover, when they entered the plush hotel function room, that the so-called school reunion consisted almost entirely of Allegra's set: the glossy girls and sporty boys of Kingsway Secondary, the best of whom wouldn't have given her the time of day back in school, and the worst would have actively sought her out to inflict some form of daily torment. Some of them she still kept up with on Facebook, and they cast vague smiles in her direction as she entered with Theo. Others, no longer even online acquaintances, looked right through her – so no change there since school. Some of the men smiled at her, however, casting unashamedly appraising glances over her legs.

'Remember, you belong here just as much as they do,' Theo whispered. 'I'm right here with you, Lex. Here, hold my hand.'

'What?'

'Come on, I'm your date for the evening. Just act like I'm your boyfriend.'

'Right. OK.' She took his hand and he squeezed her fingers tightly.

She scanned the room for Allegra, soon spotting her talking to a little group of hangers-on by a grand piano.

'I suppose we'd better go say hello, since she invited us,' she said to Theo, pulling a face.

'Nope. We're the cool kids, we don't say hello. Let her come to us.'

'All right, what do us cool kids do then?'

'We sit at the bar and look bored and aloof. Come on, I'll buy you a drink.'

They headed to the bar and Theo hoisted himself up on a stool, nodding to the one beside him for Lexie. When the barman approached, he ordered Lexie a wine and got a soft drink for himself.

Lexie cast a glance around the room and shuddered.

'Try not to look as though you're noticing them,' Theo muttered, himself managing to look entirely uninterested in his surroundings. 'Aloof, remember?'

'Aloof. Right.' Lexie fixed on what she hoped was an expression of casual unconcern as she sipped her wine.

'See anyone you know then?'

She scoffed. 'God, yes. Becky Lambert's over there with Allegra. She once swiped my schoolbag and threw it in the bin so I'd have to crawl in to get it, then called me Bin Girl for about six months after, claiming she could still smell me. And Cara Littlewood. She deliberately hit me in the stomach with a hockey stick during a game and pretended it was an accident.'

'Did she? What a bitch.'

'I know. We were on the same bloody team as well.'

'Did you ever tell anyone?'

'No,' Lexie said, bowing her head. 'I used to be terrified that if I said anything to a teacher...'

'...the bullying might get worse?'

'Yes, partly, but mainly that they'd tell my parents about it. They had their own stuff to worry about. Dad was out of work, and... well, things were tough. I didn't want to be another burden when they had so much stress already.' Her gaze wandered again to the little group surrounding Allegra. 'Ugh, Jemmy Liu's here as well. She once saw a tampon fall out of my pocket and made sure everyone in the year knew I was on my period. Cow.'

'Seriously, you got bullied by other girls for that?'

'Yep. For anything, really. Kids are dicks.'

'Aww, Lex.' He put his arm around her. 'I'm sorry, love. You had a rough time, didn't you?'

She shook her head angrily. 'You know what really pisses me off? The way they never, ever acknowledge it. They actually don't seem to remember. I can recall every excruciating, humiliating detail, how I sobbed myself to sleep at night and dreaded going to school in the morning, and there's Allegra Schofield smiling at me like an old friend to the point where I actually start questioning whether it really happened the way I thought it did. You know, every time it's National Bullying Awareness Week or whatever, she's posting anti-bullying memes on Facebook and shouting louder and longer than everyone else about what a crying shame it is that people can't just live and let live, and in a world where you can be anything, be kind – all that sort of twee inspirational bullshit. I really think she might have forgotten she ever made my life a living hell.'

'You think she genuinely has forgotten?'

'Who knows?' Lexie sighed. 'I mean, I know people change. They grow up, and when they have kids of their own it gets them looking at the world in a different way. I suppose if she found out darling Jake or Araminta had been making life miserable for some poor kid at school, she'd be horrified. But she still tries to belittle me whenever I see her, almost out of habit. Double-edged comments undermining my career, my marriage, my appearance. And always calling me bloody Jan, even now. I *hate* that fucking nickname.'

Lexie shrank back against the comforting pressure of Theo's arm, crossing her own arms as if to put up a barrier between herself and the rest of the room. Being here, in the company of these people again, made her feel the way she had as an awkward, insecure thirteen-year-old who was never allowed to feel comfortable in her own skin. She felt like a Jan again, now. The Lexie who had grown up into a glamorous, confident woman who worked in a casino, raised a son, kept a home, started her own business, was gone, and there was a frightened little girl sitting in her place.

Theo, seeming to sense how she was feeling, rubbed a comforting hand over her back.

'Told you,' he whispered in her ear.

'Told me what?'

'Allegra approaching, six o'clock. No, don't turn around. Pretend you haven't noticed. I told you she'd come to you.'

'Jan!' Allegra said when she reached them. She did the pretentious air-kiss thing that Lexie hated, then greeted Theo the same way – well, not quite the same way. She actually made skin-on-skin contact with him, spending just a bit longer than necessary with her face right up against his.

'I'm so glad you could both make it,' she said, simpering.

'Thanks for inviting us,' Lexie mumbled.

'It was me who wanted to come really. I couldn't resist meeting a few of my gorgeous girlfriend's old school chums,' Theo said with a winning smile. 'So Allegra, where does Jan come from? Is there an embarrassing nickname story I ought to know?'

His face was a picture of curious innocence as he waited for her answer. Lexie noticed Allegra's cheeks flush slightly.

'Oh, it's an old joke from school,' she said. 'I can't remember where it came from now.'

'I can,' Lexie said brightly. 'From *Grease* – you remember, Allegra? In the film, Jan was the girl who got teased for her weight. Of course I was quite self-conscious about being a big girl back in those days.'

'Oh. Yes. I suppose that, er… that might've been it,' Allegra said, her blush deepening as she glanced at Theo.

Theo frowned as if puzzled. 'That sounds rather an upsetting nickname for a friend.'

'Well, it was all meant in fun, I'm sure,' Allegra said vaguely. 'I'd forgotten that was where it came from. Old habits die hard, you know.'

'I'd think about retiring that one,' Theo said. 'I don't think Lexie likes it much, do you, sweetheart?'

167

'I'm not a big fan, no,' Lexie said, her smile all gone.

'Then you ought to have said so before,' Allegra said, looking petulant now. 'Excuse me. I must go mingle.'

'Score one to you,' Theo whispered when she'd gone. 'Now she feels ashamed of herself, as she bloody well ought to.'

Lexie smiled. 'That did feel good. Thanks, Teddy.'

'Oh my *God*!' a female voice said from behind them. 'Theo? Theo Blake?'

Theo winced. 'Shit. I know that voice.'

'Who is it?' Lexie asked.

Before he could answer, an attractive woman wearing a little pink dress that just barely covered her little pink backside had sashayed into view.

'Well, Theo, I hadn't expected to see you here,' she said with a smile evidently designed to captivate, resting long pink fingernails on his arm. She cast an approving glance over his dinner suit. 'Don't you just look divine all dressed up? It's Becky Collins, darling. You remember me, don't you?'

'Of course,' Theo said, returning a smile that didn't extend to his eyes. 'How could I forget?'

'You know, I still haven't forgiven you for ignoring my calls,' she said in an annoying infant voice. 'Still, it was a hell of a lot of fun while it lasted, wasn't it?'

'If you say so.'

Lexie had spun her barstool around to watch the scene, and Becky turned to her as if only just noticing she was there. 'Oh. Hello. I don't think we've met.'

'I think we have,' Lexie said coolly. 'It's Becky Lambert as was, isn't it? We were in the same class at school.'

'No! You're not... it can't be.' Becky skimmed Lexie's figure with surprise. 'Jan?'

'Her name's Lexie,' Theo observed, sipping his Diet Coke calmly.

Becky frowned, looking from her to him. 'Surely you two aren't here together?'

'We certainly are.' Theo put an arm around Lexie's shoulders. 'Lexie and I are deeply in love. Aren't we, darling?'

He was overdoing it a bit now. Lexie nudged him in the ribs, but his bright smile didn't fade.

Becky looked put out by this information, but she forced a laugh. 'Who, you? I thought you didn't do relationships.'

'So did I, but it turns out I just hadn't met the right girl,' he said with a fond glance at Lexie. 'I was as surprised as you are, believe me. Well, come on, Lex, let's wander over to the buffet table. I'm starved.'

Becky plucked Lexie's elbow as she hopped off her stool to follow him.

'You'd better watch yourself, Ja— Lexie,' she said in a low voice. 'That's not a man to fall for.'

Lexie frowned. 'Yes. Well, thanks for the unsolicited advice, Becky. I think that at my age, I'm capable of taking care of myself.'

'No need to be that way, hun. I'm trying to help you out here,' Becky said. 'He'll break your heart if you get too close. Trust me, I know whereof I speak. Number one with Theo Blake is Theo Blake, always.'

'Thanks for your concern. I'll bear it in mind.'

Lexie caught up with Theo and put her arm through his.

'I can't believe you shagged Becky bloody Lambert,' she muttered.

'Well I didn't know she put your bag in a bin, did I? If I had, I promise I'd never have touched her.'

'What happened between you two then?'

He shrugged. 'Her divorce had just come through when we met in a bar. We had a bit of fun for a few weeks, then she started getting clingy so I called time on it. She wasn't very keen on that. Kept leaving me pushy messages demanding I change my mind. I don't think it was that she was particularly attached really; more that she's one of those people who expects to do the dumping rather than be on the receiving end of it.'

Lexie nudged him, smiling. 'She just warned me you were going to break my heart, you unspeakable cad.'

'How little she knows, eh?'

'You were laying it on a bit thick with that "greatest love story of our age" bollocks, Theo.'

'She bought it, didn't she?'

'Hmm. Suppose.' She scanned the buffet, which consisted entirely of fancy-looking canapés she couldn't identify. 'What is all this stuff?'

Theo picked up a pink pastry thing and blinked at it. 'Dunno, beetroot? Or… maybe raspberry?'

'Oh, for a sausage roll and a cheese cube on a stick.'

The woman beside them looked up at Lexie with an expression of friendly interest. 'I recognise that voice. It's Lexie Whittle, isn't it?'

'Er, yes.'

Lexie remembered her: Jemmy Liu, whose friendship Allegra had courted after her dad was discovered to have made a bomb in property. She'd been one of the quieter members of Allegra's gang, ignoring Lexie but rarely tormenting her – apart from the time she'd told Allegra about the tampon she'd seen drop from Lexie's pocket and Allegra had spread it all over school. Lexie was surprised Jemmy should remember who she was, let alone her real name.

'How are you these days?' Jemmy asked. 'Allegra told me your marriage didn't work out. I was sorry to hear that.'

A comment like that from Allegra would usually have some sort of snide undertone that left Lexie struggling with the old feeling of worthlessness, but Jemmy actually sounded like she meant it.

'Yes, that's right. I married too young really, and… well, there were other factors.' She glanced at Theo. 'But you know, onwards and upwards. This is Theo, my… my boyfriend, actually.'

'Nice to meet you,' Jemmy said, shaking his hand.

Allegra, seeing the three of them talking, came over and fixed Lexie with a resentful look she barely tried to hide. It was evident she was still smarting from her earlier humiliation over the nickname.

'So what did you do after we all left school, Lexie?' Jemmy asked. 'Did you go to university?'

'Um, no.'

'I don't suppose that was really considered to be an option in your family, was it?' Allegra said, smiling her crocodile smile at Lexie. 'What was it you went to work as after A-levels, darling? Nightclub hostess?'

Ugh. Classic Allegra. Trust her to make it sound like she'd been some sort of cross between a stripper and an escort.

'Croupier,' Lexie muttered.

'Ooh, how exciting!' Jemmy said. 'I bet you've got some stories to tell about that.'

'One or two, yes. I once met Simon Cowell.'

'Oh my God, you never did!'

Lexie nudged Theo. 'See? Someone's impressed.'

'So is that what you're still doing now?' Jemmy asked.

'Oh, no,' Allegra said. 'Well, I suppose there'd be an upper age limit on a job like that. Jan— I mean, Lexie's a waitress now, aren't you, chick?'

'Actually she's an entrepreneur,' Theo said, drawing Lexie to his side. 'Lexie and I run a restaurant together in Leyholme, the Blue Parrot.'

'I know that place,' Jemmy said, looking interested. 'With the 1940s food, right? I took my grandma there for her birthday and she thought it was wonderful. Best spotted dick she'd ever tasted. You should've heard my brother snigger when she said that.'

Lexie laughed. 'I'll be sure to pass that on to our cook.'

'Rather a strange idea for a restaurant,' Allegra muttered, obviously feeling the conversation wasn't going the way she'd planned.

'Oh no, Leggy, it's like this brilliant little time portal or something,' Jemmy said, beaming at Lexie. 'Lexie, I must pick your brains, and Theo too. My brother's about to open a restaurant out in the Dales, his first dabble in the hospitality business. Dad put up the money so of course Leon's desperate to prove himself. I'd love some advice I can pass on if you have any.'

'Really?' Lexie said, blinking.

'Yes, of course. I think it's a real skill to make a success of something like that when you haven't got the city trade on your doorstep. Do you find it hard to promote the place?'

'It can be, but we're slowly building a reputation. And we're always on the lookout for new ways to get the word out. Theo and me have just helped set up a village 1940s festival, which we hope will raise our profile. The Parrot's going to be the main sponsor.'

'Oh, what a clever idea!' Jemmy looked genuinely impressed. 'That's just the sort of thing Leon ought to be thinking about. Look, what do you say I buy you both a drink and we have chat about it all? I mean, if you don't mind sharing a few insights.'

Lexie glanced at Theo in surprise. 'Well, yes, I'm sure we'd be happy to. Um, I'll find us a table, shall I?'

She and Theo had only planned to stay for a short time, but it was nearly half past eleven when they finally prepared to leave. Jemmy had proven to be very good company, as had her pleasant, funny fiancé, Mike. The four of them had a lot in common, and Lexie was surprised to discover she'd actually enjoyed the latter part of the evening. She knew she probably shouldn't gloat that Allegra looked pretty sick about her newfound popularity too, but she couldn't help having a bit of a smirk.

'Sorry, Jemmy, but we ought to get going,' she said, standing up. 'I told my stepson I'd be home before midnight. I'm assuming the lack of phone calls means he hasn't burned the house down, but I'd better get back and check.'

'Well, it's been lovely to catch up.' Jemmy stood too and put a hand on Lexie's arm. 'And I just wanted to say... I'm sorry. That time at school, when I... well, I wanted you to know I hadn't forgotten and to this day I feel badly about it. I'd hate to think of my young nieces treating someone the way I – we – treated you. I know it's a little late in the day for an apology, but I'd despise myself if I didn't offer one.'

Lexie was touched.

'Oh, well, it was a long time ago,' she said. 'I'm sure we're all different people now.'

'I hope so – better people. Let's stay in touch, eh? Come find me on Facebook. I'd love to do this again sometime.'

'Yes, I'd like that. Thanks, Jemmy.'

–

'I won't come in,' Theo said when he pulled up outside Lexie's place. 'It's been a pretty emotional day for us both. I don't think either of us are in the mood for the usual fun and games, are we?'

'No,' Lexie agreed. 'But... would you stay over? I don't really want to sleep alone tonight. Nothing energetic, just a cuddle.'

He reached out to run a hand over her hair. 'If you'd like me to.'

'Thanks for making me go tonight, Theo. There was a sort of closure to it, when Jemmy apologised like that. Restored my faith in people a bit.'

'I'm glad. I knew it would be good for you.'

'You were a top-notch fake boyfriend. Allegra looked sick as a dog that she couldn't manage to make me look small with you bigging me up all over the place.' She glanced at the light on behind the living room curtains. 'Looks like Con's still up.'

'He's fallen asleep on the sofa,' Theo said, smiling. 'Bet you a tenner.'

Theo was right. They found Connor with his head back, snoring nasally while an episode of *Red Dwarf* played on the TV.

'Wakey wakey, sunshine,' Theo said, shaking him. 'You're sleeping through "Gunmen of the Apocalypse". That's the best one.'

'Oh. Hey, Boomers,' Connor mumbled as he blinked himself awake.

Lexie laughed. 'I'm thirty-one, Connor. Do you actually know what a Boomer is?'

'Er, yeah. It's an old person. Like you guys.'

'It's an old person who was born in the baby boom after the war, when all our great-grandpas came back horny from overseas.'

'Right. So, like you guys.'

Theo shook his head soberly. 'Young people today, eh, Lex? No respect.'

Lexie nodded. 'Bring back National Service, I say.'

'Was your party good then, wrinklies?' Connor asked, yawning.

'Well, parts of it were,' Lexie said. 'Reluctant as I am to admit it, your uncle was right: it did do me good.'

'You'd better get to bed, kiddo,' Theo said, ruffling the lad's hair. 'It's pretty late.'

'Yeah, I was just going.'

Connor stood up, rubbing his eyes. Lexie put a hand on his arm.

'What's up?' he asked, glancing down at it.

'Nothing.' She patted his elbow. 'Just wanted to tell you I'm proud of you, that's all.'

'How come? I didn't do anything.'

'Because you're kind, and you always try to consider how your words and actions will make other people feel. Not everyone your age does that. Not everyone my age does that.'

'Er, all right,' Connor said, blinking. 'You're being sort of weird, Lexie.'

'Sorry, I've had a bit of a weird day. Here, love, give your old, wrinkly stepmum a hug before you go up.'

'Ugh. Fine.' Connor submitted grudgingly to the embrace before taking himself up to his room.

–

'He's a good lad, my lad, isn't he?' Lexie said when she and Theo were cuddled up in bed.

'He is,' Theo said, smiling. 'You're right to be proud of him, Lex.'

'You know, he's been ever so mature about this whole thing – I mean, me and you.' She yawned and snuggled against him. 'I never expected him to take it so well. It's actually got me thinking.'

'About what?'

'Dating. I always said I wouldn't while Con was at home, but I think I was underestimating how grown up he is now. And I had a chat with Tonya that made me think... well, as long as I keep home and love lives separate until the point something gets serious, I don't see why I shouldn't get out there. I wouldn't let it go like it did for you and that guy Matt.'

Theo frowned. 'Really, you think that's a good idea?'

'Yeah, my mind keeps coming back to it lately. This, me and you, it's just been so... nice. Not only the sex, but having someone sleeping next to me who cares about me, you know? I know it's only a friend sort of caring and not a romantic sort of caring, but it did make me realise how much I miss being with someone. Properly, I mean.'

She rolled over to face him when he didn't answer. 'That's OK, right? There'd be no need to stop what we've got going on. Obviously if I got serious with someone then we'd have to, but it could be a long time before that happens.'

'Yeah.' He summoned a smile. 'Of course it's OK. It's what we agreed, isn't it? I'd like to see you happy with someone.'

She looked up at him. 'We will still be the same mates after this is over, won't we?'

'Course we will.' He kissed her forehead. 'Always.'

She ran one finger over the bridge of his nose.

'You had a lot to deal with today,' she said softly. 'Are you OK, Theo?'

'I'm all right.'

'Shuffle down so I can stroke your hair.'

He smiled. 'OK.'

'You know I'll always be here for you if you want to talk about anything… your dad or whatever,' she whispered, combing her fingers through his hair. 'Or if you ever need me to do anything for your mum, I can pop over when I'm not working. Whatever you need, just ask.'

'Thanks, Lex. I appreciate that.'

He watched her as she drifted to sleep in his arms, her hand still entwined in his hair, and wondered why a sick feeling had settled in the pit of his stomach.

Chapter Twenty

Connor was in the living room channel-hopping when Theo strolled in the following Friday. It had become a routine that he would come over on Fridays for tea and TV night. Connor didn't remove his gaze from the TV, but he deigned to raise a hand to acknowledge his godfather's presence.

'All right, youngling?' Theo chucked himself down next to the boy. 'Where's your mum? Your stepmum, I mean.'

'In the bath. She says to tell you to help yourself to a beer. She got in some of that rancid stinky lager you like.'

'It's not rancid, it's the drink of the gods,' Theo said, leaning back against the cushions. 'She's really the best of women. What're you watching then?'

Connor shrugged, changing the channel again. 'Nothing really. Just in discovery mode. I've watched everything on Netflix.'

'Making good use of your summer holidays, eh?'

Connor grunted.

'Oh!' Theo put a hand on his arm. 'Stop there.'

'Nah, that's nothing good. It's just the channel where they show all the old black-and-white films.'

'I know, it's *The General*. Classic silent-era comedy. It's my favourite of all Buster Keaton's.'

Connor shook his head. 'God, Theo. I knew you were old, but I never knew you were that old.'

Theo laughed. 'Well I didn't actually catch it the first time round, hard as that might be to believe.'

'Right. Because you were off fighting in the trenches or whatever.'

'Cheeky young whippersnapper.' He nodded to the TV. 'Seriously, it's funny. Watch this bit.'

'How can it be funny? No one's even talking. I bet it's all slipping on banana skins and pianos dropping on people.'

'No, that sort of slapstick isn't Keaton's bag. Actually, one of his most famous scenes involves something not falling on him. He basically invented deadpan. Look at his face, you'll see what I mean.'

They watched for a bit, and despite Connor obviously willing them not to, his lips soon started to twitch.

'See?' Theo said. 'Keaton was ahead of his time. He did all his own stunts too, so as well as being a comic genius he was also a total badass.'

'Yeah, all right, I can see why it's funny. It's not *Red Dwarf* funny though, is it?'

'There's always been more than one kind of funny, my young Padawan. Everything has its place in the great pantheon of comedy. Well, except possibly *Mrs Brown's Boys*.' Theo shuffled round to look at him. 'You really ought to diversify your interests, Con. There's more to life than space and dragons.'

'Why should I? I like space and dragons.'

'It gives you something to talk about on dates, for one thing. And because you're missing out. There's all sorts of awesome stuff in the world that belongs to neither the sci-fi nor fantasy genres, believe me.'

'I like other stuff as well.'

'Such as what?'

Connor shrugged. 'I like musicals.'

Theo raised his eyebrows. 'Do you?'

'Yeah. Lexie's always been dead into them. I thought they were cheesy as fu— as anything when I was a kid, but after a while I got sort of hooked. Me and her are going to see *Hamilton* when we can get tickets. I mean, don't tell my mates, obviously.'

'I did not know that about you.' He clapped the lad on the shoulder. 'You're full of surprises, young Connor.'

Connor looked at him. 'You could come as well if you want.'

Theo smiled. 'I think CalderCon is probably more my scene. No, it's sweet that you and Lex have got your own special thing. Go have a nice family day out.'

'You're family too though, aren't you?'

He hesitated. 'Yes, I suppose I am. Sort of.'

Connor flicked off the TV. 'Lexie says I've got to be nice to you because your dad just died.'

Theo closed his eyes for a moment. 'She told you that, did she? Yeah, he did.'

'I thought you didn't have a dad.'

'Not one I knew, no, but biologically speaking I obviously did. I knew he was getting old and I could expect to get the news sometime. I hadn't thought I'd feel anything, but... actually it hit me a lot harder than I expected.'

'Did you wish you'd known him then?'

'I wished... he'd been better,' Theo said quietly. 'I guess I wished... not that I knew him, but that he'd want to know me. Then suddenly he was dead, and the last thin sliver of hope that I didn't even know I was still clinging to was snatched away.' He glanced at Connor's curious, half-puzzled expression and summoned a smile. 'I suppose what I mean is, it made me sad for the way I wish things could have been between us. If he'd been the dad he should've been.'

'Yeah, I get that,' Connor said, nodding slowly. 'It makes me sad too sometimes, thinking Dad doesn't give a shit about me.'

'That's not true, Con,' Theo said gently. 'I know it might not seem like it, but your dad isn't like mine. He does care about you in his own way.'

'If his own way is not giving a shit,' Connor muttered. 'He hardly ever calls me, and when he does it's just for a lecture about working hard at school or whatever, never how I feel about things. He doesn't know anything about me; what I like or who my mates are, or that I'm bi – he can't even remember what year I'm in at school. When he was here he never wanted me around. I bet he couldn't wait to get out of the country and forget about me.'

'Hang on a sec.' Theo fished out his mobile. He scrolled through until he found an old photo and showed it to Connor. 'Look. There's your mum and dad, see, with your Grandma and Grandad Carson over from Spain, and your nana and me. And do you recognise this ugly kid in the middle?'

Connor smiled at the dark-haired baby wrapped in a white shawl, snuggling deep into its mother's arms. 'It's me.'

'That's right. This is from your christening, when as your godfather I was officially entrusted with your spiritual and psychological wellbeing for evermore. Pretty heavy responsibility for a lad of twenty-one, but I've done my best to do right by you.' He pointed to Daryl, standing at his young wife's side with a look of love on his face as he gazed down at their child. 'See your dad there? How proud he looks?'

'I guess,' Connor muttered.

'He was so happy that day. Said it was the best day of his life.'

'Then if he was so happy to have me, why did he never want me around?'

'Well, only your dad can really answer that, and God knows he won't want me speaking for him. All I can say is, he changed a lot after your mum was killed.' Theo sighed. 'This'll be hard for you to hear, Con, but I think it caused him pain to see you after that. You look a lot like her, you know.'

Connor frowned. 'You think he pushed me away because I looked like Mum?'

'That might have something to do with it. But like I said, that's really a conversation you ought to have with your dad.' He looked at the christening photo and smiled sadly. 'It hardened him, losing Elise. She really was the love of your dad's life, and he was never quite the same man afterwards. I lost my best friend the day he lost his wife, although I didn't find it out until much later.'

Connor stared thoughtfully at the photo.

'Sorry, son, did I upset you?' Theo said, resting a hand on his shoulder.

'No.' Connor managed a smile. 'I'm glad you told me. I like it when people tell me things instead of treating me like some little kid who has to be protected from everything bad.'

'Well, let's talk about something happier, eh? Got your CalderCon costume ready? Only a few weeks until the big one-five.'

'Yeah, armour's all repainted. What about you?'

'Er, yeah,' Theo lied. 'All ready to go.'

'What are you going as?'

'It, um… it's a surprise. So, any progress with Sophie?'

Connor shook his head morosely. 'I tried everything to get her to talk to me before we broke up for the holidays, but she wouldn't. I mean, I'm actually sort of relieved she's not my girlfriend any more now I've had time to think about it, but it blows not having her as a mate.'

'Why are you relieved?'

'Ugh, it was just so much *stress*. Like, everything was moving too fast, you know? She was talking about being in love, and she always wanted to be taking things further with… with stuff, and I just wanted to enjoy doing normal kid things a bit longer. I wish she could be like Oli. He likes me too but he doesn't mind just being mates until I've worked out what I'm feeling. Girls give me a headache.'

Theo smiled. 'Tell me about it.'

Connor turned to him. 'Theo, can I ask you something?'

'If you want.'

'Is Lexie your girlfriend or what? I mean, you've started going on dates and stuff now, and you took her to meet your mum, so I thought maybe she was.'

Theo hesitated, wondering how to answer. He had a nagging feeling that his FWB arrangement with Lexie was setting the kid a bad example somehow, although he wasn't quite sure why, since it felt perfectly healthy – certainly a lot more than his sex life before, and Con had been well aware of his record as a serial dater. Still, he had a vague idea it was his godfatherly duty to encourage the boy to wait until he was in a loving, monogamous relationship to have sex. On the other hand, he could sense Connor was willing his stepmum and his godfather to couple up and he didn't want to create any false hopes in that department either.

'Er, not exactly,' he said. 'Those weren't really couple dates, more... friend dates. We're just mates, same as before.'

'That's what Lexie said, but I don't get what the difference is between what you guys do and dating.'

'There are lots of different kinds of relationships that exist between adults. You'll learn that when you're older,' Theo said. 'I told you, Con, we're not going to get married or anything.'

Connor shrugged and took out his phone, obviously suffering withdrawal symptoms at not having touched it for a good ten minutes. 'Don't care if you do or not. Lexie just really likes you, that's all, and I don't want her to get hurt. Have to look out for her, don't I? I'm the man of the house.'

'Well yeah, she likes me because we're mates.'

Connor shook his head pityingly. 'You are such a dumbass,' he muttered.

'Er, excuse me, you cheeky little bugger?'

He looked up from the phone. 'I mean she likes you like a boyfriend, Theo. Do you seriously not know that?'

Theo frowned. 'She didn't tell you that, did she?'

'No, course she didn't,' Connor said, rolling his eyes. 'She doesn't need to. I told you before: I'm a kid, I'm not thick.'

'Well thanks, Sigmund Freud Junior, for your helpful insight into my psyche. I'll feel free to ignore it entirely.'

Connor shrugged again. 'Suit yourself. Just don't hurt her, that's all.'

'I'm not going to hurt her.'

'Yeah, well you better hadn't.'

The door opened and Lexie poked her head around it, her hair wrapped in a towel. She was smiling, but there was a drawn, pale look on her face, as if she'd missed out on some sleep.

'Hiya Teddy,' she said. 'Can you come upstairs a sec? I need a word.'

'Sure.' He glanced at Connor. 'I mean, if it's OK with the self-proclaimed man of the house over here.'

Connor gave a shrug of either consent or indifference, not looking up from his phone, and Theo followed Lexie up to her bedroom.

'What's up, Lex? You look worried.'

She took a deep breath. 'I'm not sure yet. Maybe nothing. Or maybe... maybe something.'

He frowned. 'Lexie, what is it?'

'I'm late, Theo,' she hissed. 'Like, five days late.'

He took a step back. 'What?' he whispered.

'My boobs have been sore for ages now and I thought it was just PMT, but my period still hasn't started. I should've got it on Monday or Tuesday. So now I'm worried the breast tenderness might be a symptom of... you know, the other thing it can be a symptom of. I didn't say anything the first couple of days because it's never exactly something you can set your watch by, but it's been too long now for me to keep putting it out of my mind.'

'But... how?'

'What do you mean, *how*? You and your bloody swimmy little sperms, mate.'

'Yeah, but we've always been careful, haven't we?'

She sat down on the bed and hid her face in her hands.

'There was that one time,' she murmured. 'A few weeks ago, do you remember? The condom slipped off inside me when you were about to come.'

'But I put another one on before I did. It couldn't have been more than a few seconds we weren't protected.'

'I guess a few seconds can be long enough,' she whispered. 'I'd have been right in the middle of my cycle too, when it's highest risk.'

'Can you get a test?'

'If it hasn't started by Monday, I'll pick one up from the chemist. They're more accurate if you wait until you're a week late.' She removed her hands from her face and looked up at him. 'What do we do if this is really happening, Theo? We can't have a baby.'

He stood for a moment, staring dazedly at his reflection in her full-length mirror. Then he sank down beside her and drew her into his arms.

'That's your call, not mine,' he said, planting a kiss on her hair.

'And what if I decided to keep it?'

'Would you do that?'

'I... don't know. I honestly don't know. It's a big decision.' She looked up at him. 'What if I did though? I know this has always been your worst nightmare.'

'It has, but... it's your choice, Lexie. If you kept it then I'd do what I had to, for both of you. You wouldn't be in this alone.'

She flashed him a wobbly smile. 'Thanks, Theo.'

'Well, that's what friends are for, eh?'

Chapter Twenty-One

'I'll leave you to lock up, Charl,' Theo said after the Parrot's Sunday lunchers had disappeared. 'Somewhere I need to be this afternoon.'

'OK,' Charlene said, loading a tray with dirty crockery. 'Going anywhere nice?'

'Not really. Funeral.'

'Oh, I'm sorry. Someone you were close to?'

'No. Not at all.' He forced a smile. 'Cheers, love. See you later.'

He parked his car a little way from the churchyard, then wandered in and pretended to examine one of the gravestones. He could see the gaggle of mourners gathered around a gaping hole some distance away: a vicar, an older lady who he assumed must be his father's widow, and a few others. That was all. He knew his dad had no children other than him. The smallness of the funeral made him feel a twinge of pity for the old man, which pissed him off. He'd come for closure, for himself, not for his father. He didn't want to feel anything for that bastard.

He wandered among the stones, pretending not to observe but watching as first the priest, then the widow, threw a handful of earth into the grave. A tear escaped, and he dashed it angrily away.

No. He wasn't here to mourn. He refused to. He was here to witness the end of something; that was all.

So few people. No children except one pissed-off son, lurking nearby and refusing to grieve. An unremarkable end to a selfish life. Another tear burned Theo's cheek, and he turned away while he got his emotions under control.

Lexie was still waiting for her period. If the worst should happen – if he really was going to become a dad – Theo had sworn to himself he'd be a father his child could rely on. He'd always said that having a kid was the last thing he'd ever want, but if Fate decreed it was happening whether he liked it or not, he was resolved he wouldn't be a dad like his own father had been. He'd be involved with that kid every step of the way. He wouldn't let Lexie down either, now she really needed him.

He turned back to the little scene at the grave, and felt a surge of resentment – and determination. No, he wouldn't let any of them down. He'd be right there for that baby from the day it arrived on earth. He promised himself that.

The group of mourners were headed in his direction now, on their way from the graveside. Theo had planned to disappear before the end of the service, but for some reason he stood firm as they passed.

'I'm sorry for your loss, Mrs Chamberlain,' he found himself saying to the woman.

She looked surprised. 'Oh. Well, thank you. Do I take it you knew my husband?'

'A little. I was one of his ancient history students.'

Ancient history, like his dad's all too fleeting presence in his life. The irony of his father's specialism had never struck Theo before.

The woman, who he supposed was technically his step-mother, treated him to a warm smile. 'Well, it was very good of you to come and pay your respects. You ought to have joined us.'

'I didn't like to intrude on the family.'

'Nonsense,' she said, resting a hand on his arm. 'You'd have been perfectly welcome. Will you come along to the wake? We're just going to have a little buffet and share a few memories of Jack.'

Memories such as the brief period when Jack left her to shack up with the girl half her age who he'd impregnated? Possibly not. Theo wondered how you could manage to get a marriage back on track after something like that. Poor woman; she deserved better, no doubt. Her face was tear-stained with grief for her lost husband. She looked nice. Kind.

'No, I... can't stop,' Theo said. 'Do accept my condolences though.'

'Thank you. I really appreciate that.' She nodded to him before making her way to the funeral car.

When the mourners had gone, Theo went to stand at the graveside for a minute before the undertaker's men arrived to fill it in. He stared down into the abyss.

'Think you've won now, don't you, you son of a bitch?' he muttered. 'Well, fuck you, Dad. You don't win. You don't get to win.'

Then he fell to his knees and sobbed.

–

When Theo arrived back in Leyholme, he stopped at the old apothecary, which doubled as the village florist, and ordered some flowers to be delivered to Lexie. He wanted to do something to show her he'd been thinking about her. Poor lass must be worried sick. She was going to take a test tomorrow, if her period still hadn't started. Tomorrow they'd know for sure...

He glanced at the Blue Parrot, but he didn't really want to go back to his lonely flat just yet. A walk on the moors was a more appealing prospect, with the summer sun beating down and a radiant haze of purple heather clothing the hills. He took the path that led up past Humblebee Farm and out towards the old reservoir.

The thing was, while Lexie was worried sick, Theo himself kind of... wasn't. Not as much as he'd have expected to be. When he thought about the baby that might come to exist then yes, he felt an instinctive surge of fear and self-doubt, as he always had when considering the prospect of being a father. But when that settled down, he found himself starting to think about the kid itself. Would it look like Lexie? A little girl maybe, with the same sparkling blue eyes as her mother, filled with humour, fun and warmth. Or maybe it would look like him. When Theo pictured a boy he usually imagined Connor as he'd been as a little lad, only with fair hair like his own.

He could teach the kid things, introduce them to the stuff he liked and enjoy it again through new eyes. Help them with their schoolwork, counsel them about relationships, teach them to play rounders and how to ride a bike. Connor would go with them. He'd be a brilliant big brother. They could go on trips and holidays, the four of them, a little family…

Theo had woken from a dream last night where they actually had been a family. Him and Lexie, Connor and the little one. And it hadn't been the sort of dream you woke from in a cold sweat either; no, this had been the sort of dream you resented being pulled out of, and longed to get back into. The sort where your subconscious forces you to ask yourself difficult questions about what it is you really want.

Lexie would make a wonderful mum. He knew that from the way she'd raised Connor; the generous, loving nature that had spurred her to take the motherless little boy into her heart. Somehow, the horror Theo had always felt of parenthood shrivelled and died when he pictured Lexie at his side. He'd never known a woman like her. When she'd talked about dating, Theo had been shocked by the pain it had given him to think of her with someone else.

Damn fool that he was. When had he ever been jealous in his life before? He didn't do monogamy, everyone knew that. Theo had always believed sex was fundamentally a recreational activity, to be enjoyed with any number of enthusiastic partners. It had nothing to do with love; not for him.

And yet he was forced to admit that for the first time, he was jealous. When he thought of someone holding Lexie, touching her, giving her the feelings and sensations he delighted in giving her, he felt angry enough to punch something. It sickened him to think of her responding to someone else with the same warmth and passion she showed to him.

He wasn't only jealous on Lexie's behalf either. He hated the idea of this potential new boyfriend getting close to Connor. He'd grown to love that kid, almost like his own son. Yes, he'd always be Con's godfather, but things would have to change if Lexie fell for someone else. There'd be no more nights in front of the TV, just the three of them. No more cosy meals together, or teasing each other at the breakfast table. When the lad was in trouble and needed advice, perhaps it would no longer be his Uncle Theo he thought of calling first.

He felt a surge of anger towards this imaginary man, this future boyfriend, putting his hands all over Lexie and bonding with Connor. Taking Theo's place in the family group. Bastard! Who the hell did he think he was?

The door to Humblebee Farm opened as he was about to pass it, and Nell's mum Stevie emerged with her wife Deb and their six-year-old daughter Milly. Theo summoned a smile for them, putting his gloomy thoughts on hold.

'Hiya guys,' he said. 'Visiting the family?'

Stevie nodded. 'We popped up to see the new photos of the little one. Nell had her five-month scan yesterday.'

'Everything OK?'

'All present and correct, as they say,' Deb said, smiling.

'Do they know what they're having?'

'Yes, a little boy.'

'Oh, lovely.'

'I'm going to be his aunty,' Milly said, puffing herself up.

Stevie laughed. 'That's the weird bit. I can cope with being a granny, but the idea of Milly as an aunty somehow makes me feel ancient.'

'Mummy, can I show him the baby?' Milly asked.

'All right, Mill, go on.'

Stevie took a print of the scan from her bag and handed it to Milly. The little girl carried it to Theo, handling it with great reverence, as if it was something exceptionally delicate and precious.

'This is my baby nephew,' she told him with some importance.

Theo smiled. 'Yes, I can see that. He looks like you, Milly.'

Milly seemed delighted at this. She skipped back to her parents.

'He looks like me!' she announced gleefully to her mums. 'Did you hear the man say he looks like me?'

'Come on, tiny.' Deb held out her hand to Milly. 'Let's go home and show the baby to the doggies. See you later, Theo.'

Theo said goodbye and carried on with his walk.

Looking at the scan image had made him feel strange. Such a tiny, beautiful thing: perfectly formed, little fingers, little toes... would he and Lexie soon be looking at an ultrasound like that, of the baby they'd made together? The thought of it was terrifying, yet somehow his heart swelled. Their baby. His and Lexie's. Theo knew, before it even properly existed, that he'd do anything for that baby. Give up his life for it if he had to.

His phone vibrated, and he took it from his pocket.

'Lex,' he said. 'Is there news? Did you take the test?'

'No need.' Her voice was breathless with relief. 'It's OK, Theo. Aunt Flo is in the building. False alarm.'

'Oh.' He was silent for a second. 'Great. That's great news.'

'Christ, what a relief, right? I mean, can you imagine? What a nightmare that would've been for us.'

'Yeah. Nightmare.'

'Anyway, it's belt and braces for us from now on, mate. I'm going to the doctor's tomorrow to get a prescription for the Pill.'

'Good idea.'

'We don't want to take any chances, do we? That could've been a disaster.' She was silent a moment, as if sensing something was wrong. 'Are you OK, Teddy?'

'Mmm.' He roused himself. 'Just relieved, that's all.'

'God, tell me about it. Anyway, back to business as usual, eh? Obviously not right now, but I'll be up for some fun later in the week if you fancy celebrating.'

'OK.'

'Bye, love.'

'Yeah. Bye, Lex.'

When she'd gone, he sank down onto a tuffet of heather and gazed out over the moors, dotted with sheep and farmhouses, the occasional black mill chimney rising from out of the settlements in the lush green valleys.

False alarm. He ought to be relieved. Why wasn't he? The only thing he felt right now was sick.

He scowled, suddenly angry with himself. Had he really been allowing himself to fantasise about having a relationship; a family? What could he have been thinking?

It was his father's death; that had to be it. Like a fool he'd let himself get sentimental over it. His brain, obviously seeing it as some sort of therapy, had started constructing visions of the sort of family he'd always dreamed of having himself as a child.

But it was a nonsense, wasn't it? He couldn't be a father. Theo pitied any kid who had a dad like him inflicted on them.

Lexie obviously thought so too. He could still hear the palpable relief in her voice when she'd told him that she wasn't, after all, unlucky enough to be carrying his child. Lexie, whose dearest wish, he knew, was a baby of her own. Not with him though. No, never with him.

Of course she was relieved: what woman wouldn't be? What had she said about choosing Daryl over him the night they'd met – that he wasn't a good investment? Damn right he wasn't. A feckless, womanising manchild, hurtling towards his mid-thirties without a single committed relationship to his name.

A commitment-phobe with a lifelong fear of intimacy and some seriously mammoth-sized daddy issues. That had to be just about the last man any woman would want to have a kid with. Lexie was probably popping open the champagne right now.

Well, he ought to be relieved too. He still had his precious freedom, after all. Lex had said it was back to business as usual as far as their friends-with-benefits arrangement was concerned – hell, she was probably setting up her online dating profile this minute. Lining up a few good investments; the sort of solid, reliable men you'd want to bring up a kid with. She might be happy enough to get her kicks with a man like Theo, but when it came to settling down then those were the men she'd choose, every time.

He took out his phone and pulled up the number he wanted.

'Hi. Francesca?' he said. 'Yes, I'm sorry it's been so long. I've had some stuff going on. Look, if you're up for having another go, how do you fancy dinner later? I'm in the mood for some fun tonight.'

Chapter Twenty-Two

Lexie winced, resting one hand on her cramping stomach. While she'd never been happier to see her period, she felt seriously grotty with it. Why hadn't she asked Theo over? Just because sex wasn't on the cards didn't mean they couldn't spend a nice evening together, and she'd rather feel grotty snuggled against him.

She looked at the flowers that had arrived earlier and smiled. It was a huge bouquet, gorgeous summer blooms that seemed to cast a halo of colour all around them. The card that had come with them just said *Thinking of you. Teddy x*. It was a sweet thought, letting her know she was on his mind, especially when he must be going through horrors of his own. She well knew how the idea of becoming a dad terrified him, although it was only recently that she'd started to understand a little about why.

He was full of surprises, that man. Just when she thought she had the measure of him, she'd see a new side to him that she'd never suspected. When they'd started sleeping together, she thought she knew Theo Blake better than she knew anyone. She knew, for example, that he wasn't the irresponsible charmer she'd once believed him to be; he'd proven that when he'd been there for her after Daryl had left. Theo was a good man, despite what on the surface might seem like a selfish, libertarian attitude to life and love: compassionate, generous and principled.

But it wasn't until they'd made their FWB arrangement that Lexie felt she'd really got to know every part of him. Seeing how he cared for his poor mum; the complexity of his grief for the father he'd never known; the way he'd helped Lexie face her demons at the reunion and been there for her through this pregnancy scare, not to mention everything the two of them had been through with Connor this year, had deepened her understanding of her best friend until she felt she knew him almost as well as she knew herself.

Being with Theo had made her realise just how much she missed being in a healthy, loving relationship with someone caring and supportive. Yet somehow, every time Lexie went to set up a profile on Tinder, she couldn't bring herself to go through with it. Whenever she thought about it she pictured Theo's face, smiling at her, his eyes crinkling the way they did when she'd made him laugh, and she was overcome with guilty feelings. Yes, the arrangement was that they were both free to date whoever they liked, but it didn't feel right, somehow. Perhaps unlike Theo, Lexie's brain was just hardwired for monogamy.

Anyway, if dating meant having to end her friends-with-benefits relationship with Theo… well, she wasn't sure she was ready for that yet. Obviously it would have to end at some point – she knew Theo didn't want the things she wanted in life. But for now, what they had going on was meeting all her needs. When she thought about Theo, it produced a giddy euphoria that was almost like being on some sort of drug. He made her laugh, he made her happy and he made her feel good about herself. To throw that away for a bunch of necessary but almost certainly tedious dates with strangers as she tried to find the ever-elusive Mr Right…

She smiled at her flowers. No, there was no need to end anything yet. Not just yet.

'What do you say to a takeaway for tea?' she asked Connor when he slouched into the living room and threw himself down on the sofa. 'I don't think I can be arsed to cook tonight.'

'Can we have pizza?'

'If you like.'

'Cool. Is Theo coming over?'

'No, not tonight. Just me, you and a musical, I think,' she said, ruffling his hair. 'I'll drive out to that new Italian restaurant. They do takeaway, and I've heard good things about their stonebaked pizzas. Sound OK?'

'Yeah. Pepperoni please.'

'Right, I'll head out now,' she said, getting to her feet. 'You find us something to watch. I shouldn't be long.'

–

'Well, here we are again,' Francesca said as Theo pulled back a chair for her to sit down. 'I'm getting a strange feeling of déjà vu.'

'Except this time we're having Italian,' he said, handing her a menu.

'Not going to run out on me again, are you?'

'Nope. Tonight I promise I'm all yours.'

He smiled his most beguiling smile and took her hand to press it to his lips. If he was doing this, then to hell with it. He might as well pull out all the stops, flirting-wise.

'You know, Theo, you really didn't deserve to be given another chance,' Francesca said, pouting. 'I've never had a man walk out on me in the middle of a date before. You could have at least called me.'

'I've apologised for that. I told you, there was a family emergency. I've had a lot going on in my life recently.' He stroked one finger lightly over the back of her hand. 'You forgive me now though, don't you?' he said in a low, seductive voice.

'Well, that really depends on how you intend to make it up to me.'

'Tonight, my darling, I'm yours to command.'

She smiled. 'That's what I like to hear.'

He pressed her fingers to his lips again, and that was when he saw Lexie, standing at the hatch the restaurant's takeaway service operated from. She was watching him with an expression of hurt disbelief that was unmistakeable. Instantly, instinctively, he let Francesca's hand drop.

She frowned. 'Theo? Everything OK?'

'Of course.' He managed to smile. 'I'll go up to the bar and pick us out a bottle of wine, shall I?'

'The wine list's right here. Just call the waiter.'

'I like to see the colour though. You can't judge the, er... the body without seeing it. I'll just be a minute.'

He went to the bar, ordered the first bottle of wine he set eyes on to be delivered to their table then sidled up to Lexie.

'Lex,' he whispered. 'What're you doing here?'

'Picking up pizzas for me and Connor. What are you doing here?'

'I, um... I'm on a date.' Why did he feel so ashamed to admit it? The look of hurt on her face when she'd spotted them – had he imagined that? It was gone now, and she was smiling an unconcerned smile.

'Of course, so I see. Table Eight again.' She patted his arm. 'Well, enjoy yourself.'

'Right.' He turned to go back to Francesca, hesitated, then turned around again. 'It's OK, isn't it? I mean, it's what we agreed.'

'Absolutely. It's just what you do, isn't it, Theo? It's what you've always done. You go and have fun.'

'Have you... did you sign up for Tinder like you said?'

'Oh, yes, a week ago,' she said, picking unconcernedly at a bobble on her favourite comfy sweatshirt. 'I've had quite a bit of interest actually.'

'Really, already?'

She nodded. 'I've got a date myself next week. High hopes for him too, so keep your fingers crossed for me.'

'What's he like?'

'Oh, just my type. Well-dressed, handsome, loyal, dependable. Seriously great hair. Just a really, really nice guy, you know? We've spent hours messaging.'

'Right.' He glanced at Francesca, who'd spotted him talking to another woman and looked distinctly unimpressed. 'But me and you are still… me and you, aren't we?'

'I don't know, Theo. I'm not sure I can do what you do. I think it really has to be one bloke at a time for me.'

He blinked. 'You're not saying you want to end things?'

'I'm… not sure.' She looked over him to Francesca. 'Maybe. I mean, it doesn't matter to you, right? You'll get plenty of offers from the other women in your little black book, and I'm definitely ready to move on to something more serious. Sex is all well and good, but sometimes you just need something deeper, you know?'

'What, so after three months, that's it? So long and thanks for all the orgasms, just like that?'

'You knew it had to happen sometime, Theo. Now seems as good a time as any.'

He must have imagined the hurt look he thought he'd seen on her face earlier. She certainly looked entirely unconcerned now, not even making eye contact as she coolly called time on whatever it was they'd had together.

'Right,' he muttered. 'So… see you at work then, I guess.'

'Yeah. Guess so.' She took her pizzas from the hatch and nodded her thanks to the server.

'Lex, you're not pissed off with me, are you? Only I thought this was what you wanted.'

'Of course I'm not pissed off with you.' She smiled a dazzling smile. 'Why would I be? You're a free agent, and so am I. Just like we always said.'

'We're still friends?'

'Sure we are. See you, Theo.'

–

Lexie managed to drive home quite calmly. She'd actually convinced herself she was fine, that she didn't care a lick who

Theo was out with, until she opened the door to the living room, saw her flowers and burst into tears.

Connor looked up in alarm. 'Shit, Lexie, what's up?'

'Oh… nothing.' She wiped her eyes on her sleeve. 'Nothing. Ignore me, I'm just feeling a bit emotional. Girl stuff.'

'Did something happen? It did, didn't it?'

She managed a wobbly smile. 'Nothing you need to worry about. I'm being silly, that's all. Let's just have our pizzas, eh?'

'Is it Dad, did he do something?'

'No. Not him.' She sat down by him and took out a tissue to mop her eyes. 'Sorry, Con. I didn't mean to go off like that in front of you. That wasn't very mum-like, was it?'

'What happened?'

'Oh, I… your godfather's out on a date. I ran into him in the restaurant.'

Connor frowned. 'He's what?'

'It's all right, Connor. We always said we weren't exclusive. He's entitled to see whoever he likes.'

'Er, no he's not.'

'It's my fault,' Lexie said, blowing her nose. 'I told him I was thinking about dating again myself. He thinks I've set up a Tinder profile. Only when it came to it, I couldn't go through with it.'

'Because you're in love with him, right?'

She frowned. 'What?'

'Even I can see that and I'm bloody fourteen. Nana can too, we talked about it. You two are the only ones who can't.'

'It isn't like that, Con.'

'It's totally like that. I don't know why you don't just tell him. You're like kids about it, it's epically pathetic.'

'You think I'm in love with Theo?' She stared blankly at the wall. 'No.'

'Why not?'

'Because he's… Theo. He doesn't do monogamy and he doesn't fall in love. That's his MO, as they say in the cop shows.'

Connor shrugged. 'He does now. Are you going to tell him how you feel about him then, or are you staying in denial?'

Lexie squinted one eye at him. 'When did you get so smart?'

'I've always been smart. Smarter than you dumbass old people. Call him already, why don't you?'

'No, Con. I know Theo could never want the things I want. If I learnt one thing from being with your dad, it's not to cling to hope when something's obviously a lost cause. I'm sorry, but you're making a fairy-tale ending where there just can't be one.'

–

Theo's phone buzzed and he glanced at the screen.

'If you say you have to get that, I will be seriously unimpressed,' Francesca said. 'You already spent half our date chatting up another woman.'

'I wasn't chatting her up.' The phone stopped. 'There you go. Ignore it and it goes away. Problem solved.'

'Who was it?'

'Oh, just this kid I know.' The phone started buzzing again.

'For Christ's sake!' Francesca snatched it up and answered it. 'Look, whoever this is, Theo's out on a date right now. Can you call back another time?'

Apparently Connor couldn't call back another time. Francesca passed the phone to Theo across the table.

'He says it's urgent, Uncle Theo,' she said.

'What is it, Con?' he muttered. 'I'm a bit busy here.'

'Yeah, I fucking know you are,' Connor said. 'I'm not paying a quid for that f-bomb, by the way, because you had it coming. You made Lexie cry, you twat.'

He frowned. 'What?'

'She's crying all over the place. What did you do that for? You told me you weren't going to hurt her and now she's the most upset I've ever seen her. Even Dad never made her cry this much and he was a total prick.'

'I… didn't mean to,' Theo said dazedly. 'Why is she crying?'

199

'Er, because you're out with someone else and she loves you?'

'What? Don't be daft.'

'What is with you two?' Connor demanded. 'Are you allergic to stating the obvious or something? Just ask her to be your girlfriend already. She is anyway, which means you're basically cheating on her. She'll probably do that thing to you with the rusty penknife. I know what that means now, by the way, I googled it.'

'She's got a date arranged too. She told me.'

Theo could practically hear the boy's eyes rolling. 'God, you're thick. Course she hasn't got a date. She just wanted to make you jealous because *you* were on a date.'

'Seriously?' He glanced at Francesca. 'I didn't really make her cry, did I?'

'Yeah, loads. I think you should come and apologise. I'll give you an hour to get here, after that you're dead to me. No pressure, Unc.' He hung up.

'What was all that about?' Francesca asked.

'I'm not quite sure,' Theo said, feeling a bit dizzy. 'I think I just got roundly bollocked by a child. And I think I kind of had it coming.'

'Why?'

'Because...' He looked at her. 'You ever been in love, Francesca?'

She frowned. 'Well yes, of course I have. I mean, obviously I loved Jesse before I found out what kind of cheating scumbag he really was, and there were a few other serious boyfriends. Why?'

'I've never been in love before,' Theo muttered, half to himself. 'My mum used to fall in love every couple of months, regular as clockwork. It shattered her heart over and over, and her mind too. I grew up watching it break her apart, and I promised myself I'd never let it happen to me. But it's not that simple, is it? Not when someone comes along who's...' He laughed softly. 'Who's a once in a lifetime.'

200

'Where are you going with this, Theo?'

'I think… I've been completely blind.' He pushed his fingers into his hair. 'Christ, I'm an idiot. I mean, I'm such a fucking idiot! Through my own stupid stubborn ignorant fault I would've lost her, the best thing that ever… the happiest I've ever…'

Francesca looked completely bemused now. 'What did that kid just say to you?'

'Something I shouldn't have needed to hear from him.' He stood up. 'Sorry, I—'

'You have to go,' she said, sighing. 'Why does that not surprise me?'

'Sorry. I really am sorry. You deserve better than this.' He went round to her side of the table and planted a soft kiss on her cheek. 'You're a wonderful woman, Francesca. I hope you find someone who'll make you happy.'

'OK,' she said in a softer voice. 'I hope so too. Where are you going?'

'To say three little words I never thought would come out of my mouth to the best friend I ever had, in the sincere hope she won't give me a kick in the family jewels for my trouble.'

She blinked. 'All right, that sounds pretty momentous. In that case, good luck.'

Chapter Twenty-Three

Lexie was in bed, a hot water bottle on her tummy, when her mobile started vibrating.

She ignored it. It'd only be Daryl. He'd been leaving her messages for days, claiming they needed to 'talk' – fight, in other words – but with a potential pregnancy to worry about, she really hadn't had the energy for any more crap this week.

She'd run out of tears now. She must've squeezed the last one out about quarter of an hour ago, some time after she'd apologised to Connor and gone to her room to complete the unmumsy business of sobbing her heart out in private. Her eyes felt like ping-pong balls that had been rolled in damp sand.

She winced as another cramp tore through her. Or was that her heart ripping apart? Possibly not, unless her biology was seriously faulty, but as a metaphor it felt appropriate. Ridiculous that it had taken Connor, a child, to make her realise something she must've been lying to herself about for months. Sometimes it took a kid to see through all the bullshit and wilful blindness that adults were so fond of conjuring for themselves.

Not that it made any difference. If she'd fallen in love with Theo, he surely felt no such thing for her. If he did, why would he be out on a date with another woman the very day he'd discovered Lexie wasn't carrying his baby? Evidently his relief had been so great, he just couldn't get his black book out fast enough. Same old Theo.

She felt the sting of more tears. Same old Theo… the Theo she couldn't help loving, with all his flaws. Was he in bed with her now, the woman he'd been out with? She was very beautiful. Was he touching her like he touched Lexie? Kissing her, pleasuring her, making her... oh God.

Lexie felt suddenly nauseous. She threw her hot water bottle aside and dashed to the en suite, but nothing came out of her while she held her head over the toilet bowl except more tears.

When she stumbled back into the bedroom, her phone was buzzing again. She glanced at the screen, thinking that if it was bloody Daryl then she might just stick twenty quid in the swear jar and let rip.

But it wasn't Daryl. It was Theo. She hesitated a moment before answering.

'Hey,' she said quietly.

'Hi Lex.'

'Still on your date?'

'No. Date's over.'

'Oh.' Lexie paused. 'Listen, I'm sorry I was weird with you before. You had every right to be there with whoever you liked.'

'That's all right.'

She sighed. 'Look, Theo, I'm glad you called. I've been thinking and... I don't think I can do this any more. I thought I was a modern, liberated woman when it came to sex and dating, but I can't see you and other people at the same time. I can't think about you with someone else and not feel something. I'm just not wired that way.'

'No, you're right. I can't do it either. Not any more.'

'Right.' She pressed her eyes closed. 'So... I guess this is it then. No more friends with benefits. The end.'

'I guess it is.'

'Are we still friends?'

'No, I don't think we are,' he said quietly. 'At least, I hope not.'

She frowned. 'What?'

'Come downstairs, Lex.'

'Why?'

'Because I'm outside your front door.'

He hung up. She stared at the phone for a second before wandering dazedly down to open the door.

Theo was on the doorstep, still in the smart jeans and shirt he'd been wearing out on his date.

'Alexis,' he said, nodding.

'Theophilos.'

'Can I come in then?'

'If you like.'

As soon as the door had closed, he took her hand and led her up to her bedroom.

'Sit down,' he said, gesturing to the bed.

'Theo, what's going on? What did you mean when you said we weren't friends?'

'I said I hoped we weren't. Because… because I realised something tonight. Something I should have realised fucking ages ago.'

She sat down on the bed. Theo dropped to his knees and took her two hands in his, looking up at her earnestly.

'I don't want to be friends any more, Lex,' he whispered, pressing her fingers to his lips. 'What I mean is, I don't want to be just friends.'

'What?'

'I was wrong, what I said that night in the pub. Sex isn't like cricket at all.' He kept tight hold of her hands, as if worried she might suddenly disappear. 'You can't just take a perfectly good friendship and start throwing in the occasional shag of an evening because there's nothing good on the telly. I mean, I guess some people can, and you'd think if anyone could it'd be me, but it turns out I can't. Because of you, Lexie Whittle. You're the reason friends with benefits can't work for me.'

'Theo, I don't understand.'

He took a deep breath. 'You know when you said you wanted to start dating again and I said it was all right? That was a lie. It isn't all right. I really, really don't want you to do that.'

'Why not?' she whispered, her stomach jumping.

'Because I'm in love you,' he said simply. 'I think you're actually the love of my bloody life, and I've been hiding from it this whole time – since before we started all this, even. I don't want you to go on dates with anyone but me, Lex. I don't want anyone to touch you but me. I don't want anyone to love you but me. I think you're perfect and I want to keep you all to myself, in bed and out of it. From this moment on, you're the only one I ever want to be with. Is that OK by you?'

She laughed, feeling light-headed. 'Oh my God.'

'Well?' he said, smiling nervously. 'Do I get an answer?'

'What made you decide this?'

'Connor. Apparently I'm far too much of a delusional wanker to see these things for myself. I need a kid to point them out to me first.'

She smiled. 'Tell me about it. Here, love, come sit by me. I want to feel your arms around me.'

He sat by her on the bed and drew her against him.

'Well?' he whispered.

'The answer's yes, Theo. I mean, of course it's yes, I love you. God knows how long for. Connor forced me to confront a few home truths tonight too.'

'Lexie, sweetheart…' Theo kissed her hair, and she snuggled against him.

'Why did you go out with that girl?' she whispered.

'Because I thought you couldn't possibly want what I'd started to realise I wanted: not with me. You sounded so relieved there wasn't going to be a baby, and I…' He sighed. 'Honestly? I'd half started hoping there would be. Dreamed a little dream to myself, of me, you, Connor and the baby. A family of my own.'

'Theo…' She drew one finger over his cheek. 'Really?'

'Really.'

'I thought a family was the last thing you wanted.'

He smiled, casting his eyes down. 'I watched them bury my dad today, Lex.'

'You went to the funeral?' she said, frowning.

'Not exactly. I just lingered a little way away and watched them throw in the earth. God, I felt so angry. It just made me think that if I had a baby on the way, I'd do fucking anything for that kid. I'd never give up on them, ever. I've let my dad scare me away from being a parent because I was terrified I might turn out to be like him, but he's actually exactly the reason why I never would. I didn't realise that until it seemed like it might really happen and I was forced to delve a bit more into the man I am.' He planted a soft kiss on her lips. 'And when I thought I'd be doing it with you, Lex, it didn't seem scary at all. Not if I could do it with my best friend.'

'Aww.' She held onto him a little tighter. 'You'd be a great dad, Theo.'

'You really think so?'

'I do. You only have to see how Connor adores you to know that.'

'Well, I was in his bad books tonight,' Theo said, smiling. 'He gave me an hour to get my arse over here and apologise or – and I quote – I was dead to him. He didn't appreciate me making you cry.'

'He told you I was crying?'

'Yep. Honestly, without him interfering I'm not sure I would've had the nerve to tell you how I felt. You seemed so relieved about the baby, I was sure you thought I was still a bad investment.'

She smiled. 'Did I really call you that?'

'You did, but I forgive you.'

'He's a lamb, that boy,' she said fondly. 'Mind you, he's got a bloody nerve, ringing you behind my back when I specifically told him to keep his beak out of my love life. I don't know whether to ground him or hug him.'

'You can decide in the morning when we tell him the good news. Personally, I'm going to buy him a few more birthday presents.' He choked on a sob, laughing through his tears. 'God, Lex, I'm sorry. I nearly fucked everything right up, didn't I? If I'd gone to bed with Francesca tonight...' He sighed. 'Well, it wouldn't have happened. Even without Con's intervention, I know I couldn't have gone through with it. After being with you, the whole date felt so shallow and pointless.'

'I've been just as deluded as you. Whoever did we think we were kidding with that "meaningless sex" bollocks, eh? No one I was ever with could make me feel the way you do, Theo.' She leaned back to look into his face, stroking a tear from the corner of his eye. 'Let's go to bed. I'd like to give my new boyfriend a nice, exclusive cuddle that's just for him.'

He smiled. 'My first proper girlfriend at the advanced age of thirty-four. That's weird, right?'

'I told you you'd settle down one day.'

She got under the covers as Theo stripped to his boxers. He climbed into bed and they snuggled into each other.

'And I told you I wouldn't if I had anything to do with it,' he said, gently stroking her hair. 'I didn't realise you had a devious scheme up your sleeve to tame my wild ways.'

'Yep. I actually planned this from day one, when I knocked you back in the casino. I knew you couldn't resist falling for the only woman who hadn't gone for your schtick since you were Con's age.'

He kissed her softly. 'I love you, Lexie Whittle. You have the honour of being the first person I've ever said that to. And, I sincerely believe, the last.'

'I love you too, Teddy,' she whispered. 'I should've told you that long before now.'

He smiled. 'You're the only one who ever calls me that. I guess that's why I like it.'

'Only because you sneakily hid your embarrassing real name from me. Teddy's for Theodore really. It doesn't go with Theophilos.'

'That's another reason I like it.' He kissed her. 'Night night, beautiful. Love you.'

Lexie sighed as she buried her face in his chest, feeling that for the first time in her life, everything was just how it was meant to be.

–

When Lexie came down to the kitchen the following morning, Connor was already there.

'Morning, my little sunbeam,' she said, ruffling his hair. 'You're up early. It's a red-letter day when you manage to roll out of bed before noon in the holidays.'

'I'm going over to Oli's. We're meeting JJ and Crucial up on the moors to fly Crucial's new drone.'

'All right. Did you have your breakfast?'

'Yeah, I had some toast.'

'That's a shame. I was going to make us pancakes for a summer holiday treat.'

He looked up from his phone. 'I could still eat pancakes.'

'Well, you're a growing lad, I suppose,' she said, laughing as she searched the cupboards for pancake mix. 'Theo's here. He's just in the shower.'

Connor smiled. 'I know. I saw you let him in last night.'

'Thanks to some young busybody who can't mind his own business, I understand.' She bent to kiss his curls and he shook her away, grimacing.

'Am I in shit then?'

'You're in shit for saying shit, which is 50p you owe the jar. I can hardly tell you off for trying to make me happy, though, can I?' She put an arm round him and gave him a squeeze. 'Thanks, Con.'

He shrugged. 'Just thought you should stop kidding yourselves, that's all. So are you and him dating properly now?'

'We are.'

'About time.'

She sat down opposite him for a moment. 'You know you can't tell your father about this, don't you? It's even more important now we're making it official.'

'I don't tell him about anything else, why should this be any different?'

'I'm serious, Connor. It's eight months until we can file for divorce and I could do without your dad finding out I'm now in a relationship with his ex-best friend. He could really make like difficult for me – for all three of us.'

Connor glanced up. 'How could he?'

'Well, there's this house, for one thing. The mortgage is in both our names, but he was paying it off on his earnings alone the whole time I wasn't working.'

'Yeah, because he made you quit your job so you could look after me. That's his fault.'

'Still, I don't doubt he could make a case out of the fact he's paid more towards it than I have. He'll be able to afford a better solicitor than I can too. If he made up his mind to take me to the cleaners financially, I might find myself with not much left. And then there's you.'

'What about me?'

'You're not my son, Con. That could be a problem.'

'I'm more your son than his. He never did sh— crap for me.' Connor frowned. 'Why, what do you think he could do?'

'I guess if he wanted, he could try to cut off my access to you. Not that I think he would,' she added quickly, registering his worried expression. 'Still, you know what he's like when he gets in a temper. I think it's a good idea if we keep my relationship with Theo quiet for as long as we can – until after the divorce is final, ideally. Your dad and me are hardly the best of friends, but we've managed to keep communication channels open and I'm optimistic we can get this all sorted amicably.'

Connor still looked worried. 'He couldn't make me go anywhere with him, could he? I mean, take me away? I don't want to live with him. I want to stay with you. You're my mum now.'

Lexie felt her eyes prickle. 'Well, I don't know whether he could but I certainly don't believe he would. Daryl's not cruel, for all his faults. I know he wants what's best for you.'

'The hell he does,' Connor muttered.

'It might not seem like it, Con, but your dad loves you. His feelings are just... complicated, that's all.'

'Because of Mum, right?'

She frowned. 'You knew that?'

'Theo said something about it.'

'Well... maybe. I'm not making any excuses for him, but it is a bit less straightforward than it probably seems from your point of view.' She stood up and went to squeeze his shoulder. 'But here's one parent who always wants you around, my love. No one's going to take you anywhere against your will, I promise.'

He smiled. 'Thanks, Lexie.'

'Now then, how about these pancakes? We can have them with strawberries and squirty cream. Strawberries make it healthy so it's basically got zero calories.'

'I'm not sure that's how it works, Lex,' Theo said as he joined them. He went to put an arm around her waist and turned her face to his for a lingering kiss.

Connor grimaced. 'Bleurgh. Not sure I can keep my pancakes down if you two are going to be sucking each other's faces off in front of me. Get a room, oldies.'

Theo shrugged. 'Well, it's your own fault, isn't it? You and your matchmaking.'

'Go sit down, Teddy, and I'll make the batter,' Lexie said, patting his bottom.

'So, am I alive to you again then?' Theo asked as he took a seat next to Connor.

'S'pose,' Connor said. 'You took your time getting here though.'

'You only gave me an hour, mate. I had to ring for a cab. What, did you think I was going to fly here on the wings of love?'

'Yeah, well. You made it in the end, I guess.' He looked up from his phone. 'Last chance, though. No more making Lexie cry. Next time I'll really sort you out.'

'I don't doubt it.' Theo held out his hand. 'There, I promise. Shake on it.'

Lexie smiled as she watched the two most important men in her life shake hands.

Chapter Twenty-Four

'Come on, Lex, stop hiding. We promise we won't laugh, don't we, Con?'

'Er, no.'

Theo nudged him. 'Yes we do. Be nice or she won't tell us where she's hidden your birthday presents.'

'Ugh. Fine, we won't laugh.'

'You really promise?' Lexie called from behind the living room door. 'Because it's pretty damn hilarious. I'd have a giggle myself if it wasn't for the epic humiliation.'

'Well, maybe one little laugh to get it out of our systems,' Theo said. 'But after that, not a peep.'

'All right, here I come.' She edged around the door and spread out her arms. 'Ta-da! Go on then, mock me. I've prepared myself.'

Theo shrugged. 'I think you look hot. I've always had a thing for girls in spandex.'

Lexie scanned his tight rubber Deadpool suit. 'Not so bad yourself, Teddy. It's a bit S&M but it suits you.'

Connor made a retching sound. 'Oh God. You two aren't going to be all old and perverted on my birthday, are you? Seriously, you cannot say this stuff in front of Oli.'

'What do you think of my costume, Connor?' Lexie asked, gesturing to her red-and-black Starfleet uniform. 'You're the cosplay expert. Will I pass muster at CalderCon?'

He nodded. 'Yeah, that looks cool. Janeway was one of the best captains.'

'Janeway?' Lexie glanced down at the spandex jumpsuit. 'I thought I was Uhura. Am I not Uhura?'

Connor rolled his eyes. 'Oh my *God*. Right, just, when we get there, don't talk, all right? And whatever you do, don't tell *anyone* we're together.'

'I think since it's your birthday, we can manage to pretend to be total strangers,' Theo said. He slapped the coffee table. 'Now. Presents.'

'Wait,' Lexie said. 'Family selfie first. Con, put your helmet on, and Teddy, put your... motorcycle gimp mask thing on.'

The two of them suited up and Lexie snapped a photo.

'Aww,' she said as she looked at it. 'Don't we look adorable? You reckon we can put it on Facebook, Theo?'

'Yeah, why not?' Theo said, shrugging. 'Doesn't give anything away, does it? I don't see what's suspicious about Connor going to CalderCon with his stepmum and godfather for his fifteenth birthday.'

'You're right. I'll post it now.'

'If you tag me, you'd better not mention Uhura,' Connor said as he took his Boba Fett helmet off. 'I'm glad you're coming too though, Lexie. I mean, still don't talk to me when we get there, obviously.'

She smiled. 'Well, I suppose that's sort of sweet. Since you managed to emotionally blackmail your uncle into coming to see *Hamilton* with us next month, it seemed a fair swap.'

'Can I have presents now?'

'All right, since you're being nice to me.' She produced a pile of gift-wrapped parcels from under the sofa and put them on the coffee table. 'Here you go.' She passed one to him. 'Open this one.'

'Why're you grinning like that?'

'You'll see.'

He opened it and held up the cloth cap sitting on top of a matching beige shirt, tie and trousers.

'It's a GI uniform,' Lexie said. 'For the festival. Cool, right?'

'Oh God,' he groaned. 'I can't believe you're making me go to this stupid 1940s thing.'

'Oh, come on. I thought you loved dressing up.'

'Yeah, as cool stuff.'

'Well, what's cooler than someone who fought the Nazis to free the world from oppression? Not all heroes wear capes, Con. Besides, you'll look ever so handsome.'

'Fine, whatever. But I'm only doing it to make you happy.'

Lexie smiled. She could see her stepson was trying his best to seem unimpressed, but his eyes glinted whenever they fell on the new uniform.

'Here,' she said, passing him another parcel. 'The ones in the blue paper are from your dad.'

Connor opened it and frowned at the Marvel T-shirt inside.

'This is from Dad?'

'That's right. Don't you like it?'

'Yeah. How does Dad know I'm into Marvel though? How does he even know my size?'

'Well, I told him,' Lexie said, glancing at Theo. She didn't want to admit that Daryl hadn't chosen the presents for himself. It'd only hurt the boy, and that really wasn't fair on his birthday. 'Go on, open another one.'

'Open this one,' Theo said, sliding an oblong-shaped parcel towards him. 'That's from me.'

'Oh, awesome! Starbug!' Connor said when he opened it. He gazed at it adoringly. 'And it's in the box.'

'See?' Theo whispered to Lexie. He handed Connor another present. 'Here, I got you these as well.'

'Discworld. Terry Pratchett,' Theo said as Connor unwrapped it. 'Boxset of the first ten books. Do you know the series?'

'No. I don't read books much, unless they're graphic novels.'

'Well, you need to read these. Honestly, if you like *Red Dwarf* you're going to love them. You can thank me later.'

Connor looked up. 'Thanks, Theo. You didn't need to get me so much stuff.'

'Originally I just got you Starbug, but I felt like I owed you extra in exchange for that girlfriend you sorted out for me.' He patted the boy's shoulder. 'Anyway, you're welcome, son. I'm glad you like them.'

–

Calderdale ComicCon took place in Halifax every August. It was a relatively modest affair compared to the big events in the cities, but it was always a lot of fun. Connor and his friends had gone to every one since they started secondary school – him, Oli and Sophie, usually, and sometimes the other two if Lexie was very unlucky. For some reason, she was always the parent who ended up volunteering to go keep an eye on them.

This was the first year, though, that she was actually quite looking forward to it. With Theo along, it felt less like a chore and more like a family day out, her and her boys. Every time she looked at Connor and Theo, chatting about costumes and characters, it made her smile.

They picked Oli up on the way, dressed in a white vest and jeans as Wolverine. The outfit, fake sideburns and gelled hair made him look older, and rather handsome. Lexie noticed Connor sneaking a look at his friend when he joined them in the car. Obviously there was still an attraction there, even if officially the pair were just friends.

'Um, happy birthday,' Oli said, looking bashful as he handed over a present.

'Thanks, Ol.' Connor unwrapped it to find a little Lego Boba Fett on a keychain. He smiled. 'That's cool.'

'It's you, Con, see?' Oli said, flicking it so it swung from side to side. 'I mean, if you were Lego. And really, really small.'

'I love it.' Connor punched him on the arm. 'Cheers, bro.'

When they arrived at the venue, the place was already bustling with everything from stormtroopers to Pennywise-esque evil clowns. There were plenty of kids in fancy dress, and plenty of adults too – Lexie certainly felt a lot less self-conscious in this crowd than she had walking to the car. The Stay Puft Marshmallow Man wandered about, posing for selfies, while Shaggy from *Scooby Doo* walked arm-in-arm with the Joker like old friends. It did make her smile. This was Connor's scene, not hers, but she had to admit it looked like fun.

'Well, lads, where do you think you'll go first?' she asked Connor and Oli, who were gazing around them in awestruck delight. 'I thought you could do your own thing for a couple of hours, then we'll all meet back here at twelve for lunch.'

'There's a retro gaming area over there,' Theo said, nodding to it. 'I wouldn't mind a go at that. Might bring back a few childhood memories.'

'Did they actually have video games during the war though?' Connor asked.

'Ahahahahaha, funny child. You know, Con, that just gets more hilarious every time.'

Connor grinned. 'That's why it's never, ever going to stop.'

'I want to get a selfie on the *Game of Thrones* throne,' Oli said. 'What do you think, Con? There first?'

'I reckon autographs first.' Connor lowered his voice. 'I heard they've got Neil Carter as a surprise mystery guest.'

Oli's eyes widened. 'No way!'

'Should I know who that is?' Lexie whispered to Theo.

'Well I don't know who it is so I'm thinking no.'

Connor rolled his eyes at Oli, who nodded sympathetically. The uncoolness of parents had obviously been discussed at length many times before today.

'He's a stormtrooper,' Connor said. 'Can't believe you don't know that, Theo.'

Theo shook his head. 'I'm disgusted with myself.'

Lexie watched as a gang of about eight white-armoured stormtroopers clutching bags of pick 'n' mix passed by. 'Possibly I'm being a bit thick here, Con, but there seem to be loads of them.'

'No, I mean he's an *actual* stormtrooper, from the films. He was one of the ones who froze Han Solo in carbonite. I hope he's in his original costume for a selfie.'

'I bet there's a massive queue for him,' Oli said. 'We ought to head there now if we…'

He trailed off as he realised that Connor was staring over him to someone in the crowd.

'Sophie,' Connor muttered. 'Did you know she was coming?'

'Yeah,' Oli said, looking guilty. 'Sorry, Con. Guess I should've told you.'

Sophie had come as Princess Leia, the sexy gold bikini edition. Connor frowned at the figure with its arm around her waist, its identity hidden by a monk-like Jedi robe.

'Do you know who she's with?'

Oli grimaced. 'Look, don't freak out. It's… it's actually JJ.'

'*What?* Those two aren't here on a date, are they?'

'Yeah. Sorry, mate.'

Theo put an arm around Connor's shoulders. 'You OK, kid?'

'I'm… fine.' Connor stared at the pair for a moment before putting his Boba Fett helmet back on. 'Come on, Ol. Let's go queue.'

–

'Poor love,' Lexie said when they'd gone. 'I hope that's not going to ruin his birthday.'

'She must've known he'd be here,' Theo said. 'Is she trying to make Con jealous by showing up with another lad, do you think?'

'I can't see any other reason she'd choose to spend a day alone with JJ. That kid's an arse.' She took his arm and they started wandering around the various stalls and attractions. 'Did you notice Connor checking Oli out in the car?'

'Yeah, I think he's keen on the Wolverine look. Which are you then, Team Sophie or Team Oli?'

'Team Connor, obviously. Whatever makes him happy.' She glanced back at Sophie. 'Although I'm feeling a bit Team Oli right now. Turning up here with a date on his birthday is pretty mean.'

'Well, they're only kids.'

'Yeah, suppose I shouldn't be too hard on her. That was pretty sweet with Oli and the keyring before though.'

'Personally, I'm very much Team Nobody Until He Turns Sixteen,' Theo said. 'I've never been under so much stress as when that boy was dating. Honestly, every five minutes he seemed to be having some crisis.'

'Sophie being here reminds me actually,' Lexie said. 'Janette Cavendish emailed this morning about the flypast. She's finally had confirmation.'

'They're leaving it late. There's less than a week until the festival.'

'Yeah, I think they have to wait until they know about the weather.'

'So we're all set then, aren't we? That was the last thing we were waiting on.'

'Now all we have to worry about is whether anyone's actually going to show up on the day.' They stopped to examine a stand selling Baby Yoda bobbleheads and other assorted merch. 'How's your mum doing, love?'

'Not too bad. Did I tell you Graham got another job?'

'No.'

Theo nodded. 'Manager on his mate's building site. Have to say, that's a huge weight off my mind. I know he hates having to accept money from me.'

She squeezed his arm. 'That's great news, Teddy.'

'Yeah, I was so relieved when he rang to tell me. So was he, from the sound of it.' He nudged her. 'Come on then, Janeway. Where shall we go to amuse ourselves while the kiddies are off playing? There's a funfair out the back.'

'Hey. I'm Uhura.'

He shook his head. 'Do you not even know who Janeway is? She's actually a really cool person to be.'

'Course. She was captain of the, er... spaceship.'

'What spaceship?'

'The SS... *Spaceship*.'

'Lexie Whittle, somewhere in this room your stepson just disowned you,' Theo said. 'She was captain of the USS *Voyager*.'

'Right. And Uhura was...?'

'Comms officer on the *Enterprise*.'

'But they are all *Star Wars*, right?'

'That had better be a joke.'

She laughed. 'Yeah, all right, that one was deliberately to wind you up. I know it's *Stargate*.'

'Seriously, Lex, you really ought to keep your voice down. We're going to get chased out of here by a pitchfork-wielding mob if you keep saying stuff like that.'

She sighed. 'I must be such a disappointment to you.'

'Was just thinking that myself.' He ran one hand down the back of her uniform, letting it settle on her buttocks. 'Lucky for you you've got such a great arse. In that jumpsuit there's not much I can't forgive you for.'

'Except muddling *Wars* and *Trek*.'

'Right. You have to draw the line somewhere.'

Chapter Twenty-Five

'You OK, mate?' Oli asked, nudging Connor as they queued for Neil Carter's autograph.

'Hmm?' Connor stopped scanning the crowd for Sophie and JJ and forced himself to pay attention. 'Oh. Yeah, fine.'

Oli reached up to smooth his gelled Wolverine hair, and Connor's gaze drifted to his friend's bare arms. He'd never paid much attention to Oli's arms before. They were good arms: skinny but a bit muscly too, with a dusting of dark, curling hair. Connor found himself wondering what it would feel like to run his fingers over them.

'Look, don't worry about Soph,' Oli said. 'She's just trying to get her own back because she thinks...' He flushed. 'Well, I reckon she thinks me and you are here on a date. She heard me talking about us planning to go together and I think she got the wrong idea.'

'You mean she thinks we're here together? Like, *together* together?'

'I guess. That wouldn't be so bad, would it?'

'Well no, but we're not, are we?'

'We could be. If you wanted to be.'

'Ugh.' Connor scowled into the distance. 'All I want is my mates back. I want to have my birthday with all my mates and do cool stuff and talk about *Star Wars*. Why is everyone always trying to get me to do other stuff?'

Oli's face fell. 'All right.'

'Sorry,' Connor said in a softer voice. 'Did that sound mean? I just meant, I like us being mates. I don't really want to date anyone at the moment, Ol, not you or Soph or anyone else. Maybe next term I might feel ready, but right now I just want to keep everything in my life simple, you know? I feel like... like I'm only just learning who I am. I can't do that if I have to be learning who someone else is too.'

Oli blinked. 'Whoa. Deep, Con.'

'Right?' He glanced over the crowd again, but Sophie seemed to have disappeared. 'I wish we could get her back in the gang. This is so stupid. She should be over here queueing with us.'

'Yeah.' Oli looked thoughtful. 'Listen, bro, can you mind my place? I need to go for a piss.'

'Yeah, all right.'

Ten minutes later, Oli still wasn't back. Connor was starting to worry that his friend was going to miss getting Neil Carter's autograph. Had he got lost in the crowd?

'Hi,' a girl's voice said softly.

Connor turned around. 'Soph. Um, hi.'

JJ seemed to have disappeared, but Oli was standing beside her, smiling awkwardly.

'Brought someone to see you,' he said.

'Right.'

'Con, can we talk?' Sophie asked.

'Um...'

She glanced at the line. 'Oh. Right. Neil Carter.'

'No... no, it's fine. I can queue again.'

'I'll take your place,' Oli said. 'Meet you by Jabba's Palace after.'

Sophie took Connor's hand and led him to one of the sets that had been created for photo opportunities. She took a seat on the Wampa Beast of Hoth's hairy dismembered arm and Connor sat down in the fake snow beside her.

'I thought you were here with Oli,' she said.

'I know. I'm not though. I mean, I am. But I'm not.' He glanced at her Leia costume. 'You look, um... pretty.'

'You too. I mean, boy pretty. You've always been my favourite Boba Fett.'

He smiled. 'Cheers, Soph.'

'So Ol just marched up to me and told me I was being a douche and ruining your birthday.'

'Did he?'

'Yeah.' She sighed. 'He's right, isn't he? I've been a total bitch. I was just hurt and jealous. You know, Con, you could've told me you were gay in the first place. If you wanted me to pretend to be your girlfriend till you were ready to come out, I would've done it anyway.'

'I'm not gay though.'

She blinked. 'Aren't you?'

'No, I'm bi.' He shook his head. 'Why do people always seem to forget that's a thing?'

'So you…'

'Soph, what we did… when we were dating, you know that was real, right? I never pretended anything. I really liked you.'

'Really?'

'Yeah. I didn't even know I was bi then. That's what made it all confusing, because Oli and me kissed, and suddenly I knew – I mean, maybe I knew before and I just hadn't been thinking about it, but I dunno, it seemed pretty surprising when I worked it out. Big thing to get my head round, you know?'

'So you and Oli aren't seeing each other?'

'No. We kissed twice at your house, once in Spin the Bottle and once after, but we're not boyfriends. I mean, I like Ol, but…' He sighed. 'I kind of don't want to be dating anyone at the moment, Soph. I need some time to find out who I am. I'm only fifteen and this… this is major stuff, you know?' He took her hand. 'But I would like my friend back. I've missed you.'

She smiled. 'Aww, Con.'

'So, um… would you be back in the gang? Me and Ol need you. JJ and Crucial have been driving us insane.'

She laughed. 'Tell me about it. JJ's talked about nothing but my boobs all morning.' She glanced down at her costume. 'This bikini was not a good idea.'

Connor shook his head, smiling. 'I can't believe you went out with him.'

'I know, what was I thinking?'

'Soph, how come you never told anyone about me and Ol? I thought you'd tell everyone.'

She squeezed his hand. 'I might've been a bitch, Con, but I'm not that much of a bitch. It's up to you who you decide to tell something like that to.'

He smiled. 'You're kind of cool, you know?'

'Cooler than you,' she said, smiling back. 'I got here early so I could get Neil Carter's autograph before the queues.' She tapped her head. 'Smart, see?'

'Hug then?'

'OK.' She put her arms around him. 'Sorry for being such a dick.'

'No, it's my fault, I should've talked to you. I feel bad you got hurt because of me.'

She gave him a tight squeeze. 'Well, I'm glad we're friends again. I missed you too, Con.'

–

'...no, *Mr* Spock was the science officer on the *Enterprise*. *Dr* Spock was an eminent child psychologist.'

'Right,' Lexie said. 'So who was Dr Cornelius? Wasn't he in *Star Trek*?'

'That was McCoy. Cornelius was the head science chimp in *Planet of the Apes*...' Theo shook his head. 'All right, now you're just taking the piss, aren't you?'

She grinned. 'Maybe.'

'Well, you're lucky I love you, that's all.'

She squeezed his fingers. 'I don't think I'll ever get tired of hearing that.'

'Good, because I wasn't planning to stop saying it anytime soon.' He nodded to a group of four approaching them. 'Hello. What's this?'

Lexie squinted at them. 'So a Jedi, the Wolverine, Princess Leia and Boba Fett walk into a bar...'

'You think Sophie and Connor made up?'

'Looks like.' Lexie pulled a face. 'Ugh, but we gained JJ.'

Theo shrugged. 'You win some, you lose some.'

The rest of the day seemed to pass quickly. Crucial appeared at some point wearing a Jon Snow *Game of Thrones* costume, and Connor spent a happy afternoon with his friends getting all the autographs and selfies his fifteen-year-old heart could desire. Lexie beat Theo at *Mario Kart* in the retro gaming area; he beat her at *Mortal Kombat*. After that they discovered a pop-up pub, the Mos Eisley Cantina, which Theo discovered did a pretty good pint for a wretched hive of scum and villainy. That proved a good place to hole up until the young people had finished doing their stuff, and it was soon time to leave.

'Can you drop me off at the Parrot, Lex?' Theo asked when she'd driven Oli home.

'Aren't you staying at ours?'

'Yeah, I'll come over in a bit. I badly need to peel myself out of this sweaty suit and jump in the shower. Tell you what, both Ryan Reynolds and the entirety of the BDSM community have jumped up in my estimation today.'

'All right. Come round when you're back in your civvies, eh? Birthday Boy's requested a family curry and film night to round off the celebrations.'

'Sounds good.' He leaned over to kiss her cheek, ignoring Boba Fett's retching noises from the back seat. 'See you soon, beautiful. Bye, kiddo.'

'So did you have a good birthday?' Lexie asked Connor as they drove back home.

He shrugged. 'It was all right.'

Lexie smiled, knowing that was as much glowing praise as you could ever extract from a teen.

'I think you can take the helmet off now, Con.'

'I will when we get home. I haven't finished being Boba Fett yet.'

She laughed. 'You and Sophie made up then?'

'Yeah. We're not dating any more, though. Just mates.'

'Well, I'm glad.' Lexie frowned as she pulled into the drive. 'Hang on.'

'What?'

'Something's wrong… you didn't close the living room curtains this morning, did you?'

'No, why would I? I never do things to the curtains.'

'Well they're closed now.'

He shrugged. 'You forgot to open them then.'

'No. No, I distinctly remember opening them to get the best light for the photo of us in our costumes.'

'Maybe Nana came round.'

'She has her yoga class on Sunday afternoons.' Her brow knit into a worried frown. 'Con, I've got a bad feeling about this.'

She jumped out of the car and hurried to unlock the front door, but there was no need. It was already open.

As she'd feared, when she walked into the living room she found someone very familiar in there. He was sitting in the armchair watching TV, for all the world as if he owned the place.

'Daryl,' she muttered. 'What the hell are you doing here?'

Chapter Twenty-Six

Daryl stood up and scanned Lexie's *Star Trek* costume. 'Lex. What on earth are you wearing?'

'Why are you in my house, Daryl?'

'Our house, you mean.' He stared as Connor appeared at her side in his Boba Fett armour and helmet. 'Who the hell's this guy? Christ, Lexie, what sort of kinky shit have you been getting into while I've been away? Where's Connor?'

Connor took his helmet off. 'Here. What the fuck are you doing back?'

'Connor?' Daryl stared up at him. 'Jesus. You're enormous.'

'Well, you've not visited in nine months,' Lexie said. 'That's a long time in the life of a growing boy. Your son's fifteen now, Daryl.'

'Fourteen, you mean.'

'No, I mean fifteen,' she said, glaring at him. 'It's his birthday. Remember that, the day your only child was born? We've been at CalderCon celebrating, hence the costumes.'

'Oh. Right. Well, champ, give your old man a big birthday hug then.' Daryl went to embrace him, but Connor took a step back.

'What're you doing here, Dad?' he asked.

'Seriously, no hug?'

'We never hug. What do you want to start now for?'

Daryl sighed and sat back down. 'I was hoping you might've missed me.'

Lexie cast a worried glance at Connor before going to perch on the sofa opposite Daryl. Connor stayed where he was, watching the two of them warily.

'So are you here for a holiday?' she asked.

'No.' Daryl smiled at her. 'I'm back, Lex. Back for good.'

'What? But you've got six months left on your contract. You didn't get sacked, did you?'

'Of course not. Taro's expanding the business. He wants to open a chain of Utsukushī restaurants here in the UK and he's asked me to head it up. This way I get to come home earlier than planned and there's no need to look for another job. It's a permanent position, plus there's a pay rise included.'

'You don't mean...'

'Oh, don't worry, I'm not moving back in here,' he said. 'I'll only be staying a week until my apartment's ready.'

'A week!'

'It is half my house. There's plenty of space, isn't there?'

'Daryl, we're separated! You can't stay here. That might count as a reconciliation, legally speaking. Go to a hotel.'

'It won't count as a reconciliation. My son's here. I guess I'm entitled to have a short visit with the son I've barely seen in eighteen months, right?'

Her frown relaxed slightly. 'Well, yes, I suppose that's fair enough. You could've let me know though.'

'I've been trying to get you on the phone for weeks, Lex. You didn't return any of my calls.'

'What if I don't want you to visit me?' Connor demanded.

Daryl turned to look at him. 'Come on, lad, don't be that way. I know you're angry with me, but I'm the only dad you've got.' He glanced from Connor to Lexie. 'Look, Connor, can you go up to your room? I want to have some grown-up talk with your stepmum.'

'That OK by you?' Connor asked Lexie, flashing a resentful look at his father. 'I'll stay if you don't want to be on your own with him.'

She smiled. 'That's sweet, Con, but it's all right. Your dad's right, me and him ought to talk things through.'

'Fine. If he upsets you though, I'm coming back down.' He subjected Daryl to a hard stare before stomping off to his room.

Daryl sighed. 'I guess he really does hate me now, doesn't he?'

'He doesn't know you, Daryl. I honestly think Tony Stark could've walked through that door and Con would feel he had a closer relationship with him.'

'Who?'

'That's Iron Man to you.' She glared at him. 'Going to accuse me of brainwashing him again then?'

He winced. 'Told you I said that, did he?'

'Mmhmm.'

'Look, I'm sorry. I was angry and… well, it was out of order. I shouldn't have said it, especially not to Connor.'

'I thought we agreed that no matter how pissed off we were with each other, we'd never drag Connor in. He's a kid, not a weapon – you remember saying that?'

'OK, I was wrong. And I do appreciate everything you've done for him, Lex. He obviously feels very protective of you.' He glanced morosely at the door. 'Not so fond of me though, eh? My own fault, I know.'

Her expression softened a little.

'So you're really coming back to England?'

'That's right.' He pulled his gaze away from the door. 'I'm going to be honest with you, Lex. This job wasn't something that was offered to me. I applied, and I had to fight bloody hard for it.'

'Why?'

'Because I wanted to come home. Home to my son.' He smiled sadly. 'I know I've been a pretty useless dad, all told. I never meant to be. When Connor was born, Elise and me, we had all these plans. The three of us forever, it was supposed to be.'

Lexie bowed her head. 'I know.'

'God, I'd never been happier than the day that kid was born. This perfect little person with his mother's eyes, all ours. But after she was gone, whenever I saw him… I mean, I thought with you and me it was going to be a new start and I could put the horror of the shooting behind me. But I couldn't, Lex. I'm sorry. I tried, but… I couldn't.'

He looked so damaged and helpless, Lexie felt her heart go out to him. This was the side of Daryl that had first made her fall for him. Not the hard, success-driven career man he used as a shell, but the wounded, vulnerable person underneath who'd lost the love of his life in that horrific way. She ought to have known better than to think she could ever take Elise's place in his heart, but all she'd wanted to do, then, was to heal.

'I'm sorry, Daryl,' she said in a softer voice. 'I know it was hard for you. I tried to help, but it wasn't enough.'

'You helped more than you know.' He leaned forward, as if to take her hands, then thought better of it and leaned back again. 'Lex, I want to do better. I want to be a father to him, if it's not too late. Do you think it is?'

'I hope not. I can sense he regrets not having a closer relationship with you.'

'You'll help me then?'

'I'll do what I can, but it has to be led by Connor. He's not a little boy any more, Daryl. He's a mature, sensitive, bright young man who can make decisions for himself. If you treat him like a child, he'll just put up barriers.'

'Yes. All right.'

'Hang on. Let me get some tea on.'

She went into the kitchen, glad of an excuse to get away from Daryl for a moment so she could WhatsApp Theo.

> DON'T come over tonight. Daryl alert. Will fill you in tomorrow at work. Love you x

229

'Here you go,' she said when she went back into the living room, presenting Daryl with a cup of tea. 'White, no sugar.'

'Thanks.' He took a sip and let out a long sigh. 'God, a proper English cuppa. Now this I missed.'

'So where's the new job based? London?'

He shook his head. 'I negotiated for Manchester, so I could be nearer to Connor. Obviously I'm not planning to take him to live with me when he's settled here, but I want to be within driving distance.'

'You were threatening to move him out to Japan last month,' Lexie observed drily.

'All right, I shouldn't have said that either. I'm sorry. I get angry, shoot my mouth off and say things I don't mean, it's my thing.'

She smiled. 'You haven't been gone so long I've forgotten that.'

'Anyway, I was hoping we could set up some sort of access arrangement, with him coming to me every third weekend or something.'

'You'll need to do some groundwork first, Daz. The way he feels about you right now, I don't think he'd go if you promised to take him on holiday to Betelgeuse Seven.'

'That's why I wanted to stay here. The flat needs furnishing but I could have bedded down there at a push. I wanted a week to lay a bit of groundwork, as you put it. Try to forge a bond.'

'And you mean it? Because we've been here before, and if you hurt him this time I doubt he'll ever forgive you. I certainly won't.'

'No, Lex, this time I mean it. I've had my Damascus moment.' He put his tea down on the coffee table. 'I wanted to say something to you too.'

'What?'

'Lexie, I know you always suspected I married you more for Connor's sake than my own. That I wanted a mum for him more than I wanted a wife for myself.'

'I never said that.'

'No, but you thought it, didn't you?'

'It had crossed my mind,' she admitted.

'I wanted to tell you that wasn't the case. I loved you very much.'

'But not the way you loved Elise,' she said, smiling sadly.

'No. But I did love you, all the same.' He sighed and picked up his tea again. 'Well, I wasn't a much better husband than I was a father, I guess.'

She shook her head. 'You're being uncharacteristically nice and cooperative. You're not ill or anything, are you?'

'No. Just... taking stock of what's important to me.'

'Why? I mean, why now?'

'Well, it's partly this therapy programme I've been on. Taro put me onto it and honestly, I feel it's changing my life.'

'What is it?'

'It's like the AA Twelve-Step Programme, only this isn't for addicts. It's for people affected by grief, especially arising from traumatic circumstances. People like me, who've let it shape their lives negatively. Part of the programme is about making amends to those you've hurt.' He met her gaze. 'But healing myself isn't why I want to do it. I want to make things right with my son.'

Lexie blinked. 'Well, that's... a lot to take in. I'm glad you're finally getting help.'

'You always told me I ought to.' He smiled. 'If I wasn't such a stubborn prick I might've listened, eh?'

She smiled back. 'No arguments here.'

'So how are you then, Lex? Still at the restaurant?'

'Where else would I be?' Lexie bristled, immediately on the defensive. She hated it when he seemed to sneer at the Parrot.

He laughed. 'No need to bite my head off. I'm glad, OK? I admit I never thought that place was going to make it, but it sounds like you've made it a real success.'

'It has its ups and downs but we're always trying new things. Theo and me were instrumental in setting up this 1940s festival next week to pull in a bit of extra custom. If it goes well, we're hoping it can become a regular thing.'

He looked impressed. 'Good plan. You think of that?'

'I had the idea, yes, but Theo fleshed it out. You know how he loves everything olden days.'

'How is Theo?'

'He still hates your guts.'

'Mmm. I thought he probably would.'

'But he does a great job of looking out for Connor and me,' Lexie said, trying to fend off any hint of a blush. 'He's been a good friend, especially in the lean times.'

'Well, there'll be no more lean times. Like I said, the new job comes with a higher salary. I'll make sure Connor's provided for and you get your fair share in the divorce. I know you sacrificed your career for him and it's only fair that's taken into account.'

Lexie blinked. 'Well, that's… thanks, Daryl. And the house?'

'We'll sell it, of course. You're right, we ought to get it on the market and sod waiting to squeeze every drop of value from it.' He finished his tea. 'So… anyone new on the scene for you?'

'Er, no,' she said, once again fighting against a blush. 'I decided I wouldn't date while Con was at home with me. He doesn't need my boyfriends coming and going from his life.'

'Right. Couldn't agree more.'

'What about you?'

'No. No one for me.'

She frowned. 'Daryl… you are just here for Connor, aren't you?'

'Of course.'

'Only, me and you, that's over. I want that divorce.'

'It hadn't even occurred to me.' He stood up. 'I'd better go make up one of the spare rooms. Then I'll see if I can convince Connor to have a chat.'

'You'd forgotten it was his birthday, hadn't you?'

He bowed his head. 'Yes. But I won't forget again.'

–

Theo frowned when he arrived at Lexie's place, freshly showered and with a packet of popcorn under his arm for their film night. Did she not realise the front door was hanging open? He knew she didn't always lock it, but she really ought to make sure it was firmly closed. Anyone could wander in.

Not missing the irony, he wandered in without knocking and headed for the living room.

'Well, here I am, guys, de-gimped and ready for curry,' he called out. 'I brought popcorn.'

He opened the door and stopped short when he saw who was in there.

'You!'

Daryl frowned. 'Theo?'

Theo tossed the bag of popcorn aside, grabbed his former business partner by the lapels and within seconds had him pinned up against the wall.

'What the fuck do you think you're doing here, you back-stabbing son of a bitch?' he thundered.

'Christ, Theo! Get the hell off me!' Daryl struggled to free himself, but Theo held him hard.

'What are you doing here, Daryl?'

'It's my house, mate. I might ask you the same question.'

'I'm entitled to be here. Or at least, I'm welcome here, which is more than I can say for you.'

'You just walk in whenever you want now, do you?'

Theo stared into the eyes of the man he'd once believed he could trust with his life and gave him a shove.

'I was invited,' he growled. 'By my godson. Remember him? You and Elise once trusted me to take care of him in your place if it was ever necessary, just like I once trusted you to have my back. At least one of us kept up their end of the bargain, eh, old friend?'

233

Connor had appeared at the living room door and was watching as his godfather held his dad by the throat.

'Theo?' he said. 'What's going on?'

'For Christ's sake,' Lexie said. 'Look, there's a kid in the room. Can you two grown men put your dicks away and stop covering the walls in testosterone? Theo, let Daryl go.'

She went to put her arm around Connor. Theo glanced at them, and his scowl lifted. He released Daryl from his grip and stepped back.

'Sorry, kiddo,' he said to Connor. 'That was wrong. I was angry, but I should never... you shouldn't have to see that. I didn't mean to spoil your birthday.'

'You didn't spoil it.' Connor glared at his father. 'He did. What did you have to come back for, Dad? You've ruined everything.'

He turned and stomped back upstairs.

'What the hell did you think you were doing, Theo?' Daryl demanded, straightening his collar. 'No wonder the boy gets in trouble for fighting if this is the example you've been setting.'

Theo shook his head. 'Oh, no. You don't get to take the moral high ground. You cost me my business, you son of a bitch.'

'I didn't have any choice,' Daryl muttered. 'Anyway, it wasn't *your* business. Elise's granddad left it to me and her.'

'No, it was our business. I bought Elise's half from you fair and square. I put everything I had into Bistrot Alexandre, Daryl, because I trusted you when you told me we could make a success of it. Don't go acting like it was your fucking birthright, just because Elise's grandad was the one who trained you up in the biz.'

'I told you, I didn't have a—'

'And don't give me that bullshit about not having a choice either,' Theo snapped. 'You had a choice between discussing the state of the finances with me or stabbing me in the back so you could cut your losses and run, and you chose the latter.'

Daryl met his eye defiantly. 'I had to. We couldn't have saved the place. If you'd insisted on struggling on with it, like I just bloody know you would've, we'd both have lost everything.'

'I did lose everything, Daryl! Everything I'd invested, all those years of hard work, gone because you decided to write the place off without consulting me.'

'You didn't lose *everything*. You came away with a big enough sum to set you up with something else.'

Theo snorted. 'So you did me a favour then, did you? Well, cheers, pal.'

'I did what I had to,' Daryl said in a low voice. 'For my family. It wasn't about you, it never was.'

'That'd be the family you walked out on, right?'

'If I hadn't sold up and taken the job in Japan, I could've wound up bankrupt within the year. This way, I was able to support my son even if I couldn't be around for him.'

'And the sacrifice you were willing to make was your best friend.'

'For Connor, then... well, yes.' Daryl cast his eyes down, looking ashamed now. 'I'm sorry, Theo. It was my responsibility, as a father.'

Theo scoffed. 'A responsibility you've always taken very seriously, of course.'

'From a financial point of view, yes. You think I wanted to see the boy left with nothing? If you had kids of your own you might understand.'

'I might not have kids, Daryl, but I do have people who depend on me. Do you know how hard it was after you turned your back on me like that?'

Daryl frowned. 'Do you have people?'

'Yes!' Theo shook his head, laughing. 'Mate, we've known each other since we were fucking thirteen. The fact you still know so little about me is probably our entire friendship in a nutshell.'

'You ought to have told me.'

235

'And you ought to have talked to me, regardless of that.' Theo turned to Lexie. 'Look, I'm sorry for making a scene, Lex. I ought to go.'

He made to leave, but Daryl put a hand on his arm.

'Theo, wait. Why don't we talk about this like adults, eh? You were my best friend for nearly twenty years. You were best man at my wedding, for Christ's sake – at both of them.'

'That's right, I was. You know, Daryl, the best thing you ever did for me was to let me get to know your second wife.'

Daryl frowned. 'What's that supposed to mean?'

Theo could see Lexie from the corner of his eye, almost imperceptibly shaking her head.

'I mean, Lex was a better friend and business partner than you ever were,' he said. 'You never did realise how lucky you were to have Lexie and Connor.'

'I know,' Daryl said in a low voice. 'But I've come home to change that. I want to make amends. To them, and to you if you'll let me.'

Theo shook his head. 'Jesus. You're not telling me you're back for good?'

'Yeah, I've been transferred. I'm here for a week then I'm moving into a flat in Manchester.'

'Here! You're staying at the house?' He looked at Lexie. 'You're not having that, are you?'

'It's his house, Theo,' she said. 'He wants to spend some time with Connor before he moves to Manchester. I can't really say no, can I?'

'And what does Connor want? Not that, I bet.'

'He'll come round,' Daryl said. 'I am his father, after all – the only one he's got, for all my sins.'

Theo fixed him with a look of intense dislike. 'That's how it is, is it? You push him away for years, then you think you can just pick him up like a fucking unfinished crossword when your conscience starts to prick? Is this about Connor or you?'

'Both, I hope.'

'I'd better go, before I say something we'll all regret,' Theo muttered. 'Lex, I'll see you tomorrow at work. Daryl, if you hurt Con by messing about with his feelings – if you hurt either of them – then believe me, I'll do more than just pin you to the wall.'

He marched out, slamming the door behind him.

'Well,' Lexie said. 'Nothing like a bit of drama to say welcome home, eh?'

Chapter Twenty-Seven

The next day was the penultimate Monday of the six-week holidays, and Connor was scheduled to go on a youth club coach trip to Lightwater Valley. Lexie tiptoed past the spare bedroom Daryl was staying in to knock on her stepson's door. It had been like this all last night: creeping about, trying to avoid what felt, now, like a stranger in their home. Connor had shut himself up in his room, refusing to come down even to eat, and after pointing Daryl to the ready meals in the freezer, Lexie had gone to hide likewise.

'Time to get ready for your trip, my love,' she said in a low voice through Connor's door. 'Come get some breakfast when you're dressed.'

'Is Dad awake?'

'Not yet.'

He opened the door to peep out at her. 'I don't want to see him.'

She sighed. 'I know, Con, but you'll have to see him some-times. He's your father.'

'He might as well not be, for everything he knows about me.'

'Come on down and I'll make you a fry-up. Post-birthday treat to make up for last night, eh?'

Twenty minutes later Connor joined Lexie in the kitchen, where she was frying sausages, and flung himself into a chair. Lexie leaned over, spatula in hand, to kiss the top of his head.

'Does Dad have to stay a whole week?' he muttered.

'It's half his house, Con. We can't very well tell him to sling his hook.'

'That means Theo can't come over. Me and him were going to make the model AT-AT he bought me at CalderCon.'

'Well, I'm sure that'll keep.' She put a plate of food in front of him and took a seat opposite. 'How are you feeling, sweetie?'

'Pissed off.'

She smiled. 'I guess that's a given. But come on, isn't there a little part of you that wants to hear what your dad has to say?'

'No. He's had plenty of time to say things to me. If he didn't give a shit about me before, why should I believe he's changed now? He didn't even remember it was my birthday.'

'Oh, I'm sure he did.'

'He didn't. He couldn't remember how old I was.' He glanced up from demolishing his sausage, egg and beans. 'You got me that stuff you said was from him. Didn't you?'

'Well… yes, me and Theo did choose it,' she admitted. 'Your dad sent the money though.'

Connor snorted. 'Oh yeah, money. He'll send that if it means he doesn't have to actually think about me, right?'

Lexie reached over to squeeze his hand. 'Con, sweetheart, I know your dad hasn't always been there for you—'

'Never. He's never been there for me.'

'Well, I suppose it might feel like that,' she conceded. 'But he loves you. I genuinely believe that. And it feels like this time, he really does want to try to build a better relationship with you.'

'He's said that before. Theo's more like a dad to me than he is.'

'Did Theo ever tell you about his dad?' Lexie asked softly.

'Yeah. He said he walked out on him when he was a baby and he hated his guts for it.'

'That's right. It affected him, the fact they never had a relationship. When he and I were first…' She glanced at the door. '…first closer friends than we had been, I found out he had a lot of issues to work through because of it, especially when his dad died without any sort of closure for him. Whether or not you and your dad are able to build a better relationship, I think it would be healthy for you to talk to him.'

'He doesn't deserve it,' Connor muttered.

'But you do,' she said gently, pressing his hand. 'I know you're angry, but think about it, OK? For me.'

His scowl lifted a little. 'Yeah, all right. Only because you want me to.'

The door opened and Daryl appeared, smiling awkwardly.

'That smells good, Lex,' he said. 'Any going spare for a houseguest?'

'Help yourself,' Lexie said, gesturing to the cooker as she stood up. 'The beans'll need heating up. Sorry to leave you to it, Daz, but I have to get to the restaurant.'

Connor pushed his plate away. 'I need to get the bus to youth club.'

'You don't need to rush off, do you, son?' Daryl asked, resting a hand on his shoulder. 'I could always drive you, if your stepmum can spare me the car. I'm still insured.'

'It's fine. I like the bus.' Not making eye contact, Connor shrugged off his hand and marched out.

—

Lexie had deliberately left home early, long before she normally arrived at the restaurant. She didn't want to be hanging around the house while Daryl was there, and besides, she wanted to talk to Theo. When she arrived at the Blue Parrot, she let herself in and went to knock on the door of his flat.

'Lex,' he said when he opened it, flashing her a relieved smile. He pulled her into a hug. 'God, I'm glad you're here.'

She let herself relax in his arms. After all the drama of last night, it felt good to be held.

'I really should be mad at you after that stunt you pulled yesterday, but Jesus, do I ever need a hug,' she whispered.

'I'm sorry. Just, seeing him there... it brought it all back, you know? Here, come inside.'

She followed him in and they sat down on the sofa.

'I remember when you used to drag me up here for something much more fun than angsty chats.' She reached out to draw a finger under one puffy eye. 'Bad night, love? You look like you've been upset.'

'Yeah, I couldn't sleep after what happened. I felt bad for letting Con see, and bad for not being able to control myself, and... well, just generally bad. I didn't see your message until after.'

'I could've done without all the toxic masculinity crap, but I get why you'd react like that. I never thought about how tough it must've been for you to carry on supporting your mum when he did what he did.'

'Well. It's in the past now.'

'You nearly dropped me right in it. You were about to tell him about us, weren't you?'

He grimaced. 'Yeah, sorry. Came over all protective. I think it was the testosterone surge.'

'Seriously, Theo, we need to keep this under wraps. Daryl's all friendly right now, wanting to make amends and give me a fair deal in the divorce, but you know what a temper he's got. If he finds out we're a couple, it could all come crashing down.'

'Why's he back early anyway? Did he say he'd been transferred?'

'Yeah, he asked to be moved to his company's new UK division so he could start being a better father to Connor, apparently. He's had a Domestos moment.'

'You believe him, do you? I'd trust a sobbing crocodile before that guy.'

She hesitated. 'I actually think I do. At least, it seems like he's finally confronting a lot of things he's been pushing deep down for years. I'd say that in spite of everything, I'm willing to give him one more chance.'

Theo visibly tensed. 'What?'

'Oh Jesus, not that sort of chance. I mean one more chance to make things up to Connor.'

'Thank God for that,' he said, letting himself breathe again.

She frowned. 'You didn't really think that was what I meant, did you? Me and him?'

'Well, no. I guess not. But he is legally your husband, Lex. I can't help but remember that you picked him over me once before.'

'Things were very different back then. What we've got now… well, that's something else entirely. Come here.' She wrapped her arms around him and planted a kiss on his lips. 'You're not so insecure about us, are you? I love you, Theo.'

'I know.' He sighed. 'Sorry, I'm still new to this relationship business. You know, when you talked about dating that time, I started having all sorts of jealous fantasies about some future boyfriend who might take my place in yours and Connor's lives. Then Daryl turns up, apparently wanting to step back into the role of husband and father…'

'I talked about dating when I was still in denial about what I felt for you. I realise now there's only one man for me.' She kissed him again. 'It's you, in case you need that clarifying. You don't really think I could have those feelings for Daryl again, do you?'

'No. I mean, I hope not.' He held her tight. 'I've never been so happy as I have these past two weeks we've officially been a couple,' he whispered. 'Perhaps that's what makes me afraid of losing you. There's a part of me that keeps whispering I don't really deserve this.'

'Well, that part of you's whispering balls because you do deserve it.' She leaned back to look into his face. 'Look, Theo, Daryl's assured me he's come home for Connor alone, not me. I do think that's a good thing. But as for me and him, whatever his intentions, we are well and truly done. I love you, no one else, and certainly not Daryl Carson. So ditch the insecurity, eh?'

He smiled and stroked his fingers over her hair. 'OK. You're right, I was being daft. Thanks, Lex.'

'Feel better?'

'Definitely. I wish he wasn't staying at the house though. I know it's only for a week, but I'm going to miss you to bits.'

'You'll still see me in the restaurant, plus there's everything to get ready for the festival on Sunday. That'll give us an excuse to see each other.' She nudged him. 'We can even nip up here occasionally for a quick bounce around. Be just like the old days, eh?'

'That does sound good,' he said, smiling. 'I'll miss coming over to hang out with you and Connor though. I bloody love that kid.'

'I know. But like you say, it is only a week. Let's just be adults about it and keep an eye on how things go with Daryl and Connor. Our first priority needs to be making sure this is something healthy for him and not a recipe for more hurt and confusion.'

Chapter Twenty-Eight

Lexie wasn't back from work when Connor got home from his trip. He wished he'd remembered she had a festival committee meeting this evening so he could've hidden out at Oli's. He really didn't want to be on his own in the house with his dad.

Sure enough, he hadn't been in his room ten minutes when there was a knock at the door.

'Can I come in?' Daryl asked.

'What for?'

'I thought we could have a little chat.'

Connor scowled at the book he was reading, one of the Discworld ones Theo had given him for his birthday.

'Fine,' he said. 'But only because I promised Lexie.'

Daryl came in and glanced around at the posters and collectibles the room was adorned with.

'So I guess you like *Star Wars*, eh?' he said with an awkward smile.

'Er, yeah,' Connor said, rolling his eyes. 'For, like, the last ten years.'

'Can I sit down?'

Connor shrugged, not looking up. Daryl took a seat on his gaming chair.

'Look, Connor, I know we—' He broke off, frowning. 'Could you at least put the book away and look at me?'

'Ugh. Whatever.' Connor flung *Mort* aside and sat up, crossing his arms.

'And can we perhaps have less of the attitude?'

'Will it make you leave faster?'

'Possibly.'

'All right, then I'm listening. Let's just get it over with.'

Daryl leaned forward.

'Connor, I know we haven't exactly been the best of friends these last few years,' he began.

Connor snorted. 'Understatement.'

His dad raised an eyebrow. 'Attitude?'

'Yeah, yeah, all right.'

'Do you know why I came back from Japan early?'

'Because they offered you more money to come work in England?'

'No. Well, yes, they did, but that's not why I'm here. I came for you, Connor.'

Connor scoffed. 'Like hell you did. You always cared more about making money than about me.'

'That isn't true,' Daryl said earnestly. 'Perhaps it felt that way, but it isn't, I promise. I always cared about you.'

'It's a lie. You pushed me away from you all my life, even when I was a little kid and I still wanted you around. Theo's been more like a dad to me than you. At least he knows who I am.'

'I know who you are.'

'All right, then what do I like?' Connor demanded. 'Who are my mates? What's my favourite subject at school?'

'OK, perhaps I don't know those things,' Daryl admitted. 'But I want to learn.'

'Yeah, well, too little, too late,' Connor said, turning back to his book. 'Close the door on your way out.'

'Connor, please don't shut me out of your life.'

'Because you're the expert at that, right?'

'Look, I'm sorry. I'm sorry I wasn't the father I should've been and I'm sorry I wasn't there for you when you needed me. I want to make it up to you, honestly.'

'Heard it before. Believed it then, but I'm not making that mistake this time.'

'For Christ's *sake*, Connor! Can you please—' Daryl took a measured breath. 'Sorry. I didn't meant to get angry. Look, is there anything I can say to get you to talk to me? Please, son.'

Connor ignored him, deliberately shutting out that helpless, pleading look in his father's eyes. Daryl sighed again and stood up.

'If you change your mind, come and find me,' he said. 'I'm not giving up on this, Connor. Not this time.'

He walked to the door, then stopped and turned around.

'We never did talk properly about what happened to your mum, did we?' he said quietly.

'We never talked about it at all.' Connor blinked hard, swallowing down a sob. 'That's fine. I don't want to talk about it. Not with you.'

'It could help us both if we did.'

'No. I *won't* talk about that. You can't make me. Just… get out of my room, Dad.'

'I don't suppose you remember her at all now, do you?'

'Yes I fucking do.' Connor sat up and met his eyes. 'I remember how she sang to me and read me stories and cuddled me at bedtime. I remember that she loved me, more than you ever did. And then…' His voice trembled as a sob juddered through him. '…and then she was gone, and you took all her pictures down and stopped hugging me and you… you sent me away every time I wanted to talk about her.'

'Because it hurt me, Connor,' Daryl said in a low voice. 'I was in a lot of pain.'

'You think I wasn't? My mum was gone and I didn't understand why, and you…' A tear escaped and he dashed it angrily away. '…and you told me to shut my mouth every time I asked where she was.'

'That's not true.'

'It is! You couldn't stand to hear me talk about her. You never even told me what happened until years after. The only time you ever mentioned her after she was dead was to make Lexie feel bad. Lexie was nice and she loved you, and you never loved her back. You never tried to make her happy or asked her what she wanted because you were too hung up on Mum still. No wonder she—' He stopped.

'No wonder she what?'

'Nothing,' he muttered. 'Lexie was the one who talked about Mum to me, and helped me understand what happened. You should've done that. You were my dad.'

Daryl bowed his head. 'Yes. I should.'

'You know I thought for ages it was my fault?'

He frowned. 'You didn't, did you?'

'Yeah. Mum was gone and you were angry with me all the time, and you wouldn't tell me where she was or why she didn't come home. I was six, Dad. I didn't know what dying meant. Lexie was the one who helped me realise it wasn't anything I'd done that made it happen.'

'Yes. That was... bad,' Daryl muttered. 'I failed you badly, Connor, in a lot of ways. But I'm here now, and I want to talk. Please. I'm your father.'

Connor snorted. 'Yeah, and it only took you fifteen years to remember. Get the fuck out of my room, Dad.'

'Connor, please—'

'I said, get out! I don't want to talk about Mum to you. I don't want to talk about anything to you.' He swallowed a sob. 'I just want you to leave me alone,' he whispered. 'You've always been good at that.'

'OK,' Daryl said, blinking hard. 'If that's what you want, then... well, I'll be in my room if you change your mind.'

As soon as the door closed behind him, Connor burst into tears.

–

'Can I hang out at yours for a bit?' Connor asked Oli as they waited for the bus after a D&D session at Sophie's house later that week.

'Sure. You want to work on our characters?'

'I kind of just want to sit and talk a bit. My dad's at home and I'm trying to avoid him.'

Mr and Mrs Foster were still at work when they got to Oli's. The boys went upstairs to his room and crashed on the beanbag sofa.

'So how come your dad's staying with you?' Oli asked.

Connor shrugged. 'Dunno. He reckons he's come to make things up to me, but I know that's not the real reason.'

'How?'

'Because he never gave a crap about me before. Why would he start now? He just wants a place to crash till his new flat's ready, I guess.'

'When's he going?'

'Monday, I think. Just need to stay out of his way for another two days.'

'Will you see more of him now he's back in England?'

'Not if I can help it,' Connor said. 'Ugh, it was so cringe when he came to my room a few days ago to try this father–son bonding bullshit on me. Like he can just sod off out of my life for eighteen months then turn up again and we'll be best mates.'

'You don't think he's trying to get back together with your stepmum, do you?'

Connor flicked at some lint on his hoodie. 'He'd better not be. She wouldn't have him back anyway. Her and Theo are at the seriously vomworthy stage now.'

'I know, they looked pretty bleurgh at CalderCon. You all right about that?'

He shrugged. 'Yeah. Theo's kind of cool – way cooler than my dad. I was hoping they might move in together, once they've been dating for a bit. It's better when it's all three of us.'

'You'd still see your dad though, right?'

'Not unless he makes me,' Connor muttered darkly. 'He didn't want anything to do with me for years, serves him right if I feel the same way now.'

Oli sagged back against the beanbag and stretched out his long legs. 'Maybe you should've gone to Japan with him.'

'What, and leave school and you lot?'

Oli smiled. 'Well, I didn't say I wanted you to. I like you being here.'

Connor's eye caught the Boba Fett keychain Oli had given him for his birthday, which he'd attached to the zip on his rucksack, and he felt his cheeks heat.

'Anyway, it wasn't him going to Japan that was the problem,' he said. 'It was after my mum died that he never seemed to want me around.'

'How come?'

Connor shrugged. 'Dunno,' he muttered. 'Guess I remind him of her or whatever.'

Oli shuffled to face him. 'What happened to your mum, Con? You never talk about her.'

'She… died.' Connor stared down at his feet, struggling against a lump in his throat. 'When I was a little kid.'

'What did she die from, or don't you want to tell me?'

'Well, I guess I can, if you don't tell anyone else.'

'Course not.'

Connor was silent while he fought the choking feeling.

'She was killed,' he whispered.

Oli frowned. 'What, in an accident?'

'No. She was… her and my dad had gone down to London for a weekend break. I stayed at home with my nana. I think it was their wedding anniversary or something like that. And she…' He felt a tear slide down his cheek. 'They were out shopping and the police were chasing after this guy. I don't know what for but he had a gun and he… he was aiming at one of them, the police officers. Only he didn't hit them. He hit my mum.'

'Shit!' Oli whispered.

Almost unconsciously, Connor let his head sink onto his friend's shoulder. Oli put an arm around him.

249

'It was in all the newspapers, on TV and everything,' Connor whispered. 'Everyone in the country knew, but I didn't and she was my mum. Dad never told me, or not till I was much older anyway. I guess he told my nana she wasn't allowed to either. I think Lexie got him to in the end. She must've thought it'd be worse for me to find out by accident.'

'You must've felt like crap when he told you.'

'Yeah. I think I was nine or ten. I felt so angry at Dad, that he never told me what happened to her before. That made it even rougher between me and him. Dad didn't want me around because I looked like Mum or something, and I... before that I always secretly wished he'd decide he liked me again and we'd hang out. But after he told me, I couldn't think of him as my dad any more. Lexie was my real family, and Nana and Uncle Theo. When Dad moved to Japan, I hardly noticed any difference.'

'Jesus,' Oli said in a low voice. He reached up to stroke Connor's hair. 'Wish you'd told me before. I'm so sorry, mate.'

'I never told anyone. I didn't want to be that kid at school whose mum got shot, you know? I just wanted to be me.'

'That must've been hard for your dad, having to see something like that. I can't imagine watching something that screwed up happening to my mum or dad. It'd be like a nightmare, only real.'

Connor scuffed one shoe against the other, pressing his eyes tight shut as he struggled to stop tears escaping.

His mum's death had haunted his nightmares for years, for all that he tried to banish any picture of it from his brain. What must it have been like, to have actually seen it in real life? Did his dad have dreams like the ones Connor sometimes had? Was he, too, forced to watch her die over and over again?

'I guess it was bad for him,' Connor murmured.

'Were him and your mum, like, really in love and all that?' Oli asked.

'Yeah, since they were our age. He was mad about her – more than he ever was about Lexie. I hated him for that too; I mean, for making her sad. Lexie's dead nice.'

Oli was still running his fingers through Connor's hair, and Connor let out a soft sigh.

'You can cry if you want,' Oli said gently. 'You don't have to try not to.'

Connor managed a watery smile. 'Thanks.'

'Con…'

'Yeah?'

'All right, don't bite my head off, but I reckon you should talk to your dad like he wants you to.'

Connor frowned. 'Why? He doesn't deserve it.'

'No, but you're still upset about what happened to your mum, and sounds like he is too, so it might be good for you to talk about it together, you know? Even if you still hate him afterwards, at least you've said everything. Like, I came out to my parents last night.'

Connor glanced up at him. 'Did you?'

'Yeah. I was really worried about how they'd take it, especially my dad, but they were actually fine. Even if they hadn't been though, I reckon I'd still have felt better for telling them. It's been rubbish keeping it hidden, worrying about it all the time.'

'You really think I'll feel better if I talk to Dad?'

'I think you both will, probably. I mean, don't think I'm taking his side. He's been really shitty to you and that's totally not cool, obviously. But it must fuck you up all kinds of ways, seeing something like that happen to someone you love.'

'I suppose,' Connor muttered.

He glanced up. Oli was looking down at him, his brown eyes filled with tender concern.

'Ol?' Connor whispered.

'Yeah?'

'Will you kiss me again?'

Oli hesitated. 'You sure?'

'Yeah. Don't you want to?'

'Well obvs, but I thought you said you weren't into it right now.'

'I don't know if I'm ready for dating yet, but, um… well, a kiss might be good.'

'OK, if you really want me to.'

Connor wiped his eyes and brought his lips to Oli's. It felt different to the other times they'd kissed, or to all the times he'd made out with Sophie. This kiss was sort of… soft. Sort of easy, with nothing to think about except that it felt good and right and full of feelings that were pleasant to experience. Above all, it felt like just what he needed after reliving memories that made him feel helpless, alone and unsupported. Connor wrapped his arms around his friend's neck, allowing himself to get lost in the moment in a way he'd never been able to before.

'Thanks, Ol,' he whispered when they broke apart. 'That was really nice.'

Oli smiled shyly. 'I'd started to think you didn't like me like that any more.'

'No, I do. I told you, I just wanted space to think about some stuff.' Connor smiled too. 'Actually though, you looked really hot as Wolverine.'

'Thanks,' Oli said, flushing. 'So, um… you want to do it a bit more or you want to play *Squadrons*?'

'I guess maybe do it a bit more?' Connor said. 'I'd better go home for tea soon though or Lexie's going to stress.'

'And are we… like, boyfriends now? We wouldn't have to tell anybody. It could be secret.'

'Dunno. Do we have to say we're something? Maybe we should just see what happens.'

'Yeah, all right. Do you reckon you'll talk to your dad then?'

Connor stared thoughtfully at his trainers. 'I'll think about it. Thanks for listening, Ol. You've been great today.'

'That's OK. You can always tell me stuff, you know.'

Connor smiled. 'Yeah. Yeah, I know I can.'

Their lips met for another kiss.

Chapter Twenty-Nine

Daryl was at the cooker frying vegetables when Lexie got in from work.

'Good day?' he asked.

'Manic. I've spent most of my time between customers finalising briefs and schedules for the temps we've hired to help at the festival tomorrow. What have you been up to?'

'I picked up my rental car this morning and I've been in Manchester most of the afternoon. Had a few meetings, then spent a bit of time getting Connor's room in the flat ready. I bought him a Death Star lamp.'

'He'll like that.'

'I rented a costume too. For tomorrow.'

She frowned. 'What, you're coming?'

'Of course. I want to support your event, and I thought it'd be a good opportunity to spend some time with Connor. Is that OK?'

'I suppose, but…'

'…you're worried it'll kick off with Theo again,' he said with a wry smile. 'Don't worry, I'll try to stay out of his way. I just want to have a day out with my son, that's all.'

'Well, all right.' Lexie nodded to what he was cooking. 'Smells tasty. Are you making tea tonight then?'

'Yes, I picked up the ingredients while I was out. It's chicken chow mein, hope that's all right.'

'Sounds good to me.' Lexie leaned over him to add a splash of soy sauce. 'Here. You always make it too dry.'

He smiled. 'Just like old times, eh? You bossing me about in the kitchen.'

'Well, not quite like old times. We haven't had a row yet.' She opened the fridge. 'Glass of something?'

'Maybe later.' He glanced up from the pan. 'Connor's still not home. Does he normally stay out this long with his friends?'

'He went over to his mate Oliver's house after they'd finished gaming, I got a text. Oli only lives a few streets away. I told him to be back by six for tea so he shouldn't be long.'

'What happened to the girlfriend he had?'

'It didn't work out. They're still friends though. He's actually been at hers today.'

'That's grown up of them.'

'He's pretty mature for his age.' She smiled at him. 'Maybe we could learn a thing or two, eh?'

He shrugged. 'We do all right when we make the effort.'

'You mean when you make the effort.'

'All right, I guess I deserved that.'

'Sorry. I shouldn't have a dig when you're making me food, should I?' She went to stand by him, sipping her wine as she watched him stir the veg. 'To be honest, Theo and me were kind of relieved when Con and Sophie broke up. He's very young to be doing that sort of adult dating. I can't help worrying about things moving faster than he's ready for.'

He frowned. 'What's Connor's love life got to do with Theo?'

'He is the boy's godfather, Daz,' she said. 'The two of them have got pretty close since you moved. Connor missed having a male presence in his life, I think, and so he naturally turned to his Uncle Theo. It's tough not having your dad around when you're growing from a boy into a man.'

Daryl sighed. 'I wasn't much of a presence even when I was at home, was I?'

'Well, you're here now.'

'For all the good it does me,' he muttered. 'He won't even look at me. What should I do, Lex? I'm worried I might've alienated him for good.'

'He's got a lot to process. Let him come to you, build the relationship on his own terms.'

'And if he doesn't?'

'I think he will. Eventually.' She glanced at the sizzling pan. 'I'd stick a star anise in that, give it a bit of kick.'

'Have you got any?'

'Somewhere.'

She rifled through a cupboard and handed him a jar.

'Thanks,' he said, smiling. 'I've missed having someone to back-seat cook for me.'

'Yeah, God knows how you've managed without me. All those years in the restaurant trade and you still can't serve up a decent stir-fry.'

'It's not my fault you're a spice junkie. You've destroyed your taste buds glugging wine, love.'

'All right, don't get cheeky.'

He looked up to smile at her. 'Come on, Lex, admit it. There were times when our marriage wasn't one hundred per cent awful.'

'I never denied that. I still have fond memories of that holiday to the Highlands.'

He laughed. 'I remember. I wanted to go to Portugal, but Connor had just started Cubs and gone suddenly mad for camping so the two of you conspired against me. Three solid days of rain and my walking boots got eaten by a cow.'

'Your face, mate,' Lexie said, laughing too. 'When you woke up and found this horned, shaggy head poking into our tent, nibbling your laces.'

'One in a long line of Daryl Carson holiday disasters. Remember the day I proposed?'

'Wouldn't forget that, would I?'

'Weekend trip to Paris, picnic under the Eiffel Tower, the best champagne, and I'd got a patisserie to ice "marry me" onto an eclair. I planned it out so carefully.'

Lexie couldn't help smiling when she remembered the helpless expression on Daryl's face as he'd been about to pop the question, only to be interrupted by a Japanese tourist asking if one of them could take a photo of him and his wife.

'It was very unfair when you'd tried so hard to get everything perfect,' she said. 'I really don't think that couple knew what was going on though.'

'I was down on one knee, you'd think that would've been a clue.'

'Yeah, but holding up an eclair,' she said with a laugh. 'I said yes, didn't I?'

'I suppose that was the main thing.'

They heard the front door open.

'Lexie, I'm home!' Connor called. 'Going to my room.'

'Tea in half an hour!' Lexie called back.

'Can I eat it upstairs?'

'No, you can eat at the table with me and your father.'

'Ugh. Fine.' There was the sound of galloping feet as he disappeared upstairs.

'Think I'll be waiting a while for him to come to me,' Daryl said, smiling sadly.

'Just give him time.'

'Well, you know him best.' He turned to her. 'Lexie, I'm sorry.'

'For what?'

'For leaving you to do all the parent stuff. For all the times I flew off the handle. For the things I said that hurt you. For not being over Elise enough to appreciate how lucky I was to have you.'

'Oh.' Lexie flushed slightly. 'Well, that's… thanks.'

'I never used to have a temper. I bottled too much up when she died, I think. It felt like I was constantly simmering, ready to pop at the slightest thing, and it was you and Connor who got caught in the shrapnel.'

Lexie squinted at him. 'That therapy programme really is good, isn't it?'

'It's certainly changed me, but I've a way to go until I can say I'm healed. Managing the anger's still a big problem.' He put down his wooden spoon to squeeze her arm. 'I know it was my fault our marriage didn't work, Lex, and I'm sorry for it. You tried everything to get through to me and I gave you nothing back. Do you forgive me?'

'Well, yes. If it's important to you, then of course I do,' she said, glancing down at the hand on her arm. 'I think the best thing we can do now is make a clean, amicable break and move on with our lives. Perhaps we might even manage to be friends, now we've talked a few things over. We'll always have Connor to bind us.'

'Exactly. Connor.' He met her gaze. 'Lexie, you said he needed stability. That was why you didn't want to date.'

She felt her cheeks colour and hoped he'd blame the wine.

'I don't want boyfriends coming and going, running the risk of him becoming attached to people who might not be a constant presence in his life,' she said. 'What of it?'

'Well, I wondered… I'm not talking about a reconciliation as such, but given I'm going to be a presence in his life anyway then perhaps you might like to have dinner with me one evening.'

She shook her head. 'Come on, Daryl. After everything that's happened, you aren't seriously asking me out on a date?'

'Yes. A clean-slate date.' He took her hand. 'We had something once: something I was too damaged to appreciate. But I'm on the path to healing now, Lexie, even if I'm not quite there. It wouldn't be like it was before.'

She turned her face away. 'Daryl, I'm sorry, but no. Me and you, that's in the past. We can't go back.'

'I'm not talking about going back.' He squeezed her fingers. 'I'm talking about going forward. Not picking up where we left off, but starting again. The future could be a very different place with you in my life. And think how positive it would be for Connor if we could only—'

'What's going on in here?'

Connor was standing at the door, watching them from under a deep scowl. Lexie jerked her hand away from Daryl's fingers.

'Connor,' she said, feeling flustered. 'Your dad was just… tea's not ready yet.'

'I know. Came to get a Cheestring.'

'All right, well, help yourself. Just one before you eat though.'

He took one from the fridge and cast the pair of them a suspicious glance before going back to his room.

'I'm sorry, Daz,' she said when Connor had gone. 'I do forgive you. I don't bear any ill will, but if you want anything more than friendship from me now, well, I've got nothing to offer.'

'Why not? You said there was no one else.'

'Being single doesn't mean I'm emotionally available. I appreciate you wanting to make amends, but you need to focus on Connor.'

–

In his room, Connor threw himself face-down on the bed and rang Theo.

'Hiya kiddo,' Theo said. 'What's today's crisis then? Are my fairy godfather services required?'

'Just sick of Dad being here,' Connor muttered. 'I wish you could come over.'

'Well, it's only for another couple of days. Are you two not getting along?'

'I try and stay out of his way, but he keeps trying to talk to me.'

'Don't you want to talk to him?'

'No. Why should I? He never wanted me in his life before.' He scowled darkly at Darth Vader on his wall, quite literally the poster boy for shitty fathers. 'Now I don't want him in mine and it serves him right.'

'Lexie says he seems to genuinely want to make amends though. Perhaps you ought to hear what he has to say before you make your mind up.'

'Why are you defending him?' Connor demanded. 'Last time I saw you, you were getting ready to batter him.'

'Well, that was wrong of me. Your dad and me are never going to be friends again, but I shouldn't have been violent. That was stupid and childish.'

'Oli reckons I should talk to him too. He reckons me and Dad need to talk about Mum.'

'He's a sensible boy, that Oli. I think he's right.'

'I don't know why you're all on Dad's side now,' Connor muttered. 'I rang you because I thought you'd be on mine.'

'I am on yours, Con. That's why in spite of how I feel towards your dad, I'm trying to give you advice I think will help you,' Theo said gently. 'Trust me, as someone who let a lack of relationship with his father nearly ruin his happiness, it's something you ought to confront while your dad's still around for you to do it.'

'How did you let it ruin your happiness?'

'Because it fed into my fears about relationships and parent-hood, and made me lie to myself about my feelings for your stepmum. Good thing I had you to sort me out, eh?'

'You love Lexie a lot, don't you?'

'Yeah,' he said quietly. 'I really do.'

'What does it feel like, when you love someone like that?'

'It feels...' Theo paused. 'It's hard to explain. Like they understand you. Like they're on your side. Like you don't need to try to be anyone else when you're with them. Kind of like best friends squared, but with smooching.'

Connor smiled. 'I can't believe you just said "smooching".'

259

'Well as you're so fond of reminding me, I am very, very ancient,' Theo said. 'Why the sudden interest in The Big L, Connor?'

'Well...' He lowered his voice. 'I kissed Oli again today. Only it was different this time. He was being all nice and understanding about Dad, then we kissed and it was just really sort of easy, like you said. Like I didn't have to worry about anything while I was doing it, you know? He wants us to be boyfriends, but secretly.'

'And what do you want?'

'I'm... not sure. I think maybe I want that too. I feel like I might be ready now, if we can go slow.'

'Well, if you think it'll make you happy then I say go for it. You two seem pretty right for each other. I'm not sure I could resist someone who gave me a Boba Fett keyring for my birthday either.'

Connor smiled, glancing at the Lego figure dangling from his rucksack. 'Yeah, that was pretty sweet. Thanks, Theo.'

Lexie's voice sailed up the stairs.

'Connor! Food!'

'Ugh,' Connor said, rolling his eyes. 'I have to go. Lexie's making me eat with her and Dad so we can pretend we're a normal family instead of a bunch of freaks who hate each other.'

'All right. See you soon, eh?'

'Theo...'

'Yeah?'

'I'm worried about something,' he said in a low voice.

'About Oli?'

'No, Lexie. She was being all weird before.'

'Weird how?'

'Her and Dad were cooking together in the kitchen when I got home, laughing like twats just like they used to do in the olden days, before they started hating each other. Then I walked in on him holding her hand and saying how it would be good for me if they did something or other.'

'What something or other?'

'I didn't hear but I guess maybe stopping the divorce. Then when Lexie saw me there, she looked all embarrassed about it.'

'Right,' Theo said quietly.

'I don't think she likes him more than you, but I think he might want to get her back. Do you think he does?'

'Well, I don't know,' Theo said vaguely, as if his mind had wandered elsewhere. 'He cared about her a lot, once.'

'I wish you could come round. It feels all wrong with him here and you not.'

'Thanks, kid.' Theo sounded sober. 'Ring me whenever you want a chat, OK?'

'I will, thanks.'

Chapter Thirty

'What's this?' Connor asked when he joined Lexie and his dad at the kitchen table, eyeing the bowl of noodles.

'It's chicken chow mein,' Lexie told him. 'Your dad made it.'

'Smells weird.'

'It's tasty, I promise. Try a bit.'

Connor sniffed a forkful suspiciously before putting it in his mouth.

'Well, lad, how it is?' his dad asked.

He shrugged. ''S'all right.'

Lexie laughed. 'Don't worry, Daz. In teenager-speak that's actually a ringing endorsement.'

'So where did you go this evening then?' Daryl asked Connor.

'Why, aren't I allowed to go places?' Connor asked, immediately defensive. 'Lexie said it was OK.'

'Of course you're allowed. I'm just interested, that's all.'

'Oli's,' Connor muttered, poking at a piece of chicken.

'That's one of your gaming friends, right?'

'Yeah. He's my best mate.'

'Have you been gaming tonight?'

He shrugged. 'No, just… messing about.'

'Come on, Connor, meet your dad halfway here,' Lexie said gently. 'He wants to learn more about you. Your life, your friends, what you like. Talk to him.'

Connor looked up from his food to glare at them.

'Are you two going to get back together?' he demanded.

Lexie frowned. 'Why would you think that, Con?'

'You were being weird before. Holding hands and that.'

'We weren't holding hands and we're absolutely not going to get back together, no.'

Connor nodded his satisfaction. 'Good.'

Daryl cast a helpless look at Lexie, who shrugged.

'Was that a Starbug I spotted in your room?' he asked Connor, trying a new approach.

'Oh God, do we have to keep talking?' Connor was silent for a moment, curling noodles around his fork, before looking up. 'You don't know *Red Dwarf*, do you?'

'Course I do. It's a classic of the genre.'

'That's what Theo says. He got me Starbug for my birthday. It's never been removed from the box.'

'Impressive. What's your favourite episode then?'

'Dunno. "Dimension Jump", maybe.'

'Can't beat a bit of Ace Rimmer, eh?' His dad smiled when Connor stared at him. 'Thought I was bluffing, did you? Actually, me and Theo used to watch *Red Dwarf* together. I don't suppose we were all that different from you and your friend Oli when we were young.'

'You're totally different. You weren't a proper friend to Theo. You made him lose his restaurant and most of his money. Oli wouldn't do that to me, ever.'

'Well, there were reasons for that, Connor.'

'What reasons?'

'It was… business. It's not always straightforward.'

'It must've been a bad thing to do for Theo to hate you so much. He likes everyone.'

'It was bad but… necessary. I did what I did to make sure I could keep supporting you.'

Connor scoffed. 'Right, so it was my fault.'

'It wasn't anyone's fault, Connor. It just happened.' He paused. 'I did handle it badly though. I handled a lot of things badly back then.'

'Er, yeah you did.'

'I'm not making any excuses, but I wish you could…' He sighed and put down his fork. 'Connor, when your mum died, all the colour went out of the world for me. Everything I thought or saw or did was haunted by this terrible thing I'd seen happen to the person I loved most. I was so angry, for so long. Can you understand that?'

Connor was silent. Lexie stood up and rested a hand on his shoulder.

'I'm going to leave you and your dad alone to talk, sweetie,' she said gently.

He looked up at her. 'I wish you wouldn't.'

'I have to, Con. This is important. Just listen to what he has to say, OK? One day you'll be grateful that you did.'

She kissed the top of his head and left the room with her food.

'Connor, please hear me out,' Daryl said, a pleading expression in his eyes. 'You have to understand that what I saw happen to your mum, it… did things to me. No one expects to lose their wife the way I lost Elise, and suddenly I found myself having to deal with this crippling grief, with being a single dad, and still only in my mid-twenties. And I saw so much of your mum in you, it made it hard for me to… well, I'm not proud of the person I became after it happened. That man I was then, he wasn't me. Not really.'

Connor stared down into his chow mein.

'Theo told me losing Mum made you hard.'

'It made me… cold,' Daryl admitted. 'Not because I didn't care. Because I knew I was in danger of caring too much, letting my emotions spiral out of control. I never used to get angry at the drop of a hat before I lost Elise. The unfairness of what happened, the fact I felt guilty it had been her and not me… it felt like I was on a knife edge, constantly trying to stop myself getting overwhelmed with all these things I was feeling. It felt like… almost like I might lose my mind unless I kept tight control of every emotion. I know that must be hard for you to understand.'

264

'So you shut me out.'

'Not just you, Connor. Everyone. Theo, Lexie, your grand-parents, they all tried to help me, but I just threw myself into work and bottled everything up. Told myself it was all for you, as if by making sure you were provided for financially I could convince myself I was doing my duty as your father. It's only been these last few months, since I started therapy, that I've begun to confront everything my grief turned me into.' He sighed. 'Connor, I'm sorry. You were a child and you were grieving too, and I wasn't there for you. I never have been. But I do want to change that.'

'Why should I believe you?'

'Son, you're a young man now, so I'm going to talk to you as one adult to another,' Daryl said quietly. 'I know the time's passed when I could shield you from what's painful. The truth is...' He looked down, and for a moment it seemed as though he was struggling against tears. 'The truth is, it did prey on me, the shooting,' he said in a choked voice. 'When I closed my eyes it was your mum's face I saw, as she was in her last moments. When I slept, the memory of it woke me up, struggling to breathe. I've got no excuses – you deserve better than that – but I would like you to try and understand how that must have felt for me.'

Connor was silent, fighting against tears of his own. He'd always tried so hard not to think about how his mum died; never to picture it...

'You really loved Mum, didn't you?' he whispered.

Daryl bowed his head. 'More than anything in the world.'

'More than you loved Lexie?'

'Differently than I loved Lexie. Lexie was... a waste.'

Connor frowned. 'She's not a waste. She's my mum. My other mum.'

'I mean, it was a waste for me to have met her when I did. My mind was full of Elise, and I couldn't appreciate the different but equally amazing woman I had in my life then. I loved Lexie, but not as she deserved to be loved, and I regret that.'

Connor looked up to meet his eyes. 'Dad, can I ask you something?'

'Of course.'

'And you'll tell me the truth? You promise?'

'I promise. What is it?'

'Are you here for me or Lexie? I heard you before, talking about it being good for me if you guys got back together.'

Daryl paused for a long moment before he answered.

'Well, I am here for you,' he said finally. 'But as I said, I do regret not having been in a place mentally to make a proper go of things with Lexie. If she told me she wanted to give me another chance, have us be a family again, I wouldn't say no.'

'She won't. She doesn't feel like that about you any more.'

'You sound very sure.' Daryl narrowed one eye. 'There isn't anything you and her are keeping from me, is there?'

Connor flushed. 'No. Like what?'

'She hasn't had any boyfriends since I've been gone?'

'That's none of your business.' He hesitated. 'She hasn't though.'

'You're sure?'

'Yeah. She says she doesn't want a boyfriend till I leave home.'

Daryl gave a satisfied nod. 'That's a good plan. I approve of that.'

'She won't get back with you though, not ever, so I'd leave her alone about it if I were you. You said you were here for me, not her.'

'That does rather depend on you deciding to talk to me, don't you think?'

'We're talking now, aren't we?'

Daryl smiled. 'Well, I've talked quite a lot at you, I suppose. What are you feeling then?'

'I think…' Connor took a deep breath. 'I think I understand why Mum getting killed made you weird. But I'm still angry about it. It wasn't my fault and you made me feel like it was.'

'Yes, I understand that. Go on.'

266

'And for most of my life I felt like you never gave a shit about me.'

'That isn't true, Connor.'

'You didn't ask what was true, you asked how I felt. Well, that is how I felt. And I think I was right to feel like that when you ignored me all the time and never hugged me or told me you loved me or... or anything. So if you want me to forgive you or whatever then you'll have to show me you mean it about wanting to be in my life.'

'That's all I'm asking for: a chance to prove that.'

'Right. Then I get to make the rules.'

Daryl frowned. 'Rules?'

'Yeah. Rules are: don't boss me about. Lexie gets to because she earned it but you don't. Don't keep going on about working hard at school, like the only thing you care about is whether I do well in my exams. Don't tease me about girlfriends or try to have cringey sex talks with me because I already know everything I need to know. And leave Lexie alone because she isn't ever going to get back with you, ever.'

Daryl blinked. 'That's a lot of rules.'

'Well?'

'OK, if that's what it takes.'

'Promise?'

'Promise.'

He held out a hand, and Connor eyed it warily before deigning to shake it.

Daryl smiled. 'So come on, is it true you don't know Monty Python?'

'Never heard of him.'

'It's not a him, it's a they... look, it's better if I show you. How about we have a film night tonight, just us boys? You're in for a treat if you've never seen *Holy Grail*.'

'Well... we can have a film night, I guess,' Connor said. 'But Lexie has to be there. I don't want it to be just us.'

'All right, if it'll make you feel more comfortable.'

'And can we have popcorn? Theo always brings popcorn.'

'If you like. I can go to the shop for some.'

'OK. It doesn't mean you're forgiven though.'

'Well, for now I'll settle for you not shunning my company,' Daryl said, smiling. 'Do I get a hug as well as the handshake? I'd like to start as I mean to go on.'

Connor hesitated. 'Well… all right. I guess so.'

They stood up, and his dad clapped him on the back as Connor submitted awkwardly to an embrace.

'It's good to feel like a dad again,' Daryl whispered. 'Thanks for hearing me out, son. I promise you won't regret it.'

Chapter Thirty-One

The next day was the outcome of months of planning as the village prepared to celebrate the first ever Leyholme 1940s Festival. Lexie was up early and dressed in her waitress uniform, ready to get everything set up at the restaurant. The festival officially began at one, kicking off with a costume parade down the main street.

With all her worry being expended on Connor, Daryl and the drama at home, Lexie had barely had any to spare for the festival, but the nerves hit her in force as she walked into the village. What if hardly anyone came? What if all the time and public money the committee had invested was for nothing – and after it had all been her idea? She wondered if Theo, down in the park setting up the refreshments marquee, was thinking the same.

The Blue Parrot was going to be fighting on two fronts today. A special festival menu of hot food was being served up at the restaurant, while the marquee cafe in the park – run jointly by the Parrot and the Highwayman's Drop – would be serving cakes and sandwiches, hot drinks and bottled beer. She and Theo had hired a handful of extra servers for the day, with their team on rotation between the marquee and restaurant.

It looked as though the villagers had done their bit to get Leyholme looking the part, anyway, which gave Lexie a glimmer of reassurance. Red, white and blue was everywhere: in the bunting that decked the old Victorian primary school, on the Union Jacks and American flags draped from shop windows. An Austin utility vehicle, swathed in Tonya's rainbow-coloured bunting, had been parked outside the bakery. Scarecrows in military uniforms formed a guard of honour up to the door of the Mechanics' Institute, where the village dance society was advertising drop-in sessions teaching jive, swing and the Lindy-Hop.

Tonya was outside the Parrot when Lexie arrived, pinning bunting across the large front window.

'Morning.' Lexie glanced down at the grey boiler suit her friend was wearing. 'What uniform is that? Munitions?'

'Nope, Holloway Prison. I've come as a conscientious objector unfairly imprisoned for her pacifist convictions.'

'Naturally.'

Tonya finished pinning up the string of bunting and turned to face her. 'So, have you murdered Daryl and buried him under the patio yet then?'

Lexie laughed. 'Not yet. Actually, he's coming along later. Things are going pretty well, considering.'

'Oh?'

'Yes, Connor's finally decided to give him another chance. We had a family film night last night.'

'And how are you feeling?'

'It does feel awkward having him in the house, I must admit. Still, I was wondering if I ought to invite him to stay for another week. It seems a shame for him to leave just when him and Connor are getting close.'

'No temper tantrums?'

'No, he's been ever so well-behaved. This therapy he's having really seems to have made a difference.' Lexie glanced behind her to make sure no one was in earshot. 'I am a bit worried though.'

'About Theo? I don't suppose he's very happy about the arrangement.'

'No, Daryl. Yesterday… well, he seems to be nursing a hope that me and him can try again. Obviously that's never going to happen, but I'm not sure he was entirely put off when I shut it down.'

'Hmm. You need to nip that in the bud before you invite him to stay longer, Lexie. He might take that as encouragement.'

'I know.' She unlocked the door to the restaurant. 'Here, come on in. We'll get sorted out in here while the others are putting up the marquee.'

–

The first guests started to appear about half past twelve, ready for the costume parade. By that time, the pavements of the main street were lined with stalls and games run by members of the festival committee and other volunteers. Lexie was chatting to Stevie Madeleine's wife Deb on the tombola when she felt someone tap her shoulder.

Daryl had appeared behind her. He was wearing an American army captain's uniform, with Connor beside him looking terribly grown-up in his own GI costume.

Lexie smiled. 'Aww. Look at you two in your matching outfits.'

'Can I take this stupid cap off yet?' Connor asked, rubbing his head.

'No you can't,' Daryl said.

'Why not?'

'Because it'll ruin the whole effect. And because I'm a captain and you're only a private, and I say so. Now drop and give me twenty.'

Connor looked puzzled, and Lexie laughed.

'He's joking, Con.'

'You're wearing the thing wrong anyway.' Daryl reached up to push Connor's cap to a more rakish angle. 'This is how they used to wear them, not sticking straight up like that.'

'I feel like a right twat,' Connor muttered.

'Well you look as cute as a button,' Lexie said, pinching his cheek. 'Just think of it as a convention, Con, only with fewer superheroes and more... you know, history.'

Connor glanced across the crowd and groaned. 'Oh God, Oli's here. And he's not in fancy dress. Can't believe he has to see me like this.'

'Honestly, sweetie, you look great. Ever so handsome.' Lexie took out her phone and held it out to Deb. 'Would you mind? I need a picture of this.'

'No problem,' Deb said, smiling.

The three of them clustered together, Connor in the middle with his parents either side, as Deb took the photo.

Lexie glanced in the direction of the park when the brass band who were playing on the bandstand struck up 'In the Mood'.

'That's my cue to get to work,' she said. 'You boys go enjoy yourselves. I'll see you both later.'

'Sounds good to me,' Daryl said. 'What do you think, Con, shall we have a wander? Perhaps you can introduce me to your friend.'

'Yeah, all right then.'

They disappeared into the now sizeable crowd and Lexie headed in the direction of the park.

There were loads of people out now, many of them in costume, lining the main street in readiness for the procession. Lexie recognised a lot of them from the village, but there were plenty she didn't know, which was heartening from the Parrot's point of view.

Nell Shackleton was there, heavily pregnant now in a maternity Land Girl uniform. Her little sister Milly gripped her hand, looking adorable in pigtail plaits and a beret as an evacuee. Ryan Theakston and the other members of his re-enactment group were forming ranks behind a utility vehicle, dressed in full combat gear. There were spivs, French Resistance fighters, Home Guard members, WAAFs, Wrens and ATS girls, nurses, munitions workers, a few Rosie the Riveters; even a Churchill. It was a better turnout than Lexie could ever have hoped for.

Theo was serving cream teas and plates of sandwiches when she joined him in The Victory Cafe, as the refreshments marquee had been christened.

'Hey, this is all right, isn't it?' she whispered. 'We haven't even officially opened yet and we've already got customers. You should see the main street, it's crammed.'

'I know. Looks like we're going to have a good day.'

She smiled at him in his RAF uniform. 'You know I can't resist you in that thing. What do you reckon, can we fit in a quickie at the flat later?'

He didn't respond, and she frowned. 'You all right?'

'You didn't call me last night like you said you would.'

'Oh God, sorry.' She put a palm to her forehead. 'I totally forgot. Sorry, Teddy. The boys wanted to have a family film night and I got distracted.'

'Film night?'

She nodded. 'Daryl introduced Connor to Monty Python. He loved it, naturally, so that's one thing they've found to bond over.'

'Con decided to give Daryl a chance then?'

'Yeah, they made a breakthrough during a heart-to-heart about Elise. I wouldn't say Connor's exactly in the adoring son category now, but he's cautiously allowing his dad to spend time with him. I hope today goes well for them.'

'What, Daryl's here?'

'Yep. Connor's introducing him to Oli.'

Theo knew it was daft, since he'd been the one to encourage Connor to give his dad a chance, but nevertheless he felt a surge of jealousy.

'That's good news then,' he said, trying to ignore it.

'Yes, I thought it was pretty encouraging. Daryl seems determined to prove himself this time. If it goes well today, I might ask if he wants to stay at the house for a bit longer. I know it's a pain as far as me and you are concerned, but it could be a great thing for Connor.'

She looked very happy. Was that for Connor's sake, or for Daryl's? They seemed to have transformed into a model happy family almost overnight. It sounded like the bloody Waltons over there.

He handed her a plate of sandwiches, trying to ignore the sick feeling in his stomach. 'Here, you'd better take these to the old dears at the corner table. I'll be over with their teas in a minute.'

—

Some hours later, Theo watched as Lexie carried a couple of buttered scones to one of the tables. The brass band had given way to a ukulele-strumming George Formby impersonator, and the chirpily phallic innuendo of 'With My Little Stick of Blackpool Rock' was doing nothing to improve his mood.

Not a good investment. The words kept jumping into his head, every time he looked at her. Ever since Connor had told him Daryl had plans to win his estranged wife back, Theo couldn't stop thinking about it: how eight years ago, Lexie had chosen Daryl – steady, reliable Daryl – over his philandering, immature excuse for a best friend.

He took out his phone and brought up the photo he'd saved from Facebook earlier.

They looked so happy, the three of them. Connor and Daryl looking handsome in their army uniforms, grinning the same grin – everyone said it was Connor's mum he most resembled but there was plenty of Daryl in the boy, especially when he smiled – and Lexie beside them, stretching a proud arm around her stepson. The perfect family.

Lexie had told him he had nothing to be jealous about, but it was hard not to feel a bit green when he thought about her husband right there, living in the house with her. Yes, Daryl had hurt Lexie in the past, and their marriage had probably had as many unhappy days as happy ones. Nevertheless, there had been good times; Theo had been there through all of them. He

274

remembered Lex sitting on his best friend's lap as the three of them had sat around playing cards and drinking wine in the evenings after Connor had gone to bed; the way Lexie and Daryl laughed and pawed at each other, gazing sickeningly into each other's eyes until Theo had started to feel it was time for this furry old gooseberry to roll itself home and leave his friends to get themselves a room. He remembered how loved up they'd been on their wedding day, when as best man he'd stood at Daryl's right hand, making a complimentary speech about his friend's beautiful bride and never knowing that one day he'd long to make the same vows to her himself.

Why had things gone so wrong for Lexie and Daryl? The answer to that, of course, was Elise; or rather the ghost of her, haunting Daryl's imagination, an ideal no other woman was ever going to live up to. If it hadn't been for that, Theo didn't doubt that the two of them would be happily married to this day.

And now Daryl was back, full of regret for his past, desperate to show his family he was a changed man ready to be the husband and father he always should have been. Theo couldn't help thinking, had anything really altered since the day Lexie had made her choice? Daryl was still steady and reliable, even more so now he seemed to have dealt with some of the character flaws he'd developed in the wake of Elise's death. Meanwhile, Theo wasn't far removed from the reckless, emotionally stunted fuck-up he always had been. One three-week relationship hardly made him Mr Dependable now, at least probably not in Lexie's eyes.

Christ, she'd never even have ended up in a relationship with him if she hadn't been randy and seen him as a good bet for a regular shag, with his well-known predilection for no-strings-attached sex. She'd actually chosen him for his *lack* of ability to commit – the exact opposite reason for choosing Daryl originally – and only a trick of Fate had brought them to where they were now.

He knew she loved him, but she'd loved Daryl too, once; loved him enough to become his wife, only eight months after they'd first met. Lexie's generous heart had naturally gone out to that broken man who'd lost his first wife in such a tragic way, just as it had to little motherless Connor. Could she fall for Daryl again if he made up his mind to win her back? He was still her legal husband, and Connor's father. They owned a home together. Lexie had a lot invested in Daryl Carson one way or another, and if what Connor had said was true, he was already giving it his best shot.

What's more, it sounded as though Lexie wasn't exactly fighting him off with a stick. Holding hands? What had that been about? Theo had been torturing himself with jealous visions of Daryl putting his hands all over Lexie most of last night, made worse by the fact that these weren't simply fevered imaginings but his actual memories. He knew Lexie had once welcomed Daryl's touch just as much as his own. Maybe more…

'All right?'

Theo looked up from the butterfly cake he'd been glaring at to find that Daryl himself had appeared in the marquee and was smiling awkwardly at him.

'What the hell do you want?' he demanded.

'Lexie. Is she here?'

'You can see she bloody is.' A couple of customers looked up from their tables, eyebrows raised at his angry tone, and Theo lowered his voice. 'She's over there.'

Daryl glanced over his shoulder. Lexie had just finished serving one of the tables and was walking towards them.

'Daz,' she said, smiling. 'Hiya. Where's Connor?'

'That's what I came to tell you. He asked if he could go over to Oliver's for a bit. I said that was OK and I'd give you the message.'

Theo raised an eyebrow. 'You said it was OK, did you? Who asked you?'

'He's my son, Theo. I could ask you the same question.' He looked at Lexie. 'You don't mind, do you? Sorry, I should've checked first.'

'No, that's fine. As long as he's home for tea.' She rested a friendly hand on Daryl's arm, and Theo tried not to glare at her fingers on his body. 'Have you two had a nice afternoon?'

'Yes, I think we've made some progress. How's it been here?'

'Great. Trade's been non-stop.'

'That's good, right? Lots of publicity for the restaurant.'

'That's the idea. Everyone seems to have enjoyed themselves too. The committee were thinking we might make it a full weekend event next year.'

'Look, there's customers waiting,' Theo snapped. 'Can you two make chitchat in your own time? Me and Lexie have got work to do.'

Lexie frowned at him. 'No need to be like that, Theo. It's not that busy, is it? The other staff can handle it.'

'It's all right, Lex,' Daryl said in a soothing voice. 'I don't want to cause any trouble. I'll go.'

'Good,' Theo said. 'Don't let the door hit you on the way out, will you?'

'We're in a tent, mate.' He squeezed Lexie's arm. 'See you back at home, love. I'll get a bottle in for us, eh? You'll need it after today.'

'Yeah, thanks.'

When he'd gone, Lexie turned to glare at Theo. 'What the hell is wrong with you?'

'What the hell is wrong with *him*? Did he just come to gloat or what?'

'He was being perfectly polite and you bit his head off for no reason. Everyone was staring at us.'

'It's fine. We'll just tell them it was a battle re-enactment.'

'Seriously, Theo. Can't you at least manage to stay civil?' She lowered her voice. 'He's going to get suspicious if you start acting all jealous.'

'Sorry.' He sighed. 'Sorry, you're right. Look, can we have a word in private before you go swap with Claire at the restaurant?'

'I guess. We can talk at HQ.'

'Just taking a quick break, you guys,' Theo called to the other servers. 'Back in five.'

HQ was what they called the gardening association hut to one side of the bandstand, which the festival committee had requisitioned for the afternoon. Theo unlocked the door and Lexie followed him in.

'What's up?' she asked when they were inside.

'Oh, nothing. Give us a hug, can you?'

She blinked. 'All right.'

He sighed as he wrapped his arms around her.

'Sorry,' he whispered. 'I was just... well, it doesn't matter. I needed to touch you, that's all.'

'Come on, talk to me. You've been on another planet all day, and there was no need to have a go at Daryl like that in front of people.'

'No, that was stupid. It's just... Connor rang me last night, Lex.'

'About his dad?'

'Among other things. I encouraged him to hear what Daryl had to say.'

'It must've worked then.' She gave him a squeeze. 'Thanks, Teddy. It's big of you to put Connor first given your own feelings about Daryl.'

'Lexie... Connor told me Daryl wanted you and him to work things out.'

She frowned and let him go. 'That's not what you're worried about, is it? Theo, we talked about this.'

Theo lowered his eyes. 'I know, but I couldn't help feeling... he said you guys were holding hands.'

'We weren't holding hands. Daryl took my hand and then I took it away.' She shook her head. 'Do you not trust me or something?'

'No, of course I do,' Theo said, rubbing the back of his neck. 'But, well, he is your husband, Lex. Your stepson's father. And now he's back in your house, sleeping there night after night, and you're posting cosy family pics on Facebook and sharing bottles of wine with him while I'm hidden away in the flat like some dirty little secret you hook up with for the occasional quickie. And now you're talking about inviting him to stay for even longer – well, how am I supposed to feel about that?'

'You're supposed to feel fine, Theo, because you know I'm in love with you. Daryl's staying at the house for Connor, not me, something which the sleeping arrangements very much reflect.'

'OK. So are you saying he hasn't talked about you two getting back together?'

She flushed slightly. 'Well, no, he has. But that's neither here nor there.'

'Lex, come on! Neither here nor there? That your husband wants you back and is staying in your house? You seriously think that ought to be no big deal for me?'

'It shouldn't be any sort of deal if you trust me.'

'When we met, you said you chose him over me because he was a better investment. Isn't that still true? He's wealthier than I am, more successful, not to mention you've been married for seven years – are married still, for fuck's sake! You own a home together, you've got a kid together; tell me you really think I'm the one being unreasonable here.'

'Yes I bloody do,' she said. 'Not a single thing you've just mentioned is important, Theo, for the simple reason that I don't love Daryl. I love you.'

'We've only been seeing each other officially for a few weeks. He can offer you a family life, a comfortable home—'

'I don't give a shit about what he can offer me!' Lexie snapped. 'He can't offer me *you*, which is the thing I actually want.' She scowled at him. 'I can't believe you're being like this. What are we, twelve? Connor's more mature about relationships than you are.'

'Yeah, well he's had more experience of relationships than I have.'

'Christ, Theo! You've slept with nearly every woman this side of the Pennines. Ever since I've known you, just the word "commitment" has been enough to bring you out in a cold sweat. Do I get jealous or paranoid? No, because I trust you, for one thing, and I genuinely believe that you love me for another.'

'Lex, come on. Don't be that way.'

He reached for her hand, but she jerked it away.

'How do you expect me to be?' she demanded. 'You've all but accused me of shagging another man, which is a bit bloody rich coming from you.'

He frowned. 'What's that supposed to mean?'

'Come on. It was only three weeks ago I caught you out on a date with another woman right after I seriously believed I might be pregnant with your baby; literally on the brink of going home to have sex with her. And now you've got the chutzpah to accuse me of seeing someone behind your back? Really?'

'I didn't accuse you of anything,' he muttered. 'And Daryl isn't just someone, is he? He's your husband.'

'He's my husband on paper. Emotionally speaking, he's not even on my radar.' She glared at him. 'So you actually believed I'd consider ditching you to go back to him, did you? Well thanks, Theo. Thanks a lot.'

Theo's cheeks were flaming with shame and humiliation. Why did he have to go and open his big, insecure mouth? They could have been holding each other now, finding comfort in one another; instead they were trapped in a blazing row.

'I just thought, if you felt it would be good for Connor to have his dad at home...' he mumbled.

'You what?' Lexie laughed. 'So you think I'd sign my life away to Daryl, sleep with Daryl, throw aside the man I actually love, just for the sake of convenience? Of... of fucking *accessibility*?'

'Look, I'm sorry.' He sighed. 'I don't want to lose you, that's all. It literally terrifies me, Lex; that's what makes me paranoid. I've never had anything this good in my life before and I can't help worrying there's been some terrible mistake. That the universe is just waiting to snatch it all back from me.'

She scoffed. 'Really, you're terrified of losing me? Am I supposed to think that's sweet? I mean, nice job trying to keep me. I always dreamed of being with a man who's so possessive and insecure he's afraid to let me out of his sight in case I start shagging my exes the minute his back's turned.'

'Don't take it that way. I was worried, that's all. Don't you think I had a right to be worried? Connor tells me Daryl's been making advances to you, then you don't call me when you say you will because you're snuggled up watching films with the pair of them, like...'

'Like?'

'Well, like the three of us normally do.'

She shook her head. 'That's it, isn't it? This is some chest-beating silverback gorilla bullshit where you're worried Daryl's going to jump in and take your place. You really think there's room for only one father figure in Connor's life? That I have to pick one or the other of you to be his dad and therefore my official alpha male concubine in the family group? There really isn't any excuse for thinking I'd behave like I'm in the midst of some sodding... mating ritual, Theo.'

'I don't think that. That's ridiculous.'

'So do you trust me or don't you?'

He flinched. 'I... I mean, yes, I do, obviously, I just...'

'You just what?'

'Well, he's your husband, Lexie.'

'He's my separated, soon-to-be-ex-husband. Not my current boyfriend. Not someone I have any sort of romantic feelings for: not any more.' She sighed. 'Teddy, I love you, I do, but if you can't learn to trust me... well, I think you need to have a long, hard think about how you do grown-up relationships. Goodbye.'

She walked out to the angry sound of a Spitfire zooming overhead, Theo staring after her.

Chapter Thirty-Two

Daryl had changed out of his GI uniform and was in the living room reading the paper when Lexie arrived home after her last shift of the day. She still kept forgetting she was going to find him there. It gave her an uncomfortable jolt every time, as if she was somehow walking back into her past.

She summoned a feeble smile for him. 'Oh. Hi. Is Connor still at Oli's?'

'No, he's upstairs writing notes on Mordecai the Slaughterous. I was pretty disturbed by that until he explained it's some character he plays in Dungeons and Dragons.' He frowned as he put down his newspaper. 'What's up, love? You seem depressed.'

Oh, right. All those years of marriage and it was only now, when it was least convenient, that he started being perceptive about her moods…

'No, just exhausted,' she said. 'Obviously it's great we managed such a roaring trade, but it does feel a bit like I've been fed through a mangle.'

'You do look tired,' he said, examining her face. 'You want me to cook?'

'No, you stay put; it'll help me wind down. I've got the ingredients for macaroni cheese, Connor's favourite.'

She was hoping Daryl would take the hint that she wanted to be left alone, but no. He stood up and followed her into the kitchen.

'So what did you and Con get up to today?' she asked, to make conversation as much as anything.

'Well, he introduced me to Oliver and I bought them a hot dog each, so that's progress. He seems a nice lad, his friend.'

'Yes, they've been best mates a while. They're well suited, I think. They look out for each other.'

Lexie reached up to rub her temples. She had a throbbing headache after a long day at the festival and her first big row with Theo, and being forced into making small talk wasn't helping.

'You look knackered, Lex,' Daryl said gently.

'I am. Early night for me tonight.'

'You're sure there's nothing else wrong?'

'I told you. Long day, that's all.'

He went to stand behind her as she chopped spring onions and started massaging her shoulders with his fingertips. Lexie tensed at his touch.

'What're you doing, Daz?'

'Giving you a shoulder rub. You used to like me doing this when you'd had a stressful day.'

'Daryl, I told you—'

'Come on, Lex, it's only a massage. Although...' He leaned around to softly kiss her neck. '...I remember when you used to like me doing this after a stressful day too,' he whispered.

She turned to face him, and he put his arms around her waist.

'Daryl, you need to stop,' she said firmly. 'Look, I don't want to start an argument when we've been getting along but I told you before: I'm pleased you're making progress with Connor, but I just don't see you like that any more, I'm sorry.'

'You could if you tried, surely,' he said, his voice husky and insinuating. 'Like I said, we'd be starting again rather than picking up where we left off. Isn't that worth a shot? You loved me once, Lex. Found me attractive... exciting...' He trailed his fingertips over her hips. 'Sexy.'

'I did, but I don't now.' She pushed his hands away from her body.

'You might be able to again, if you just gave it a chance. Don't you think Connor deserves the opportunity to have his dad back in his life full-time?'

'No he fucking doesn't,' a voice growled. Daryl hastily moved aside, and Lexie saw that Connor had appeared in the doorway and was watching them with an irate look on his face.

'Jesus, kid,' Daryl said, patting his heart. 'You really need to stop sneaking up on people like that.'

'Yeah, you'd love that, wouldn't you? Get me out of the way.'

'Now, Connor—'

'Don't "now, Connor" me like I'm the one who's done something bad.' Connor shook his head. 'You know, Dad, I actually believed you this time. I really thought you meant it when you said it was me you were here for. Jesus Christ, I can't believe I was so stupid!'

'I am here for you.'

'Yeah? Then you remember my rules, right? My rules, that you agreed to and shook hands on? You promised you'd leave Lexie alone.'

'Your stepmother and I were just… having a discussion.'

'I'm not an idiot, Dad. I saw it all. I saw you touching her even after she asked you to stop, which everyone knows is a proper dick thing to do to girls. I heard you trying to use me as blackmail to get her to go back to you. That's sick, Dad!' His voice sank to an angry whisper. 'I'll never, ever believe a word you say to me again.'

'Connor, sweetie, calm down a little,' Lexie said gently.

'Why the fuck should I calm down?' Connor's cheeks were feverish, and he sounded like he was on the verge of tears. 'He *promised*, Lexie. He said he wanted to make it right with me but all he wanted was to use me to get you back. He doesn't care about me, or want me in his life – he doesn't even know me! He can't tell you a thing about me except that I like *Star Wars*, and that's only because he saw my posters. He doesn't know what my favourite food is, or the stuff I like to do, or even… or even that I'm bi.'

'Your favourite food's macaroni cheese.' Daryl frowned. 'Hang on, you're what?'

'I'm bi, Dad. Bisexual – you know what that means, right? They had that in whatever bit of the past you come from?'

'I know what it means, young man, thank you.'

'Yeah, well, finding that out's been a pretty major deal for me this year and you don't even know a thing about it. You don't know why me and Soph broke up, or that Oli's my boyfriend now—'

'Oli? Your best friend Oli who I met today?'

'He's not just my best friend. We're together, Dad. Like, dating. Maybe if you ever called to actually ask me about myself, if you even cared who I was any more, you might know some of this stuff.'

'I can't… Jesus, Connor.' Daryl turned to Lexie, his brow knitting into an enraged scowl. 'When the hell were you going to tell me all this then, Lex? My son's been going through this massive change that could affect his whole life and you didn't think I had a right to know about it?'

'No I didn't,' she said, frowning. 'Only Connor gets to decide when, or if, he wants to tell you something like that. I'm his mum, not your personal spy.'

'Except you're not his mum, are you, Lexie?' he countered, his face pale with anger. 'His mum's dead.'

'Lexie is too my mum!' Connor's fists had clenched so tight his knuckles had turned white. 'You throw that in her face every time you two fight, but she's been my mum since I was seven and loved me and everything, and I reckon that counts just as much as if she'd had me as a baby. Her and Theo have been more of a mum and dad to me than anything you've ever been. All you care about is yourself, and how to get the things you want. I wish Theo was my dad and not you. No wonder Lexie loves him more than she ever—'

He stopped, looking horrified at what he'd let slip.

'What?' Daryl turned to Lexie. '*What?*'

'Nothing,' she murmured. 'It's nothing, Daryl.'

'Theo? Theo's your… he's your lover? Christ, Lexie!'

'Daryl, just stay calm, can you?'

'So that's it! That's why you didn't want to know when I suggested giving us another chance. That… that backstabbing little *shit*! He's been round here screwing you every day since the day I left the country, hasn't he?'

'Now you're being ridiculous.'

'Or before, for all I know,' Daryl said, carrying on as if he hadn't heard her. 'That's why he strolls into my house like he owns the place: because he's been doing exactly the same thing to my wife. Fuck!' He shook his head. 'I should've known he'd try to get his revenge on me somehow for what happened with the restaurant. Not content with sleeping with my wife, he's managed to turn my son against me as well.'

'No, Daryl, because as hard as it might be to believe, this isn't actually about you,' Lexie snapped. 'This is about Theo and me. What we feel for each other.'

'Oh for fuck's sake, Lexie, don't be such a child!' he exploded. 'He's using you, can't you see that? All he ever wanted was to get back at me for this so-called Great Betrayal, and you were naive enough to open your legs for him. All his life Theo's been jealous of me. Oh, I bet he's so proud now he thinks he can finally *be* me.'

'He'd *never* want to be you!' Connor yelled. 'He's a better person than you'll ever be, Dad. He's not selfish like you, and he actually cares about me and Lexie. We were all happy until you came back.'

Daryl stared at him for a moment, silent and seething, his breath ragged.

'So he's completely poisoned your mind against me then, has he?' he said finally in a voice so low it was almost a whisper. 'I should've known there was a reason you were dead set against building any kind of relationship with me.'

'Right. Because it couldn't just be that you've been acting like a dick to me for most of my entire life.'

'And you,' Daryl growled, spinning to face Lexie. 'I trust you with my son and you do what? Bring another man into my home for sex? His godfather, no less – my oldest friend! Then you hide things from me, never saying a word while Connor's getting into fights and sleeping his way around his school friends, both male and female? What's next, letting him join a cult?'

Lexie shook her head in disgust. 'Sleeping his way around his school friends? Jesus, Daryl, what world are you in?'

'Well, I suppose it shouldn't surprise me that he's obsessed with sex, with the sort of example he's been set at home,' Daryl went on, ignoring her. 'I mean, Theo Blake, Lexie, Christ! You'd seriously talk about being in love with a man like that? He works his way through women like bloody penny sweets and he never has just one on the go at a time. Since we were sixteen he's been that way. You do know that, right?'

'You're wrong. Lexie's been a great mum to me,' Connor said, sticking out his chin. 'She's had to do everything on her own and even when I've been a total brat she's been there for me, and Theo too. They'd never give up on me, no matter what stupid shit I did. Those guys are my family now, not you.'

Even through her anger and panic, Lexie managed to flash him a fond smile.

'You would think that,' Daryl snapped. 'They've brain-washed you, Connor. Don't worry, I know it wasn't your fault.'

Connor rolled his eyes. 'Yeah, whatever. And where the hell were you while I was being "brainwashed" then? Because it wasn't fucking here.'

'I was trying to earn enough to make sure you had food, clothes, a home, that sort of minor thing. I'm sorry if living off my money all these years was so offensive to you both.'

Lexie went to Connor, who was visibly shaking with anger and hurt, and put a supportive arm around his waist. He put an arm around her too, and she took a deep breath to calm herself.

'Look, come on. Let's stop yelling and talk about this like civilised adults,' she said as evenly as she could manage.

'Oh, no. The time for talking's past.' Daryl marched forward and jerked Connor away from her by his elbow. 'Connor, go upstairs and pack a bag. We're going.'

Connor frowned. 'What? I'm not going anywhere with you.' He yanked his arm from his dad's grip. 'Don't you touch me, either.'

'Yes you bloody are, you're going to Manchester to stay in my flat. I'm not leaving you in this vipers' nest to have poison poured into your ears a second longer.'

'Daryl, don't be ridiculous,' Lexie said in a low voice. 'You know you can't take him against his will.'

'You think I can't take him, do you? He's my son, Lexie, and he's a child. I have every right to remove him from undesirable influences, both morally and legally, regardless of what he believes he wants. I'm acting in his best interests, which is more than you've been doing while you've been getting your cheap thrills riding Theo bloody Blake.'

Connor looked helplessly at Lexie. 'That isn't true, is it? He can't really force me to go with him?'

'No, it isn't true.' She gave him a squeeze. 'Don't worry, my love. You're not going anywhere.'

'He certainly is, unless you want me to get the police involved,' Daryl growled. 'You don't have a single legal right to stop me, Lexie; not one.'

'I've got a parental responsibility agreement.'

'That doesn't overrule my rights as his father. By law, he's got one parent only and it's me.'

'Daryl, this is cruel,' she said in a low voice. 'Please, you have to reconsider. He's distressed, look.' She nodded to Connor, who was pale and trembling, his eyes filled with tears. 'Is that really what you want, to cause your son even more pain? He's going back to school next week. Just calm down and we'll talk about it properly.'

'All right, on one condition,' Daryl said, his eyes narrowing.

She frowned. 'What condition?'

'You end whatever you've got going on with Theo. Right now.'

'What?' she whispered.

'I won't have him being a part of my son's life, not now I know what he's capable of. I want all ties severed between this household and that man or I'm removing Connor from its influence this minute.'

'Daryl, come on. This is childish and wrong: somewhere inside, you must know that.'

'I'm sorry but those are my terms.' He snatched her phone from the table and held it out to her. 'Go on. Let me hear you do it. Otherwise my next call, if you insist on obstructing my rights as Connor's father, will be to the police.'

Lexie looked at Connor, took in the helpless, frightened expression on his face, and bowed her head.

'OK,' she whispered, pressing her eyes closed. 'If that's what it takes... I'll do it.'

She reached for the phone but Connor put his hand on her arm.

'Please don't,' he said quietly. 'I really don't want you to do that.'

'Connor, I have to.'

'No. I won't let you, Lexie. You'd be sad forever and I'd know it was my fault.'

'Sweetie, nothing about this – *nothing* – is your fault.'

'I won't let you break up with Theo. It isn't right to make you do that.' He squared his shoulders, although his Adam's apple was bobbing with suppressed emotion. 'I'll... I'll go with Dad then. If that's what he wants.'

'Con, no,' Lexie said, shaking her head. 'I can't let you.'

'You don't have any choice,' Daryl said.

She turned to look at him, feeling more helpless than she ever had in her life.

'Daryl, please,' she whispered. 'I'm begging you not to do this dreadful thing. Don't take my boy from me. I'll do anything you want.'

'He never was yours, Lexie. I'm sorry, but you've proven yourself unfit to care for him and so I'm left with no choice but to remove him from your and your boyfriend's influence before any more damage is done.' Daryl clapped Connor on the back. 'I'm glad you've finally seen sense, lad. Go pack a bag and we can get the rest of your things sent on.'

'Can I say goodbye to Lexie?' Connor demanded. 'That's OK, isn't it?'

Daryl nodded. 'Go on.'

Connor put his arms around Lexie, who gave him a tight squeeze.

'Don't worry,' she whispered. 'I promise I'll get you home again. On my life, I promise. I'll see a lawyer as soon as I can.'

Connor let out a sob. 'I'll miss you loads.'

'I'll miss you too, my love. Ring me when you can, OK? We'll get this all sorted out, you'll see.'

'I wouldn't give the boy any false hopes if I were you,' Daryl said. 'Connor. Bag.'

Connor let Lexie go and flashed his father a look of pure, unadulterated hate before turning to trudge upstairs.

When he'd gone, Lexie snatched her phone from Daryl and pushed hard against his chest, making him stumble backwards.

'Of all the shitty things you've done to that boy, Daryl Carson, this is by far the worst,' she said in a low voice. 'Do not fucking think this is over, you son of a bitch. I'm going to throw everything I've got at this. I'm going to fight you every step of the way until my son is back at home with me where he belongs.'

Chapter Thirty-Three

'Are you ever going to take Table Four's bill over?' Claire asked Theo as she sailed past him with a tray of Woolton Pie.

'Hmm?'

'Table Four. She asked for her bill five minutes ago.' She stopped a moment to look at him. 'What's up with you anyway? You've been away with the fairies all evening.'

'Sorry, just… daydreaming. I'll sort it now.' Theo pulled his gaze away from the beer pump he'd been scowling at and rang up the bill for Table Four.

It had been a busy evening at the restaurant, packed with festival stragglers keen to keep the party going. Theo was glad they were down to the last few customers as the clock ticked towards seven p.m., closing time. He'd been struggling to concentrate ever since his fight with Lexie.

Bloody idiot that he'd been! Of course she was right. He'd been totally out of order to get jealous of Daryl like that. After all, what better way was there to convince the woman of your dreams that you're the one for her than by accusing her of wanting to be with another man, right? When Lexie had stormed off earlier, she'd really looked like she never wanted to see him again. Hell, he'd probably sent her straight into Daryl's arms with his pathetic insecurities.

The thought of it made his heart plunge. He knew he was doing it again, the exact thing that had driven her away, and yet there it still was: this childish, gnawing jealousy of his former friend, who was still lucky enough to be married to the woman Theo loved. And if she did decide to give Daryl another chance, where would that leave him? Without Lexie and Connor in his life, it felt like there was no point to anything any more.

He forced a smiled for the customer at Table Four as he put her bill down in front of her, although smiling was the last thing he felt like doing. Would she still tip if he burst into tears over her? She might offer him a Kleenex, at least.

'Sorry for the wait,' he said. 'Cash or card?'

'Card, please.'

He'd noticed the woman before, around the village. She was the sort of woman you would notice in Leyholme: tall and slender, very attractive and always immaculately dressed. Today she was in a sexy pencil dress with fishnet stockings, appropriate for a wartime pin-up girl, with her blonde hair fashioned into shining Veronica Lake waves.

She looked up at Theo through long lashes, smiling at him while he tapped at the card reader. So ingrained was his response to those sorts of signals from women, he almost found himself sending the appropriate body language back – until his brain overruled other parts of his anatomy and reminded him not to hold eye contact for too long.

'I like your costume,' she told him. 'You suit the navy.'

'RAF, actually. But thanks.' Ignoring the provocative little smile, he passed her the card reader. When she was done, he tore off her receipt and handed it to her.

'I did include a tip, but it doesn't seem enough when I know you must have been hard at work all day,' she said. 'Perhaps this might make up for it though.'

She took a pen from her handbag and scribbled something on the back of the receipt before handing it back to him.

'What's this?' he asked.

'What do you think it is? My name and phone number.' She followed his gaze to the ring on her third finger. 'Oh, don't worry about that, my divorce came through ages ago. I don't know why I still wear it – just used to feeling it on my finger, I suppose. Believe me, I'm one hundred per cent unattached and up for some fun.'

'Oh.' He stared at the phone number for a moment. 'Well, that's, er… that's very flattering' – he squinted at the writing – 'Jolene, but I'm… I won't be able to call you. I mean, I'd love to get to know you better, but, well, I can't. Sorry.'

'Oh. OK.' Jolene looked disappointed. 'You've got a girlfriend, have you? Or a boyfriend? Sorry, I shouldn't assume.'

'No. Yes. I mean, maybe.'

'What, aren't you sure?'

Theo was grateful to be interrupted by the ringing of the restaurant telephone.

'I have to get that.' He put the receipt with its scribbled phone number back on the table. 'Thanks again, Jolene, and… well, sorry.'

Claire had just beaten him to the phone as he approached the bar. She was frowning as she listened to whoever was on the other end speak.

'Whatever's wrong, love?' she was saying. 'Now, calm down, I can't understand you. Tell me again.' She paused. 'Theo? Yes, he's right here. Hang on.'

She covered the mouthpiece.

'It's Lexie,' she whispered. 'Theo, she's bawling her eyes out. I can barely make out what she's saying. All I can get out of her is that she wants you.'

He frowned. 'What? Here, pass it over.'

She handed it to him and left to start clearing tables.

'Lex, what's up?' he asked.

'Theo, he…' Lexie broke off with a shuddering sob. 'Theo, he… he's gone. He's gone, Theo.'

'Sweetheart, calm down a little. Who's gone where?'

'Manchester,' she gasped. 'He… took him. You have to come.'

Theo felt a dark foreboding settle on him.

'Who took who, Lex?' he asked in a low voice.

'Connor. Daryl took Connor. He took… took my boy. Help me. Please, you have to help me.'

Connor sat hunkered under the highsleeper desk-bed in the room his dad had put him in, hugging his knees. He'd only just stopped crying – not because he wanted to, but because he seemed to have run out of tears. Once his body had made a new load, he'd probably cry a bit more. It didn't help, but it made him feel like he was doing something to manifest his utter misery at the situation he found himself in.

What was going to happen to him? Lexie had said she'd get a lawyer, but then she'd have to go to court and that could take a long time, couldn't it? All he wanted was to go home, right now. This place – this bare, unfamiliar flat – felt far away and frightening, and his dad like a stranger who'd ripped him from everything he knew. Connor would never, ever forgive him for this, not if he lived to be a million. In three years he'd be eighteen, and after that he'd never see or speak to his father again for the rest of his life.

Daryl knocked gently on the door.

'Come on, Connor, come out,' he said. 'We need to talk.'

'I've got nothing to say to you,' Connor called back. He sniffed. 'I want to go home, Dad.'

'You are home.'

'This is not my home,' Connor snapped. 'My home's with Lexie.'

'You agreed to come with me.'

'Only because you told Lexie she'd have to break up with Theo, and I knew if she did that then she'd be sad forever. What, do you think you can blackmail me into coming here and then we'll just be mates? Don't you get that I hate you?'

'I didn't want you staying there. Lexie's let you down badly, bringing men into the house for sex when you were there, letting you get into fights and God knows what else – none of which she saw fit to tell me while happily living off the money I send her. I'm sorry, but it's obvious that I just can't trust her to be a parent to you.'

'It wasn't *men*, it was Theo. He's her boyfriend and she loves him, so I don't see what's wrong with that. You're jealous, that's all, because she picked him instead of you.'

'That's a very childish view to take, Connor. It was you I was looking out for.'

'Yeah, bullshit. You were thinking about yourself, same as always.'

'I promise you. You're at an impressionable age when it comes to your feelings – your sexual feelings in particular. It sounds as though you're very confused about a lot of things right now, and I don't think Lexie is either mature or responsible enough to help you deal with that.'

Connor frowned. 'You don't mean because I'm bi?'

'I'm sure you believe that, Connor, but I think now that you've been removed from an unhealthy influence at home...'

Connor snorted. 'What, I'll be cured, will I? Are you from the eighties or something?'

'I just mean that what you are – who you are – is often in a state of flux at your age. You need a parent who's able to guide you through that, not encourage you to indulge in all kinds of toxic experimentation.' He sighed. 'I should've realised Lexie was too young to cope with you at this age.'

'What? I haven't done anything toxic. That's bollocks, Dad.'

'Connor, I'm sure something like being bisexual sounds very cool and modern to you and your friends. It probably all seems like good fun at your age, but what you don't seem to realise is that it will affect your whole life,' Daryl said gently. 'The way people treat you, your opportunities, your health. I don't suppose Lexie has talked to you about any of this, has she? You need to think very carefully about whether this is what you really want.'

'It's got nothing to do with what I want, it's what I *am*. Don't you get that? This isn't some new hobby, Dad, it's me.'

'Well, we'll see about that. You're very young to be making a permanent decision on something so important. I think you might find that in a year or so, you'll feel differently.'

'Why, are you going to send me to one of those torture clinics where they electrocute you in the balls until you're fixed?'

'Don't be facetious, Connor.'

'Ugh, I don't even know what that means!'

'It means that this isn't something to joke about.'

Connor sniffed and rubbed his eyes. 'Aren't you going to let me see Lexie ever again?'

'Well, I'm not saying that,' Daryl said in a softer voice. 'She has been close to you for a long time, I suppose, despite her failings as a substitute for your mother. Once we're settled into a new routine, we can arrange some supervised visits.'

'Supervised by you, right?'

'That's right.'

'But not with Theo. I can't see him at all.'

'Absolutely not,' Daryl said firmly. 'Connor, can you come out of your room, or let me come in? I'm sick of having a conversation with a door.'

'All right, then sod off and don't bother,' Connor muttered. 'You know I hate you, right? That as soon as I'm eighteen, I'm never seeing you or speaking to you again as long as I live? I wish you were dead – or I was.'

'Now, you don't really mean that.'

'I fucking do. Are you going to give me my phone back or am I a prisoner in this shithole?'

'Yes, you're welcome to have it back now. I've got it here.'

Connor wiped his eyes and went to open the door a crack.

'Here you go,' his dad said, passing him the phone.

Connor frowned at it. 'What've you done to it then?'

'I've installed a parental filter. Just to block any undesirable numbers, messaging app contacts, that kind of thing.'

'You mean you've blocked Lexie and Theo.'

'For now. I'm sorry, Connor, but it's the only way. Perhaps tomorrow you can call Lexie on my phone, with the speaker on so I can hear what's being said.'

'Christ, this really is a prison,' Connor muttered. 'Can I at least have the Wi-Fi code for my laptop?'

'Of course. Once I've installed a filter on it.'

'For God's sake, just look at what you're doing, Dad! You're like the bloody Gestapo or something. This is so wrong, don't you see that?'

'I'm trying to keep you safe, Connor,' Daryl told him. 'Now, why don't you come sit in the living room and watch something on my tablet while I go out and get some food? I've got some more Monty Python. You'll love *Life of Brian*, it's the best thing they ever did.'

'Not a chance.' Connor thrust the phone into his pocket. 'This is the last time I'm ever going to speak to you, all right? You can force me to live here, but you can't force me to talk to you and you can't ever make me stop hating you.'

He closed the door in his father's face.

Chapter Thirty-Four

When Theo had hung up, Lexie threw aside her phone and fell back onto Connor's bed, giving in to the gasping sobs she could no longer control.

For the first hour after Daryl had walked out with Connor, a deathly calm had settled on her. She'd tried to stay focused. First, she'd done an internet search for solicitors specialising in family law, but the legalese on their websites had made her already aching head spin. The repeated phrase she kept coming across on different family law sites – 'a stepparent has no legal custody rights' – made her feel sick to her stomach.

Eventually she decided that hiring a lawyer was something she would have to come back to when she'd spoken to those of her friends who might be able to advise her. Desperately needing to be doing something practical, she'd gone up to Connor's room to pack some of his things for the hopefully short period he'd be staying with his dad. Useful things, but things that might give him comfort too. Things to remind him of home, and of her.

She'd been fine, still in calm and practical mode, until she'd gone to his bookshelf. On it she found an old storybook that had belonged to Lexie as a child. She'd taken it out to put in Connor's case, but instead found herself staring at it, stroking it; remembering.

It had been her first gift to the little boy after she'd started seeing Daryl, when she'd discovered to her shock that her new boyfriend never read to his son. That ought to have been a wake-up call, but the young Lexie had just told herself it was Daryl's grief that prevented him from reading to Connor. Perhaps Elise had done the bedtime story, and Daryl found it too painful, now, to take over the role. So Lexie had taken over it instead, filling Elise's place everywhere but in Daryl's heart, just as she was to do throughout their marriage.

She turned the book over. The story titles on the back made her lip quiver as she remembered reading each of them to the shy, trusting little curly-haired boy she'd found in her care. 'Todd the Naughty Farm Cat' had been Connor's favourite: the one he'd ask for over and over until he could tell her the story from memory without even needing to open the book. 'The Dragon Who Loved Ice Cream' had been another favourite, and any of the ones with magic and wizards, of course.

But still Lexie had held back her tears, until she'd opened the book and seen the inscription there.

> *For Connor. I hope these stories make you as happy as*
> *they made me when I was as small as you are. Sunshine*
> *for my sunbeam! Lots of love always, Lexie xxx*

Underneath, little Connor had crayoned a drawing: a couple of stick figures holding hands, one tall with a scribble of yellow hair, the other small, curly-topped and grinning. When she'd first seen it, Lexie had thought it was a picture of Connor and Elise. It wasn't though: she knew that now. Elise's hair had been brown and wavy, like her son's. The woman in the picture wasn't Connor's mother. It was her.

That was when the tears came. That was when Lexie had collapsed onto the bed and hidden her face in the pillow, paralysed by hyperventilating sobs for a good ten minutes before, with a trembling hand, she managed to call Theo at the restaurant.

By the time she heard him walk in, she'd managed to get her tears under control enough to at least breathe properly, although hiccuping sobs still racked her body.

'Up here,' she called to him. 'In Connor's room.'

He bounded up the stairs and within seconds she was in his arms, sobbing into his chest while he soothed her.

'Sweetheart, what happened?' he asked.

'He… he took my Connor. He found out about us and… Jesus, Theo, he's had some temper tantrums in his day but this was off the chart. When he knew me and you were together, it just brought on this insane jealous rage. He threatened to call the police if I didn't let him take Connor away with him. Said it was his right as a parent.'

'Seriously? I can't believe the police would make Connor go with Daryl against his will.'

'He never actually called them. He sounded so sure they'd be on his side though,' Lexie murmured. 'He said I don't have a single legal right when it comes to Connor and he's right, isn't he? I'm not his mum, in law or in fact. A parental responsibility agreement isn't an adoption and it doesn't give me any rights in the event of an acrimonious separation – that's what the family law sites I've been looking at say. Everything I've ever been to Connor has been dependent on Daryl's goodwill.'

'You're Connor's mum in practice, if not in law.' Theo shook his head angrily. 'What the hell does Daryl think he's playing at? Christ, I know he can have a mean streak a mile wide when he's got a monk on but this is fucking abhorrent. Poor Con must be terrified, being dragged from his home like that.' He looked at her. 'How did Daryl find out about us anyway?'

'Connor let it slip,' she whispered. 'He didn't mean to. He was angry when he caught his dad… caught him touching me.'

Theo frowned. 'Touching you?'

'Yes, he was holding me – well, he was trying to. I'd told him there was no reconciliation on the cards but he wouldn't take no for an answer. When Con thought his dad was just using him to get me back, he flew right off the handle.'

'I don't blame him. Bastard!'

She looked up at him. 'Theo… Daryl asked me to choose.'

'What, between me and him?'

'No, between you and Connor. He said he'd let Con stay if I broke it off with you.' She lowered her voice to a whisper. 'And I agreed. I'm sorry. Connor was so afraid, and... well, I'm his mum. First and foremost, it's my job to protect him. Do you forgive me?'

Theo was silent for a moment, looking down into her tear-swollen face.

'Theo?' Lexie said.

'Don't be daft. That's not something I need to forgive you for,' he said softly. 'I'd have been shocked if you'd behaved any differently. I know you'd do anything for that boy. It's one of the many reasons I love you.' He planted a tender kiss on her forehead. 'Do you forgive me?'

'What for?'

'For being a jealous prick. For not trusting you like I obviously ought to do.' He held her tighter and blinked back a tear. 'Lexie, sweetheart, I really thought I'd lost you today.'

'Lost me?' She leaned back to look into his face. 'Why would you think that?'

'Well, you were so angry, and then you said goodbye like that and stormed off...'

'That's just a fight, Theo. All couples have fights. Not every argument is a break-up.'

'No. That was... naive of me.' He frowned. 'Hang on. If you agreed to break up with me, why did Daryl still take Connor?'

She lowered her head. 'Con wouldn't let me go through with it,' she whispered. 'He said he'd rather go with his dad than let me do something he knew would break my heart. Not in those exact words, but that was the gist of it.'

'God, did he?' Theo swallowed a sob. 'That kid.'

'I know.'

Theo's gaze landed on a photo of the three of them – himself, Lexie and Connor – in a frame on Connor's desk. Con must've been about nine at the time it was taken, his big brown eyes full of fringe. He was grinning as he stood between them, clutching a bucket and spade and some sort of giant teddy Theo remembered winning for him at the funfair.

'I remember this trip,' he said, smiling as he reached for it. 'It's sweet that he keeps it in his room.'

'He must've put it there recently. I never noticed it before.' Lexie frowned and took it from him. 'Hang on.'

'What?'

'I know this photo. The guy who ran the donkeys took it for us.'

'So?'

She opened the frame to take out the photograph. Part of it had been folded back – the part that showed Daryl, standing on her other side.

'Con folded him out of the picture,' she muttered as she smoothed it out.

She glanced around the room. There was another framed photo of Lexie with Connor on the day he was invested at Cubs, looking proud in his uniform. The one on the bookcase showed him as a toddler wearing a Christmas-cracker hat, being cuddled by his mum and Tonya. But there wasn't a single family photo that included his father.

Theo sighed. 'Poor messed-up kid. What can we do, Lexie? Have you got a solicitor?'

'Not yet, but I'm going to get one,' she said, her brow knitting. 'Will you help me find one? I've got no idea what the hell I need but I want legal advice ASAP.'

'Of course I will,' he said gently, brushing his fingers over her cheek.

'I bookmarked a few family law websites earlier. They all say stepparents have no automatic custody rights but it must be different for me, surely. I brought him up as his mother and I've had pretty much total parental responsibility for him since Daryl left the country. That has to count for something.' She pressed her throbbing temples. 'Oh God, why didn't I legally adopt him after I married his dad? Daryl always said he couldn't

303

see the point, but... shit, I should've seen a lawyer about this years ago. It's all my fault, Teddy.'

'Come on. That type of talk isn't going to get our boy home, is it? Now, did you find any relevant case studies on these websites?'

'There was one that wasn't dissimilar to my situation. Hang on.'

Lexie wiped her eyes and took out her phone, instantly feeling if not better, then at least like she was moving things forward. Everything seemed easier with Theo there. The sense of despair that had settled on her when Connor had walked out shrank ever so slightly.

She pulled up a website and handed Theo the phone. 'See, here's a case where a man was denied access to his little stepdaughter by his ex-wife, even though he'd provided the majority of the childcare. In the end, a court granted him the same visitation rights as the girl's biological father. Not custody, but I do think in my case they'd surely consider it, since I've raised him alone for so long. There's something called a Child Arrangements Order that can grant custody to a stepparent. They're rare but they do exist.'

Theo skimmed the text. 'This stepfather was only granted access after a lengthy legal battle, though. God knows what it cost him to fight it.'

Lexie stuck out her chin. 'I don't care about that. I'll sell the car, my half of the restaurant, release equity from my share of the house, get a loan – whatever it takes. I'll bankrupt myself before I'll let that bastard take my son.'

'But it could take ages to get a court order, Lex – years, maybe.'

'No. Con needs to come home.' She pondered for a moment. 'Surely we can make a strong case, can't we? I mean, it's not just about my relationship with him: his life's here. His friends, his boyfriend, his school, his community. Not to mention that he wants to be here – it's already causing him distress to be ripped from his home, and at fifteen he's close enough to an adult that his views should be taken into account. Surely any judge will take my side like a shot.'

'Hmm. You'd hope so, but… well, Daryl's bound to hire a pretty hotshot solicitor.'

'It can't be hopeless. It can't.' She clutched at his arm. 'I mean, for Christ's sake, he's my son, Theo! They can't just take him away from me. Sod the law, I'm talking about fucking basic humanity here. It's… monstrous.'

'I know.' Theo sat in silence a moment, his brow furrowed in thought. 'Lex, what did Daryl actually say when he found out about us?'

'Oh God, he was like a caveman. The words "my wife" featured frequently, as if you'd stolen a valuable bit of property from him rather than me actually having any sort of decision-making capability. He told me I was a fool to believe you cared about me, given your track record with women, and that obviously you were just using me to get him back for what happened with Bistrot Alexandre. Oh, and he said we were irresponsible sex maniacs setting a bad example to Connor and deliberately trying to turn him against his father.' She sighed. 'I guess he'll use the sex thing in any legal case, make it sound like something really seedy. We'd have to come clean about our pre-commitment FWB arrangement. That won't look good if Daryl decides to present me as some sort of nymphomaniac swinger intent on corrupting the morals of youth. And then there's my age, the fact I'm only—'

'Lexie. Shh.' Theo silenced her with a kiss. 'If you dwell on stuff like that, you'll only work yourself up into a panic. Let's keep practical, all right?'

'Yes.' She took a deep breath. 'Yes. Thanks, Theo.'

'So. Our goal is to get Connor home, as quickly as possible.'

'Right.'

'If we seek legal advice, we've got a strong case but it could take a long time to fight a custody battle, and potentially cost more than we can afford.'

'We?'

'Of course, we,' he said, kissing her again. 'Anything I've got, financial or otherwise, I'm ready to throw at this alongside you.'

She summoned a weak smile. 'Thanks, love. So what do you think our best course of action is?'

He was silent for a moment.

'Lex, before Daryl flew into a temper, were you still convinced he meant it when he said he wanted to make things up to Connor?' he asked at last.

'Well, yes.'

'And now what do you think? Was it all a charade to win you back or what?'

'I think...' She paused. 'I still believe his main intention in coming here was genuinely to fix his relationship with his son. Connor thought Daryl was just using him to get to me, but I'm certain it was the other way round: that he wanted to give our marriage another go so we could be a family, for Connor's sake. That's why he was so persistent in pressing for a reconciliation – for his son, not because he still has strong feelings for me.'

'You really believe that?'

'Yes. I know Daryl can be selfish, but this time... I was married to that man for years, Theo. I know him. There was something in his expression, when he talked about Connor and about Elise, that makes me think he really wanted to be a father again. Then he saw red and threw away all the progress he'd made by being a jealous, possessive wanker, as usual.'

'Right.' Theo passed back her phone. 'In that case, I think the logical course of action is to try to reason with him. If underneath the anger he really does have his son's interests at heart, then that's our best bet for getting Connor home again.'

'What, so you think I should skip the lawyer and try talking to him first?'

'No. I think I should try talking to him.'

She frowned. 'You? But he hates you.'

'Exactly. That's what this is all about. He threw a paddy not because he found out you were seeing someone else: it's because he found out you were seeing me. I'm the only one with any chance of making him bin the Othello act and see sense.'

'I don't know, Theo. If he thinks you're rubbing your relationship with me in his face, it might just make things worse. I don't want to jeopardise any legal case we go on to make.'

'Trust me, it needs to be me. I've known Daryl Carson a long time and I really think I can get through to him on this.' His gaze fell on the seaside photo, with the fold down the picture clearly showing where Connor had tried to remove his dad from the family group. 'Anyway, who's better placed to talk about fractured father–son relationships than I am?'

'He won't answer the phone to you.'

'No, but he'll answer the door. I'm going to sit outside that bloody flat of his until he opens up, and I'm not leaving until I've made him hear what I've got to say.'

Chapter Thirty-Five

Theo took a deep breath before knocking on the door of the flat at the address Lexie had given him.

He didn't know how his former friend was going to react to him turning up out of the blue but he was guessing, not well. He'd told Lexie he felt he had the best chance of appealing to Daryl's better nature, but first they had a lot to deal with – Theo's still simmering anger about his old friend's betrayal, for one thing, and of course the not insignificant fact that Daryl had recently discovered Theo was sleeping with his wife.

Theo didn't actually know what he was going to say to Daryl to get through to him; only that this was something he needed to do. Lexie and Connor needed him now like never before and letting them down simply wasn't an option. He didn't have any sort of neat little speech prepared, but he did have a lifetime's supply of daddy angst and a couple of props. All he could do was pray that would be enough.

Theo held his breath as the door opened.

'Hello, can I – oh shit, it's you.'

Daryl made to slam the door but Theo jammed it with his palms, leaning his full weight against it.

'Don't,' he said in a low voice. 'I'm only here to talk, Daryl.'

'Well he doesn't want to talk to you, and I'm sure as hell not letting you anywhere near him, so you can just fuck off home again.'

'I'm not here to talk to Connor, I'm here to talk to you.'

Daryl shook his head. 'So she sent you, did she? Realised she couldn't afford the sort of legal help she needs to fight this and sent you here to threaten me. Yeah, nice try, Theo. If you think I can be intimidated into giving up my son, you really don't know me at all.'

He gave the door another push, but Theo held it hard.

'No one sent me and I'm not going to make any threats,' he said. 'I just want to have a conversation, one old friend to another.'

Daryl snorted. 'Friend, that's a laugh. How long did you wait after the wedding until you jumped into bed with my wife? Was it going on while I was still in the house? No, don't answer that, I don't want to know.' He shook his head. 'I should've known better than to trust you around any woman of mine. Just couldn't help yourself, could you? Always thinking with your cock, just like when we were kids.'

'Oh, you're really going to try the injured friend routine, are you, after the way you screwed me over with the bistro?'

'Yeah, and you had to have your revenge, didn't you? Regardless of who might get hurt in the process. I knew you were a selfish, feckless womaniser, Theo, but I never believed you were fucking petty enough to target Lexie. I thought you had more respect for her than that.'

'It wasn't revenge, Daryl. I love her. More than you ever did.'

Daryl laughed. 'Yeah, till the next one comes along. You've never been in love in your life.'

'You don't know a thing about what I feel for Lexie so you can just—' Theo stopped himself and took a measured breath. 'Look, I'm sorry. I didn't come here to fight. Just let me in and we'll have a civilised conversation like the two grown men we are, eh?'

'Not a chance.' Daryl finally managed to give the door a powerful enough shove to break Theo's hold and slammed it shut.

'Daryl!' Theo called through it.

There was silence, but Theo knew Daryl was still there, hovering, waiting to see if he'd leave. He'd been prepared for this. He crouched down and slid something under the door.

Everything was quiet, then the door opened a crack.

'What's this then?' Daryl muttered.

'It's a photo. You remember that weekend we hired a caravan up in Morecambe, the four of us? You managed to maintain your record of holiday misadventures by getting bitten on the arse by a donkey while this picture was being taken.'

'Why's it been folded like that? There's a big crease between me and Lexie.'

'Connor made it,' Theo said. 'He had it in a frame in his room, only you were folded out of the picture. Out of the family.'

Daryl scowled. 'Because you and Lexie have been poisoning him against me.'

'No, Daryl. Hard as this might be for you to believe, as angry as I've been with you for the last eighteen months, I've never said a word against you in Connor's hearing. Nor has Lexie. The fold you're looking at entirely represents Connor's own feelings based on your treatment of him.'

Daryl was silent, frowning down at the photo, but he didn't try to close the door again. Theo followed up on his advantage.

'You know who Connor was talking to on the phone before your Monty Python breakthrough last night?' he asked.

'You?'

'Yes, me. I was the one who convinced him he ought to hear what you had to say. I told him he'd regret it one day if he didn't at least give you a chance to make things up to him.'

'Why the hell would you do that?'

Theo gave a little half-smile. 'Do you know what the last thing I ever said to my dad was, Daryl?'

'What?'

'"Fuck you." Those were pretty much the last words I ever spoke to him, and he wasn't even alive to hear them. Standing at his graveside, this total stranger who'd created me and broken my mum, and all I had left for him was a curse.' He looked into Daryl's eyes. 'Do you want that to be Connor?'

'No,' Daryl whispered, still staring at the photo. 'I just... want to do what's best for him.'

'And so do I. So does Lexie. When we let our emotions about each perceived wrong we've done one another control us, it's Connor who gets hurt. If you've really got his welfare at heart and you're not just trying to score some petty points against me and Lexie, then we ought to be able to discuss this like civilised human beings. Let me in, eh?'

'Yes. I suppose... all right, you can come in for a minute.' Cautiously, Daryl held open the door. 'This doesn't mean he's going back with you.'

'Never mind that. Let's just talk a few things out, shall we?'

Theo followed Daryl to a small open-plan living room and kitchen, still bare and full of cardboard boxes.

'Not much room, is there?' he observed.

'Well it was supposed to be a bachelor pad. I hadn't expected Connor to be coming to live with me.' Daryl gestured to a box and Theo sat down on it. 'Anyway, it's only for the time being. Now I've got Connor I'll start looking for somewhere a bit bigger, closer to his school. I don't want to interrupt his education this close to his exams.'

Theo bit his tongue for the moment. It wasn't the time yet to talk about bringing Connor home. They had things to discuss first.

'Look, shall we get our issues out of the way before we start talking about Connor?' he said. 'I think we need to if we're going to dial down the tension.'

'You slept with my wife,' Daryl muttered.

'And you lost me my business. That makes us even, don't you think?'

Daryl scowled. 'So it was revenge.'

'It was no such thing. You really think I'd use Lexie as a pawn like that?'

'Well, what then?'

'It wasn't going on when you were still living together, I promise you. I'm not a complete bastard,' Theo said. 'We've only been together four months.' He decided now wasn't the time to start a discussion with his girlfriend's husband about whether their arrangement prior to three weeks ago constituted being 'together' or not.

Daryl flinched. 'I'm not sure I want to hear this.'

'You don't still have feelings for her, do you?' Theo asked in a gentler voice.

'Perhaps. At least, I thought we had a shot at making it work. The reasons our marriage crumbled, Elise and how I was then... maybe I'm not fully healed yet, but I'm at least aware of the mistakes I made before. I thought we could try to be a family again — a happy one this time.' He glared at Theo. 'I didn't realise you'd already swooped in to take my place.'

'We keep talking about places like there's only one to spare, but there can be room for both of us. There's no reason Connor can't have a bond with you and with me. Lexie's right, we're not bloody gorillas.'

'How did you two end up together then?'

'Well it wasn't planned,' Theo admitted. 'I'd never really thought about Lex in that way — at least, not since that night we both met her. Then Connor was going through a tough patch. He needed us both to support him through it, emotions started to creep in, and... well, long story short, we fell for each other.'

'This tough patch of Connor's: it was to do with that boyfriend of his, right?'

'The relationship with Oli's very recent. At the time he was just trying to get his head around this new thing he'd discovered about himself.'

Daryl shook his head. 'I should've been told about that.'

'No, Daryl, you shouldn't. Connor's not a little kid, he's a young adult. It's not a case of being told things about him, it's a case of having mature conversations with him until he feels like he wants to confide in you.' Theo shrugged. 'Perhaps he felt you wouldn't take it well. Not every parent does.'

'I didn't take it very well,' Daryl said, rubbing his ear. 'I'm not a bigot — I hope I'm not — but it was... a surprise. When

I thought about all the problems it could cause for him when he's older, the prejudice he might experience, whether he'd still have kids of his own... well, I ought to have dealt with it better.'

'It's not something he's chosen, Daryl, it's something he is. You get that, don't you?'

He sighed. 'I don't know. If he'd told me he was gay I could get my head around that, but the bisexuality thing... I've not had much cause to think about it before. Perhaps I'm not as progressive as I ought to be, but it really was Connor I was thinking of.' He fell silent. 'You know, I really thought this therapy programme was changing me as a person. Helping me find the way back to the man I was before I lost Elise. But when Connor told me about you and Lexie, I just lost control. The anger was still there, waiting to be triggered, and I let it take over me entirely. I think... I've still got a long way to go.' He looked at the photo he was holding, staring at the crease that separated him from the rest of the family. 'Connor told me that once he turns eighteen, he'll never speak to me again.'

'It doesn't have to be that way,' Theo said quietly. 'If we work together, the three of us, we can make things right.'

Daryl was silent, gazing at the photo. Feeling he was nearly at his goal, Theo took Connor's old storybook from the satchel he was carrying.

'Remember this?' he said, showing it to Daryl.

He smiled slightly. 'I remember. Lexie gave it to him, not long after we met. There was a cat called Tim or Tom or something that he was always chattering to me about.'

'He took to her right away, didn't he?'

'I suppose that was only natural, when he missed his mum. Lex was warm and kind, and he needed love so badly. God knows I was no bloody use to him.'

Theo opened the book at the title page and passed it to Daryl so he could see Connor's scribbled drawing.

'Lexie,' Daryl murmured. 'Connor drew this?'

'Yes, back when he was still biting ankles. Him and her.'

'But not me.' He sighed. 'He really did love her.'

'And still does. She's his mum, Daryl,' Theo said. 'You know she's done nothing but sob hysterically since you walked out with him? She loves that boy just as much as if he were hers – as much as Elise would if she were here. She's never done anything but love him and try to do right by him.'

'Yes. Yes, I know she loves him.' He looked at Lexie's inscription and blinked a couple of times. 'I was grateful to her for the way she looked after him, but it hurt too, seeing how quickly she took his mum's place. I half resented her for it – and Connor – even though I knew that was illogical. It felt like an insult to Elise's memory, how soon she was replaced.'

'Yet it was your decision to marry again so soon after her death.'

'Yes,' Daryl said, half to himself. 'There was a hole in the family. In me. I thought I could fill it with Lexie, but it was too soon. All I did was end up hating myself and resenting my wife and child. The guilt was worse than the grief.'

'You never did replace Elise with Lexie, you know,' Theo said softly. 'Connor hasn't forgotten his mum. He talks about her all the time, and Lexie encourages him to hold on to his memories. It's like me and you. There isn't a quota on how many people you can love, Daz.'

Daryl looked up in surprise when he heard the old nickname. 'Never thought I'd hear you call me that again.'

'Well, then you thought wrong.' Theo held out his hand. 'Go on.'

Daryl hesitated for a moment before shaking it. 'I'm sorry. I was wrong to react the way I did, and to say what I said to Lexie. I do believe she always did her best for the boy.'

'Yes she did. Connor's wellbeing has been number one with her since the day she married you.'

'It was cruel to take him, wasn't it?' Daryl muttered, half to himself. 'God, the pain in his eyes... all I could feel was this overpowering resentment, that Lexie had turned my boy away from me and filled my place with someone else.' He looked up at Theo. 'Is it too late, do you think?'

'It's never too late when we make up our minds to do better,' Theo said quietly. 'Go to him now. Talk to him, explain what you were feeling. Then I'll take him home to his mum, eh?'

'Yes. That's the right thing to do, isn't it? Thanks, Theo.'

Daryl went out to knock on the door of Connor's room. Theo picked up the storybook again, smiling at the little boy's drawing.

He frowned as Daryl came back in, looking pale. 'What's up?'

'It's Connor,' he whispered. 'He's gone.'

Chapter Thirty-Six

'Where are you going to, my love?' the kind-looking woman in the ticket office at Manchester Piccadilly asked Connor.

'Leeds,' he said. 'How much does a ticket cost please? A single, not a return. I'm not coming back here again, not ever.'

'Have you got a young person's railcard?'

'Um, well, I've got this.' Connor handed her the discount travel card he used to get to school and back.

The woman glanced at it. 'Oh, I'm sorry. This is only valid in West Yorkshire. It's no good here, I'm afraid.' She frowned at the card, then glanced up at his tear-swollen face, half hidden by his hoodie. 'You're a long way from home on your own, duckie. How old are you?'

'Er, eighteen. I've been to a… college open day. How much does it cost without a pass please?'

'Leeds… now, let's see.' She tapped something into her computer. 'That'll be seventeen pounds twenty for a seat on the next service.'

'What? But I've only got ten!'

'I'm sorry, I'm afraid that's what it costs for a standard ticket.'

'Well… is there a cheaper train I can get?'

'If you wait a couple of hours, I can find you an economy seat for ten pound thirty on the Hull train. That stops at Leeds.' She lowered her voice. 'I'm sure my boss would say I shouldn't be telling you this, but if you're strapped for cash then the coach is your best bet. It takes a little longer but the tickets are cheaper. The 962 goes from the coach station in about half an hour, I think. That's only a ten-minute walk from here.'

'You're going to Leeds, did you say?' a voice from behind Connor asked.

He turned to see who'd spoken. A man, pleasant-looking and quite young, was sipping a coffee at a nearby Costa.

'Er, yeah,' Connor said.

'I'm driving to Leeds this evening myself, as it happens. You're welcome to cadge a lift. No charge except some conversation.' The man spotted the wary look on Connor's face and laughed. 'What, eighteen and you've never hitch-hiked before? Come on, kid, have an adventure.'

'Well, duck, do you want this ticket for the Hull train or not?' the ticket office lady asked. 'There's a queue behind you.'

'Um, no. Sorry. Thanks for your help anyway.' Connor left the queue and went to join the young man at his table.

–

Daryl hung up the phone. 'Well, my mum and dad haven't heard from him and nor has Tonya. Any joy getting him on his mobile? He's more likely to answer to you than me.'

Theo shook his head. 'I just get an engaged tone. Maybe he's talking to Lexie.'

'Oh. No, of course.' Daryl rubbed his temples. 'You won't be able to get through to him, or Lexie either. I blocked your numbers.'

'What? For Christ's sake, Daryl! He's out there on his own and you've cut off his lifeline to—' Theo took a deep breath, forcing himself calm. 'Well, never mind, we don't have time for that. We need to work together.'

'Yes. Right. I'll try him.'

Daryl called Connor's number, but quickly hung up again.

'It rang for a second then went dead. Someone switched it off, I think,' he said in a low voice. 'Shit, Theo, you don't think he's got into any trouble, do you?'

'He's a sensible lad. He knows better than to put himself in danger,' Theo said. 'He'll be trying to get back home to Lexie.

When could he have slipped out? You were here in the flat the whole time, weren't you?'

'Apart from fifteen minutes when I went out to the deli.'

'Well, that must've been when he ran for it. When was that?'

'About an hour and a half ago. Does he know Manchester?'

'Pretty sure he's never been here apart from to go to the Arndale with Lex.' He glanced at the phone in Daryl's hand. 'I think... I think you'd better call the police, Daz.'

'Will they treat him as a missing person this soon?'

'Surely they'll do something when it's a kid. He's vulnerable, he's probably broke and he's out there in a strange city at night, alone. We can't take any chances.'

Theo watched as his friend dialled 999 and furnished the police with a description of Connor and the situation they were in.

'They're going to put out an alert on social media and notify all officers in the area to be on the lookout for him,' Daryl said when he'd hung up. 'What should we do? Wait here and see if he comes back or go out looking for him?'

'Get out there and try to find him before he gets into trouble, definitely,' Theo said. 'I guess he'll be heading for a train or bus that could take him to Halifax. Is there a station near here?'

'Manchester Piccadilly isn't far.'

Theo glanced at the phone in his hand. 'Should we tell Lexie?'

'Let's try the station first. Hopefully we'll find him there safe and sound and there'll be no need to worry her.'

'Right.' Theo grabbed his jacket. 'Let's go.'

–

'Just here in the NCP,' Connor's new friend David said as Connor followed him down the narrow streets to his car. 'Costs a bomb but what can you expect in a big city, right?'

'Right.'

'You don't drive, I'm guessing?'

'No,' Connor said. 'I'm, er, learning.'

'What brings you to Manc then? Open day, did you say?'

'Yeah. I'm… looking at courses. You know, now that I've left school.'

'You won't believe me but you will miss it,' David told him, smiling. 'Funny thing about school: feels like hell when you're there, but you spend the rest of your life wishing you could go back.'

'So how come you're going to Leeds?'

'I've got a friend up there who's having a house party tonight. I'm just back from a business trip to London so I wasn't going to go, but when I heard you say you were heading in that direction it seemed like a sign I should get off my arse and make the effort. You're welcome to come along if you want; should be pretty wild. Always plenty of sex, drugs and banging tunes at his bashes.'

'Thanks, but, um, I need to get somewhere.'

'Sure. Course you do.' He glanced sideways at Connor. 'So you got a girlfriend then, kid? Or a boyfriend maybe?'

'Yeah, a boyfriend. Oli.'

'Well, he's a lucky lad.' David nodded to a silver Prius parked in one of the bays. 'Here we are then. Climb in.'

–

'You're sure you haven't had any kids here buying a one-way ticket to Halifax?' Daryl demanded of the woman in the Piccadilly ticket office.

'I told you, love. No Halifax tickets bought today.'

'You're positive? You remember every single ticket you've sold, do you?'

The woman frowned. 'Look, you can ask as many times as you like, it won't make the answer any different. I can see right here on the computer: no Halifax tickets.'

'Here, get out of the way.' Theo elbowed Daryl aside to talk to the woman, managing, even through his panic, to summon the smile that always worked when he needed to launch a charm offensive. 'Sorry about my companion here, he doesn't mean to be rude. He's just worried. We're looking for his son, he's run away from home.'

'Oh dear,' the woman said, her brow furrowing. 'Are you a policeman then?'

'Er, no, I'm a godfather.'

The woman blinked. 'Oh. Well, like I said, there've been no Halifax tickets bought from this station today. I'm sorry I can't be more help.'

'What about from the other windows, or the machines?'

'They all go onto the central system here. The last ticket to Halifax was sold two days ago.'

Daryl nudged him. 'Come on, we're wasting our time. Let's go.'

'Hang on.' Theo turned back to the ticket-seller. 'Listen, the kid we're looking for is called Connor, Connor Carson. Fifteen years old, six foot tall, curly brown hair, brown eyes... probably wearing a hoodie with a superhero of some kind on the front.'

'The Flash,' Daryl muttered. 'It was red and it had a yellow lightning bolt on it.'

'Oh!' Theo produced the photo of their family trip to More-cambe and passed it through the hatch. 'This is him, when he was a lot smaller. I've got a recent pic on my phone if you just wait a second...'

He started fumbling for his mobile as the woman took the photo, frowning.

'No, that's all right. I recognise this boy,' she said. 'He said he was eighteen.'

'Well, he isn't. Do you know what train he caught?'

'He wanted tickets for the Leeds train but he didn't have the fare. I told him he ought to try the coach if he wanted to get there any cheaper.'

Daryl frowned. 'Leeds? Why Leeds? He lives near Halifax.'

'I can't answer that, I'm afraid,' the woman said as she handed Theo back the photo. 'Sorry.'

'Thank you, that's a big help,' Theo said. 'You don't happen to know which coach he might have gone for, do you?'

'Oh, he didn't get the coach in the end. A young man overheard him trying to get tickets and offered him a lift.'

Theo frowned. 'What? He... you're not saying he left here with a stranger? Christ, he's a kid!'

'Shit,' Daryl whispered. '*Shit!*'

The woman looked faintly guilty. 'Well, if I'd known his real age then perhaps I might have said something, but at eighteen, what was I supposed to do? He said he was an adult and it's not my job to babysit customers.'

'No.' Theo forced a smile, willing himself calm so he could get the information he knew they needed. 'Of course it isn't. Can you describe this man he went with?'

'Well yes, he was... I'd suppose about twenty-five, with red hair and one of those bushy lumberjack beards the young people all seem to wear now. He had a tattoo on the back of his hand – a dolphin, I think – and he was wearing grey chinos and a blue-and-white-checked shirt.'

'Thank you.'

'I do hope you find your son soon. He was a lovely, polite boy.'

'I bloody hope we do too,' Daryl muttered. 'Theo, come on.'

–

'What do we do now?' Daryl asked when they were outside. 'Jesus, what could he have been thinking, getting into a car with a stranger?'

Theo flinched. 'Shit. This is... this is bad. Right, we need to stay calm and make a plan. I think you'd better call the police and give them the description of this guy he went with. Then... well, we can either sit in your flat and wait for news or try to work out where he's going.'

'If he gets there. God knows what this guy's motive is for offering him a lift.'

'Christ, don't say that. He'll be OK. He has to be OK.' Theo glanced at the family photo he still had in his hand. 'We'd better tell Lexie, hadn't we?'

'We'll have to, now. If the police put his picture on social media and she sees it, it's going to send her into a fit. You can call her from the car. I'll drive, I know the way.'

'Where are we going?'

'Leeds.'

Theo shook his head. 'I don't get it. Why Leeds and not Halifax? Con doesn't know anyone in Leeds, does he?'

'He knows one person,' Daryl muttered. 'I think I know where he's trying to get to. Let's just hope we find him when we get there.'

Chapter Thirty-Seven

'Look, try to stay calm, Lex,' Theo said in his gentlest voice. 'I'm sure he's OK. Daryl and me are on the case now, we'll ring you as soon as we know anything. Love you, all right?' He ended the call.

'How did she take it?' Daryl asked.

'God, she was half out of her mind with worry. Tonya's with her now so at least she's not alone. When I told her we'd called the police… I just bloody hope we find Con at this place, that's all.'

'You didn't tell her about this hipster bloke who offered to drive him, I noticed.'

'No. She was already borderline hysterical, I didn't think she needed anything else to worry her. I mean, it's easy to assume the worst but he might genuinely just be offering a favour.'

'Who sits around train stations offering lifts to kids?'

'The guy didn't know he was a kid. Connor told the woman in the ticket office he was eighteen. This bloke might be a sleazeball, but it doesn't necessarily mean he's a pervert as well.'

'Shit, Theo,' Daryl whispered. 'I've seriously never been more terrified than I am right now.'

'Tell me about it.' Theo rested a hand on his arm. 'You want me to drive, mate?'

'No, thanks. I know where we're headed.' He cast a sideways glance at Theo, noting the worry etched on his face. 'You care a lot about that boy, don't you?'

'Well, you trusted him to my care. I've always tried to live up to that responsibility, even after me and you fell out. He's a brilliant kid, Daz.' He summoned a feeble smile. 'Honestly, I'm amazed something that good could've come from you.'

'No credit to me, I reckon. He gets his best qualities from his mums. Elise made him thoughtful and shy, and Lexie taught him right from wrong. All I did was teach him not to be a dad like I was.'

Theo sighed. 'We've fucked things right up between us with all that macho posturing. If he's hurt or... if anything happens to him, I'll never forgive myself.'

'It's my fault,' Daryl muttered. 'Me and my bloody temper. Christ, if his mum could see me, she wouldn't recognise me.'

'Oh, I don't know. The old you is in there somewhere. I realised that today.'

'You've been a far better godfather than I was a father. Or a friend.' Daryl looked at him in the rear-view mirror. 'I never did apologise, did I?'

'No. Well, you'd have to admit you were in the wrong first, which you've also never done.'

'Then I will now. I was in the wrong. I mean, I still don't believe we could've saved Bistrot Alexandre without some kind of miracle, but I should've talked to you. It was one of those things that just spiralled out of control. I hid the finances in a panic, hoping I could turn the tide, then it started to get worse and...' He sighed. 'Sorry. I really am sorry. It's true I was worried about Connor, but that doesn't excuse what I did.'

'No. It doesn't. Like I said, I had people to support too.'

'Who?'

'My mum. Her mental health's been worsening for years and I relied on the income from that place to keep a roof over her head.' He managed a smile. 'Anyway, that's the past. Apology accepted.'

They were silent for a long time while they drove, watching the lights on the motorway as each of them sat alone with their worries.

'So, you and Lex are serious about each other then,' Daryl said at last.

'You really want to talk about that now?'

'Christ, Theo, I want to talk about anything now.'

Theo could hear the quiver of desperation in his friend's voice. 'OK,' he said quietly. 'Then yes, we are.'

'That's not like you.'

'I'm not like me any more. Not like the old me.'

'Why?'

Theo shrugged. 'Lexie. She made me realise that a relationship with someone I really loved could give my life all the meaning it lacked, if I just stopped being afraid and opened myself up to it.' He smiled. 'And Con might've had something to do with it. I spent my life being terrified of fatherhood, thanks to the shining example set by my old man, then discovered I'd become a sort-of dad almost by accident. It made me think it wouldn't be so terrible, having a family, if I could have someone like Lexie to do it with.'

'I thought that once too,' Daryl murmured. 'Well, I'm not sure I can quite give my wholehearted blessing. I mean, it does hurt. But... I suppose I'm glad she's happy.'

'She told me you asked her to choose between me and Connor.'

'Yes. She chose him.'

'Of course she did. She'd always choose him. You should've known that without asking.'

'He wouldn't let her go through with it though.' Daryl stared out into the night. 'That was pretty fucking noble, wasn't it?'

'I told you, he's an amazing kid. You should get to know him a bit better and find out for yourself.'

'If he'll let me after this.' Daryl indicated for the next left. 'Nearly there.'

'You said Connor knew one person in Leeds. Who is it? A relative?'

'Yeah.' Daryl nodded to a sign showing they were heading for Lawnhill Crematorium. 'His mum.'

It was dark when they pulled up in the cemetery car park and got out of the car.

'I haven't been here since the funeral,' Daryl muttered. 'I never could bring myself to visit the grave.'

'I hope you're right about this,' Theo whispered.

'This must be where he's heading.' He pushed open the iron gate that led inside. 'I just hope he's here and not still with this sleazy bloke he went off with.'

Theo and Daryl both turned on their phone torches and shone them around the cemetery. Theo felt himself shudder. Being here reminded him of the last time he'd set foot in a graveyard, when he'd gone to deliver a final 'goodbye and fuck you' to his dad.

The phone beams were pretty weedy, but as they walked across the damp grass they could just make out a lanky figure sitting cross-legged in front of a headstone in the distance.

'Connor,' Theo whispered. 'Is it? Is that him?'

'Oh, thank God,' Daryl muttered. 'Thank God!'

'It is him.' Theo let out a laughing sob, clutching at Daryl's arm. 'He's safe, Daz.'

'Who's there?' Connor's tear-choked voice called into the darkness.

'It's OK,' Daryl called back. 'Don't be afraid. It's me, Connor. It's Dad.'

The relief that surged through Theo felt like a lead weight being lifted from his chest. He was about to run to Connor and pull him into a hug when he stopped himself.

'No,' he said. 'Daryl, you need to do this.'

'Both of us. Come on.'

Theo shook his head. 'No, you're his father. I'll wait in the car. I can ring Lexie, let her know he's safe and we'll be bringing him home soon, and tell the police they can call off the search. You go win back your son.' He pressed the Morecambe photo into Daryl's hand. 'Good luck, mate.'

'Who's there?' Connor called out. All he could see through his swimming eyes was a wobbly torch beam pointed in his direction, and a man's silhouetted figure. Or were there two? He couldn't tell through the tears.

'It's OK,' a voice called through the darkness. 'Don't be afraid. It's me, Connor. It's Dad.'

Connor scrambled back against the gravestone, hugging his knees to him, as his father approached.

'Oh, thank Christ you're safe,' Daryl said, exhaling with relief. 'I was so worried.'

'Yeah, well don't bother trying to ground me. You can call the police or do whatever you want, but I'd rather go to prison than go back with you.'

'I'm not going to make you go anywhere you don't want to.' Daryl sank to his knees beside his son. 'Are you OK? You're not hurt or anything?'

'I'm OK.'

'Thank God.' Daryl looked at the white marble gravestone and flinched. He was silent for a moment, as if struggling with strong emotion, before speaking again. 'Did you come to ask Mum for some advice?'

'Yeah.' Connor choked on a sob. 'I didn't know where else to go,' he said in a low, tremulous voice. 'I was scared and I thought if I went to Lexie, you'd probably get her arrested or something for having me there, and I… I wanted my mum.'

'Of course you did,' Daryl said gently. 'I did a terrible thing to you, Connor. It was cruel and… and inexcusable. You're right, I was jealous, and I let my anger get the better of me.' He looked at Elise's name on the gravestone. 'Your mother would be ashamed of me. I'm ashamed of myself.'

Connor stared at him, watching as the tears streamed down his dad's face.

'You're crying,' he said in disbelief.

'I'm crying because you're safe,' Daryl said with a wet laugh. 'Connor, you don't know the hell I've been through tonight. God, I was so afraid you were in some kind of terrible danger. Who was the man you left the station with?'

'How do you know about that?'

'Me and Uncle Theo have been all over the place trying to find you. Your mum's worried sick – I mean, your other mum. The police are hunting for you all over Manchester.'

Connor frowned. 'Theo?'

Daryl nodded. 'He's waiting in the car.'

'What, you two came here together? You hate each other.'

'Well, we discovered tonight that we don't hate each other as much as we thought we did. Not when someone we both loved was in danger.'

'So you're friends again?'

'Yes, I think we are. Not the same as before, but… let's say we understand each other again. Can I have a hug then?'

Connor hesitated before nodding, and his dad hugged him tightly.

'Thank God you're safe,' he whispered. 'I thought I might lose someone else I love tonight.'

'Sorry,' Connor whispered. 'I didn't know what else to do.'

'Who was the man you got a lift with? Did he try to hurt you or… or anything?'

'I didn't go with him in the end. I was being stupid. I knew Lexie would kill me if I got into a car with a stranger, and he was being pretty sketchy, asking me about boyfriends and that. I told him I had to take a slash then ran off and caught the coach.'

'Well thank goodness you had that much common sense left,' Daryl said as he let him go. 'Connor, I'm sorry. I treated you like a child while behaving like one myself. I promise that from now on, nothing happens without us discussing it as a family: you, me and your stepmum.'

Connor blinked. 'You mean it?'

'Yes, I mean it. And I'm sorry I acted like a pillock when you told me about your sexuality. I suppose… I suppose I'm not as modern about these things as I ought to be. Your boyfriend seems like a nice lad.'

'Yeah, he's great.'

'Well I'd love to get to know him better, if you still want a relationship with me after the way I behaved. That's entirely up to you, Connor. Just know that I'll be happy with whatever makes you happy.'

'Are you really letting me go home?'

'I am, but I'd like it if we could still see each other. I know it's hard to believe, but I really did come back to England for you.'

Connor shook his head. 'You wanted to get back with Lexie. I heard you say so.'

'I hoped there was a chance we could all be a family again, yes. I think what I've learnt today is that we're going to be a different sort of family, if you'll have me, and, well, that's fine too.'

Connor still looked wary. 'You won't get mad and act like a dick again, will you?'

'Not this time,' Daryl said. 'I'm going to talk to Lexie about her legally adopting you, like I should've let her do years ago. Then we'll have equal parental status in law and you won't need to worry. How does that sound?'

For the first time since his dad had shown up, Connor smiled. 'Yeah. I'd like that loads actually.'

Daryl reached into his pocket for the Morecambe photo and handed it to his son. 'You think you might fold me back into the picture one of these days?'

'I might. If you deserve it.'

'That's the only opportunity I want. To earn my place again.' Daryl glanced at the gravestone and blinked hard. 'I found it very hard to deal with having you around me after I lost your mum, Connor. There was so much of her in you that even seeing you triggered this unspeakable pain and guilt. Her eyes in your face, looking at me with so much trust and love and hurt, just as they had that awful day when I couldn't... God, it was a daily torture to me. That's the stark truth, son, and I hate myself for it. But now I've absorbed some of that pain and you've grown up to become this amazing young man, I just think what a miracle it is that a part of the woman I loved is alive inside you. I know I haven't truly lost her while I've got my boy. As long as he still wants me as his dad.'

'I guess I do,' Connor muttered. 'I always did, only I thought you didn't care about me any more.'

'That was never true, Connor,' Daryl said softly.

'No. I get that now.'

'So did Mum give you any good advice then?'

'Yeah, kind of. Being here made me think about her, and that made me think about you. I imagined her telling me to try to understand why you acted the way you did and not hate you for the rest of my life, like Theo did to his dad.'

Daryl smiled. 'Told you not to be too hard on me, did she? That sounds like my girl.'

'You miss her?'

'Every day.' Daryl bowed his head, and his voice trembled. 'Every day, Connor.'

'I do too. I'm sorry, Dad.'

Daryl glanced at a wreath of flowers resting on the grave-stone. 'You brought these?'

'Me, Lexie and Nana brought them on Mum's birthday.'

'I should've been up here before now,' Daryl murmured.

'What was Mum like? I mean, when she was my age. Nana tells me about her when I ask, but she always talks about when she was a little girl. I guess that's how she likes to remember her.'

'Well, she was very pretty,' Daryl said, a distant look coming into his eyes. 'And funny, really funny. Bright too. She could've gone out with any lad in our year if she'd wanted.'

'How come she went out with you then?'

He laughed. 'I've often wondered. I think it must've been my bad-boy charm. I was going through a grunge phase at the time.'

Connor smiled. 'Really, you?'

'Yep. Green hair, earring, the lot.'

'I never saw any photos of you with green hair.'

'No. I put them all away when Mum died.' He looked at Elise's name again and closed his eyes for a moment. 'I wasn't stupid, I knew my luck had come in the day she agreed to go out with me. Knowing someone like your mum wanted to be with me... it made me a better person. Made me feel like I had to earn it. I wish I'd known how short the time we'd have together would be. I'd have savoured every minute, if I'd known. Every look, every touch, every smile. Some mornings I still wake up and reach out for her, then it hits me all over again that she's...' He swallowed a sob. 'I thought we'd grow old together, Connor,' he said in a broken voice. 'Watch you grow up and have kids of your own, maybe even live long enough to see them have kids. I never thought...' He trailed off as he gave in to tears.

'I'm sorry, Dad. That wasn't fair, what happened to you.' Connor hesitated before putting an arm around his father and patting him on the back. 'I think about her all the time, you know.'

'I thought you must've forgotten her,' Daryl whispered. 'Lexie's your real mum now, I suppose.'

'They both are. And I haven't forgotten her. I never will, I promise. She'll always be my mum.'

Daryl wiped his eyes and smiled. 'You're a clever little sod, Connor Carson. How did you know I needed to hear that?'

He shrugged. 'It's how I feel, that's all.'

'Well, come on.' Daryl stood up. 'Let's say goodbye to this mum and get you home to the one who's currently worrying herself sick about you. I think you're in serious danger of Lexie hugging you until you pop when I take you back.'

Epilogue

Eight months later...

Lexie knocked on the door of Connor's room in the snug little Leyholme cottage they'd moved into after the big house had finally been sold.

'Come on, Cap,' she called. 'Your dad'll be here to pick you up any time now. Don't want to be late for your first Pride, do you?'

She went down to the kitchen, where Theo was crying his eyes out over the red onion he was chopping.

'Aww, Teddy, don't cry,' she said, putting her arms round his middle. 'The onion had a good life. It was just his time.'

'So you've come to mock me, have you?' He wiped his eyes with the back of his hand and turned to give her a kiss. 'Lucky for you you're such a hot piece of ass. Where's Con? Daz'll be here in a minute.'

'Polishing his adamantium shield or something.' There was the sound of thundering feet coming down the stairs. 'Ah, there we go. That's either Con or the elephant stampede from *Jungle Book*.'

A second later Connor appeared in his Lycra Captain America costume, gripping a round cardboard shield painted in the colours of the rainbow flag.

'How do I look then, oldies?' he asked.

'Pretty awesome actually.' Theo turned to Lexie. 'How come I never get to wear something like that when he takes us to these bloody cosplay things? I want to be Captain America.'

'Captain America doesn't cry while chopping onions, he's far too old-school butch. You're definitely more of a Thor.' Lexie approached Connor and put her hands on his shoulders. 'Aww. Look at you.'

'What're you looking at me like that for?' Connor stared. 'Lexie, are you crying?'

She smiled and wiped away a tear. 'I'd like to say it was the onion but that'd be a lie. I'm so proud of you, Connor Carson, do you know that?'

'What for? You know I'm not really Captain America, right?'

'No, but you'll always be my little superhero.'

'Wow.' Connor shook his head. 'You really just said that, didn't you?'

She laughed. 'Not so little these days, I suppose, but I'll still have the power to embarrass you no matter how big you get. Here, give us a hug.'

'Ugh. All right.'

He put his shield down so he could hug her.

'Have fun today, sweetie,' she whispered. 'You look amazing. Take lots of photos of you and your friends for me.'

'I will.' He gave her a squeeze. 'I wish you guys were coming.'

'So do I, but it'll be good for you to do this with your dad. I was pleased when he offered to drive you all. Pride's not exactly his scene so I think that constitutes progress.' She let him go. 'So which Avengers are Oli and Sophie going as?'

'They've done a gender swap thing because Soph didn't want to wear a catsuit. She's going as female Thor and Oli's going as male Scarlet Witch. Like, Scarlet Warlock. He's got this long red coat thing.'

'You'll approve of him in that costume, will you?' Theo said, smiling.

Connor flushed. 'I guess. He looks great whatever he wears.'

Outside, a car horn sounded.

'There's your dad.' Lexie gave him a peck on the cheek. 'Go on then, handsome. Try not to break too many hearts.'

'We'll see you all afterwards,' Theo said. 'I'm sure Sophie and Oli won't object to homemade pizza for tea.'

When Connor had gone, Lexie pulled off a sheet of kitchen roll to dab her eyes, laughing. 'God, I'm a soft old thing. He just looked so grown up suddenly, off to his first Pride with his boyfriend and best friend. Whatever happened to my little boy?'

'Right there with you, love. I only started chopping the onion because I knew I wouldn't be able to hold it in.' Theo went to wash his hands so he could give her a hug. 'Makes you proud, eh? Watching our gawky kid grow into this incredible young man; happy, confident, building a relationship with his dad, falling in love for the first time...'

She raised an eyebrow. 'You think?'

'Yeah, I can tell it's going that way for him and Oli. I consider myself a bit of a love expert these days, with all my vast experience of the tender passion.' He kissed her. 'Oh, and happy anniversary, by the way.'

She smiled. 'I thought you'd forgotten.'

'Certainly not. A year to the day that I let my best friend get me drunk and have her wicked way with me, and still paying the price. In fact...' He let her go. 'I even got you a present.'

'Did you?'

'Yep.' He opened the kitchen drawer and took out a little parcel in sparkly wrapping paper. 'There you go.'

'What is it?'

'Friendship bracelet. I braided it myself.'

She blinked at it. 'Oh.'

'Well, open it.'

Inside the wrapping was a little leather jewel box. When Lexie snapped it open, she discovered it contained a white-gold eternity ring studded with diamonds, fashioned in a twisted, braid-like style.

'Theo, it's beautiful,' she whispered.

Theo lifted it from the box. 'For the only woman I ever loved, and the best friend I ever had.' He took her left hand and slid it on. 'I think you should wear it on this finger.'

She stared at him. 'You're kidding.'

'Er, insulting. No, I'm not kidding: why would I be? I can get down on one knee if that's what it takes.'

She laughed. 'Oh God, please don't. It really wouldn't suit you.'

'Well then, Lex? What do you say that after your decree absolute comes through, we make those benefits we've always been so fond of legally binding? I've already earmarked young Connor as my best man.'

'Sounds good to me.' She kissed him softly. 'Theo Blake a married man. I never thought I'd see the day.'

'All it took was you,' he whispered, holding her tight. 'I love you.'

'I know. I love you too.' She smiled. 'It means a lot that you even love me enough to let our nearest and dearest find out your full name when we say our vows, Theophilos Timothy Blake.'

He groaned. 'Oh God, I hadn't thought of that. Is it too late to take that proposal back?'

'Nope, sorry. I couldn't bear to part with my new ring, it's far too shiny.' She gave him another lingering kiss before stepping away. 'I've got an anniversary present for you too actually.'

'I bet it can't beat mine.'

'How much do you bet?'

He laughed. 'Seriously, what's better than an engagement ring? Is it tickets to Disneyland?'

'Nope. Hang on, it's in the bedroom.'

Lexie went upstairs to fetch the gift-wrapped parcel she'd hidden under the bed that morning. She jogged back to the kitchen and presented it to a bemused-looking Theo.

'Well it's too small to be sexy underwear, which was my next guess,' he said, squinting at it. 'What is it?'

Lexie smiled. 'Friendship bracelet.'

Theo tore off the paper. Inside was an old Parker pen case, which, when he opened it, he found contained a little white stick. A white stick with two strong, clear pink lines in the middle of it...

'It's a stick with wee on, I wrapped it for you,' Lexie said. 'And they say romance is dead, right?'

Theo stared at it dazedly, the pink lines swimming before his eyes. He clutched at the kitchen counter.

'You need to sit down, love?' Lexie asked gently.

'I'm OK,' he whispered. 'Lex, I think you win that bet.'

Suddenly, vividly, the fantasy he'd concocted when Lexie had briefly believed she might be pregnant appeared in his mind again. His dream family – him, Lexie, Connor and the baby – now about to become all too real. But he didn't feel afraid, not this time. No, not even a little bit. All he felt was a deep, overwhelming joy that something he'd once believed was the last thing he wanted was finally happening to him.

He laughed as the full meaning of Lexie's gift sank in. 'Oh my God! Is it really real, Lex? Tell me it is.'

'Yes, it's really real.' Lexie put her arms around him and stood on tiptoes for a kiss. 'You're going to be a dad, Theo.'

A letter from Lisa

Hi everyone, Lisa here! I wanted to say a big thank you for choosing to read *Friends With Benefits*. It was wonderful to be back in gorgeous Leyholme, and to get to know Lexie, Theo and Connor as they told me their story. Not to mention meeting up again with some of the characters I fell in love with on my first visit to Leyholme while writing *The School of Starting Over* – it was so nice to catch up with Nell, Xander, Stevie and some of the other villagers and find out what had happened in their lives since the last book.

This story was written at a time of great international anxiety as the world struggles to deal with the Covid-19 pandemic, and writing it provided me with the perfect balm for the frightening reality of the real world: its core themes of love and family had never felt more relevant or poignant. As with my two previous books for Hera, *The School of Starting Over* (which features the same setting and some of the same characters) and *When You Were Mine*, the story explores the concept of family: those we're born with, those we make and those we choose. If you enjoyed this book, I do hope you'll consider checking the previous titles out too.

I'd also absolutely love to hear your thoughts on this story in a review. These are invaluable not only for letting authors know how their story affected you, but also for helping other readers to choose their next read and discover new writers. Just a few words can make a big difference.

If you would like to find out more about me and my books, or contact me directly, you can do so via my website or social media pages:

Facebook: /LisaSwiftWrites
Twitter: @LisaSwiftAuthor
Web: www.lisaswiftauthor.co.uk

Thank you again for choosing *Friends With Benefits*.

Best wishes,

Lisa

Acknowledgements

As always, huge thanks to my agent, Laura Longrigg at MBA Literary Agents, and to Keshini Naidoo, my editor at Hera, for once again going above and beyond to get this book out into the world.

Big thanks to all of my talented, supportive writer pals: Rachel Burton, Victoria Cooke, Sophie Claire, Jacqui Cooper, Rachel Dove, Kiley Dunbar, Helena Fairfax, Kate Field, Melinda Hammond, Marie Laval, Katey Lovell, Helen Pollard, Debbie Rayner, Rachael Stewart, Victoria Walters, Angela Wren, and many others! Thanks, too, to the Romantic Novelists' Association for being such a wonderful and supportive organisation, and its members. I'm also grateful for the support of the RNA's Rainbow chapter, which provides support for RNA members who identify as LGBTQIA+ and/or write novels featuring LGBTQIA+ characters.

As ever, thanks to my family, friends and colleagues – my partner and long-term beta reader Mark Anslow, to whom this book is dedicated; friends Robert Fletcher, Amy Smith and Nigel and Lynette Emsley; Firths, Brahams and Anslows everywhere, and my ever-supportive colleagues at Dalesman Publishing.

And finally, thanks to Keshini, Lindsey and the gang at Hera. Thank you so much, again, for everything you do for your authors!